Praise for the novels o

"Suspenseful, atmospheric, and l
—Ashley Weaver, author of the Amory Ames My...

"Readers looking for atmospheric mystery set in the period following the Great War will savor the intricate plotting and captivating details of the era." —*Library Journal* (starred review)

"Action-filled . . . Huber offers a well-researched historical and a fascinating look at the lingering aftermath of war." —*Publishers Weekly*

"Masterful. . . . Just when you think the plot will zig, it zags. . . . Deeply enjoyable . . . just the thing if you're looking for relatable heroines, meatier drama, and smart characters with rich inner lives." —*Criminal Element*

"Huber is an excellent historical mystery writer, and Verity is her best heroine. Sidney and Verity are a formidable couple when they work together, but they are also very real. They don't leap straight back into life before the war but instead face many obstacles and struggles as they readjust to married life and post-war life. Nonetheless, the love between Sidney and Verity is real and true, and the way that Huber creates their reblossoming love is genuine. Topped off with a gripping mystery, this will not disappoint." —*Historical Novel Society*

"A smashing and engrossing tale of deceit, murder, and betrayal set just after World War I. . . . Anna Lee Huber has crafted a truly captivating mystery here." —*All About Romance*

Novels by Anna Lee Huber

*This Side of Murder*

*Treacherous Is the Night*

*Penny for Your Secrets*

*A Pretty Deceit*

*Murder Most Fair*

*A Certain Darkness*

# SISTERS *of* FORTUNE

## ANNA LEE HUBER

KENSINGTON
PUBLISHING CORP.

www.kensingtonbooks.com

For my cousin, Jackie.
Thank you for being such an uplifting, faithful, and
remarkable friend.

# CAST OF CHARACTERS

## The Fortune Family from Winnipeg, Canada

- Mark Fortune—64-years-old millionaire. Self-made man.
- Mary—60 years old. Mother of six.
- Flora—28 years old. Engaged to Crawford Campbell, a banker.
- Alice—24 years old. Engaged to Holden Allen, an insurance broker.
- Mabel—23 years old. Involved with Harrison Driscoll, a musician from Minnesota.
- Charlie—19 years old.
- Robert—34 years old. Married to Alma. Lives in Vancouver.
- Clara—30 years old. Married to Herbert Hutton.

Chess Kinsey—tennis star and attorney from New York.
William Sloper—amiable young man from Connecticut whom the Fortunes met while traveling to Europe.

## The Three Musketeers—congenial bachelors who traveled from Winnipeg with the Fortunes.

- Thomson Beattie—friend of Flora.
- Thomas McCaffry—originally from Ireland.
- John Hugo Ross—falls ill with dysentery while in Egypt.

Thomas Andrews—shipbuilder and naval architect who designed the *Titanic*.
J. Bruce Ismay—managing director of the White Star Line.

## Titanic Officers and Crew

* Captain E. J. Smith
* First Officer William Murdoch—Scottish.
* Second Officer Charles H. Lightoller—"Lights."
* Fifth Officer Harold G. Lowe—Welsh.
* Dr. William O'Loughlin—ship's surgeon.
* Steward Ryan.
* Stewardess Bennett.
* Stewardess Mary Sloan.

Colonel Archibald Gracie—affable author of a Civil War history book.

Mr. and Mrs. Straus–former congressman and co-owner of Macy's Department Store and his wife.

Jacques and May Futrelle—author of popular Thinking Machine mysteries. Wife also an author.

Charlotte Drake Cardeza—wealthy widow who reserved one of the deluxe parlor suites.

Thomas Cardeza—Charlotte's 36-year-old son.

Colonel John Jacob "Jack" Astor and second wife, Madeleine—wealthiest man on the *Titanic*.

Karl Behr—tennis star who travels to Europe following Miss Helen Newsom, whom he intends to marry.

Sir Cosmo Duff-Gordon—Scottish baronet and sportsman.

Lady Duff-Gordon—fashion designer Lucile.

Helen Churchill Candee—author, interior decorator, and suffragette.

Margaret Brown—socialite and philanthropist from Denver.

Helen Newsom—19-year-old friend of Karl Behr's sister.

Mr. and Mrs. Beckwith—Helen's mother and stepfather.

Mr. and Mrs. Ryerson and children—traveling home after eldest son's tragic death.

Mr. and Mrs. Thayer and son, Jack—vice president of Pennsylvania Railroad Company; wife, Marian; and 17-year-old son.

Quigg Baxter—former hockey player from Montreal escorting his mother and sister home from Europe, and secretly bringing his mistress, Berthe Mayné, to marry.

Mrs. Hélène Baxter—wealthy widow from Montreal.

Zette Baxter Douglas—Quigg's sister.

Mr. and Mrs. Charles Melville Hays—president of Canadian National Railway and wife.

Orian and Thornton Davidson—daughter of Mr. Hays and husband.

Francis Browne—amateur photographer who traveled on the *Titanic* from Southampton to Queenstown.

Major Arthur Peuchen—president of Standard Chemical Company and commissioned officer in Queen's Own Rifles. From Toronto.

Dr. Alice Leader—female physician who runs a practice in New York.

Mrs. Margaret Swift—friend of Dr. Leader. Possesses a law degree.

Marie Young—companion to Mrs. White. Former music teacher to Roosevelt children.

Ella White—wealthy widow traveling with Miss Young.

Mr. and Mrs. Hudson Allison and family—young, self-made millionaire; wife, Bessie; 2-year-old daughter, Lorraine; and 11-month-old son, Trevor.

Alice Cheaver—Trevor's new nanny.

Henry B. and René "Harry" Harris—theater managers and producers from New York.

Hugh Woolner—English businessman. Admirer of Mrs. Candee.

Harry Widener—bibliophile and businessman. Son of George and Eleanor Widener.

Dr. Washington Dodge—physician and banker from San Francisco.

Harry Markland Molson—richest Canadian on board the *Titanic*. Survived two previous shipwrecks.

Dorothy Gibson—model and film star.

Michel and Edmond Navratil—two young boys traveling with their father under the assumed name Hoffman.

Neshan Kreckorian—Armenian immigrating to Canada traveling in third class.

# SISTERS *of* FORTUNE

# PROLOGUE

❧

*February 12, 1912*
*Cairo, Egypt*

Alice Fortune was captivated. From the verdant green branches of the dwarf palm trees in their stone pots flanking the broad stairs to the vibrant blue, green, and orange tiles covering the terrace floor, and the jasmine- and fig-scented breeze playing with the strands of hair that had escaped their pins to tickle the base of her neck, it was all she could do to drink it all in.

This feeling was new for her. This desire to see and do and experience everything around her. She had never been farther from home than Toronto and she was almost insatiable with the appetite to explore.

However, her mother had wanted to rest during the heat of the day, and the remainder of her family had agreed to join her. But Alice was too excited to lie down. Not when there was still so much to discover. While she couldn't leave the hotel, when a friend of the family and fellow traveler had fortuitously appeared in the templelike main hall just as they were returning from their morning excursion, she'd seized the opportunity he'd presented to escape the purgatory of staring out the window while her sisters napped.

Which was how she found herself taking tea on the veranda of Shepheard's Hotel in the heart of Cairo with the handsome, fair-haired William Sloper of Connecticut. He smiled at her indulgently as she lifted her glass of cool hibiscus tea and turned to look at him for perhaps the first time since they'd sat down at one of the rattan tables. Another man might have been offended by her inattention, but not William. He was an incorrigible flirt, but a harmless one, and good-natured enough not to take himself too seriously. She laughed, a bright note against the chorus of low, cultured voices and the rattle and hum of the carts and motorcars passing along the street.

"I can't imagine you would ever be able to enjoy a cup of tea on the terrace at your home in Winnipeg at this time of year," he remarked.

"Good heavens, no," she agreed. "Not unless we wanted it to freeze solid in a matter of minutes. Although Winnipeg in winter does have its compensations," she felt compelled to add out of some sense of loyalty, even if she was hard-pressed to remember what those were at the moment.

Sloper hummed and nodded. "No need for an icebox, I suppose."

She smiled. "I can't imagine Connecticut is much warmer."

"Which is why I'm here and not there."

She took a sip of her tea. There was just enough sugar to sweeten it but not enough to cloud the tartness of the hibiscus. "I thought you were intent on adventure?"

"Yes, but it's always best to do one's adventuring in the winter." William's pale blue eyes sparkled beneath the brim of his Panama hat. "And return to New England just as the daffodils are heralding spring."

Alice couldn't counter this argument, for it was clearly also what her father, Mark Fortune, had in mind when he had surprised the entire family with this trip—a grand tour of Europe and the Mediterranean. Ostensibly, it was a reward for her younger brother Charlie's graduation, but they'd all been invited to go. It had taken little effort to persuade the four youngest Fortune children to join in on such an extravagant voyage. Even

Flora, Alice's older sister by four years, had seemed perfectly willing to postpone her spring wedding in order to join them and act as a chaperone for her three younger siblings. But of course Flora was dutiful like that. Whatever Father and Mother thought best, she inevitably acceded to.

The Fortunes had boarded a train from Winnipeg shortly after the start of the new year and set sail from New York to Trieste on the Cunard *Franconia*. Which is where they'd met William Sloper, along with about a dozen Canadian acquaintances, all embarking on their own holidays. A number of them appeared to be following the same route as the Winnipeggers, through Italy and on to Egypt and Cairo's Shepheard's Hotel. Everyone who was anyone stayed at Shepheard's Hotel when they were in Cairo, or at least dined in its illustrious restaurant.

"When are you off?" William asked.

Alice knew he was asking about their boat trip up the Nile to Luxor and Thebes, for she'd been talking of temples and pyramids for the last half hour. "In a few days' time."

She turned to allow her gaze to skim over the other patrons seated at the tables along the terrace on either side of the main entrance to the hotel. Most were gathered under the canopy, shaded from the sun's brutal rays, but one pair of ladies in gauze tea gowns had opted to settle beneath the branches of another dwarf palm tree farther along the veranda—half in shadow and half in bleached light. "We're touring the Museum of Antiquities this afternoon. You're welcome to join us," she told him.

"Perhaps I will."

A stream of guests emerged from the hotel, pausing to allow their vision to adjust to the brilliant sunlight. Even the shade of the terrace did little to soften the transition from the dim but opulent interior, with its lotus-topped alabaster pillars and marble and ebony furnishings. An elegantly attired couple blinked several times before continuing across the tile floor and down the steps to the street, where a motorcar was waiting for them.

William remarked again upon the stifling weather, but Alice

spared him only half her attention, the rest of it being drawn to a little man wearing a maroon fez who stood on the opposite side of the balustrade, speaking to the couple. Whatever he had to say, the smartly dressed man didn't want to hear it, for he turned resolutely away, assisting the woman into the vehicle.

The blast of a lorry horn distracted Alice momentarily as she turned to see a donkey cart driver raise his arm and holler in response, but when she looked back, she discovered the little man was now staring rather intently at *her*. A tiny smile played across his mouth, and he reached through the wrought-iron railing to gesture to her. At first, she wondered if he was another one of the street vendors she periodically heard cry out, offering up their wares to passersby, but he clutched nothing in his hands, nor would such a peddler have been permitted to display his goods so close to the hotel entrance.

"Now, what do you think he wants?" she observed offhandedly.

William followed the direction of her gaze toward the man who beckoned again. "Why, to tell you your fortune, of course. Have you never had it done?"

"No. But . . ." She wasn't certain her mother and father would approve, nor her older sister Flora, but, after all, they were on this grand tour to experience other cultures and continents. "Oh . . . what could be the harm?"

"I will go fetch him for you," William said with a smile.

Alice brushed her hands over her cornflower-blue skirts, smoothing out the wrinkles but careful not to dislodge her gloves where they were draped over her lap, and adjusted her wide-brimmed straw picture hat, suddenly nervous as well as excited.

The Egyptian soothsayer's dark skin was creased with wrinkles and his clothes were soiled with dust, but his eyes gleamed with warmth and almost merriment. He bowed politely to her before speaking in a melodic accented voice. "Does the young lady wish me to read her palm?"

She offered him her hand, watching with great interest as he turned it over to examine it, tracing the lines with his short fingers. William adjusted his gray linen suit jacket and settled back into his chair, offering her a wink.

"You are in danger every time you travel on the sea."

Alice's eyes snapped back to the fortune teller, noting that much of the man's good humor had faded from his weathered features.

"I see you adrift on the ocean in an open boat," he continued, almost as if speaking to her from a distance. "You will lose everything but your life. You will be saved, but others will be lost."

Silence stretched following this pronouncement, broken only by the clink of glassware and the clopping of donkey hooves. It felt as if a cool breeze had blown across the back of her neck, pebbling the skin there and along her arms. It took a considerable amount of her self-possession not to react.

Fortunately, William was not similarly affected. He huffed a dry laugh. "A little dire, don't you think? Here's a word of advice, old boy." He lowered his voice. "Tell them a happy fortune if you wish to be paid well. One filled with the peal of wedding bells, and golden sunsets, and the pitter-patter of little feet."

At these words, Alice reached into her purse for a coin. She passed it to the soothsayer, who had not reacted to William's prodding but kept his eyes trained on her. He nodded once again as he backed away and then turned to hurry down the steps and disappear into the crowd streaming down the street.

"What a funny little man," William mused, shaking his head.

Alice lifted her hand to finger the string of cultured pearls draped around her neck, continuing to stare at the spot where the fortune teller had vanished from her sight. She wished her fiancé, Holden, was here. He would know what to say. Although she thought of herself as a logical person, one not inclined to superstition or flights of fancy, she couldn't deny that the soothsayer's words—and the manner in which he'd spoken them—had stirred something unwelcome inside her. It wasn't fear, exactly, but uneasiness.

Apparently, this didn't go unnoticed, for William cast her a look of pitying disbelief. "You aren't actually taking that fakir's words seriously, are you?"

"No . . ." Her voice trailed away uncertainly.

"Because he's likely told dozens of tourists the same fortune. He realizes Americans, and Brits, and Canadians"—he gestured to her—"have to travel by sea to get here, and we'll have to travel by sea to return home. And he knows precisely where to find us." He looked around, indicating their current setting.

"True," she conceded, able to draw a breath deeper into her lungs. Shepheard's Hotel *was* at the social center of British and all English-speaking Cairo. It was the place where those of wealth and distinction from those nations gathered.

"He saw a beautiful young woman seated here, shielding herself from the sun's harsh rays, and calculated which of his patented fortunes would cause the greatest impact."

"Is that really how it works?" she asked, unable to deny that William's explanation had reassured her. *Not* that she'd genuinely believed the little man could read her future inscribed on her palm, but there was comfort in hearing how dismissive her better-traveled companion was of the fakir's prediction.

His expression was almost patronizing. "I'm afraid so, my girl."

She nodded, smarting a bit from her naivete, and lifted her glass of tea. She frowned at the deep pink contents. "But it seems rather cruel of him to foretell such a dreadful fate."

"Perhaps, but I imagine it's how he earns his living. And to some degree, it's what tourists expect. After all, no one wants to be told their future will be dull and predictable. Better to send a shiver down your spine than bore you with complacency."

She supposed he was right. Truth be told, she wasn't certain she wouldn't have been just as unnerved to hear that she would marry, give birth to half a dozen children, and never bestir farther than one hundred miles from her comfortable home again—the future she fully anticipated. But she wasn't yet ready to accept that reality, not when there was still so much left to experience of their grand tour. In another month or two, surely her desire for adventure would be sated and she would be more than content with such a fate, but to hear it pronounced as such now would be disheartening.

And didn't that make her the most wretched fiancée ever, especially after receiving Holden's last letter? He was everything that was adoring and attentive, and she missed him terribly. But that didn't mean she was willing to sacrifice her enjoyment of this opportunity to see the world. Particularly when it might be her only chance.

Still, a part of her struggled to dismiss the fakir's words entirely. They niggled at the back of her mind like an unwanted guest who wouldn't leave. All she could do was hope that time and happier concerns dislodged them. Until then, she would pretend it was so, and took a determined drink of hibiscus tea as if to prove it to herself as well as to Mr. Sloper.

*The New York Times*
April 10, 1912


THE TITANIC SAILS TO-DAY.
Largest Vessel in World to Bring Many Well-Known Persons Here.
Special Cable to THE NEW YORK TIMES.

London, April 9.—The White Star Liner Titanic, the largest vessel in the world, will sail at noon.

Although essentially similar in design and construction to her sister ship, the Olympic, the Titanic is an improvement on the Olympic in many respects. Capt. Smith has been promoted from the Olympic to take her across. There are two pursers, H. W. McElroy and R. L. Baker.

Among the passengers to sail to-morrow on the Titanic are Mr. and Mrs. H. J. Allison, Mrs. Aubert, Major Archibald Butt, Mrs. Cardeza, Mr. and Mrs. W. E. Carter, Mr. and Mrs. Herbert Chaffees, Norman Craig, Mr. and Mrs. Washington Dodge, Mr. and Mrs. Mark Fortune, Mr. and Mrs. W. D. Douglas, Col. Gracie, Benjamin Guggenheim, Mr. and Mrs. Henry Harper, Mr. and Mrs. Frederick Hoyt, Mr. and Mrs. Isidor Straus, Mr. and Mrs. J. B. Thayer, and Mr. and Mrs. George Widener.

# CHAPTER I

*Wednesday, April 10, 1912*

Flora Fortune was grateful for the steadiness of Mr. Beattie's arm as they hurried along the platform at London's Waterloo Station, slicing a swath through the sea of humanity separating them from the first-class special boat train bound for the new London & South Western Railway facilities at Southampton's berth 44. A cacophony of sounds echoed off the soaring ceiling of the station—whistles and escaping steam, grinding wheels and the slam of doors, raised voices and pounding feet. Flora didn't even attempt to speak.

In any case, she needed all her breath to keep up with the porters hastening ahead of them, carrying poor Mr. Ross on a stretcher. He was so weakened from dysentery that he couldn't even walk to his train compartment, but nonetheless he was determined to return to Winnipeg. She couldn't blame him. Being ill was miserable enough without being so far from the comforts of home.

Flora hunched her shoulders against the icy breeze that whisked through the station. She hoped the temperatures were more favorable along the coast in Southampton, for they had woken to a decided chill in the air. After spending months in the warmer climes of the Mediterranean and southern Europe, their bodies were no longer acclimated to the cold, forcing them to pull topcoats and hats from the depths of their trunks. Father had even jested about donning his old buffalo coat, matted and moth-eaten though it was, and far from gentlemanly in appearance. Fortunately, Mother had been able to convince him to wear a dark woolen coat instead. Though Father had then insisted on taking up valuable space in the trunks bound for their ship cabins rather than those tagged NOT WANTED, which would be stored in the holds until they reached New York.

Flora exhaled in relief as they spied Mr. McCaffry and his brown overcoat in the doorway to a compartment just ahead. He was the last of the trio of Winnipeg gentlemen who had accompanied the Fortunes on their grand tour. Mr. Beattie, Mr. McCaffry, and poor Mr. Ross, now relegated to his stretcher. A fellow traveling companion had genially dubbed them the Three Musketeers, and the ridiculous sobriquet had stuck. Not that the bachelors seemed to mind. They were often lumped together.

Mr. McCaffry had hurried before them to ready the space for his sick friend, while she and Mr. Beattie waited for the porters to see to Mr. Ross. Mr. McCaffry stepped to the side, stroking the sides of his light mustache as he watched the porters begin the delicate work of maneuvering the stretcher and its occupant into the train.

"Won't be much longer, Hugo," Mr. McCaffry told him encouragingly. "Thomson, why don't you escort Miss Fortune to her family," he suggested. "I'll see Hugo settled."

Mr. Beattie nodded, turning their steps. "This way."

Accepting there was nothing more she could do, Flora allowed herself to be guided into the train, carefully maneuvering the broad rolled brim of her picture hat through the doorway. The confection of silk, ribbons, and feathers might be the height of fashion, as was her smart plum-and-cream traveling suit, but that didn't mean it was practical.

Exchanging nods with fellow passengers, they strode down the aisle to her family's compartment. It wasn't difficult to find. The Fortunes had never been a staid or quiet bunch. Even without the two eldest of the six children, there was no lapse in discussion or laughter, and Mr. William Sloper's presence helped fill any gaps there might have been. He had met their party at the station and been invited by their mother to join them in their compartment. It was his voice she heard as Mr. Beattie opened the door for her.

"My friends will all be green with envy when they hear I've sailed home on the *Titanic*. I suspect I shall be dining out on it for weeks," Mr. Sloper declared, laughing at himself.

In all honesty, none of them had expected to sail home on the maiden voyage of the White Star Line's new flagship. It had been their father's last surprise. Initially they'd been scheduled to sail the third week of April on the *Mauretania*, but several members of their party had been exhausted and anxious to return home, including poor Hugo Ross.

Flora sat next to her nineteen-year-old brother, Charlie. "They say she made twenty-one and a half knots during her sea trials," he chimed in, his blue eyes alive with enthusiasm. "And they say once she's at sea, with all her boilers lit, she may be able to go as fast as twenty-four knots."

"That may be so," Mr. Sloper countered. "But she was never built for speed. The White Star Line is all about size and luxury. After all, *Titanic* is fifty percent larger than Cunard's *Mauretania*. She can't hope to best her."

"I don't care how fast she goes as long as we arrive safely," Mother declared, opening the book that rested in her lap. As ever, Mother dressed for comfort as much as style. She had been raised on the plains of Manitoba, one of fourteen children born to her Scottish mother and father. She said that when you grew up understanding what it meant to be well and truly chilled to the bone, you never forgot it. As such, she'd eschewed a picture hat for a more sensible black velvet cap with a chinchilla band accented by a gold brooch sporting two ostrich feathers.

"And she will." Mr. Sloper turned to Alice, the middle Fortune sister, seated on his right in a dress dyed the shade of fresh raspberries beneath her aubergine coat. "Lest you should worry. They say she's unsinkable. The safest ship ever put to sea."

"I'm not worried," Alice replied, looking wholly unperturbed, but perhaps now a little annoyed.

Mr. Sloper had been separated from the Fortunes since they'd departed Cairo, having taken a different itinerary during his travels, but upon their meeting again in London, he'd professed his intentions to sail home on the *Mauretania*. However, as soon as Alice mentioned the Fortunes had booked passage on board the *Titanic*, he'd exchanged his ticket as well. When he'd returned to tell them so, Alice had reminded him of the Egyptian fortune teller's prediction, jesting that she was a dangerous person to travel with.

Their brother Charlie now spoke up once again. "When the *Olympic*—*Titanic*'s sister ship—collided with the *Hawke* last September, it ripped a twelve-foot and a seven-foot gash into her side and damaged the starboard propeller blades, but she never even came close to sinking." This remark was presumably meant to reassure Alice.

"I just said I'm not worried," she retorted.

The blast of the train's whistle signaled their imminent departure, spurring a flurry of emotions inside Flora. There was excitement, yes, for how could she resist her siblings' enthusiasm, especially since *Titanic* was supposed to be such a magnificent ship and they would be some of the first passengers to sail aboard her. There was also the familiar flutter of nerves that began in the pit of her stomach before starting any journey and a touch of sadness that their grand tour was nearly at an end.

But lurking amid it all was also a disconcerting sensation of dread. Not for their safety. Flora had never believed in superstitious nonsense like fortune telling and séances, and she wasn't about to start now. No, this dread had more to do with what was waiting for her back at home. She'd tried to forget about it, to push it to the back of her thoughts, but now that their feet were actually turned in the direction of Winnipeg, it pressed on her ever more insistently.

She clasped her hands in her lap, trying to quiet her mind as Father returned from speaking with Mr. Beattie to sit on her other side. Father sank into the plush leather with a sigh that reminded her that at sixty-four, he was no longer young, and this trip had undoubtedly been more exhausting for him than it had been for those who were decades younger.

"Mr. Beattie and Mr. McCaffry are going to attempt to exchange their cabin for one closer to Mr. Ross," he confided to her while Charlie and Mr. Sloper continued to expound on *Titanic*'s merits. "Given the circumstances, I presume the purser will be happy to accommodate them if he can."

"Is the ship fully booked?" Flora asked.

"We'll have to wait to find that out." He reached over to pat her hand where it was resting in her lap. "You and your sisters are free to visit Mr. Ross if you wish. I assume he would welcome the sight of your cheery faces. But I don't want any of you playing nursemaid." His voice and his gaze were firm. "Beattie and McCaffry and the stewards will be there to help him, as well as the ship's surgeon, so there is no need. I want you to enjoy yourselves, not spend the last few days of your tour trapped in a cabin with a man with a violent stomach complaint. Understood?"

She nodded, recognizing why he'd directed this speech at her and not her sisters, for Alice, with her past health troubles, would never be allowed to nurse Mr. Ross in the first place, and the youngest sister, Mabel, would never volunteer.

"Good." He patted her hand once more before removing his hat to sink his head back against the seat. A sparse covering of brown hair threaded with silver clung to the sides and back of his head—a match to his thick mustache—but the top was bald.

Seeing him thus, with his frame grown to portly, it was difficult to imagine him as the young, adventurous man who had set out for California to pan for gold. Two years later, Mark Fortune had found himself in Manitoba at a fortuitous time, acquiring a thousand acres along the Assiniboine River, where a few years in the future, Portage Avenue, Winnipeg's main thoroughfare, would be built. By the age of thirty, he had become not only a wealthy man but a well-respected one. He was a Freemason and a member of the St. Andrew's Society. He'd served as a city councillor and as a trustee of Knox Presbyterian Church. And just the year before, he'd built the family a thirty-six-room Tudor-style home in one of Winnipeg's finest neighborhoods. But despite the changes physically, Flora could still see the determination and brash self-confidence glinting in his eyes that had propelled him from a man with barely two cents to rub together to a millionaire.

"I know we asked a great deal of you by urging you to postpone your wedding and chaperone your younger siblings, but I hope it proved to be worth it," he said.

"Of course it has," she assured him.

He closed his eyes. "Once we return, you and Campbell set the date as soon as you like. I'll make it happen."

She felt she should say something, but her throat closed around any response. Fortunately, her father didn't seem to require one.

Last autumn, when she'd informed her fiancé, Crawford Campbell, that she wanted to delay their wedding so that she could take this grand tour with her family, he hadn't seemed to mind in the least. Worse still, *she* hadn't minded. In truth, it had felt like a reprieve. A sad thought, indeed.

It wasn't that she didn't like Crawford. He was handsome and courteous, and a rising Toronto banker. Her parents certainly approved. Her father had been the one to introduce them, and they had promoted the match every chance they could. Perhaps because, at twenty-eight, Flora wasn't getting any younger. It would be a comfortable marriage, a sturdy one.

The trouble was, she didn't feel anything stronger for Crawford, and she was fairly certain he was the same. At least, his actions thus far and his dearth of correspondence led her to believe that. If absence was supposed to make the heart grow fonder, it hadn't worked in either direction.

In stark contrast, Alice and her fiancé, Holden Allen, had exchanged dozens of letters, at great difficulty, in some instances. More than once, Holden's letters needed to be forwarded on to them at their next destination or held in anticipation of their arrival. Meanwhile, Flora had received one note from Crawford, and a rather dry one at that. She understood that, in general, men weren't purported to be very good correspondents, but all the same she couldn't help feeling disappointed and uneasy.

She looked up at the sound of Alice's bright laughter, finding her head tilted toward Mr. Sloper to hear whatever he'd said that was amusing. Another muffled whistle pierced the air, and the train lurched ahead with a small jolt as the brakes were released, and they began to roll forward.

"Not concerned about Sloper, are you?" her father murmured.

She turned to find him peeking at her from beneath one eyelid. It unnerved her to think he might have been observing her this whole time. "No," she replied honestly. "Alice is devoted to Holden."

The youngest Fortune daughter, Mabel, on the other hand, seemed to wield the name of the ineligible ragtime musician from Minnesota she had formed an attachment to as a blunt instrument, usually when their parents were within hearing. Mabel knew perfectly well that their parents had hoped separating her from Harrison Driscoll for the duration of their grand tour would sever the connection, and she seemed determined to let them know every chance she could get that they'd failed. But Flora had noticed that Mabel rarely mentioned Harrison's name unless their parents were within earshot.

"Mr. Sloper is simply an inveterate flirt, and Alice is indulging him," Flora informed her father.

"And enjoying it," her father asserted with a chuckle. "But I agree." He settled himself more comfortably, lacing his fingers together where his hands rested in his lap. "In any case, Sloper isn't strong-willed enough for your sister. Though one can't fault him for admiring her."

Flora had to agree. She would be the first to admit how beautiful Alice was, with her delicate porcelain features, blue eyes, and cloud of sandy hair. Most people took one look at her lovely face and petite figure and all but sighed at the ethereal picture she presented. Just as they couldn't help but smile in approval at Charlie, with his similar coloring and clean-cut good looks. Which wasn't to say that Mabel didn't possess a beauty of her own. It was merely bolder. A fact she enhanced with the deep colors she chose for her garments, such as the rich admiral blue of her suit, with its cardamom trim. They complimented her dark mahogany hair and wide gray eyes and softened the effect of her large mouth and pronounced chin. Of all the daughters, Mabel resembled Mother most. Which might explain why they butted heads so often.

Being constantly compared to her striking sisters, Flora might have been pitied and dismissed, but for two redeeming qualities: her height and her figure. It was difficult to ignore a woman who stood as tall as some men, but with a decidedly shapelier silhouette. A less confident woman of such features might have slumped or slouched, but Flora had learned that the key was to hold her head high and package it in elegant, expertly tailored clothing.

The next few hours seemed to crawl by as the train made its way southwest. The English countryside, while lovely, couldn't hold their attention or properly be appreciated while their thoughts were bent on the mechanical wonder they were steaming toward. Even Flora, despite her conflicted emotions about returning home, couldn't stop checking the watch pinned to her bodice or noting their progress as they passed through each successive station en route. Their entire party was all breathless anticipation as they entered Southampton and the train began to slow. They crowded by the window, straining to catch their first glimpse of the ship as they neared the docks.

Charlie was the first to spot her. "There!" he cried. "You can just see her between the buildings."

They were but fleeting glances, but he was right. Her black hull was a steadily growing mountain in the distance, with her four black-and-gold funnels piercing the flat gray sky. It was all Flora could do not to gawk. The others chattered excitedly, but she was too awed to speak, for the *Titanic* was *enormous*! Hadn't Charlie said she was the largest moving object ever built? She could well believe it. When the train finally pulled to a halt on the tracks running parallel to the ship's side, she positively towered above them.

But there wasn't much time to sit marveling over its size. Not when there was luggage to gather, tickets to check, and family members to be counted as they joined the flow of passengers exiting into the large shed nearly seven hundred feet long constructed next to the tracks. An army of porters bustled beneath the skylights, wrestling with the cargo and steamer trunks to be transferred to the ship and directing passengers toward a set of stairs.

Flora spied Mr. Beattie speaking with one of the porters, likely asking for assistance with the ailing Mr. Ross. She wondered if she should offer her assistance but then remembered Father had ordered her to leave the matter in Mr. Beattie's and Mr. McCaffry's capable hands. Having dawdled, she had to hasten to keep up with her family and Mr. Sloper as they began climbing the stairs, which led up several flights to an enclosed balcony. Here they joined the queue to present their tickets, and then were being ushered over a gangplank toward the ship itself.

At the edge of the balcony just before she stepped into the open air, Flora hesitated, feeling at the precipice of something monumental. The cool sea breeze kissed her cheeks, toying with the tendrils of copper-brown hair that had escaped their pins to curl against the nape of her neck. She squinted against the sudden glare of the brilliant white superstructure before her and realized the sun had peeked its head through the heavy clouds, as if it, too, couldn't resist the urge to gawp and stare at the magnificent ship. Turning her head to the side, she realized at what a dizzying height they now stood, and they weren't even crossing into the uppermost deck. Two more levels soared above them.

Below on the dock, bystanders milled about, pointing up at the riveted hull and waving to a few people far above them on the ship's decks. A larger mass of people had congregated near an aft gangway, presumably waiting to board in third class. On her same level, about five hundred feet or so aft, stretched another walkway, where she supposed the second class were crossing into the ship. The chill in the air they'd first felt in London had not abated with their journey south, and the wind fluttered the flags hung from the ship's masts—a Blue Ensign, the American flag with its forty-six stars, and the swallow-tailed White Star house flag. Seagulls wheeled about the snapping tails, their cries competing with the growl of the crane engines at either end of the ship still hard at work loading cargo.

Perhaps it was the disorienting height. Perhaps it was the grandeur of the ship herself. Or perhaps it was the tumult of emotions their journey home aroused in her, and the fact that once she stepped aboard, once they cast off, there would be no turning back.

Whatever the reason, didn't matter. And after but a moment of wavering, she took a deep breath in and plunged forward, grasping the sides of the gangway and keeping her eyes trained through the doors at the end of the walkway and not on the intimidating clifflike sides of the *Titanic*.

The first thing she noticed as she entered the ship was the scent of flowers. It was like walking into a floral shop or a garden in full bloom, and entirely unexpected after the salty bite of the sea air. A few steps later she understood why the rooms had been so liberally embellished with blossoms, for the sharp smell of fresh paint began to pierce through the haze of gardenias and hyacinth. The crew must have been working until the last moment to ready the ship for its first passengers.

Stewards and stewardesses in crisp uniforms stood waiting in the white-paneled vestibule beyond the teak-framed doors, as well as several of the officers. Father had paused to speak with them and shake their hands, while Charlie and Mr. Sloper allowed a pretty young stewardess to give them a flower for their buttonholes. A couple entering before the Fortunes was directed to the location of the kennel on the Boat Deck for the dog trailing along behind them on a leash. His claws clacked against the black-and-white-patterned floor, the sheen of which was so lustrous that at first Flora mistook it for marble.

One of the stewards peeled away to escort Mother and Father through one of the sets of doors into the Entrance Hall foyer, at the center of which stood the Forward Grand Staircase. Constructed from solid oak, it boasted hand-carved panels and balustrades of the highest craftsmanship and sturdy Tuscan columns. Tucked into a corner of the hall sat a four- or five-man orchestra, playing a lively tune that Flora couldn't quite identify, but it certainly lent a festive atmosphere to the proceedings.

Just forward of the staircase stood a trio of lifts, their lift boys ready to ferry passengers to their assigned decks. At the moment, there was a line waiting to use them, but the Fortunes' steward informed them that their cabins were on C-Deck, just one floor below where they currently stood on B-Deck, so they opted to take the stairs instead. They said farewell to Mr. Sloper, whose cabin was located above on A-Deck, and turned to follow their steward. Flora couldn't resist trailing her hands over the smooth finish of the wood, astonished by the sheer splendor and size of everything around her. She found herself grinning almost stupidly, but then her brother and sisters were doing much the same thing.

Emerging on C-Deck, they discovered a foyer much like the one above, and found another crowd clustered before the Purser's

Enquiry Office to the left, on the starboard side of the ship. The Enquiry Office was always a hive of activity on sailing day. It was there that people went to deposit their valuables for safekeeping, to exchange foreign currency, to rent steamer chairs or rugs for the duration of the voyage, and to arrange a specific table assignment in the Dining Saloon for their meals, among other things. As they passed near the front of the line to turn down the forward starboard corridor, Flora heard a woman in a fur stole arranging for a rebate since she intended to take all her meals in the À la Carte Restaurant on the Promenade Deck rather than the Dining Saloon.

"Well, aren't we flush," Mabel quipped under her breath, for only the wealthiest of passengers chose to dine in the restaurant, since it cost an extra tariff.

"Don't be crass," Flora scolded.

"We're all thinking it," her youngest sister replied, undaunted. "I'm simply the one brave enough to say it."

Flora stopped herself from retorting that some things were better left unsaid. It would only be a waste of breath. Mabel viewed plain-spokenness as a virtue, but often confused candor with impudence.

The Fortunes didn't have far to walk, finding their cabins C-23, 25, and 27 grouped together as a suite with a private bath. The steward paused before a short corridor leading toward starboard, explaining that the sisters' and Charlie's staterooms would be just off the next passage, before leading their parents to their door. True to his instructions, Charlie found the door to C-23, an interior cabin, while the sisters entered C-25, an exterior one.

Flora felt the bedroom was everything they could ever want in a floating palace. A small chandelier illuminated two brass beds covered in rose-pink eiderdowns, two mahogany wardrobes positioned in opposite corners, a dressing table, and a folding washbasin. Three-armed candelabras were mounted throughout the room and pastoral scenes graced the walls. The first bed was positioned before the curtain-draped porthole, while an upper pullman berth was fitted over the second. Mabel immediately moved toward the first bed, but Flora blocked her, plunking down on the firm mattress.

"I've been more than fair in sharing accommodations with you both the past three months, but in this I will not be budged from exerting my privilege as the eldest sister."

Mabel scowled down at Flora.

"She's right," Alice agreed, fingering the white daisies and lavender chrysanthemums overflowing the vase placed on the table at the center of the room, and drawing Mabel's ire. "I'm sure all the beds are just as comfortable. I'll even take the upper berth if you wish."

"And have Mother scowling at me for risking your delicate constitution?" Mabel retorted. "Oh, no. I'll sleep on top."

"If you wish," Alice repeated as Mabel stomped across the cabin to the other beds. The tiny smile that played across Alice's lips made Flora suspect that had been her intention all along.

Flora didn't care which bed her sisters slept in as long as it wasn't this one. She reached across to twitch open the rose-printed curtains to peer out the porthole at the steel-blue waters. Multiple tugboats idled nearby, billows of smoke emitting from their stacks, waiting for the signal to be given and the *Titanic* to be cast off so that they could pull her away from her berth.

A light rap sounded on a door across the room from the one through which they'd entered. "Come in," Flora called.

The dark-haired steward who had shown their parents to their cabin opened the door. "Pardon, misses. Is everything to your liking? Do you have any questions?" He spoke with a slight accent and flashed them a merry grin that revealed both a gap between his front teeth and the fact that he was slightly younger than she had first assumed. "Your bath is just through here," he said, gesturing behind him.

Charlie strode past him with his hands tucked into his pockets. "Through my cabin."

"Or you can circle around to the door on the interior corridor," the steward added. He nodded to the trunks already on the floor—those they had wanted for the voyage rather than the rest they'd stored in the hold. "A stewardess will be in shortly to unpack your things."

Father had decided there was no need to bring a maid on the trip, since the sisters could act as one for each other and their mother, and every ship and hotel in which they stayed would have staff to see to those needs beyond simple dressing, such as laundering and unpacking.

All the sisters and Charlie listened attentively as the steward explained how to utilize some of the room's features, including the electric heater and a metal panel of bells and electrical fixtures affixed to one wall that would enable them to summon him, among other things.

"What's this for?" Alice asked, pointing to the green mesh bag hanging on the wall next to her bed.

"That's for your valuables, miss," the steward replied with a grunt as he lowered the upper pullman berth at Mabel's request. "Those you don't want stored in the safe in the Purser's Office, that is. You can tuck your watches and whatnot inside at night, so they don't fall to the floor and get lost."

He meant if there were rough seas, but Flora had to wonder if they would even feel it on board such a colossal vessel.

As Mabel clambered up to her bed, the steward stepped back, scrutinizing the cabin, as if searching for any detail he'd forgotten to share. "Is there anything else I can do for you?"

"If the *Titanic* is unsinkable, why on earth are there life belts on top of the wardrobes?" Mabel taunted, clearly having just spied them from her loftier perspective.

The steward's grin returned. "Purely a matter of precaution, miss. She's got to follow the same rules as everyone else, now, don't she? But have no fear. All those watertight compartments. She'll never founder." He opened their outer cabin door to depart, and Flora rose to see him out. "If that's all, then. My name's Ryan, miss. Ring if ye should need anything."

"We will. Thank you."

He bowed his head before departing, closing the door behind him.

Flora turned to find her brother Charlie bending over to peer through the porthole over her bed. His sandy hair appeared almost ashen in the muted sunlight. "Are Mother and Father getting settled?"

"Mother said she had a letter to write before we depart and then she wishes to lie down for a spell." He straightened, forcing her to look up to meet his eye, something she was still growing accustomed to even six months after his graduation. For all her life, her little brother had been . . . well, littler than her. But at some point during his past two years at Bishop's College School in Quebec, he'd grown over six inches, rivaling their older brother Robert for tallest. "I'm going up on deck to watch her depart."

"I'll join you," Mabel declared eagerly, hopping down from her berth.

One look at Alice told Flora she also didn't want to miss the excitement.

"Why don't we all go," she suggested, as Mabel pulled a half dozen flowers from the vase.

"To throw to those watching," she replied in answer to Flora's arched eyebrows.

Alice smiled at her and reached out to take half a dozen for herself.

# CHAPTER 2

❧❦❧

Alice could hear bells clanging as she and her siblings once more avoided the crowds clustered around the lifts and took the stairs up to the Boat Deck, enjoying the sights and sounds of the glorious ship. She had been impressed before, but she couldn't withhold an actual gasp as they reached the foyer on A-Deck. A cherub figure perched on the central newel post of the Forward Grand Staircase, hoisting aloft a lamp, which pointed upward toward the wrought-iron-and-frosted-glass dome overhead. Sunshine filtered down into the space, bathing everything in warm light, including the ornate wood carving on the landing of allegorical figures depicting *Honour and Glory Crowning Time* with a clock inset at its center.

"All the clocks on board, including this one, are operated by a Magneta system," Charlie informed them, apparently not yet having exhausted his knowledge of all of the *Titanic*'s features. "There are two 'master' clocks in watertight cases in the Chart Room that are then tied to almost fifty 'slave' clocks throughout the ship. This way, as we travel west, they only have to change the time on the 'master' clocks, and the 'slave' clocks will adjust accordingly." It was clear from his tone of voice that he found this to be brilliant.

"Where did you learn all this?" her younger sister Mabel demanded to know, her skepticism all too apparent.

"Journals and newspapers." His gaze sharpened. "Instead of

spending all my time in London shopping and gamboling about the city, I chose to better myself in the library."

"I resent that," Mabel retorted. "Wasn't I the one who requested we visit the British Museum?"

"Children, let's not squabble," Flora chided as they climbed toward the Boat Deck, a statement certain to unite rather than divide their younger siblings. They hated to be treated like children, even when acting like them.

Alice kept her eyes trained on the dome above, marveling at the light fixture installed at its center. Even on such an overcast day, the gilt metal frame and glass-beaded panels shimmered and glistened. So absorbed was she that she nearly collided with a crew member as he was coming down. He smiled politely before continuing to the landing to holler, "All ashore!"

As they were crossing the Boat Deck Entrance foyer, they felt a faint hum beneath their feet. Alice turned to her brother.

"The engines."

A knot formed in her throat, competing with the excitement bubbling just beneath the surface of her skin. A knot that was not eased when she caught sight of the lifeboats hanging on the newly designed Welin davits Charlie had told them about at some point in the last few days. They were supposed to make swinging the boats over the side and raising and lowering them all swifter than the old-fashioned davits used on other ships. They certainly looked sleek and efficient overarching the deck in a cluster to the front and another much farther aft. But to her eyes, the lifeboats, while by no means tiny, appeared incredibly flimsy and exposed when compared with the stalwart and enormous *Titanic*.

*I see you adrift on the ocean in an open boat. . . .*

It was all she could do to push the fortune teller's words from her mind. His fortune had not bothered her much during the past two months of travel, and she was not about to let the warning of some theatrical soothsayer who had been pandering for money from gullible tourists ruin this last leg of her journey either. Not when it was practically all that remained of her adventure.

Her latest letter from her fiancé, Holden, seemed to burn a hole in the beaded bag draped over her elbow. For all the comfort she derived from his declarations of love and admiration and his avowals that he missed her, she couldn't help but wither at his descriptions of the cozy, cosseted life he was planning for them in Toronto once they were wed. A life in which she need not set a foot outside Rosedale, the neighborhood where he intended for them to live.

Alice knew she should be grateful Holden cared for her so. She was perceptive enough to recognize that few women were granted such a luxury. Yet she still couldn't halt the disappointment and, dare she say, dread she felt at the idea of returning home.

No, that couldn't be right. She adored Holden. She *wanted* to marry him. She was simply being selfish and overwrought.

She watched as Flora stepped up to the rail to peer over the side of the ship, wishing she could be more self-contained like her older sister. Here Flora had been coaxed into postponing her wedding, and she'd raised nary a fuss over the fact. She *must* be eager to return to Winnipeg, and yet barely a ripple of emotion showed on her face, just as barely a ripple had shown when they departed. Not for the first time, Alice envied Flora's cool aplomb, and sought to emulate it, moving forward to stand beside her.

Apparently, they'd become turned around and exited on the starboard side of the ship, for instead of the dock, they were met by the sight of half a dozen or more tugboats each securing their lines to the ship and awaiting the order to tow *Titanic* away from the quay and turn her into the narrow deep-water channel of the River Test. A man in a dark suit hovered just to their left, taking photographs of the proceedings. Alice watched as he gingerly lowered his camera over the side of the ship, snapping a picture of the tugs.

The smell of coal smoke teased at her nostrils, both from the boats below and the funnels of the *Titanic* above. By now, the ship's stokers would be below, building up a full head of steam.

At least, that was what Alice believed they called it. She half expected her brother to try to find an excuse to go down to the boiler rooms to watch the proceedings, but perhaps he was saving that request for later. At the moment, another novelty had caught his eye.

"Come see," Charlie exclaimed behind them. "There's a gymnasium."

Alice and her sisters followed their brother into a room lined with large arched windows, allowing natural light to spill across the wooden floor. All manner of contraptions filled the space, such as rowing machines and stationary bicycles, and a pair of devices the robust man with an impressive mustache explained were an electric camel and an electric horse. Several other passengers were already testing out the equipment with varying degrees of success. One pair of ladies couldn't seem to stop giggling over the electric camel. All while the instructor in white flannels bounded about the place, offering guidance and encouragement and the occasional demonstration.

Flora appeared more interested in the large map on the wall that displayed *Titanic*'s current location with a tiny flag. Alice wondered if they intended to chart the ship's progress across the Atlantic here throughout the voyage. While their brother seemed enamored with the facilities, the sisters quickly grew tired of indulging him and turned to go. Charlie caught up with them as they were passing through the First-Class Entrance to the door opening on the port side of the ship.

Here, the deck was far more crowded and noise rose from the people gathered on the dock below. They managed to secure a spot along the rail. Stacks of deck chairs were lined up in the white-walled alcoves between the various entrances and quarters behind them, waiting to be used.

Two gentlemen stood at the railing immediately to their right, speaking quite earnestly. From the snatches of conversation Alice managed to catch, it had something to do with a battle. A historical one, she hoped.

Soon after their arrival, the man with a head full of graying dark hair and a deep drawl turned to greet them. "A good morning to you, ladies. Or rather"—he snapped open his pocket watch to consult it—"I suppose I should say, good afternoon." He bowed and his mustache twitched as he offered them a smile. "And what a splendid one it is shaping up to be, indeed. Please, allow me to introduce myself. Colonel Archibald Gracie, at your service." He nodded toward his companion. "And this is Isidor Straus."

The owner of Macy's department store in New York? Alice eyed Colonel Gracie's companion, a bald older man with a well-trimmed white beard.

"Lovely to meet you," Mr. Straus said simply as the sisters greeted them in return.

As the eldest, Flora was the one to make their introductions, naming each one in turn before swiveling to look for their brother, who apparently had wandered off to examine something else on the ship that had intrigued him.

"But do not tell me you are traveling alone?" Colonel Gracie replied before observing to his friend. "Such intrepid females there are now adays. I have already offered my services as an escort to a trio of sisters traveling together, all friends of my dear wife. I do so hate to see a lady without the protection she is due."

Alice was beginning to form an idea of what a loquacious individual the colonel was, and how quiet and indulgent his friend was.

"We are traveling with our parents, Mr. and Mrs. Mark Fortune, and our brother," Flora finally managed to interject.

"Ah . . . from Winnipeg," Colonel Gracie said, clasping his hands behind his back. "Your father and I have met. I dabble a bit in real estate myself," he explained. "Good man."

Suddenly the deafening triple-toned whistles atop the two forward funnels pierced the air, making them all jump and then wince as it sounded twice more, signaling the ship's departure. Charlie joined them at the rail in time to witness an altercation that appeared to be going on below between someone aboard the ship and a group of stokers rushing toward it as the last gangway connecting *Titanic* to the shore was pulled back. But not before one final man dashed across the ever-widening gap back to shore. The group of stokers was too far away, and the crowd gathered on the ship and the pier too loud for them to hear what they were saying, but from their angry motions and the manner in which one of the men threw his kit to the ground, Alice gathered that the stokers were being left behind and none too happy about it.

"Won't they be short on crew?" Alice worried.

"No, they've always got extra men ready to sign on if the others fail to show," Charlie answered, displaying once again knowledge that she had not expected him to possess. "But those fellows will be furious to have lost a good wage. Especially given the lack of vessels leaving the port due to the coal shortages from the strike." He gestured toward the crowded quays adjacent to them, some of which were tied up two to three ships deep.

Colonel Gracie spoke, raising his voice to be heard. "I was told that White Star and International Mercantile Marine"—a trust operated by J. P. Morgan, which owned White Star—"had to transfer coal from several of their existing ships already laid up in Southampton and Liverpool just to have enough for *Titanic*'s maiden voyage."

While in London, Alice had remembered hearing about the coal strike. It would have been impossible not to, for it had caused considerable disruption to both train and shipping schedules, among other things. Though recently ended, it would take a number of weeks if not months before stores of coal could be built back up to the levels needed to resume normal service. However, the maiden voyage of White Star's new flagship was plainly of tantamount importance, and thus other ships had been docked and pilfered of their coal.

Just then there was a sensation of movement, and with a silent thrill Alice realized that the ship was shifting away from the dock. Having moved up onto deck, the ship's band struck up a lively tune—one that was almost drowned out by the cheers of the passengers and those people who had gathered along the waterfront to watch the *Titanic* depart. All the siblings—even Flora—were caught up in the excitement. Alice and Mabel threw the flowers they'd pulled from the floral arrangement in their stateroom to the crowd below, while Flora waved her handkerchief over her head.

Everyone's spirits were high. Passengers leaned over the rails, calling goodbye to their friends on the dock, who answered with cheers. Toots and whistles came from the water around them, as fellow steamers and tugboats sounded a farewell. Alice couldn't help but grin from ear to ear, wondering if there had ever been a merrier send-off.

Slowly the ship turned to point downriver, moving almost parallel with the neighboring berths and hugging the line of quays as it passed. Alice assumed this must be where the deepwater channel had been dredged to allow ships as massive as the *Titanic* to use the port. Several large liners were tied up just before them. The one closest to the quay was an older White Star steamer with twin funnels—the *Oceanic*, Colonel Gracie said. While the one lashed to the *Oceanic*, making double use of the existing berths in the crowded port, and floating nearest to the *Titanic* as the ship approached was the *New York*.

There was an almost imperceptible change to their momentum—one that was most notable by the swift current suddenly running along the entire length of the ship.

"They've engaged the engines," Charlie announced eagerly, leaning farther out to watch their effect.

Alice started at the sound of a sharp report and reached out a hand to steady her brother as his foot slipped and he nearly tumbled over the side. A series of harsh pops like shots from a revolver soon followed, reverberating through the air. Alice turned in time to see several snaky coils of thick rope hurtled high above before crashing down on a crowd of people who had climbed onto the *New York* for a better look at the *Titanic* as the ship passed.

They shrieked in panic, scrambling to retreat from the flailing ropes. Alice sucked in a breath through her teeth, hoping they were all successful. Unfortunately, it soon became evident they were not, as several people rushed back, dropping to their knees to minister to someone in skirts laid out on the deck.

A ripple of alarm passed among those watching from the rails of the *Titanic*, and Alice quickly grasped why. *New York*'s hawsers had snapped, and the stern of the ship shuddered and began to swing out into the river directly toward the *Titanic*. The crew of the *New York* dashed up and down her length, paying out ropes and putting mats over the side.

"The force of *Titanic*'s engines is too much," Colonel Gracie remarked.

Alice looked about her and then toward the Bridge, wondering where the *Titanic*'s officers were. Could they see what was happening?

"Hold fast for the shock," shouted a large, somewhat disheveled man on their other side.

Alice gripped the rail, her heart in her throat.

Suddenly the vibration they'd barely felt beneath their feet stopped. *Titanic*'s engines had ceased. They all leaned farther over the rail, anxiously watching the progress of the *New York*'s stern, and compelling the ship to stop her forward momentum. But it was to no avail. The steamer continued its arc toward *Titanic*'s after-port flanks.

A light pulsing began again on the wooden deck, and Alice looked with wide eyes toward her brother.

"They've likely reversed the port engine to try to halt the *New York*'s motion," Colonel Gracie said, in answer to Alice's unspoken question.

However, even that did not stop the ship's stealthy crawl toward them.

They watched as a tug, which had come rushing forward to assist, was thrown a line from the port stern of the *New York*. The crew of the little tug tied her up, and the captain engaged her engines at full throttle. Groans and gasps of disappointment emerged from the lips of several of the *Titanic* passengers gathered around them as the line parted almost immediately under the strain. A second, and hopefully sturdier, line was affixed to the tugboat and she began to drive at full power to halt the *New York*'s harrowing advance.

"I told you that sailing on a ship's maiden voyage is never a good idea," the woman with the disheveled man chided shrilly. Alice turned to study the woman in interest, surprised to hear someone else held some sort of superstition about the favorableness—or lack thereof—of the *Titanic*'s journey. The woman's round cheeks looked pale, and dark circles surrounded her fretful eyes beneath a large picture hat with a wide cream bow.

Alice's curiosity was piqued by the couple, but before she could endeavor to find out who they were, someone behind them jested, rather in poor taste, "Now, for a crash."

Her attention lurched back to the debacle unfolding below. The man with the camera they had witnessed on the starboard side had crossed over to join them on the port side, and he leaned far over the bulwark rail to snap a photograph. If the *New York* collided with the *Titanic*, at their current speeds it might not cause a great deal of damage, but both would be forced back to dock at least temporarily to be assessed and repaired. The much-lauded first sailing of White Star Line's flagship—the Ship of Dreams—would be over before it had even begun. This would delay the Fortunes' return to Winnipeg—a not wholly unhappy result—but one that would be incredibly inconvenient and disappointing to her siblings, and possibly detrimental to Mr. Ross's health.

Then, just as the collision seemed inevitable, the *New York*'s forward progress halted and ever so slowly began to reverse. Everyone heaved a collective sigh of relief. Whether it was the reverse wash from *Titanic*'s port propeller or the quick action of the tugboat that prevented the accident, Alice didn't know. But any way you sliced it, it had been a remarkably close shave.

# CHAPTER 3

⌇⌇⌇

"Well, she got that out of her system, anyway!" the large, rumpled American standing next to Mabel told his wife with a laugh. At least, Mabel assumed the woman was his wife. They were of an age and appeared respectable, even if the man vaguely resembled a shaggy dog.

"Futrelle, my good man," Colonel Gracie declared, his drawl less languid than the Futrelle fellow's. "Good to see you." He shook the other man's hand, though it wasn't clear whether it had been offered. "I would love to get your opinion of my book. I've written one, you know. *The Truth About Chickamauga.* A history of the battle. My father commanded a brigade in Bragg's army, and I thought it was high time someone set the record straight. But you must give me your opinion, being a writer yourself."

"You wouldn't happen to be Jacques Futrelle?" Flora stepped forward to ask. "The author of the Thinking Machine stories?"

Mr. Futrelle flushed, brushing the overlong hair that fell over his brow out of the way, so that he could better see through his pince-nez. A string ran from the side of the spectacles to his earlobe in case they fell from his face. "I am," he replied.

Even Mabel recognized the name of the popular series of mystery novels that featured the brilliant amateur sleuth Professor Augustus S. F. X. Van Dusen. She eyed Futrelle with new interest. The man had been dubbed the American Conan Doyle, after all. Though he looked nothing like the tidy, tall, mustachioed creator of Sherlock Holmes whose photographs she'd seen in the newspapers.

"What a delight to meet you. I've long admired your books," Flora told him sincerely. "And this must be your wife," she declared, shifting attention to the round-faced woman beside him. "Are you not a writer as well?"

"Why, yes, I am," she responded with delight.

Flora turned to Alice. "Mrs. Futrelle is the author of *Secretary of Frivolous Affairs*."

Alice gasped in recognition. "Oh, how wonderful!" She looked at both her sisters in turn, lingering longer on Mabel. "I believe I can safely speak for us all when I say we greatly enjoyed it."

Colonel Gracie chuckled to his companion, Mr. Straus. "Yes, the ladies usually do enjoy such things."

Mabel gave the colonel a withering look, but before she could make a sarcastic retort, Alice stepped back toward the rail. "What are those tugboats doing? Pulling the *New York* around the corner of the quay?"

"Yes," Mr. Straus said. "It looks like they intend to warp her into a berth farther from the deepwater channel and the *Titanic*'s path to avoid any further incidents." Though not a tall man, he possessed a commanding presence. Particularly when standing straight with his hands clasped behind his back. He nodded toward the ship that was sitting behind the *New York*. "And it looks like they're attaching more hawsers to the *Oceanic* to be sure she holds fast to the dock. They're not taking any chances of it happening again."

That was a relief to hear.

The maneuvers did not take long, and *Titanic* soon resumed its journey downriver. However, after the excitement of leaving port, there was a score of land miles to endure before she reached open sea, and Mabel had no interest in standing about in the chill breeze, staring at the dull shoreline. She had just turned to tell her siblings so when the ship's bugler began to play "The Roast

Beef of Old England," the traditional signal aboard ship that lunch or dinner was now being served.

Mabel's stomach asserted itself, making a loud growl.

"Haven't swallowed a bear, have you, Mabes?" her brother Charlie jested with a wide, boyish grin.

She linked her arm with his. "No, but I might turn into one if I don't have some sustenance."

With a laugh, they all headed down to D-Deck, where the Dining Saloon was located.

As they emerged from the lifts and moved around the staircase, they entered the main First-Class Reception Room, which filled the entire width of the ship. With its dark Axminster carpet, palm trees, and white cane chairs and settees cushioned by green pillows, it resembled an English lounge. Even the tapestry depicting a hunting party, hanging on the wall opposite the staircase—a reproduction of some famous piece, undoubtedly—lent the same aesthetic to the space. As they crossed the plush rug, Mabel noted the Steinway grand piano situated in one corner, likely for the band's use.

They joined the queue of other passengers slowly filtering through the two sets of double doors thrown open to the Dining Saloon. The first meal aboard ship was always a confusing affair as passengers searched for their assigned tables. This was no small task in a room as immense as the one aboard the *Titanic*, even with the assistance of the dining stewards. Mabel estimated the space must be over one hundred feet long and filled with more than one hundred tables varying in size from two to a dozen or so occupants. There were very few of the larger tables, as most passengers preferred to sit with their own party, lest they be forced to endure all their meals aboard ship with a bore or an annoying prattler or, worse, someone who chewed with his mouth open.

The Fortune family had been assigned its own six-person table near a trio of portholes covered with backlit leaded glass.

The room's décor was Jacobean in style, with Tudor roses depicted in scrollwork across the Saloon's roof and decorative columns. It was undeniably lovely, though not as striking as one might have expected.

One thing Mabel certainly appreciated was the sturdy oak-framed, leather-padded chairs. They were not affixed to the deck like most saloon chairs on Atlantic liners, being heavy enough to stay in place. Which allowed her to enjoy her meal at an appropriate distance from the table instead of being forced to hover at the edge of her cushion.

The crisp white linens, spotless napery, and fine bone-china plates edged with twenty-two-karat gold and bearing the White Star logo at the center did nothing to distract from the meal, allowing the food to shine. And shine it did. Turbot in Homard sauce, mutton cutlets and green peas, beef sirloin with chateau potatoes, roast duckling with apple sauce, and more. Everyone declared it all delicious, and Mabel pushed back from the table feeling plump as a pigeon.

They didn't linger, for Mother was eager to finish unpacking—a task Mabel and her sisters were content to leave to the stewardesses—and Charlie and the sisters wanted to be on deck when the ship steamed down the Solent—the waterway between England and the Isle of Wight—and out into the English Channel.

However, it wasn't long before Mabel grew impatient gazing out at the shores of the island flushed brilliant green with new spring foliage—a bright speck in their otherwise gray surroundings. "How much longer until she reaches open water?" she asked. There was an entire ship to explore, after all.

"See, there in the distance," her brother Charlie replied, pointing toward a growing speck ahead of them that they could just make out, standing as they were on the forward promenade of A-Deck. Above them was the Bridge where the harbor pilot, quartermaster, and officers on duty would be positioned. "That's Nab Light. Once we pass it, we'll have entered the Channel."

It appeared to her as if they were already entering the Channel, but she knew maritime boundaries were sometimes not as straightforward as they seemed. A small tugboat to their right flying a White Star flag bobbed about on waves that Mabel and the others on the massive ocean liner couldn't even feel. The tug tooted her horn in salute as they passed, and the *Titanic* answered. Farther out, a number of warships dotted the horizon with their attendant black destroyers standing by like sentinels to the harbor.

Mabel tugged at her brother's sleeve. "It will be hours before we reach Cherbourg, and I intend to see every inch of the ship before then." Without waiting to see if the others followed, she turned to hurry aft along the deck, nodding periodically to those she passed. This forward section of the Promenade Deck was proving to be popular, particularly on such a cool afternoon, since it was enclosed by walls and windows to protect those strolling and lounging on the deck chairs from the brisk sea breeze.

"There's no need to race," Flora chided, easily catching up with Mabel on her long legs.

Mabel felt a stirring of irritation, but when she turned to make her retort she caught the spark of amusement in Flora's blue-gray eyes.

"Besides, you'll leave our naval instructor behind."

She peered over her shoulder. "Charlie is rather enamored with the ship."

A wide grin brightened Flora's face. "That he is. Perhaps he'll become a shipbuilder."

"In Winnipeg?"

She laughed. "He would have to move to the coast. Perhaps British Columbia or Nova Scotia."

"British Columbia would make more sense," Mabel said. "That's where Robert and Alma are." Their older brother and his wife.

"British Columbia it is, then."

"Are you going to tell him we've arranged his future for him or shall I?"

Flora laughed again—a merry, tinkling sound. "We'll let him figure it out."

The Fortune siblings explored the ship from top to bottom, just as Mabel had insisted. On A-Deck, they visited the soothing Reading and Writing Room, with its thick rose-colored carpet and delicate feminine touches, and then strolled through the Lounge—the gaudiest of all the public rooms. Its décor had been inspired by the palace of Versailles, with a dash of English coziness mixed in. Beyond the Lounge, down a long corridor, stood the aft staircase and its foyer, and then the Smoking Room. That room being a male preserve, they exited onto the Promenade Deck again to circle around to the entrance to the starboard side Verandah Café and Palm Court. The starboard-side café had been designated for non-smokers, while the port side was almost an extension of the Smoking Room, with just a revolving door between them. The large windows offered wide ocean vistas while surrounding passengers with trellis-covered walls adorned with climbing plants.

From the aft staircase, they made their way down to B-Deck and the chic À la Carte Restaurant, where passengers could choose to dine instead of in the Saloon, albeit for an extra tariff. Mabel entertained no expectations of dining there, for she knew her father would find such an expense frivolous when the meals offered in the Saloon already bordered on the extravagant. However, she fully intended to make time to visit the Café Parisien along the restaurant's starboard side. Resembling a sidewalk café in Paris, it exuded a Continental flare. It was enough for Mabel that it smelled of strong coffee and sugar—her favorite combination. She was tempted to remain there even then.

The remainder of B-Deck and all of C-Deck and E-Deck amidships, save for the staircase foyers and the Purser's Enquiry Office, were given over to passenger cabins and private quarters. Having already visited the Reception Room and Dining Saloon—the only public spaces on D-Deck—they continued down to F-Deck via a secondary staircase at the foot of the Forward Grand Staircase. There they found a thirty-foot-long swimming pool filled with heated seawater. Next door were the Turkish and Electric Baths, which were rumored to be quite opulent and strikingly Moorish in decoration, but in order to enter, they would have to pay a fee and come at the prescribed time for their gender. Charlie was quite taken with the two-story-high Squash Racquet Court, which they could view from above in the Spectators' Gallery, and he arranged a time with the racquet professional to use the court the next morning.

By the time they reemerged from below, they discovered it was already midafternoon and the band was playing in the D-Deck Reception Room, where tea was being served. The four siblings decided to partake of the restorative, relaxing on a settee and adjoining armchair. Mabel noticed Flora's eyes periodically drifting toward the stairs.

"I hope Mother didn't have need of us," she fretted.

"Oh, you know her," Mabel added, shifting aside a pillow and sinking deeper into her corner of the settee. "She can smell a pot of tea brewing from a mile off. I suspect she'll join us shortly."

As if on cue, their parents made their way slowly down the staircase arm in arm. Mother appeared serene in a medium shade of blue, her white hair glistening in the light of the candelabra at the foot of the center balustrade. They paused near the bottom as a tall man with dark brown hair joined them.

"Who's that with Father?" Mabel asked.

Charlie swiveled in his chair to look. "Why, I believe that's Thomas Andrews, the ship's architect and chief shipbuilder!"

Mabel and Flora looked at each other. Of course Charlie would know such a thing.

"As I understand it," Charlie continued, "he and a group of men from the shipbuilding firm sail on each maiden voyage to inspect the liner and address any issues that arise."

"I thought Mr. Ismay was in charge," Flora said, lowering her gaze to conceal her amusement as she adjusted the drape of her skirts. News had spread quickly at lunch that the managing director of White Star Lines was on board.

"Not of the shipbuilding firm—Harland and Wolff. That falls under the purview of Mr. Andrews's uncle, Lord Pirrie. But I suppose since *Titanic* is now in White Star's hands, that means that, overall, you're correct, and Ismay is in charge." Charlie tilted his head. "Though, while at sea, the captain is supposed to have ultimate authority. In any case, Andrews is the one who knows the ship's every bolt and rivet. He's a genius!"

Their parents and Mr. Andrews joined them, and Father performed the introductions.

"Well, this has been an exciting day," Flora said. "Even more so for you, I imagine."

"Aye, and it isn't over yet." There was a tinge of weariness at the edges of his voice. One he pushed aside, broadening his smile. "Are you enjoying yourselves?"

"We are, indeed," Charlie proclaimed. "She's a marvel, a real marvel." Mabel listened in amusement as her brother launched into an enthusiastic endorsement of the ship, rambling off statistics.

"You've toured the ship, then?" Mr. Andrews managed to slip in between sentences.

Flora nodded, lowering her teacup after taking a drink. "Yes, we've explored her from stem to stern."

"All the rooms we're politely allowed to enter, anyway," Mabel couldn't resist adding.

"Because I was going to offer my services as an unofficial tour guide, but if—"

Charlie practically leapt out of his chair, interrupting Mr. Andrews with his eagerness. "Would you? That would be all to the berries!"

Mother frowned, evidently not appreciative of this bit of slang he must have picked up while away at school. It was times like this that Mabel was reminded her brother was still only nineteen and far from sophisticated.

Mr. Andrews laughed before asking in his lilting northern Irish accent. "How about Friday morning?"

Mabel turned to listen to the band as Charlie and Father arranged to meet Mr. Andrews the day after tomorrow. They had struck up a ragtime tune—one by Joplin, she believed. The last time she'd heard it was when Harrison's band had performed it at a soiree shortly before their departure from Winnipeg.

She'd met Harrison Driscoll the previous summer and was charmed by his dark eyes and the syncopated rhythm of his music. But while she was fond of the handsome musician and flattered by his attentions, she wasn't in love with him. However, it suited her purposes to let them believe that she was.

She waited until Mr. Andrews walked away and then let out a dramatic sigh. "Harrison played this song for me. Oh, how I miss him."

Out of the corner of her eye, she saw her parents exchange a look, but continued to stare forlornly at the orchestra in the corner. One of the violinists—a young, attractive fellow—must have thought she was gazing dreamily at him, for he flashed her a cheeky grin. One she struggled not to return, for he was a rascal. She was certain of it.

Later, when they returned to their cabin, they found a stewardess still at work hanging the last of their garments in their wardrobes.

"I do beg your pardon," the pretty brown-haired woman told them. "It should never have taken so long for me to finish unpacking your trunks, but with learning to navigate the new ship and the other passengers constantly ringing for things, well, I'm afraid time got away from me."

"Not to worry," the oldest sister Flora reassured her. "We're not unfamiliar with the rigors of the first day aboard ship."

"Aye. I'm Bennett, by the way."

Eyeing the young woman's sharp chin and cheery smile, Mabel decided to plumb her for information. She'd already wasted much of the day, allowing herself to be distracted by the excitement of sailing on the *Titanic*. It was time to refocus her efforts to convince her father of her greatest desire in the world: to be allowed to attend university like her brothers.

Once they returned to Winnipeg, they would be surrounded by the same circle of acquaintances they had always known, and few of them supported the notion of allowing women to obtain a university education. Most of them believed a young lady risked her femininity by embarking on such a masculine pursuit. Some were even convinced it would render her infertile.

All of which was utter balderdash, but she was still left with the onerous task of proving it such. There must be at least one or two enlightened women sailing on the *Titanic* who could guide her in her efforts. Who might even be willing to speak to her father to further her cause. She simply needed to find them.

"Rumor has it, a number of notable people will be boarding the ship at Cherbourg," Mabel posited, sinking down into an armchair positioned near the foot of Flora's bed. "And that several of them are outrageously wealthy."

"Aye, we should be nearing the port within the next hour. I'm to help greet the new arrivals," Bennett admitted, sliding one final gown into the wardrobe before closing its door.

"Have they told *you* who will be boarding?" Mabel pressed, hoping the stewardess would prove eager to share.

Sandy-haired Alice cast her an indulgent look, evidently believing her awestruck by the company they were about to keep, before returning her attention to the stack of correspondence tied together with yellow ribbon resting in her lap.

"Well . . . ," Bennett began slowly, lengthening the moment for dramatic effect, "I've heard that Colonel John Jacob Astor and his new bride will be sailing with us."

This captured all three sisters' attention.

"Isn't he the wealthiest man in the world?" Alice asked.

"Or very near it," Flora responded.

Alice set her letters aside and began removing her hat. "They must be returning from their honeymoon. How romantic."

"Maybe, but it seems as likely they were trying to escape the gossip," Mabel said. Neither the press nor society had been kind to the second Mrs. Astor. For Colonel Astor had notoriously divorced his first wife and two years later wed a woman almost thirty years younger. Even in Winnipeg, the gossip columns carried the news, though the juiciest details came from the clippings from *Town Topics* and other American gossip rags that had been mailed by friends and family to their northern neighbors.

Alice's brow furrowed in concern. "Oh, well, I do hope no one says anything hurtful to her once they board."

"I gather that it's more that they don't say anything at all." Mabel eyed her sister cynically. "But don't tell me you pity her. She must have known what she was getting herself into. It's not as if they treated her any differently before they were wed. And the gossip sheets have been calling him Jack Ass-tor for ages now." His reputation for pawing girls and brawling seemed well documented. "Money doesn't buy happiness."

Alice planted her hands on her hips. "She didn't marry him for money. She couldn't have. Not if she'd 'known what she was getting herself into,'" she countered, throwing Mabel's words back in her face. "It must have been a love match."

"For her sake, I hope so." Mabel gave a mock shudder. One that made Flora cast a scolding glare her way. But, honestly, she didn't care how much money he had. There was no way she would let a man thirty years older than she was touch her, let alone wed him. Especially not Jack Astor. Some ladies found him to be dashing, but to her eye he was too tall, too skinny, and his head with its smarmy mustache far too large for his frame.

The stewardess had observed this exchange with avid interest, enjoying their banter. She would undoubtedly share what they'd said with some of her crewmates. A fact that, judging from Flora's disapproving frown, she realized as soon as Mabel did. So before her older sister could dismiss Bennett, Mabel leaped into the lull.

"Who else is joining us?"

"Let's see, a number of wealthy businessmen from Pennsylvania. A few artists and writers. A pair of tennis stars." Bennett's grin turned sly. "I've never laid eyes on them, but some of the other stewardesses tell me Karl Behr and Chess Kinsey are quite the sight to behold."

That she'd thought this would draw a reaction was obvious, but unfortunately for her, Alice was besotted with her fiancé, Flora was far too respectable to comment on a gentleman's good looks, whether she noticed them or not, and Mabel wasn't in the least interested in handsome men or romantic entanglements. Not when her goal was the exact opposite.

Bennett seemed disappointed by this, but then her eyes widened, as she recalled someone else important. "Sir Cosmo Duff-Gordon and his wife, Lady Duff-Gordon, are also rumored to be boarding. You might know her as the dressmaker Lucile." Glamorous company, indeed.

"We strolled by her new shop when we were in Paris," Mabel replied. "I wanted to go in, but Mother disapproves."

Without even looking, she could feel Flora shooting daggers at her, but Mabel thought Bennett deserved something in compensation for the information she was sharing. In any case, Mother wasn't the only woman who disapproved of the lingerie Lady Duff-Gordon designed and her tea gowns, which could be worn without a rigid corset. Mabel thought they were fascinating.

"What about her sister? Is she boarding at Cherbourg?" she asked.

Bennett's lips twitched, evidently aware of who Elinor Glyn was, or at least the racy novels she wrote. "No, I'm afraid not."

Mabel sighed. "Too bad." Not that she'd ever read one of Mrs. Glyn's novels, though not for want of trying.

Bennett's eyes lifted toward the ceiling. "There will be a few correspondents joining us. Miss Edith Rosenbaum is a fashion writer for *Women's Wear Daily*, I believe. And Mrs. Helen Churchill Candee is another columnist, as well as an interior designer."

Mabel straightened and then struggled to temper her reaction. Even so, the others had noticed, so she couldn't let the moment pass without comment. "I find her accounts on the history of design to be fascinating."

Mabel winced, realizing too late that her sisters would never believe such taradiddle. The truth was, it was less her books on rugs and tapestries, and more her book *How Women May Earn a Living* that interested her. Mrs. Candee had penned it following her divorce from her abusive husband. She was also a suffragette. Surely, *she* must have some advice for Mabel on how to further her cause. For despite Mrs. Candee's status as a divorcee and her need to earn her own living, she was still widely accepted in society and had even decorated the homes of several notable figures in Washington, DC, including former President Roosevelt.

Mabel felt a surge of hope, sharp and swift, in her breast. Surely, Mrs. Candee could help.

# CHAPTER 4

❦

The station at Cherbourg was hot and noisy. For about the tenth time, Chester Kinsey—better known as Chess—checked his pocket watch, wondering how much longer they would be left to cool their heels. The manager from White Star's Paris office who had greeted them as they'd disembarked the train from that fair city had told them that the *Titanic* had been delayed in leaving Southampton. But that the great ship was crossing the Channel as he spoke, and in an hour to an hour and a half's time, they would all be boarding the tenders which would take them out to meet her. Well, that hour and a half had nearly passed, and yet here they still sat.

Even though it wasn't the manager's fault, Chess found he couldn't summon an ounce of sympathy for him as the fellow struggled to placate the more demanding passengers in their midst. Jack Astor, in particular, looked angry enough to spit nails. His new young bride had arrived looking wan and ill, and this echoing hot box couldn't be helping matters. But she also had a nurse and a maid to see to her, and Astor's Airedale terrier seemed smitten with her. He doubted there was another person here more indulged. Anyone else in her situation would merely have had to tough it out. But she was an Astor now, certainly not just anyone, so that simply wouldn't do.

His gaze shifted from Mrs. Astor's pale face to that of Mrs. Margaret Brown, seated next to her. The lively woman from Denver, the wife of the millionaire James J. Brown, was watching him pace up and down in front of the windows overlooking the quay. Or rather she was watching him watch Madeleine Astor.

Mrs. Brown seemed more subdued than past experience had shown her to be, whether out of genuine concern for the young lady or some other reason. Either way, she didn't suffer fools gladly. So if she thought Mrs. Astor deserved her care, then she undoubtedly did, and his uncharitable thoughts were uncalled for. They simply proved what he already knew. He was cross and grumpy.

He offered Mrs. Brown a commiserating smile. One she returned with a nod before turning back to her friend. Chess pivoted on his heel, returning toward the seat he'd given up to a harassed-looking woman a short time before. Next to her sat his friend—and sometimes rival—Karl Behr. His knees jounced up and down, the only indication in his otherwise placid demeanor of his impatience to board.

When he'd bumped into Karl on the streets of Paris a week prior and Karl had told him he'd trailed a girl across the Atlantic, Chess had thought he was pulling his leg. But the more Karl had elaborated, having pretended that business in Europe had just happened to take him to some of the same cities as the young lady, the more Chess had begun to believe him. Having just spent the interminable six-hour train ride from Paris listening to him expound on Helen Newsom's every winsome trait, he no longer held any doubts. His friend was smitten.

Chess had yet to lay eyes on Miss Newsom, but he knew that her lips were like roses and her hair as fine as silk. At least, according to Karl. Chess had no doubt she was a looker. Karl was charming and handsome, after all, and was forever being swooned over by female admirers, the same as Chess. Karl never stepped out with anyone who wasn't beautiful. But *this* was decidedly different.

For one, Miss Newsom was a friend of his sister, and every gent knew you didn't trifle with your sister's friends unless you were serious. At nineteen, Miss Newsom was also young, and it seemed her mother and stepfather—Mr. and Mrs. Beckwith—had taken her to Europe in the first place to slow down the courtship. Chess might have thought Karl was purely responding to the challenge this presented by pursuing her. He was a dashed good tennis player, after all. Not as good as Chess, but close. And highly competitive. However, Karl would never have taken it to this extreme if his feelings weren't truly engaged.

Karl's blond head was turned toward the windows of the Gare Maritime, his gaze never wavering from the long jetty, with its timeworn stone tower at the end. Chess stopped to watch as the remainder of the luggage and sacks of mail were loaded onto the pair of White Star tenders—*Traffic* and *Nomadic*. White Star's newest liners were too big for Cherbourg's harbor, so the *Titanic* would have to anchor beyond the breakwater and wait for the tenders to bring the passengers out to her. The weather that day had been mild but cloudy. As such, night would fall fast, and there was already a sense that the day was fading. Yet there was still no sign of the *Titanic*.

Despite this, he heard a murmur of excitement run through the crowd of first- and second-class passengers behind him and turned to find many of them rising to their feet. The man from White Star's Paris office was passing through the passengers, having apparently made the decision to go ahead and have them board the *Nomadic*.

There was a decided chill in the air as Chess strolled up the gangway next to Karl. So they followed the majority of the other passengers down into the lounge, where there were ample roll-backed slatted benches. The walls were paneled in white and covered with little decorative flourishes, but beyond that there was little of interest to look at. Especially when the passengers had already been observing one another for ninety minutes, albeit in a different stuffy room.

Some minutes after boarding, they felt the floor begin to vibrate and the boat pulled away from the quay. "It won't be much longer," Karl declared eagerly.

Chess didn't offer an opinion, even though he had his doubts. He wished now that he'd kept the copy of Sir Ernest Shackleton's *The Heart of the Antarctic* he'd been trying to read on the train with him. Then he might have at least had some way to pass the time. But it was too late now. He crossed his arms and closed his eyes, hoping the remainder of the day's journey would pass without incident.

It was not to be.

The moment the *Nomadic* left the safety of the harbor, the calm water turned decidedly choppy, rocking the boat from side to side. Chess heard the sound of someone in distress and opened his eyes to discover more than one passenger's features exhibited a rather greenish hue. The pitching waves didn't bother him. His stomach was made of iron. But he could tell that quite a few of those around him were about to be actively ill. Given this, and the fact that the enforced closeness of the room might be contributing to their nauseas, he decided to abandon the warmth of the lounge for the deck above. Karl joined him.

Above deck, he buttoned his wool coat around him and pulled his hat lower on his head against the brisk breeze. The single stack of the tender belched smoke as it maneuvered them to a spot just outside the breakwater, waiting for the *Titanic*'s four stack silhouette to appear on the horizon. They were by no means the only people on deck, and more than once someone gave a shout, pointing toward something that, after raising everyone's hopes, proved to be nothing.

Chess began to wonder why he'd allowed Karl to convince him to join him on *Titanic*'s maiden voyage. Though, truth be told, he hadn't needed much convincing. He enjoyed an adventure as much, if not more, than the next fellow, and this was exactly the sort of escapade his family and society expected of him. He was a Kinsey, after all, and a second son, at that. All Kinsey men were good-looking, but second sons were also supposed to be charming and a little feckless, essentially drifting along as lovable rascals. Or so they'd been since Great-Great-Great-Uncle Daniel Kinsey charmed his way across the Atlantic to America by escorting an English earl's two daughters—one of whom he married and was nearly shot for doing so, only to wind up inheriting the bulk of the earl's unentailed fortune. Kinsey second sons were adored, but never taken seriously.

Chess had more or less conformed to this mold. At least ostensibly. He'd attended Yale and obtained a law degree, and he was now employed as an attorney for one of the family's many businesses, where he was never tasked with anything of importance. That was the extent of his family's expectations of him.

What they hadn't expected was for him to be such a brilliant tennis player, or that he would excel enough to be ranked as one of the top players in the country. They explained it away by pronouncing him a virtuoso, a natural. One of those fellows who either by fate or blind luck proved to be exceptional at something. And Chess didn't correct them or the journalists who seemed to prefer to believe the same twaddle, even though the truth was he'd worked dashed hard to get where he was. His athletic prowess might have helped him take to the court easily to begin with, and his enjoyment of the sport might have kept him playing, but his excellence certainly wasn't fate or luck.

Not that anyone would believe him if he asserted that. Not that anyone would want to. It was easier to see him as unnaturally blessed than determined and hardworking.

He entertained himself by observing a fishing boat for a time, until that turned tedious. Even Karl, who had until that moment been in such high spirits, began to become fractious. Then finally, on the far horizon, backlit by the setting sun, they spied the *Titanic*'s funnels.

The crankiness and vexation of the last few hours began to melt away as the ship steamed toward them, growing ever nearer and ever larger. Chess was simply no match for the awe and excitement of witnessing such a massive object glide across the water, particularly knowing he was about to board her. Night was falling as the *Titanic* dropped anchor and the *Nomadic* and *Traffic* put on steam to pull alongside. The ship towered above them, eleven tiers of glittering electric lights illuminating the ship's clean and gracious lines. It was almost impossible not to gape.

"What a ship," Karl proclaimed. "The greatest ship ever built, they say. And Miss Newsom is aboard her."

Chess turned to find his friend grinning rather stupidly up at the liner, but instead of being annoyed this time, he slapped him heartily on the back. "Then let's go find her."

They waited as the tender's gangway was affixed to the ship and the ladies—especially those who had been ill, such as Mrs. Astor—were helped across the shaky expanse by their male escorts and the *Titanic*'s staff. For the most part, the process moved smoothly, but then a stout woman stumbled and fell, and had to be carried the remainder of the way across. It appeared she'd twisted her ankle, but it would be for the ship's doctor to determine how badly she'd injured herself.

Eventually it was their turn to cross the gangway to the ship, something he and Karl both managed agilely. They entered a sort of vestibule paneled in white with a black-and-white patterned floor. From there they proceeded into a reception room covered in a dark Axminister carpet to be met by a line of stewards ready to assist them. The room resembled a palm court, with numerous cozy groupings of furniture, most of them wicker, and a number of potted palm trees. Nearest them, they could see a panel of lifts ready to transport passengers, and then the curved balustrades of the grand staircase. On the far side of the room, he could see people watching them through a wall of windows as they supped. Dinner must have already begun.

One man in particular stood out from the phalanx of white-coated stewards. Dressed in a smart three-piece suit, a tall fellow with a dark mustache, somewhat similar in appearance to Jack Astor, warmly greeted the wealthy and famous. Chess soon discovered it was J. Bruce Ismay, White Star's chairman. Rumor had it his manner was equally as aloof and sometimes as obtuse as Astor's. However, for the moment Ismay seemed to be acquitting himself admirably enough.

Chess had heard the whispers about the Ryersons, a prominent family from Cooperstown. The Ryersons were hurrying home draped in black, having learned their eldest son—a sophomore at Yale—had been killed in an automobile accident. Their large party included children and a number of personal servants, and Ismay was offering them not only his condolences but also an extra stateroom, which adjoined the cabins they'd already booked, and a personal steward to see to their needs.

Chess thought this quite decent of the chairman. It was difficult to look at Mrs. Ryerson's grief-stricken face and not be overcome with pity and compassion. It was also understandable why she kept her three other children huddled around her.

A gray-haired steward stepped forward to assist Chess and Karl, leading them up one floor to C-Deck and down a long corridor toward the port-side aft of the ship. The two tennis stars had been assigned cabins near each other, but while Karl's was an interior cabin, Chess had paid for an exterior one. He'd never liked closed-off spaces and, in any case, had decided it simply wouldn't be in keeping with his image not to indulge in a more deluxe stateroom. He—and his family—could certainly afford it.

After a brief glimpse over his room, he rejoined Karl in the corridor. It being the first evening aboard ship, the normal dress code of formal attire at dinner was usually eschewed, as Ismay's appearance in the vestibule had confirmed. So neither of them wasted time in changing clothes. Not when the tempting odors that were wafting into the Reception Room while they were boarding still lingered in their nostrils. Chess was fairly certain he'd smelled lamb loin chops, and he was already anticipating the taste.

"These are quite the digs," Karl remarked as they fell easily in step.

"That they are," Chess agreed.

"Did you notice the doors are connected with a clip to the electric light? The steward told me the lavatories are fitted with them as well. The rooms are in darkness until you close the door, and then the light turns on until you open it again. There's a clip by the door and also one at the head of the bed, so you don't have to get back up to turn out the light after you've retired."

"That's convenient."

They nodded and exchanged polite greetings with a number of other passengers who were either standing in their doorways, waiting for the rest of their party to join them, or still making their way to their respective cabins. Chess was fully aware, as he knew Karl must be, of the effect they had on people, particularly when they stood side by side—one light and one dark, but both tall and athletic, and too handsome for their own good, as one female admirer had phrased it. So he was prepared for the stir they caused and the eyes that followed them, ignoring them as best he could.

Though, in Karl's case, he seemed all but oblivious, being too intent on reaching the Dining Saloon. "I can't wait to see Miss Newsom's face once she realizes I'm here," he remarked gleefully.

"And Mr. and Mrs. Beckwith?"

His bright grin turned to one of mild chagrin. "I trust they won't be too put out with me."

"They shouldn't be," Chess said, taking gentle umbrage on his friend's behalf. Miss Newsom's mother and stepfather would be lucky to have Karl as a son-in-law.

A spark of mischief lit his blue eyes. "But I'll still play it off as a happy coincidence all the same."

Chess's lips quirked. "That's probably for the best." He suspected the Beckwiths must have already guessed the truth, but for politeness's sake wouldn't press the issue.

Forgoing the lifts, they jogged down the single flight of steps to the Palm Court and then into the Dining Saloon, where dinner was already in full swing for many of the passengers, if not nearly finished. But accommodation would be made for the late arrivals, particularly given the fact it hadn't been their fault that the *Titanic* was delayed. Chess turned to speak with the steward positioned near the door to locate their table, while Karl searched the assembly for a certain pair of doe-like eyes. He found them as the pair were striding toward their table, and the pure joy that lit Miss Newsom's face as she spotted Karl sparked a bolt of unexpected jealousy in Chess's gut.

Had anyone ever looked at him like that? Yes, he was admired and courted and even lusted over, but he couldn't recall ever being greeted with such untempered pleasure and sweetness.

Chess realized, rather astonishingly, that he envied his friend. Actually *envied* him. Not because of Miss Newsom herself, though she was undoubtedly beautiful and engaging, but because of their happiness. Because of the life together they both seemed intent on building. That discovery was a disconcerting one.

Falling back on his breeding and manners, he went through the motions of greeting Miss Newsom and the Beckwiths, charming them almost by rote. While in truth, his thoughts were still all a jumble. It was a relief when he was suddenly hailed by another acquaintance who'd risen from his table and crossed to greet him.

"Quigg?" Chess exclaimed in surprise, accepting the younger man's hearty handshake. "What are you doing here?"

Quigg Baxter was a star athlete in his own right—a football and hockey player. Or he had been until a blow from a hockey stick had cost him the sight in his left eye. Now he coached. That is, when he wasn't escorting his mother about Europe, which is what he'd been doing when Chess had last seen him in Brussels. Or what he was supposed to be doing.

"Maman decided it was time to return to Montreal." He nodded toward the table where a lovely white-haired woman was seated with a younger version of herself. "So Zette and I are escorting her home. Maman isn't feeling well. *Mal de mer*, I suspect.

I'm going to shepherd them back to their cabin. But I had to say hello first." He leaned forward then, lowering his voice. "She's here."

Chess was momentarily distracted by the long, elegant neck of the woman seated just behind Quigg, and the single twist of medium brown hair with just a glint of copper at its nape. "She who?" he replied, returning his attention to his friend. Studying Quigg's lopsided grin, he began to have an unsettling suspicion he knew, but part of him didn't want to believe the brawny, big-hearted bonehead had done such a thing.

"Berthe."

Chess realized, with horror, he had.

"Maman and Zette don't know, of course. She's staying in a cabin on the deck below ours." His voice rose with his elicit excitement. "Registered under Mrs. B de Villiers, so if you see her, be sure not to give her away."

Chess nodded. "Of course." He wasn't about to step into the middle of the mess the other man had created. Not when it was certain to be sordid and unpleasant. For Berthe Mayné was a cabaret singer and almost certainly a courtesan of some variety. Quigg had fallen hard for her in Brussels and apparently taken her as a mistress. What Madame Mayné's actual feelings were for Quigg, he couldn't begin to guess. He was handsome despite his scars and possessed a kind heart, but he was also wealthy and besotted. Her affections could have many motives. None of which would matter to Quigg's mother or the rest of society if they found out.

The woman with the elegant neck's back stiffened, indicating she'd overheard them. Just as she overheard Quigg's next statement.

"I'm going to marry her once we reach Montreal."

His eager expression told Chess he was entirely serious, and it was all Chess could do not to laugh in morbid horror at his friend's monumental folly. "Won't that be a joyous occasion," he couldn't resist saying.

Quigg nodded, evidently not catching Chess's cynical undertone, but the woman with the elegant neck's head suddenly snapped around, pinning Chess with a pair of eyes the same shade of blue as the sea holly he'd once seen while hiking through the Alps, and just as prickly. Faced with such disapproval, his first instinct was to flash her a roguish grin. Most women—young and old—proved helpless against it, even the prickly ones, but not this elegant lady. She merely arched a single eyebrow—arched it in a way that was far more eloquent than any words could have been—and resolutely turned away.

Absurdly, he found himself grinning even wider and wondering foolishly just what else that eyebrow could communicate. He had a strong suspicion he would enjoy finding out.

# CHAPTER 5

❦

Flora could feel the sun-bronzed gentleman's eyes still on her, but she refused to dignify him with another glance. He was a handsome one, she'd give him that—with russet-brown hair and eyes the warm shade of bleached prairie grass. Because of that, he would undoubtedly view any further interest on her part as encouragement. In fact, he probably expected it. His cheeky, remorseless grin certainly indicated as much.

Well, she wasn't about to give him the satisfaction. Not when his counsel to Quigg Baxter had been so dreadful.

Honestly, what was Quigg thinking? Bringing a fiancée home with him, without his mother's or sister's knowledge or approval. And a scandalous fiancée, at that, if this Chess fellow's reaction was any gauge. Flora certainly didn't derive any of the amusement from the situation that he seemed to.

Mrs. Baxter would be extremely hurt. Hadn't she suffered enough? But then Quigg had always taken after his father, to an unfortunate degree. Flora doubted he would ever turn his charm and good looks toward making crooked business deals and end up in prison like "Diamond Jim" Baxter, but that didn't mean Quigg was ruled by his good sense any better than his papa was. How on earth did he expect to keep this secret until they reached New York or, worse, Montreal? And what did he think would happen once it was revealed?

Clearly, that was the problem. He wasn't thinking. And so his friend should have advised him. Quigg owed his mother his respect, and he also had a responsibility to listen to her guidance. She would help him select an appropriate spouse, just as her parents had helped her and all her siblings.

Her gaze slid to Mabel. Well, most of her siblings. Harrison Driscoll, the ragtime musician, was not exactly her parents' choice for their youngest daughter.

Mabel turned and caught her looking at her. Her mouth shriveled into a little moue before she leaned toward her to speak in an undertone. "You can't still be angry with me for speaking out of turn in front of our stewardess."

"I can," Flora replied, though it wasn't the main source of her agitation.

Mabel rolled her eyes. "It was a bit of harmless entertainment in exchange for valuable information."

"It was gossip that will likely be planted in half the ears on board ship before midnight."

"If it reflects poorly on me, it's nothing half the passengers don't already know, and that I don't care if the other half discovered," Mabel scoffed.

Flora's face flushed with temper. "It reflects poorly on all of us," she hissed, though she knew this remark would have even less of an impact on her sister.

She sat back, angry that she'd let Mabel rile her so. Or rather that Quigg's friend Chess—what kind of name was that, anyway?—had riled her, and she'd taken it out on Mabel. She inhaled deeply through her nose, focusing on the fillet of plaice set before her. She'd managed little more than two bites. Something her mother soon noted.

"Is the fish not to your taste?" she asked in concern. "Or has this day seen too much excitement?" Fortunately, Quigg Baxter and his friend had already returned to their respective tables, for Mother then turned to scold her siblings. "Did you not think your sister might have desired a rest this afternoon? She's no longer as young as you."

Yes, at eight and twenty she was practically rolling in her grave, she thought sourly.

"Your father and I have conferred"—Mother turned to him—"and we believe that, while aboard ship, Flora, you may relax your chaperoning duties."

"Yes, by all means." Mabel's gray eyes glinted with more than mischief. "Flora should have a much-deserved holiday after the hardship of the past few months."

"I've enjoyed traveling with all of you," Flora protested as their stewards began whisking away their plates, in preparation for their next course.

"Oh, we know you have," Alice assured her. "But you can't deny some of our adventures weren't your first choice." She arched her eyebrows. "Remember the camels."

Flora preferred not to.

Charlie chuckled. "And the pigeons in St. Mark's Square."

Flora wasn't certain she would ever be able to think of Venice without remembering the mess the birds had made of her hat, and it had been her favorite. But that didn't mean she couldn't smile now at her folly in tripping and throwing the birdseed skyward rather than toward the ground.

"And we all know what a good sport you've been, postponing your wedding to Crawford." Alice's features softened with a sympathy that made Flora uncomfortable. Her eyes dipped guiltily to the pristine white linen. "It's only right that you take some time for yourself."

Charlie looked toward the backlit portholes a short distance away. "I wonder if we've departed Cherbourg yet. Can you hear the engines?"

They all stilled, listening for their hum, but the rumble of voices and the clink of china and silverware overshadowed any other sound.

"We must not have left port yet," Father said as a steward set a plate of loin chops with cauliflower and fried potatoes before him.

"Excuse me, sir," the same steward leaned in to interject. "We have been outside the breakwater for more than ten minutes."

Charlie grinned. "We're bound for Ireland, then."

"Mrs. Hays and Mrs. Davidson told me there will likely be a number of bumboats that pull up to the ship while we're at Queenstown," Alice informed them as she adjusted the gauze sleeve of her primrose gown. "That they'll have vendors selling Irish linen and lace and other trinkets. They say the products are very fine, and you know Mrs. Hays," Alice said, appealing to their mother. "She would never purchase an inferior product."

Mrs. Hays was the wife of Charles Hays, president of the Canadian National Railway, and Mrs. Davidson was his second daughter.

"Might we visit the vendors when they pull up to sell their wares?" Alice asked Father with wide, earnest eyes.

"I see no problem with it," Father said around a bite of chop. "So long as you take your brother or one of your sisters with you," he added after swallowing.

Mabel agreed to accompany her, and Mother urged them to see if they had a nice length of lace for a christening blanket. Neither their older sister Clara, nor their brother Robert's wife, Alma, was expecting, but they'd been anticipating such news from both of them.

Charlie was pleased to hear that the Davidsons were on board, for he and Thornton were of a similar age and both avid sportsmen. "I'll have to ask him to join me for a game of squash."

Father took a long drink from his glass. "I need to speak to Hays about this hotel the Grand Turk line is opening in Ottawa. I've heard they propose to build one in Winnipeg as well."

Flora knew her father well enough to recognize he saw this as an investment opportunity.

"Well, save that discussion for the Smoking Room," Mother reminded him with a teasing smile.

The remainder of the meal passed pleasantly enough, and

when the first notes of the band began to drift through the open doors to the Reception Room, their party rose to follow the others out to the Palm Court. Flora wasn't surprised when they were soon joined by Mr. Sloper, who was in as good spirits as ever, and full of praise for the splendor of the ship.

They found seats for the ladies as stewards moved through the room with cups of coffee. A number of passengers paused to exchange greetings, including Mr. Beattie and Mr. McCaffry, who informed them Mr. Ross was still too ill to leave his cabin but was resting comfortably. Father and Mother soon drifted off to their cabin or other pursuits, and Charlie had cornered Thornton Davidson, but Mr. Sloper and the Fortune sisters lingered, listening to the music.

Flora's eyes grew heavy and her heart suddenly full at the haunting melody of *Cavalleria Rusticana*. It must be fatigue, she told herself. Exhaustion could make one maudlin. She blinked away the burning at the back of her eyes and attempted to tune out the melancholy notes, lest she begin weeping in earnest.

"Sloper, is that you?"

Flora stiffened at the sound of the familiar voice as Mr. Sloper rose from the settee. A wide grin stretched his face as he declared, "Chess Kinsey! I heard you and Behr were coming aboard, but I wasn't quite sure if I should believe it." The two men shook hands. "It's good to see you. Going to make another run at the Davis Cup this year?"

"We shall see," Mr. Kinsey answered. "But what are you doing here? And with such lovely companions."

As Mr. Sloper introduced them, Mr. Kinsey dipped his head to each of the sisters in turn, but it was to her that his laughing regard returned, and Flora suddenly suspected that his hailing Mr. Sloper while he was in their company had not been a coincidence.

"We met in January on the *Franconia*, of all places," Mr. Sloper explained. "And when Miss Alice told me they were sailing home on the *Titanic* and I must join them, I jumped at the chance."

"Is that so?" The mocking manner in which Mr. Kinsey uttered the words made the hairs on the back of her neck bristle.

"Ladies, this is an old college buddy of mine, Chess Kinsey."

"The tennis player," Mabel stated as more fact than question.

"Best in the country," Mr. Sloper declared proudly.

Mr. Kinsey rocked back on his heels, his sardonic grin never slipping. "That point is debatable. But Winnipeg? So that's why we've never been introduced."

"We don't have much cause to travel to Connecticut," Alice replied with a light laugh. "Is that where you're from?"

"New York, actually. Though, truth be told, I'm away as much as I'm there."

"Yes, I suppose your tennis requires a great deal of traveling."

He shrugged one shoulder. "In addition to other things."

"But I suspect you've spent time in Montreal," Flora couldn't stop herself from pointedly prying. "So perhaps you are acquainted with Mr. Baxter?"

"Quigg?" he queried, feigning ignorance in a manner that made her grind her teeth. "Why, yes, I am. I believe I saw him in the saloon."

"Of course, you did," Mabel muttered dryly. "You spoke with him."

"I did, didn't I?" he responded with undaunted cheer. "You must forgive me. The long day seems to have muddled my brain."

Mabel scrutinized him for a moment, then a spark of quicksilver lit her gray eyes. "Yes, I can't quite recall the discussions I had at dinner either," she quipped with a smirk before turning to Flora. "Except . . . didn't Father say you could relax your chaperoning duties?"

Flora glared at her sister in warning, wondering why she was intent on mischief.

"Ah," Mr. Kinsey said, looking at Flora. "Then perhaps you'd like to join me tomorrow morning for a stroll along the promenade?"

The request was so unexpected—as well as her reaction to it—that she was momentarily at a loss for words. Because for the flicker of a second, she wanted to say yes. She wanted to stroll along the promenade with this attractive man and take him to task for his poor behavior and ask what else took him away from New York other than tennis.

But fortunately, a moment later, reason reasserted itself. After all, she was engaged to be married, and had no business ambling with strange men, no matter how disarmingly charming or hand-some they were.

"Thank you, but I don't think so," she replied coolly as she rose to her feet. "Though you are right about one thing. It has been a long day, and I'd like to retire."

Mr. Kinsey didn't respond, but the glint in his eyes suggested he'd deduced something of her brief inner struggle. There was nothing for Flora to do but ignore him, shaking her skirts out as she turned to go.

But then Mabel surprised her by agreeing, "Yes, I suppose we should retire as well,"

Flora had fully expected her youngest sister to take advantage of her lack of a chaperone to remain among the public rooms until the stewards closed them for the night simply because she could. It was actually Alice who seemed most reluctant to depart, though even she bid goodnight to Mr. Sloper and Mr. Kinsey and returned with her sisters to their cabin.

However, Mabel proved not to be finished with her foolishness. Not five seconds after the door to their stateroom shut, she turned to Flora to announce, "I think he likes you."

Flora frowned. "Who? Mr. Kinsey?"

Mabel gave her a long-suffering look before turning her back to Alice so she could begin unbuttoning her bodice for her. "Of course, Mr. Kinsey. We already know Mr. Sloper is smitten with Alice."

A pleat formed between Alice's eyebrows. "He's not smitten. He flirts with everyone."

"Not that I blame you," Mabel continued. "Mr. Sloper *is* a handsome fellow, as is Mr. Kinsey. . . . And neither of you is married yet."

"I *love* Holden. I'm *marrying* Holden," Alice retorted. "Nothing is going to change that."

"And I'm devoted to Crawford," Flora added primly, removing the Egyptian enamel bracelet around her wrist and her opal ring.

"Oh, you're *devoted* to him?" Mabel queried derisively.

"You don't *love* him?" Alice prodded.

Flora scowled at them both and turned away. "Of course, I do. Devotion implies love."

Though, if she was completely honest with herself, then, no, she didn't love Crawford. But it seemed disloyal to admit such a thing about her fiancé, even to her sisters.

Removing her morganite pendant, she dropped it and her other jewelry into the green mesh bag provided for her valuables and hung it on the hook by her bed. Then she backed up so that Mabel could begin unfastening her mauve crepe brocade dress as Alice still worked on her gown.

"All I'm saying," Mabel began again, "is that a stroll is meaningless. Alice well knows this—ouch!" She broke off as Flora imagined Alice had made her displeasure at this remark known. But Mabel was undeterred. "So why not enjoy Mr. Kinsey's company? Perhaps you'll be saving him from one of those obnoxious American women with tiny dogs, bossing everyone around."

"I doubt Mr. Kinsey needs saving from anything," she muttered wryly. Men like him rarely did.

As Mabel finished unbuttoning her gown and loosened her corset, Flora turned to assist Alice, who stood staring at the door, fingering the strand of pearls still draped around her neck. "Alice?" Flora queried.

"I . . . I thought I might go to the Lounge or the Reading Room for a time," she said after some hesitation. "I'm too excited to sleep."

This wasn't like Alice, who was typically the first to rise in the morning and the first to fall asleep in the evening. "Has Charlie returned?" Flora asked, moving toward the door connecting the family's cabins. "Maybe he would be willing to go above with you."

Alice reached out a hand to stop her. "No, that's not necessary. I just . . ." She grunted in frustration and turned to throw her beaded purse down on her bed. "Never mind. I can see it would be easiest if I just stayed."

Flora looked at Mabel, who mouthed, "Should we fetch Mother?"

Flora scowled and shook her head at the ridiculous notion. Alice wasn't ill, merely acting out of character. Perhaps she was simply more tired than she realized. As a child, Alice would sometimes walk and talk in her sleep, especially when her body was weighted with fatigue from her sickness. They'd once caught her halfway across the lawn to the neighbor's house.

As a precaution, Flora decided she'd wait until Alice had drifted off to sleep and then find something to bar their cabin doors to alert them lest Alice fall back into childhood habits.

# CHAPTER 6

❧

*Thursday, April 11, 1912*

Alice drifted awake slowly at first, then with a sudden jerk as she blinked open her eyes, struggling to recall where she was. The past few months had seen the Fortunes frequently change locations and lodgings, so more often than not, it took Alice several moments each morning to remember the city and country in which she was now resting. Except for the glow from the room's electric heater, the room was dark. Dawn was merely a softening around the edges of the curtain that covered the porthole across the room.

The porthole. That's right. She wasn't currently in *any* city but traveling across the sea on the largest ocean liner ever built, probably somewhere near the Scilly Isles off the southwestern tip of England, if her sense of geography was correct. She lay still, trying to feel any sense of rocking or movement, any vibration of the engines, but all seemed calm and even to her, as if they were on land. It truly was amazing.

Even though she'd lain awake for some time the evening before, Alice almost always woke with the dawn. No matter where she was or what she'd been doing the day before, her eyes popped open with the first ray of sunrise. At home in her own bedroom in Winnipeg, this wasn't an issue, but sharing a room with her sisters on their travels, she'd discovered Flora and Mabel were not early risers. And they became rather annoyed when she began moving around, making noise. Mabel was not so easily roused, but Flora stirred at the slightest sound.

So Alice remained snuggled in her cozy bunk under the eiderdown blanket, listening to Mabel snore softly overhead while the sunlight grew brighter at the edges of the curtain, tinting the white walls pink, then orange, then yellow. Her gaze drifted to the small leather valise Flora had removed from the wardrobe to set in front of the door. Alice had not quite been asleep when Flora stole out of bed to set this alarm, and Alice had felt a prick of anger at her presumptuousness. But just as swiftly her irritation abated, as she considered the fact that her sister was simply trying to protect her.

Alice heaved a quiet sigh and was surprised when the bedclothes overhead rustled and Mabel suddenly poked her head over the side of the bed, gazing down at her, upside down. Her long braid trailed nearly to the edge of Alice's mattress. She couldn't see her eyes—Mabel's face was naught but a dark smudge—but she could imagine her dazed expression.

"Breakfast?" Mabel whispered.

Alice almost giggled aloud. "I don't think they serve it until eight."

Mabel looked at the porthole. "What time is it now?"

"No later than six."

They fell quiet as Flora shifted in her sleep. Once she settled, Mabel began to slide out of her bed, dropping to the floor on silent feet like a cat. "Let's go find something to eat anyway. They won't deny me a biscuit."

In short order, Alice and Mabel found themselves in the foyer on C-Deck, opposite the lifts. Though, technically, most of the public rooms did not open until eight o'clock, they managed to convince their steward to bring them a cup of tea and a biscuit there, so as not to disturb the rest of their family.

After donning hats and warm fur-lined coats, they made their way up to the Promenade Deck, discovering they weren't the only passengers already about. The weather was clear and calm, if cool, with the sun glinting off the water. The wind created by the *Titanic* slicing through the seas was a bit cold for lounging on deck, but it was just the right amount of briskness for a stroll.

The sisters walked arm in arm, nodding to those they passed as they circled the ship. At the aft section, a father watched as his young son, wearing a flat cap and short pants, spun a top across the deck's surface. Alice and Mabel paused for a moment to watch, too, smiling at the child's enthusiasm. Alice noticed the man with the camera again, snapping a photograph, and decided to approach.

"Are you a reporter?" she asked.

The tidy man chuckled. "Far from it. I'm on my way back to Dublin to continue my studies. I'm simply an amateur photographer."

"You're disembarking at Queenstown, then?"

"Aye." He lowered his head, fiddling with his camera. "That's why I don't intend to waste a minute of the day. I haven't much longer to see everything." His eyes lifted briefly. "I noticed you and your sisters. Returning home to America?"

"Canada, actually." She offered him her hand. "Miss Alice Fortune."

He smiled, clasping it warmly. "Pleased to meet you, Miss Fortune. I'm Francis Browne."

"What are you studying, Mr. Browne? Back in Dublin, that is."

"I intend to be ordained as a Jesuit priest."

Alice's eyebrows lifted. "A priest with a penchant for photography."

"Aye." His eyes twinkled. "I don't suspect there are many of us." He lowered his head again to adjust something. "Perhaps you and your sisters would be willing to pose for me?"

"Oh, I don't know," she answered, suddenly bashful. She pressed her pale blue velvet hat trimmed with roses tighter to her head against the wind. "I'm not sure that's such a good idea."

She was grateful when he didn't press. "'Tis not for everyone.

Even Mr. Futrelle, the writer, was reluctant at first. But you let me know if you change your mind."

Alice watched as he carefully leaned over the rail to take a photograph of the wake trailing out from the ship along the starboard side. "I imagine your pictures will be worth quite a great deal. Do you intend to sell them?"

"Oh, I don't know about that," he demurred. "There were newspaper reporters clambering all over the ship at Southampton, and there are bound to be more in Queenstown and New York. Why would they pay for mine when they can use their own? But I do intend to send copies to the captain and crew, and to Mr. Andrews. I'm sure they'll find them of interest."

"I'm sure they will," she agreed, leaving him to his contemplation of the gleaming rails and decking, stretching into the distance toward the fore of the liner.

Mabel stood at the aft banister, her dark hair grazing her shoulders, staring down at the Well Deck, where a number of third-class passengers were milling about. A group of children were running around, playing some sort of game in which they appeared to pretend to be horses, while another cluster of rowdy boys scaled the sides of the baggage crane in order to swing out over those below. As the boys dropped to the deck below, they came away with their hands covered in black grease.

"They'll be filthy," Alice remarked, feeling pity for their mothers or whoever their caretakers were. She couldn't imagine they'd brought many clothes with them. Not when most of them were immigrating to a new country and carrying everything they owned with them.

"Oh, leave them be," Mabel countered. "They're having fun." Her features turned contemplative. "This may be the only time in their entire lives when they're free to do as they please for a whole week for the simple reason that they *can't* work while they're aboard ship."

Alice was much struck by this observation. "I suppose I never thought about it." A single day's holiday was an enormous luxury when they were accustomed to working every day from sunup to sundown, so seven days on board a ship where they *couldn't* work, and even had their food prepared for them, must seem wondrous to these children.

She turned to look at Mabel, wondering where this insight had come from. "What made you realize it?"

Mabel shrugged. "Maybe I'm not as obtuse as you all think I am."

Lacing her arm through Mabel's, Alice guided her around the corner moving forward into the wind. "Do you know what the *Titanic* needs? A crane over the swimming pool! Like that rope swing at Gran and Grandad McDougald's that swung out over the pond! Can you imagine how some of our fellow passengers would react?"

"Oh, I imagine a few of them would give it a try. Mr. Sloper, for one. And that Kinsey fellow. The one who couldn't stop smiling at Flora. . . ."

"Oh, now, don't start that again. Flora is engaged." Alice clutched her ermine collar tighter around her throat with her free hand. "I know you haven't forgotten."

"Maybe so, but have you noticed she hardly ever mentions Crawford?"

Alice frowned, thinking back over their more recent conversations. "That doesn't mean anything. Flora is circumspect."

"What about the fact that I don't believe she's received more than one letter from good old Crawfy this entire trip. And I bet that one was as dull as ditchwater, too."

"You've never liked Crawford," Alice pointed out.

"Because he's dull," Mabel retorted with what she seemed to think was an unassailable truth. "As ditchwater," she added in emphasis, turning it into a refrain. Her cool gray eyes cut sideways to look at her. "Flora is only marrying him to please Father and Mother."

But this was too much for Alice. "That can't be true. Just because *you* find him dull, doesn't mean she does."

Except, thinking back now, she couldn't recall ever seeing Flora more than mildly pleased with her fiancé. Even when they'd announced their engagement, she hadn't glowed or laughed but worn a polite smile while accepting everyone's congratulations with her carefully modulated voice. What was just as bad, Crawford hadn't been giddy or excited, either. For Alice, who had worried she might burst with happiness when Holden asked for her hand in marriage, it was a stark realization.

She turned to gaze out over the endless expanse of water, watching the sun ripple and play over its surface as the sun climbed higher in the sky. Flora deserved happiness, as much if not more than any of them. But that didn't mean it was any of their business to interfere. Not like she could tell Mabel wished to.

Alice reached over to cover Mabel's gloved hand with her own where it rested against the balustrade. "We are not going to meddle in Flora's affairs. Flora is perfectly capable of managing her own life."

"Of course, she is," Mabel agreed, but the quirk of her lips at one corner made Alice suspicious.

# CHAPTER 7

❦

Mabel lingered over breakfast. Having sat with Alice at their family's assigned table promptly at eight, she might have finished her baked apples, tomato omelet, and grilled sausage and departed by half past. But Charlie joined them then, freshly bathed after his squash match with Thornton Davidson, and launched into a play-by-play description, so she'd elected to stay, sipping her coffee and listening to her younger brother with half an ear. The other was tuned to the voices around her, attempting to identify those passengers she most desired to meet. Eventually, her parents and Flora arrived at the table, trading places with Charlie, yet Mabel still remained. Her family thought she couldn't be patient, but in truth, she could be every bit as persistent as she needed to be when there was something she wanted.

She didn't tell Flora she'd seen handsome Chess Kinsey not ten minutes before, dining with an equally attractive blond fellow. Mabel also didn't tell her father that Major Arthur Peuchen had been looking for him. She knew Father found the president of Standard Chemical Company mildly annoying if well meaning. However, she liked the bluff, talkative Torontonian better than most of the prominent Canadians in their circle of acquaintances. At least his stories were interesting. He also didn't take care to guard his tongue like some, a trait she appreciated. Why, just that morning he was telling her what rotten luck he found it to discover that the captain at the helm of the *Titanic* was Edward

J. Smith. Thus far, Mabel had heard only glowing praise for the captain. There were even passengers who claimed they went so far as to travel specifically on liners under Captain Smith's command. So, to hear someone say otherwise was rather intriguing.

She'd strained all morning to hear Helen Churchill Candee's name, eager to speak with the author and designer she'd learned had boarded at Cherbourg, but had no luck. However, she heard a pale-haired lady address her darker-haired companion as "doctor" as they passed near their table.

Mabel excused herself, following the women as they passed through the Palm Court, and climbed several flights of stairs to the A-Deck. Both women were dressed in expertly tailored, high-necked suits with lace at the collar and cuffs. As they crossed the foyer toward the corridor that led to the public rooms, Mabel hastened forward.

"Excuse me," she called out twice, before the two women turned to her. She took a moment to gather herself and catch her breath, wishing the ladies had taken the lift. That would have presented a far more natural opening for their conversation.

"I beg your pardon," Mabel began again, addressing the lady with the sharply restrained tight brown corkscrew curls. "But did I hear that you are a doctor?"

The woman gave her a brief once-over with her dark eyes. "I am, but if you're having some sort of complaint, it would be best to speak with the ship's surgeon. Dr. O'Loughlin is amiable and eminently qualified," she added as she turned away.

"I'm sure he is, but that's not why I asked," Mabel replied before she could be summarily dismissed. "I asked because . . . well, I wish to attend university, and I . . ." She flushed as she fumbled her words, unused to feeling so flustered in front of others. Normally other people's opinions mattered little to her, but this was different. *This* was important. "Well, my father, he . . ." She halted once again, hesitating to speak negatively about her father.

The dark-haired lady exchanged a look with her friend. "Let me guess. Your father does not approve?"

Mabel nodded. "How ever did you convince your father to let you study medicine?"

The woman offered her a tight smile. "Come with us."

Mabel eagerly joined the ladies as they headed for the entrance to the Reading and Writing Room.

The pale-haired woman looked at the watch affixed to her bodice. "Perhaps the Lounge," she suggested to her friend, seeing that this room was not intended to be a social space. "There should still be plenty of time to finish our letters before the mail is taken off in Queenstown."

From the number of people seated at the desks scattered about the Reading and Writing Room, their pens scratching across White Star-embossed stationery, these ladies weren't the only ones keen to post letters at the last stop before the *Titanic* set off across the Atlantic to New York. In fact, a steward was just departing with a handful of envelopes and postcards to be taken to the Enquiry Office, where it would be dropped down a chute to the post office near the bowels of the ship. The *Titanic* was a Royal Mail ship, after all, and one of her chief duties—besides ferrying passengers—was to transport the mail.

The dark-haired lady nodded, leading the way to the Lounge next door, which boasted high ceilings and ample windows. Walnut furnishings and comfortably upholstered chairs were situated in cozy little groupings across the expanse of the green-and-gold carpet, while Aubusson tapestries hung from the walls paneled in the finest English oak. These panels were engraved with delicate reliefs of shell, floral, and musical themes. Along one side of the room, a massive mahogany glass-fronted bookcase offered a selection of books that passengers could borrow for their enjoyment. There was even a bar in one corner for their convenience, though ten o'clock was early for such indulgences.

The women chose a green velvet settee in front of the hearth, leaving space for Mabel to perch between them. The electric fireplace threw off a welcome amount of heat and a cheery light, and while it did not flicker or crackle like a real fire, it still left Mabel feeling soothed. She noted a small golden statue perched on the marble mantelpiece—one lovingly crafted of a Greek or Roman goddess. Artemis or Diana, from the looks of it, for she'd been depicted as a huntress.

"Now, tell us," the dark-haired woman urged. "Is that what you wish to do? Study medicine?"

"Truthfully . . . I'm not sure what I wish to study," she admitted. "Did you know? Did you always know you wanted to study medicine, Doctor . . ." She broke off, realizing they hadn't yet introduced themselves.

"I'm Dr. Alice Leader," she replied with a smile, before nodding to her friend. "This is Mrs. Margaret Swift. But to answer your question, no. No, I didn't always know." She scrutinized Mabel. "But by your age I did."

Mabel stared down at her fingers. "Probably not medicine," she conceded. "But I do know I want to attend university. I want to study *something*. Law, perhaps. I just . . . I want there to be more to my life than marriage and motherhood. There must be more. Or at least the opportunity for it," she pleaded with them.

The two women shared another speaking glance.

"I'm Mabel Fortune, by the way," she added in a small voice, knowing she was being incredibly forward.

"Miss Fortune," Mrs. Swift said gently. "I admire your courage in approaching us. I suspect there are few among your circle of acquaintances who understand this desire. I also attended university. I have a law degree, and I've lectured to women's groups upon occasion, though I've never practiced. I certainly don't fault you your eagerness to learn." She reached out to touch Mabel's hand. "But it is a difficult road. There will be people who discount you at every turn, who believe that you're destroying your femininity. That you're acting against God's intentions."

"Such a ridiculous notion," Dr. Leader pronounced. Her hands tightened into fists in her lap. "The Lord gave us brains as well, and the will to help others. As if He would have us confined to the home when He gives us the gifts and the longing to do more." She inhaled and exhaled sharply through her nostrils. "But Mrs. Swift is right. You will confront all of this and more. Perhaps your entire life." She arched her chin. "Though thankfully there are more and more of those among us who accept reason."

"And among them were our dear husbands, may they rest in peace," Mrs. Swift said in a soothing voice. Of the two women, she seemed the more willing, or at least better able, to accept things as they were. But perhaps that was because she had never actively attempted to practice law.

"Do you have a medical practice?" Mabel asked Dr. Leader.

"Yes, in New York. Before that, I worked alongside my husband, who was also a physician, in his hometown of Lewiston, Maine. And before that at a number of asylums." Her expression turned sardonic. "Though you will often enough find your position described as a social service nurse or visitor rather than as a fully fledged physician because the hospitals fear offending their patrons and patients."

This, too, might explain why Dr. Leader was not able to remain as sanguine as her friend about the matter.

"So, you see, this isn't a matter to be treated lightly," Mrs. Swift cautioned, pressing a hand to the fuzzy blond hair of her pompadour.

"I understand, and I assure you I'm quite serious. If I could just convince my father to allow me." She looked back and forth between the women. "How did you do it?"

"My father was not without his arguments against it, but . . ." Dr. Leader released a sigh that was more mournful than exasperated. "He also highly valued education, for his daughters as well as his son." She smiled tightly. "In that regard, I was fortunate."

"My father did not come from money," Mrs. Swift said, "so once he'd made his fortune, he was anxious to see that his daughters were well cared for. He saw it as a mark of success, of breeding, you see, that we wouldn't have to work like our ancestors had."

Mabel lifted her gaze toward the gilt ormolu clock hanging on the wall, wondering if her father held similar notions. After all, she knew that he was proud of the fact that by the age of thirty he'd already become a tremendously wealthy man, even though he'd started life with almost nothing. Perhaps, in his eyes, the notion of one of his daughters attending university was seen as a failure. *His* failure.

"How did you overcome his reticence?" Mabel asked.

"With time. And patience," Mrs. Swift replied.

"Both of which I have tried," Mabel huffed. "But he seems no closer to agreeing now than he did five years ago."

She couldn't wait another year. Not again. She would rather marry Harrison and cast her lot with him. Perhaps he would be more amenable.

Yet, inside she squirmed at the very idea. It would be dishonest and underhanded, and unfair to both Harrison and herself. She didn't *want* to marry. But she also couldn't go on living another year under her parents' roof, with Mother playing matchmaker and Father denying her only desire. Once Flora and Alice were wed and Charlie was off to university, it would just be her and her parents in that enormous house Father had built for them on Wellington Crescent. She had to do something!

"Maybe you could talk to him," she told the two women, hearing the desperation in her voice. "Convince him that it's not as terrible as he believes."

Both women seemed momentarily at a loss for words.

Mrs. Swift found her voice first. "My dear, we're more than happy to meet your parents if you introduce us. But . . ."

"We're not going to intrude into the middle of a family affair," Dr. Leader finished for her. "It would be uncivil for us to do so."

Mabel's heart sank.

"*However*," Dr. Leader went on, "you introduce us and include our credentials—smoothly, mind you—and if they ask questions, as most curious people do, then we will do what we can." Mrs. Swift pushed to her feet. "And now, we really must finish our letters."

"Of course," Mabel said, knowing it was time to retreat. "Thank you."

# CHAPTER 8

❧✽❧

Flora found her sisters on the Boat Deck, leaning over the rail in a rather unladylike manner, but they were far from the only ones doing so. Hurrying forward, Flora discovered why. A small whaling boat had been pulled alongside the ship so a man could clamber aboard.

"The harbor pilot," the man with the camera from the day before was explaining to Alice. He was wielding the black contraption yet again.

"This is Queenstown Harbor, then?" Flora interjected, squeezing up to the rail next to her sisters. She'd heard the murmurs a short time before that Ireland's coast had been sighted.

Rugged gray cliffs rose out of the water, topped by the brilliant green hillsides Ireland was so famous for.

Alice's eyes sparkled with anticipation. "Mr. Browne was just explaining to us how the harbor isn't deep enough for the *Titanic*. So a harbor pilot who knows the bay well will be guiding the ship the rest of the way, edging her as close as possible before she drops anchor a couple of miles offshore."

Flora looked out over the sea toward the gap between the two rock-strewn headlands. On the eastern bluff perched a white lighthouse, guiding ships toward the entrance to the harbor, while to the west sat a massive turf-and-concrete structure.

Someone behind them asked about the building, echoing

Flora's curiosity. If she squinted, she could just make out the gun emplacements marking it a military installation.

"Fort Templebreedy," Mr. Browne answered.

"I suppose Redmond and his gang are at it," a deeper voice remarked, sparking a debate with a third person about his derogatory tone.

Flora had heard enough talk among her parents' British friends to know that John Redmond was an Irish Member of Parliament and an advocate of Irish Home Rule—an issue that was currently a hotly debated topic—and one she had no desire to venture an opinion on, let alone listen to an argument over. Fortunately, her sisters appeared to agree. Even Mabel, who sometimes ventured into disputes or played devil's advocate just to stir the pot. But she also seemed preoccupied by something. Flora could see it in the tiny pleats between her eyebrows and the distant look in her eyes.

They moved a short distance away from those who were arguing, watching as the whaling boat departed and the *Titanic* advanced slowly into the harbor. As the door to the First-Class Entrance opened behind them, the sound of instruments tuning drifted out, and Flora realized the band was about to begin playing, likely clustered around the piano situated in the corner of the entrance foyer beneath that glorious roof.

"How is Mr. Ross?" Alice asked politely, evidently realizing Flora had paid a call on their ill friend that morning.

"The same," Flora reported. She was tempted to make a pointed comment about how he would undoubtedly welcome a visit from her sisters as well, but she elected to hold her tongue. In any case, Mr. Ross wasn't despairing for company, despite his dour mood. His fellow Winnipeg Musketeers had told her a number of visitors had stopped by to cheer him up, including Mr. Sloper and Major Peuchen from Toronto.

In the distance, the city of Queenstown came into focus, hugging the edge of the harbor. At the top of the town stood a cathedral, its tall gray spire visible against the blue sky, while the waters near the shore were dotted with boats. Two of them were undeniably the tenders bringing more passengers and the mail bound for America to the *Titanic*, and some of the others must have been transporting the vendors Alice and Mabel hoped to purchase wares from.

A flock of gulls swarmed around the ship, drawing Flora's eyes upward as they hovered overhead, seeming never to move their wings. Pressing her hand to her head so that her champagne straw hat wouldn't topple off, she stared up toward the towering gold-and-black funnels and gasped in shock as a head poked out from the top of the fourth funnel. She wasn't the only one surprised. Several other shrieks were heard along the length of the deck.

Alice and Mabel followed her gaze toward the face covered in soot. Evidently the fourth funnel must be false, installed merely for appearance's sake and perhaps ventilation. But until that moment, Flora hadn't known it.

She gave a little laugh, feeling silly for reacting so. Who could blame the stoker for wanting a bit of fresh air? And, if he was from Ireland, a sight of his homeland.

"What's all the excitement?" a familiar, deep voice declared.

Turning reluctantly, she found herself noting in annoyance how Mr. Kinsey looked even more handsome in the bright light of day. Clearly, *he'd* not lost any sleep the night before, for he appeared vital and refreshed, his amber-brown eyes seeming to take in everything, including her, with one glance. He'd forgone a hat, allowing the wind to tousle his dark hair, and for a moment she envied it.

No, wait. That wasn't right. She felt herself begin to flush at the thought. Rather, she envied *him*, for she wished she could remove her hat and loosen the pins restraining her waves. But that would be scandalous, not to mention embarrassing to her family. Except now it was all she could think of. She frowned at him, irritated he'd placed the consideration in her head. Or, at least, inspired it.

"Mr. Kinsey," Alice exclaimed. "How lovely to see you again."

"Yes," Mabel added, making Flora's lips purse in aggravation.

"But who are your friends?" Alice asked.

"Karl Behr and Miss Helen Newsom, allow me to introduce the Fortune sisters." Mr. Kinsey gestured to each of them with a flourish as he stated their names.

"You're also a tennis player," Mabel said to the blond fellow who was nearly as tall as his friend.

"I am," Mr. Behr confirmed with a smile. "Or, as Chess might say, I try to be."

Mr. Kinsey simply grinned.

"He's awfully good," Miss Newsom chimed in to say, her eyes soft as she stared up at Mr. Behr.

They made an attractive pair—her delicate, brunette loveliness next to his blond ruggedness. Judging from the way they looked at each other, Flora wondered if they were engaged. Or if they would soon be.

"Are you planning to visit the vendors from the bumboats as well?" Alice asked.

"Vendors?" Miss Newsom queried in interest.

Flora noticed Mr. Kinsey smirking at her as Alice explained. Flora tried to ignore him, but the smile he aimed at her and the way his gaze never wavered was far too vexing, and she soon found herself glaring back at him.

"Do you intend to purchase some lace?" he asked her once Alice and Miss Newsom had stopped speaking. "Perhaps for a special occasion."

He was baiting her, Flora realized, and she arched her chin in defiance. "No, I've already purchased my wedding gown from Worth. It's in the hold, as we speak."

Miss Newsom clapped her hands together. "Oh, how marvelous! You must describe it to me."

"I should be delighted to," Flora told her.

"But not now, I'm afraid," Mr. Kinsey announced. "Not if you don't want to miss those bumboats."

They all turned as one to peer over the side of the ship at the approaching boats. They looked so tiny next to the massive hull of the *Titanic*, and the waters that had previously seemed so calm now exhibited a slight swell as the smaller crafts rode up and down on them.

"One of the crew members told me the licensed vendors usually set up their wares on the promenade," Alice told them, hurrying toward the entrance so that they could take the stairs down to the deck below. Miss Newsom, Mr. Behr, and Mabel followed her. The latter of whom cast an amused look over her shoulder at Flora as she stood trapped against the railing by Mr. Kinsey.

Well, perhaps "trapped' was an uncharitable description. She was certain that if she had decided to follow her sisters, he would have willingly allowed her to pass. But there he stood, smirking at her all the same.

"Perhaps you would stroll with me." He turned, offering her his arm.

"I believe I already told you that wouldn't be a good idea."

"Surely you're not afraid to walk with me in broad daylight on a deck full of people." He peered around them. "I recognize I'm quite irresistible." He leaned closer. "But I suspect you can resist."

"Don't do that."

He straightened abruptly at the harsh tone of her words.

"Don't mock me." Her skin prickled with anger. "Do you honestly think I'm foolish enough to be dared into doing something? Don't belittle me."

"I didn't—"

"And don't belittle yourself!"

His mouth snapped shut as he stared down at her.

"Or are you truly this"—she waved her hand, searching for the right words—"roguish ne'er-do-well you present yourself to be?"

She glowered up at him, waiting for him to answer. When he didn't, she turned to walk away.

"I'm not."

She turned back, looking up at him from beneath the wide brim of her hat.

He swallowed. "I'm not just a roguish ne'er-do-well, as you so elegantly put it."

In that moment, gazing up into his wary eyes, she realized that it had cost him something to admit that.

"Then . . . why do you pretend to be?"

"I suppose because it's what's expected of me," he murmured, raising more questions than he'd answered. But before she could ask them, he shifted a step closer. "I know you are perfectly within your rights to say no, especially after the way I've behaved, but . . . I would still like to stroll with you. If you're willing—and if I promise not to behave like a 'ne'er-do-well'?"

She didn't quite understand why sharing such a moment of simple honesty had made him suddenly so much more appealing, but instead of firmly refusing once and for all, she found herself saying yes instead. However, she declined the offer of his arm, clasping her hands before her instead as they walked side by side slowly down the deck.

"So, Mr. Kinsey, you said you hail from New York. Is that where your family lives?" she asked, deciding that was a safe topic.

"Yes."

"Is it a large family?"

His lips curled upward at the corners. "I have a brother and a sister, and enough cousins to fill a brownstone, but no more." He clasped his hands behind his back, allowing the sides of his black wool greatcoat to gape and reveal the gray tweed suit beneath. "What about you? Do you have a lot of cousins?"

"Dozens. As well as an older sister and brother back in Canada."

"So, there are six of you? Why didn't the others join you on your grand tour?"

"Robert and Clara are both married," she replied. "They have their own lives, and leaving it for four months was out of the question."

"I imagine Robert and your brother-in-law have careers to think of. As does your fiancé."

"Ah . . . of course. My fiancé," Flora said, smiling, having already guessed this was where the conversation was headed.

"Am I so predictable?" he asked.

"Not so very," she teased, wrinkling her nose. "But it seemed the question must arise at some point." She took in a deep breath, preparing herself to speak about the man she had been trying not to think of for the past three and a half months. "Crawford Campbell is a banker. A rising one at a firm in Toronto. He's . . . well established, but not yet at a place where he can abandon his responsibilities for months at a time."

"A banker," he ruminated, as they came to the end of the First-Class Promenade on the Boat Deck and made an about turn in the opposite direction.

"I suppose that's not very exciting to someone who plays tennis."

"No. But tennis isn't all I do. I'm also an attorney for one of my family's companies." He grinned more broadly. "This surprises you?"

"No. Well . . . yes," she admitted somewhat abashedly that he'd so easily been able to read her rather insulting shock. "I apologize."

"Please don't." He turned his head to gaze out over the water toward the far shore. "I'm afraid I'm not very good at it. Even my family knows better than to assign me any important tasks."

She wasn't sure what she was detecting in his tone. Frustration? Discontent? Embarrassment? Whatever it was, despite the seeming candor of his revelation, she felt certain there was more he wasn't saying.

"But you *are* a good tennis player."

"I am." He turned to her with a confident smile. And this time, instead of wanting to wipe the smug smile off his face, she was glad to see it. This time she smiled in return.

# Chapter 9

In all his thirty years, Chess had been smiled at by hundreds, if not thousands, of women. Women who found him charming and handsome. Women who wanted to squeeze his cheeks and tousle his hair. Women who wanted to crawl into his bed or be called Mrs. Kinsey. He took those smiles as his due. But never in all his life had he realized until the moment Flora Fortune smiled at him—really, *truly* smiled at him—how dangerous a smile could be.

Because the fact was, she wasn't smiling at him because he was attractive or because he was witty or even because she wanted something from him. She was smiling because he was happy. Because ever since her unexpected forthrightness had knocked him back on his heels and made him admit things he never in his sound mind would have, he'd been scrambling to regain his footing. And when he *had* recovered his balance, she'd known. She'd *known*. And she'd been happy for him, too.

Now it felt as if his mental faculties were scrambled all over again. This time simply from the curl of a lovely set of lips and the glint in a pair of blue-gray eyes.

"What of you?" he said after clearing his throat. "How do you like to spend your time?"

"Well, my sisters and I help with a number of charitable institutions around Winnipeg. And I teach Sunday school at our church."

"Yes, yes, very admirable," he replied with mock impatience. "But I asked how you *like* to spend your time?"

She blushed prettily. "I like doing those things."

"Of course, you do. But what else?"

"I like music," she admitted. "I play the piano. But Alice is much more lyrical than I am."

"Do you sing?"

"With precision, if not emotion."

He turned to look at her, knowing without her saying so that she was repeating other people's opinions of her abilities, not her own. "Do you read?"

Her head whipped around, her eyes widening in surprise. "Of course." It took her the space of two seconds to realize he was teasing her.

"What do you like to read?"

She opened her mouth to respond, but he spoke over her.

"And if you tell me John Bunyan or George Whitefield's sermons, I shall call you a bald-faced liar."

She lowered her chin, and he thought at first he had offended her with his wry humor, but he soon realized her shoulders were shaking with laughter, not tears.

"No," she said with a chuckle, swiping at the corner of her eye. "No, I like history books and tales of exploration."

"Exploration?"

"Yes." She appeared endearingly uncertain.

"Such as Sir Ernest Shackleton's *The Heart of the Antarctic*?"

Her face became alive with interest. "Yes! Have you read it? Wasn't it fascinating?"

They spent several minutes sharing their admiration for the Irish explorer and his adventures.

"My mother and sisters much prefer works of fiction," she admitted, still sporting a soft smile. "But at least my father and brother Charlie share my taste in reading." Her skirts brushed his leg as she shifted closer to him to avoid a group of men clustered near the rail. "What of you? Does your father or brother or your sister enjoy the same books that you do?"

"My family doesn't discuss literature much."

She must have heard something in his voice he'd not wanted her to, for she looked up at him in concern. "I suppose there are so many other things to occupy one's time in New York." She gave a half-hearted laugh. "I'm afraid the same can't be said of Winnipeg, especially in the winter."

Her brow furrowed as if in unhappy memory, and he was about to ask her about it when he realized her sudden displeasure wasn't aimed at him but at the man walking toward them with a woman dressed in a long woolen motor coat and an elaborate hat with a veil that, rather than mute her presence, in fact accentuated it. Chess inwardly groaned at Quigg's stupidity in strolling here with his mistress in broad daylight.

Miss Fortune abruptly veered toward the railing, pausing to gaze out toward the sea. He imagined she was torn about what the proper etiquette was in such a situation. From her reaction to the conversation she'd overheard between him and Quigg the previous evening, Chess had already deduced that she and Quigg were acquainted. So if hailed, should she greet him and his mistress or should she snub him? Better to attempt to avoid the awkward encounter entirely.

Chess stood silently beside her while she waited tensely for Quigg and his paramour to pass by. "I wish you had counseled Mr. Baxter differently," she told him stiffly, still staring down at the murky water, which had been stirred up by the propellers churning so near to the bottom of the seabed.

Chess felt a pulse of irritation at her inference. "I might have, had we not been standing in the middle of a dining saloon filled with hundreds of people, and had my words any chance of piercing Baxter's thick skull." He sighed. "In any case, there's little that can be done now."

"Quigg could still inform his mother and sister and save them the shock and embarrassment of finding out from someone else. Before they arrive in Montreal and he springs it on them. From what I know of the Baxters, Quigg is nothing if not doted upon. He at least owes them his respect." Miss Fortune's face had flushed through this recitation, so she inhaled a calming breath before adding, "But you're right. I should not have blamed you for Quigg's poor decisions or for exercising prudence."

"Is that an apology?" he quipped, feeling startled by how easily she'd admitted her error. In his world, such behavior was rare.

A pale wash of color returned to her cheeks, which at this distance he could now see were lightly freckled, but this time her heightened color was not due to anger. "Yes. Yes, it was."

He couldn't help but smile.

"Do you accept my apology?"

"I do. Though . . . I now feel like I owe you one, too."

She tilted her head quizzically.

"For provoking you. I suspect my cheeky grin did not help matters."

She snorted in amusement. "No, it did not. Rather like baiting a bull." Her eyes narrowed up at him. "But somehow I suspect you enjoy provoking others. It must be the attorney in you."

"The 'Kinsey' more like. Regardless, I assure you I am properly chastened."

Her eyes laughed at him. "Are you?"

"You doubt me?" He reared back in mock affront. "You are a mistrustful lady."

"No, just one who is used to making little boys turn out their pockets before they enter Sunday school lest they sneak in a frog, and who checks the seat of her chair before she sits lest it be covered in chalk."

"You have some naughty boys in Winnipeg."

A laugh escaped her lips, making several people turn their way. She pressed the back of her gray suede glove to her mouth, stifling her merriment. "Now, why do you sound so impressed?"

He glowed with pleasure at having made her laugh so, and wanted to hear it again, despite the interest they were arousing. "I was never very good at catching frogs, and I didn't learn the chalk trick until I went away to boarding school."

She kept her hand over her mouth as her shoulders shook with mirth. "I think I am very glad you are not from Winnipeg," she finally managed to say. "You would be a terrible influence."

"I take it your fiancé is not."

As soon as the playful words were out of his mouth, he wished he could take them back. Her sparkling eyes dimmed, and her posture straightened.

"Crawford is . . . well respected."

If that's all she could say about him, Chess decided he must be a dead bore. No wonder her sisters—at least the dark-haired one with the wide mouth and saucy grin—seemed intent on pushing them together. She seemed like the type to stir up trouble whenever she could.

"So, the type to tattle on the boys with frogs in their pockets?"

She frowned.

"And bring the teacher an apple every week."

"There's nothing wrong with being honest and respectable," she retorted.

"Not as long as your honesty isn't at the expense of others. Not as long as you know the teacher truly appreciates the apple rather than imposing upon her gratitude for appearance's sake."

Miss Fortune didn't seem to have an answer for this, but her scowl did not abate. Given this, he wasn't surprised when she soon made some sort of excuse about her mother requiring her assistance and disappeared into the domed Grand Staircase entrance. He didn't turn to watch her go, though he felt her absence more keenly than he'd expected.

He surveyed the activity below as the tender tied up to the ship below, and debated what to do with himself. The Gymnasium was just behind him, but he'd already spent an hour earlier that morning on the stationary bicycle and with the punching bag. He could undoubtedly find some jovial male company in the Smoking Room, but that held less appeal than usual. Instead, he elected to join Karl, Miss Newsom, and the other Fortune sisters on the Promenade Deck to see what wares the vendors had brought over in the bumboats.

But soon enough, Chess realized his presence there was redundant. The ladies were absorbed with the lace, linen, and other trinkets, and Karl was absorbed with Miss Newsom. He spoke to Jack Astor for a moment, but even he was more interested in haggling with a shawl-clad Irishwoman over the price of a lace jacket for his new bride.

Lunch passed without incident, except that after one peremptory nod of her head across the room in greeting, Miss Fortune seemed somewhat determined not to meet his eye. Chess couldn't decide if this was because she was still vexed at him or because she was embarrassed now by the manner in which he'd made her laugh. Although their acquaintance was new, he'd observed enough of her interaction with her family to tell that she was supposed to be the steady, responsible one. It was obvious in the way she carried herself, in the way her parents addressed her, and in the manner in which her siblings looked at her.

If he was honest with himself, he felt slightly envious of that fact. His family only ever eyed him with fond tolerance. If he ever attempted to broach something serious, he suspected his mother would send for the family physician.

Except Miss Fortune didn't seem happy in this role. Not truly. She was stiff and almost stilted. The light that he'd seen sparkling in her eyes when they'd jested was now muted to a dim glow.

He knew it wasn't any of his business. Six days from now he would never see her again. She would return to Winnipeg and marry the dull, respectable Crawford, and he would carry on with his life as before. With spring came a new season of tennis, and he wagered he had at least a few more good years of play left in him. Particularly since his role as an attorney demanded so little of him. After that . . . well, he didn't know what he would do. But it wasn't as if anyone was counting on him.

Now, why did that make that last bite of lamb with mint sauce taste so bitter?

With his appetite spoiled, Chess returned to the aft Promenade Deck just as the last tender was pulling away. He glanced overhead as *Titanic* gave three long blasts of her whistle and the tender honked in reply. While the First-Class Promenade was fairly empty—as the ship's passengers were inside dining and the vendors had all packed up their wares and departed—the rails of the aft Well Deck and Poop Deck below were lined three deep with people in some areas. The plaintive notes of some sort of bagpipe filled the air, and Chess looked up to see a man dressed in a kilt and full regalia standing near the stern.

As the *Titanic* slowly turned a quarter circle and began to move out to sea, the music swelled, reaching out to wrap around him and anyone who was listening. Chess didn't consider himself an emotional man, but he felt a clutch in his chest all the same.

Though he'd seen them but once before, he recognized now that the instrument was the uilleann pipes. His Irish nanny had once taken him to a wake where he'd heard them played. She'd risked her position in doing so, but the wake had been for her dear cousin, and his parents were out of town and would not allow her the day off, so she'd taken him with her. Chess had been fascinated by the ritual and the dourly sweet music, and he had never told a soul about it, not wishing to lose Nanny Murphy. Not when she seemed to be the only person in the world who had ever expected more from him than mere amusement.

Well, Nanny Murphy and Miss Fortune.

Chess realized then that this mournful song was a goodbye— for the piper and for the Irish surrounding him. Many of these third-class passengers were immigrants bound for new lives in

America and Canada. And while those who had traveled from eastern Europe and Palestine had long since said farewell to their homelands, this was likely the last time the Irish among them would ever see the shores of Erin again.

For a man who had the means to sail back and forth across the Atlantic whenever he wished, this was a harsh reality. One Chess was not entirely comfortable with. Yet he could not help but feel empathy for the poor chaps.

# CHAPTER 10

❧

*Thursday, April 11, 1912—3:00 p.m.*

Alice was restless. Queenstown Harbor had long since receded into the distance, and while the windswept southeastern coast of Ireland was lovely—in a bleak and melancholy sort of way—as they continued to steam past it, she could stand staring at gray cliffs and gaunt and desolate settlements for only so long without her eyes glazing over. Most of the other passengers had lost interest in the scenery after the *Titanic* had rounded Daunt Rock, the official starting point of the transatlantic crossing, so they'd gone off to find other diversions.

Diversions that, for the most part, did not interest Alice. She did not want to read, or write letters, or even play the piano. Those were all things she could do in Winnipeg. The Gymnasium was open to ladies exclusively only at midday from ten to one. Likewise, the Turkish Bath. She tried to convince Mabel to visit the Swimming Pool with her, but her younger sister surprisingly had no interest, and neither did Charlie nor Flora. She'd joined a game of bridge in the Lounge for a short time but now she'd taken to wandering again, searching for something—anything—to engage her wayward thoughts.

If this was how the next six days were to pass, she might as well be home in Winnipeg. Her adventure couldn't be over yet. It just couldn't!

She was passing through the foyer of the Forward Grand Staircase on A-Deck for perhaps the third time, when a voice called out to her from a settee in the corner. "Good heavens, my dear! You're making my head spin. Come here," she beckoned. "Have you lost someone or have you merely gone stir-crazy?"

Alice didn't know exactly what the woman dressed in an elegant gown of black chiffon trimmed with cerise meant, but she could infer that she'd not managed to conceal her agitation as well as she'd believed. "My apologies," she said, pinkening with embarrassment. "I'm afraid I simply can't seem to settle."

The woman with hennaed hair flicked her wrist. "No need for apologies. I'm Mrs. J. J. Brown, by the way."

"Miss Alice Fortune."

She nodded. "I know your father. From Winnipeg, aren't you? I'm from Denver, Colorado. Now, why don't you sit and tell me why you can't settle?" She patted the cushion next to her. "You're not nervous about sailing, are you?"

Alice sank down as directed, straightening her pink linen skirts.

"No, not really. I mean, if I could go on sailing forever, I think I would. Well, not forever," she amended. "But I'm in no rush to reach New York."

Mrs. Brown tilted her head in scrutiny. "Is something dreadful waiting for you there?"

"No. Not dreadful. I mean . . . there is actually something quite marvelous at our journey's end, but . . ." Her voice fell away, uncertain how to explain.

Mrs. Brown hummed to herself before pushing to her feet. "I need some fresh air. Come out to the promenade with me."

Alice followed, slowly at first and then more willingly.

Rather than stroll, she discovered Mrs. Brown intended for them to sit in a pair of deck chairs gazing out at the sky on the starboard side. While striding toward the chairs Mrs. Brown had rented for her use, Alice heard a faint eruption of raucous laughter and looked about to try to figure out where it was coming from.

"The deck below," Mrs. Brown explained in answer to her unspoken question. "The Cardezas are staying in the starboard parlor suite on B-Deck, which has its own private promenade. And apparently Thomas is putting it to good use for poker games and such. Do you know Mrs. Cardeza?"

Alice shook her head. Though she knew she shouldn't be, Alice was intrigued. Now, *that* was something she'd never be able to indulge in once she returned to Winnipeg—poker games . . . and such. And they sounded as if they were having so much fun. But she knew her father definitely would not approve. For that matter, neither would Holden.

"Lucky you," Mrs. Brown quipped beneath her breath as they settled into the beechwood chairs with caned seats and slat backs. A steward soon appeared to hand them rugs for their laps and offered to fetch cups of warm beef tea. Both ladies declined.

"What brought your family across the Atlantic?" Mrs. Brown asked as she snuggled beneath her cozy rug.

"My father gifted us all with a grand tour."

Mrs. Brown nodded to a passing acquaintance who tipped his hat to them. "What was your favorite destination?"

"Oh, I'm not sure I could choose just one," Alice breathed. "Paris and Venice were ever so lovely. And the Adriatic Sea. I've never seen such a shade of blue. But Jerusalem was also amazing. And Egypt . . ." She sighed. "The temples and pyramids. It was just all so wonderful."

Mrs. Brown smiled. "I myself have just come from Egypt, and I agree. It's all quite wonderful." She reached into the pocket of her coat and extracted a small figure, which she held out to Alice.

She examined it closely, realizing it was an Egyptian tomb figure.

"I picked it up at a market in Cairo. It's supposed to be a good-luck talisman. Or so the man who sold it to me said," Mrs. Brown added with a twinkle in her eye. "I adore traveling. Exploring new places. Trying new things. It's good for the soul. And now that you've had your first taste of it, I imagine you'll wish to continue."

Alice turned to gaze out at the endless blue sky, where seagulls still trailed alongside the ship. "Perhaps."

"There's no 'perhaps' about it. You've got the bug," Mrs. Brown stated definitively. "I can see it in your eyes. You won't be satisfied 'til you see the world."

Alice plucked at the button on her white kid gloves. Was she deluding herself to think that she could ever be happy back in Winnipeg, being cosseted and sheltered at every turn? She wondered what would happen if she simply told her fiancé the truth and tried to coax him around to her way of thinking. Except Holden believed he would be getting a certain type of wife, and if she suddenly revealed otherwise, he might no longer want her. Besides which, there was the more practical issue of Holden's seasickness. The only time he'd traveled to Europe, he'd spent the entire trip confined to his cabin.

"For now, I'm bound for home," she finally answered in a subdued voice.

"Then I suppose it's no wonder you're a bit restless. I always find myself a bit out of sorts at the end of a journey," Mrs. Brown said sympathetically. "Sad that it's over. Wishing I could relive parts of it over again. Anxious to squeeze every last drop of enjoyment from the experience."

Then Mrs. Brown did understand. At least, partially.

"So you feel the same way that I do?"

"Well, this trip is a bit different. I received word that my grandson is ill, so I booked passage home as quickly as possible."

"Oh, I'm so sorry."

"The little mite will probably be recovered before I even reach New York," she declared, folding her hands in her lap. "But I simply couldn't chance it. So, you see, this time I'm far more anxious to arrive home than distressed by my travels ending."

Alice brushed a stray strand of hair out of her face. "Yes, that does make a difference."

"My advice, Miss Fortune, is to ease yourself back into your normal life. To spend some time reflecting on your favorite memories and what they might mean for your future. Maybe keep a journal, if you haven't been doing so already. Or consider taking a hobby inspired by your travels or learning something new. A language or whatnot. We can always better ourselves." Mrs. Brown chuckled. "Why, I'm sure one of the handsome young men on board would be happy to teach you deck quoits or shuffleboard, if you're so inclined."

Alice squirmed under Mrs. Brown's amused stare.

"And if all else fails, you can always throw yourself into some worthy cause. There's bound to be some issue that needs to be addressed, some improvement that needs to be made." Her lips quirked wryly. "I'm afraid I'm not very good at sitting still myself. Not when there's something to be done."

Alice was helpless not to smile in return, recognizing what an understatement that must be even on such a short acquaintance. Mrs. Brown was like a whirlwind, carrying everyone along with her.

Conversely, until this journey, Alice had always excelled at stillness. Being sick so often as a child and later coddled, she'd had to. Now that she'd been freed from those restrictions, she felt like a shooting star released upon the heavens. And the thought of falling to earth so soon made her restive and melancholy.

# CHAPTER 11

Had Mabel realized what an inquisition she would be facing once she returned to her cabin to dress for dinner, she might have delayed her arrival.

"And just where have you been?" Flora demanded to know, pausing in her efforts to tighten Alice's corset. Alice stood glaring at her from her position, gripping the footboard of the bed, waiting for Flora to resume her tugging at her corset ribbons.

Mabel slowly closed the door, trying to deduce the reason for their icy greeting. She hadn't seen either of them since lunch, but perhaps that was the problem. They both seemed to think she needed minding like a toddler.

She moved toward the washstand, deliberately taking her time. "Here and there," she answered blithely before splashing water on her face, knowing the vagueness of her response would irritate her sisters. When she opened her eyes, patting her face with a towel, she could see Flora scowling at her in the reflection of the mirror.

"Is that so?" Flora exchanged a look with Alice. "Then it's strange we couldn't find you when we went looking for you."

Mabel dropped the towel on the marble and turned to face her sisters, folding her arms over her chest. "It's been *hours* since I last saw you, and you can't very well have expected me to remain in the same place that entire time. Anyway, you can't have looked very hard. I was seated in the Verandah Café for quite some time."

"Oh." Alice gasped softly. "On A-Deck beyond the Smoking Room? I'd forgotten it was there."

"And why were you there?" Flora persisted as she tied off Alice's ribbons.

Mabel crossed the room. "Miss Young asked me to have tea with her." At her sisters' blank looks, she went on. "She's companion to Mrs. White, the woman who twisted her ankle boarding the ship at Cherbourg."

Mabel began to rifle through the clothes hanging in the wardrobe. "She's a music teacher as well. Used to teach piano to President Roosevelt's children." Locating the lapis lazuli shade gown with asymmetrical draping she'd been searching for—the one her mother had initially balked at—she pulled it from the confines of the wardrobe to lay it across Alice's bed next to her sister's more modest pink chiffon.

"The president's children? Really?" Alice exclaimed.

"How did you meet?"

"Outside the Enquiry Office." She'd been perusing the notices posted on the walls nearby without truly reading them, struggling to master her frustration at having been unable to introduce her parents to Dr. Leader and Mrs. Swift at lunch. "I'd just picked up a copy of the *Atlantic Daily Bulletin*"—the *Titanic*'s daily newspaper—"when I heard a woman asking after her poultry. Can you imagine?"

Mabel explained how Mrs. White had purchased two prized French roosters and three hens while she was in Europe, and it was left to Miss Young to ensure they were being well cared for, as Mrs. White had broken her ankle at Cherbourg and Dr. O'Loughlin had ordered her to rest in her cabin for the duration of the voyage. This meant that Miss Young had to be accompanied each day by a crewman named Hutchinson to the place where the poultry was being stored. Upon discovering that Miss Young had a delightful sense of humor, Mabel indulged her curiosity and invited herself along.

Mabel elected not to mention to her sisters that this meant descending into one of the cargo holds, where the poultry were being kept, knowing precisely what her sister Flora would have to say about that. But it had been exciting to venture into areas of the ship where the lovely white paneling and carpeting of the passenger areas were replaced by utilitarian metal and bare wood. Though she found herself wishing she could tell them about the stacks of barrels, sacks, boxes, trunks, and crates filling the massive hold, including a motorcar. Fancy shipping one of those across the Atlantic on the *Titanic*!

"Then after Miss Young gave Hutchinson a gold coin for his trouble, which is apparently quite lucky on a ship's maiden voyage." Mabel laughed lightly. "Or so he said. Anyway, afterward Miss Young invited me to join her for tea."

"Perhaps we should all take our tea in the Verandah Café tomorrow?" Alice suggested, tugging at the bottom of her chemise before reaching for her petticoat. "After all, it does have an unobstructed view of the sea."

"True. But I must warn you it was nearly overrun with young children and their caregivers." Mabel supposed there were few places on board where governesses and nannies would be welcome with their young charges, and isolated as the trellis-covered café was from the other public rooms on the ship, it would be the perfect place for them to go. Green plants climbed the lattice walls, while large bronze-framed windows allowed ample light to spill across the white wicker tables and tile floor. It was redolent of a conservatory near the seashore, as wisps of briny air swept through the space whenever the door to the aft Promenade Deck was opened.

"I even spied Mrs. Allison there with her two children and nanny," she added.

Mrs. Allison was the wife of a Montreal stock promoter with whom they had a slim acquaintance. Mabel recalled how the young Allison girl, who couldn't have been more than three, had sat very properly in her crisp white dress with a large bow affixed at the side of her dark hair, her legs swinging beneath her chair as she watched the other children play. It had been evident she was torn between wanting to join in the fun and wishing to earn her mother's approval by behaving correctly. It had reminded Mabel acutely of her sister Flora, particularly when Mrs. Allison had barely spared her daughter a glance, but pressed her hand to her leg as she continued her conversation with the lady next to her, silently urging the girl to halt her movements. The little girl complied, turning rather dolefully back to her half-eaten tea cake.

Mabel had wanted to urge the child to jump up and play, but fortunately Miss Young had appeared before she could give in to temptation.

They had spent a pleasant few hours discussing their lives. Miss Young had told her about her time in Washington working as a music teacher. Some of her famous pupils had indeed included former President Roosevelt's children. Miss Young possessed a dry wit and a natural gift for storytelling and had painted the amusing picture of young Archie Roosevelt hammering out the notes to "Over the Waves" on the piano during one recital while his father looked on with pride. "One would have thought his son was storming the San Juan heights alongside him," she'd quipped, referring to President Roosevelt's time commanding the Rough Riders during the Spanish-American War.

Flora and Alice both smiled as Mabel relayed this anecdote.

But Miss Young's life had not been all happy. When she was just fifteen, her musically talented father had suffered a head injury and was never the same again. He had fallen into depression and turned to drink between stints in an insane asylum. When he'd attempted suicide a second time, he succeeded. Then she nursed her mother through a long illness, only to see her die two years later.

It was after that she'd met Mrs. White and become her traveling companion. Friend rather than employee, or so she explained. Though it seemed Mrs. White was also quite generous, for while in France, she'd purchased Miss Young a trousseau for her upcoming marriage. One that apparently was not meant to be, for her fiancé had died just a few weeks earlier.

Mabel's heart ached afresh for her new friend and all the tragedy she'd suffered. Yet Miss Young was still so warm and hopeful. Her soft smile and gentle laugh drew one in. And Mabel had found herself eager to make Miss Young like her, even remaining in her delightful presence when she should have excused herself to go in search of the author and interior designer Mrs. Helen Churchill Candee. Few people, if anyone, gazed at her as fondly or spoke to her as confidingly as Miss Young, so she was reluctant to give it up.

"I'm sure I would enjoy meeting her," her sister Alice remarked.

Mabel studied her sister's perfectly coiffed appearance—even dressed in naught but her unmentionables—and suddenly felt a twinge of regret that she'd mentioned Miss Young at all. For she didn't want to share her with Alice, or Flora, for that matter.

Mabel gave a noncommittal little grunt and turned to search through the drawers for the appropriate undergarments for her dinner dress even as she racked her brain for a subject to distract her sisters.

"I never got to ask," she said innocently. "How was your stroll with Mr. Kinsey?"

A flush crested Flora's cheeks even as she frowned. "It was . . . pleasant." She turned away, searching for her own corset and chemise to wear underneath her lemon-yellow gown trimmed with lace. "Though I initially had my doubts."

Mabel exchanged a look with Alice. If Flora's blush was any indication, she wasn't unaffected by the attractive tennis star. Which was more of a reaction than Mabel had ever witnessed from her in regard to Crawfy. She arched her eyebrows, silently emphasizing this point to Alice.

"But you could have been a bit less obvious with your maneuverings," Flora drawled, casting a sharp-eyed glare their way.

"I have no idea what you're talking about," Mabel replied breezily, picking up the underdress of Alice's gown and urging her to turn away from their older sister's eagle eyes.

"Mmm-hmm," Flora hummed, clearly unconvinced.

Fortunately, a knock at the inner door halted any further questions.

The door opened the merest crack. "Flora, your mother requires your assistance," their father's deep baritone pronounced.

Mabel waited until Flora disappeared through the door and shut it behind her before she pinched Alice's arm.

"Ow!" Alice protested.

"You can't give up the game so quickly!"

She turned to scowl at her sister, rubbing her arm. "I didn't."

"You were about to. Have you never lied in all your life?"

Curiously, this made the tips of her ears turn red.

"Obviously not as often as you have," Alice shot back. "But I can prevaricate when necessary."

"Well, this is one of those necessary times. Did you see her reaction?"

Alice crossed her arms over her chest. "I did."

"And?"

"And I admit you are right. Flora is in no way enamored with Crawford. Not if a simple stroll with Mr. Kinsey made her blush so." Alice appeared troubled by this discovery.

"I told you we would be doing her a favor by throwing them together. But we can't stop now. Not if we don't want her turning into a martyr and marrying Crawford out of pure sainthood."

Alice frowned. "That's a vulgar way to put it."

"But true. I have it in mind to ask Mr. Sloper to assist us with our endeavor."

"No," Alice stated emphatically. "You promised not to meddle." Her voice lowered. "If Flora discovered we'd conspired with William to test her loyalty to Crawford, she would not only be hurt but mortified."

Mabel exhaled in aggravation and then reluctantly nodded. She looked toward the inner cabin door. "What about Charlie?"

Alice glared at her. "That's still meddling."

"Fine," she grumbled, allowing her sister to spin her around and begin working on the fastenings of her dress, careful to conceal her crossed fingers within the folds of her skirts.

# CHAPTER 12

◈

By the time Flora and Alice reached D-Deck, the two sets of double doors leading to the Dining Saloon had already been opened and passengers had begun to proceed to their assigned tables. Flora's irritation at her youngest sister continued to rankle in her breast, but even that proved powerless before the awe she felt seeing the crowd gathered below as she descended the stairs.

Ladies and gentlemen in evening attire fashioned of the finest satins, chiffons, crepes, and velvets, in almost every hue of the rainbow, save purple—which tended to be eschewed because it appeared brown under gaslights—glided and rustled across the floor. The previous evening, the first one aboard the ship, few had bothered to change their clothes. But tonight, and every evening after, formal dress was *de rigueur.* The jewels draped around the women's throats and wrists and nestled in their hair caught the light, and sparkled and shimmered like fallen stars. Feathers wafted, fans stirred, voices rumbled, and beaded overskirts clacked. Yet not a hair was out of place in the women's pompadours or the men's slicked heads, save for dear, funny Mr. Futrelle, whose hair seemed incapable of being controlled, much like the Thinking Machine sleuth in his novels. Flora smiled at the sight of him, feeling a pulse of excitement to be included in such an esteemed affair.

She had, of course, attended dinners and balls before. She had dined with many of the same passengers on other ships. But somehow this voyage, this ship, was different. Perhaps it was the novelty, the very fact that they were the first ever to sail on the grandest ship ever built, to dine in its saloon. Or maybe it was the company, as the combined wealth in the room was positively staggering. Whatever the case, a sense of enchantment was cast over the proceedings, one that made Flora anxious not to put a foot wrong. Gripping the banister tighter with one hand, and the train of her lemon-yellow underskirt with the other, she resumed her descent more slowly.

Her eyes lit on a number of their acquaintances before catching sight of her parents, with Mabel and Charlie. They had been speaking to a pair of women in their forties or fifties who were now excusing themselves. As they reached the bottom of the staircase, Flora grasped Alice's hand so that they wouldn't become separated, and they merged with the flow of passengers into the saloon. No one hurried or rushed, but the mood was convivial, even festive. Flora found herself struggling not to smile too broadly, knowing it would be deemed unbecoming.

And then her gaze collided with a pair of warm brown eyes. Eyes that twinkled devilishly at her, as if they knew exactly what she was restraining. She didn't know how Chess Kinsey had deduced that, or how she'd deduced his thoughts in return, for thirty feet must have stood between them, but she was confident of her impressions. As confident as she was that he looked utterly devastating in a white waistcoat and black tails. His appearance in a day suit had been arresting enough, but somehow his evening kit only accentuated his height and athleticism even more.

The crowd shifted, blocking him from her sight, and she began to scold herself for her wayward thoughts. He was just a man. An attractive one, yes, but a man all the same. And *she* was an engaged woman. She should not be feeling flustered simply because an admittedly handsome man had smiled at her.

When they reached their table, Flora was surprised to find Mabel looking sullen. She had breezed into their cabin last and yet still was the first one to finish dressing, hustling off with their parents to the Reception Room, intent upon some objective other than assisting her sisters in turn. As the youngest, Mabel often finagled her way into doing the least, relying on her older sisters to help her but doing little in return. Normally this didn't irk Flora overly much. She knew it was simply Mabel's way. But tonight, after her teasing remarks about Mr. Kinsey and her determination to leave early for dinner with her parents, Flora's suspicions had been aroused. Mabel was up to something, and it almost certainly involved mischief.

However, her grim expression now seemed to indicate that whatever her objective had been, she'd not achieved it. Flora searched her parents' faces as a steward helped her into her chair, curious if they'd had some sort of quarrel with Mabel, but she saw no sign of it.

"Are you excited for your tour of the ship with Mr. Andrews tomorrow morning?" Flora asked Charlie after taking a drink from her glass.

Her brother's face lit up like an incandescent bulb. "Am I ever! I'm hoping he can take us to the Bridge and the Marconi Room as well." His sandy brown hair was still damp at the temples, making him appear all the more boyish in his earnestness.

Flora smiled. "Did those journals you read include information about their equipment as well?"

"Indeed. It's one of the most powerful—"

"Oh, please, don't encourage him," Mabel cut in. "He's been nattering on all evening to whoever will listen."

Undaunted, Charlie favored his sister with a smug look as he served himself some of the cold asparagus in vinaigrette. "Only when people ask. I can't help it that people find all of it as interesting as I do."

"They don't."

Mother reached over to lay a quelling hand on Mabel's arm before addressing Alice. "This shade of pink looks lovely on you, dear. I had my doubts, but Worth was right. It's just perfect for your pale complexion."

Even Mabel wasn't insolent enough to defy Mother at the dinner table and remained silent as they discussed their new Paris gowns and acquaintances whom they'd discovered to be fellow passengers.

Midway through the meal, Mabel leaned toward Flora to murmur, "Someone has his eye on you."

Flora struggled not to react when Mabel flicked her gaze in the direction where she knew Mr. Kinsey was seated. Out of the corner of her eye, Flora noted her father turning to look, though Flora kept her eyes averted. She swallowed a drink of her wine before giving in to the temptation to sneak a look of her own at Mr. Kinsey's handsome profile.

"Perhaps his eye is on *you*," she countered calmly, though her pulse was hammering in her ears.

Mother turned to them in interest. "Of whom are we speaking?"

Mabel smiled at Flora with tight lips, forcing Flora to answer. "Chess Kinsey."

"The tennis player?" Charlie asked keenly before casting a long look over his shoulder.

"Mr. Sloper introduced us," Alice explained between displeased glares at her younger sister, which Mabel ignored.

"I shall have to ask Mr. Sloper for an introduction as well." Their brother grinned. "I wonder if he'd like to join me and Thornton on the Squash Racquet Court tomorrow morning."

"You'll be trounced," Mabel stated bluntly.

"Oh, undoubtedly." Charlie seemed to relish the prospect.

Father dabbed at his mustache with his napkin. "Don't discount your brother so easily. You'll recall he received a citation for athletic as well as academic excellence."

"Yes, but I'm nowhere as good as Kinsey. They say his overhand serve is spectacular. And the sidespin he puts on the ball."

Objectively, Flora had known Mr. Kinsey was a tennis star, for Mr. Sloper had introduced him as such. But the discovery that her brother not only knew of him but admired his play cast a sort of mythical aura over his personality. It was no wonder he got away with smirking and mockery much of the time.

Interestingly however, when he greeted her in the Palm Court following dinner, she noticed that his roguish ennui was absent.

The Fortunes had all clustered together again, along with a number of their friends and acquaintances, to listen to the band play and to trade gossip from the day. Many of the other passengers were doing likewise. She spied the elegant Countess of Rothes seated with her cousin on one of the settees closer to the Steinway grand piano around which the orchestra clustered. A trio of Americans stood to her left, debating loudly whether Roosevelt would challenge President Taft for the Republican nomination. She watched as one distinguished-looking gentleman with a trim mustache caught wind of their exchange and reversed course to avoid it.

Most of the men in their party were otherwise preoccupied with the betting pool on the ship's run for the next day. It was a popular practice aboard ocean liners for the male passengers to purchase bids on the nautical miles traveled by the steamship from noon one day to noon the next. The faster the ship, the more fevered the betting became. Even though the *Titanic* was allegedly incapable of traveling fast enough to take the Blue Riband for the fastest Atlantic crossing, that didn't seem to dampen the men's interest in her speed. Even her father seemed eager to debate her merits and capabilities.

Flora didn't know whether to be amused or annoyed by the entire matter.

"You must forgive us, Miss Fortune," Mr. Kinsey's deep voice rumbled on her right as he came to stand beside her. "We men are, at heart, simple creatures. Give us something foolish to wager over and we will leap at it like an oasis in the desert."

"You're not going to bet on the day's run?" she asked in genuine surprise, for she would have thought such a pastime would be irresistible to someone like him.

"Oh, I will. But I'm not so invested in the outcome as to bore my female companions with all the therefores and what-ifs," he quipped, turning to meet her gaze. His lips quirked upward at the corners just as the previous evening, but the gleam in his eyes was decidedly less jaded and more genuinely amused.

Flora narrowed her eyes playfully. "Or perhaps you're simply clever enough not to divulge the method of your calculations."

The creases at the corners of his eyes deepened. "Precisely." He peered about them furtively before leaning toward her to whisper, "Don't tell anyone."

She bit back a laugh. "Your secret is safe with me."

He arched his chin, clasping his hands behind his back as he focused his eyes once more on the band. "I knew I could rely on your discretion."

Flora snorted, and Mabel turned in her seat to glower at them from the settee in front of them where she was seated with Mother and Mrs. Hays.

"Is your sister a music lover? Are we ruining her enjoyment of the performance?" Mr. Kinsey leaned close again to murmur.

"No, she's just incurably nosy." Flora watched as Mabel's eyes narrowed. "Just wait. She's going to suggest we've been talking about her."

True to her statement, her youngest sister shifted in her seat so that she was almost facing them over the back of the settee. "Are you telling secrets about me?" she demanded to know.

Both Flora and Mr. Kinsey burst into laughter.

Mother hushed Mabel, who then pushed to her feet and rounded the settee to stand glaring at them with arms crossed.

"That will do you no good," Flora informed her. "For we've not even been speaking about you. Or we weren't," she amended. "Not until you started giving us the evil eye."

Mabel rolled her eyes. "Then what were you talking about?"

Flora shrugged. "This and that." She knew perfectly well this vague statement would drive her sister batty, but Flora liked the idea of her and Mr. Kinsey having a private jest.

"This and that about what?" Mabel persisted, appealing to him when Flora remained silent. "Tell me!"

"Nothing noteworthy," he replied with a mischievous glint in his eyes.

Eager to change the subject, Flora caught Charlie's eye across the room and beckoned him closer.

"Mr. Kinsey, this is our brother Charlie. Charlie, allow me to introduce you to Chess Kinsey."

Charlie looked so excited that she thought he might leap out of his shoes. As it was, he shook Mr. Kinsey's hand so vigorously, Flora feared he'd dislocate it. "Wow! You're *the* Chess Kinsey. I'm so pleased to meet you."

"Likewise," he responded, reaching out to clamp his other hand on Charlie's upper arm to stop him. "Do you play?"

Charlie's cheeks pinkened with pleasure. "Why, yes. Yes, I do. Though not at your level. I've read in the papers all about how brilliant you are. They say your serve is faster than a cannonball."

"Nearly," Mr. Kinsey conceded good-naturedly, rolling his right shoulder almost unconsciously.

"Boy, I'd like to see that. Say, I know it's not the same as a tennis court, but would you want to join me on the Squash Racquet Court tomorrow morning? Thornton Davidson and I have it reserved for half an hour, and I'm sure we could convince the racquet professional to join us for a game of doubles. I mean, you're Chess Kinsey, for goodness' sakes. He wouldn't want to miss out on *that* opportunity."

"I suppose I could do that," Mr. Kinsey replied before flashing a sly grin at Flora. "Perhaps your sisters would even like to watch."

"There is a spectator's gallery," Charlie informed them, sending a teasing glance her way. "But good luck getting Flora, or Mabel," he added as almost an afterthought, "out of bed at such an hour."

"Not a morning person, is she?" Mr. Kinsey remarked, as if

she weren't standing right there, though his eyes remained locked with hers.

She didn't know why such a subject was making her cheeks warm. "I thought your tour with Mr. Andrews was tomorrow morning?"

"It is. At nine." Charlie turned to Mr. Kinsey. "Perhaps you'd like to join us for that as well." He peered over his shoulder toward the men conferring over the ship's speed before confiding. "I think Father is hoping to obtain some inside information."

"As are all the men," Mr. Kinsey replied. "Officers, stewards, engineers. They're all fair game for anyone hoping to gain some sort of advantage."

The swish and rustle of elegant garments preceded Alice's excited gasp. "Did you see her?"

"Who?" Mabel asked.

"Mrs. Astor," she replied, as if her sister was very dull. "She's been keeping to her cabin, but she came down to dinner and is now listening to the band." She nodded toward the woman seated listlessly in a chair a short distance away, with Colonel Astor standing behind it.

Rather than the dazzling woman Flora had been expecting—one who glowed with contentment and triumph at having wed the man she had desired—Flora saw a pale, somber young lady. Madeleine Astor was alleged to be a great beauty—one would have to be to capture the eye of the wealthiest man in America—and her features bore the traces of that. But it was severely tempered by a dreary sort of disinterest in everyone and everything around her. Had Colonel Astor not been hovering over her, she would never have believed this young woman was his second wife.

Flora couldn't help but feel her heart go out to Mrs. Astor. In all honesty, she felt a little ashamed of herself now, gawking at her as if she were some sort of circus sideshow. She wondered if this was what it was like everywhere Mrs. Astor went.

Turning away, Flora found Mr. Kinsey observing them and flushed. What must he think? Especially with his also being a celebrity, of sorts.

"Famous people are rarely who you imagine them to be," he said softly. "Or, rather, who society and the press make them out to be." His lips flattened into a humorless smile. "And if they are, then you haven't scratched deep enough."

"I suspect you're right," she answered, curious what society and the press portrayed wrongly about him.

Flora's gaze shifted to the right, finding her mother watching her, and it was all she could do not to fidget like a guilty child. She nodded before turning back to her sisters, who were discussing in hushed voices whether Mrs. Astor was wearing one of the daring new corsetless gowns. Then anger stirred within Flora at the fact she felt discomfort at all. Merely speaking with another man was no cause for concern.

Her sisters fell abruptly silent as Mother joined them.

"Am I correct in deducing this is the tennis player you were all discussing?" she asked.

Mr. Kinsey bowed his head in greeting. "Chess Kinsey at your service, Mrs. Fortune. And may I say what charming company your children are."

"You may," she replied, a shrewd look in her eye. "I hear you hail from New York. That your family is quite well connected there."

"Indeed."

Mother nodded, though her eyes still weighed and assessed him like a bolt of fabric or a choice cut of meat. Father might have had the eye for real estate and investments, but Mother could calculate the value of nearly any object down to the penny. It was a skill that had served her well early in life, and even now, when she needn't make her own purchases at the butcher or stitch her own gowns, she still knew the precise value of any good. They'd lost more than one servant because of her demanding accounting.

She turned to Flora with a weary smile. "Your father intends to join the other men in the Smoking Room, but I wish to retire. Accompany me."

"Of course," Flora answered, for as a dutiful daughter there was nothing else she *could* say. She opened her mouth to say something to Alice and Mabel, but her mother pressed her hand to her arm, halting her.

"Leave them be. I expect them to retire soon enough." This last was spoken for her sisters' benefit, a reminder to mind themselves. But Flora couldn't help but feel a trace of resentment that they were allowed to stay, and she was not.

She frowned, then turned to Mr. Kinsey as her mother began to lead her away. "Good night."

"Good night," he said, his eyes watchful.

Though their cabins were just one deck above, Mother insisted on taking the lift.

"He seems like a sturdy enough fellow," she remarked as the lift boy slid the gate closed. "His family are certainly prosperous."

A response seemed unnecessary, so Flora remained quiet, wondering where this conversation was leading.

Mother waited until they'd exited the lift and begun striding down the corridor toward their staterooms. "Perhaps he'll manage to turn Mabel's head away from that jazz musician."

Flora felt as if she'd been punched in the stomach.

Mabel and Mr. Kinsey? The thought made her go hot and then cold. Though she had no right to such a reaction.

She was engaged, for heaven's sake. To Crawford Campbell. She had no right to Mr. Kinsey's affection. No right to deny them to Mabel. But the idea of them together still made her wish her corset was laced a little less tightly.

She was thoroughly aware of the commitment she'd made to Crawford. A commitment her parents desired. And she wasn't about to do anything rash to jeopardize that.

At the same time, she couldn't help but recognize how different Mr. Kinsey made her feel. While helping her mother change for bed, Flora found herself listening with only half an ear to her mother's commentary. The other half of her mind couldn't help ruminating on whether she and Crawford had ever laughed together.

It was true, Crawford was a decidedly more serious fellow, and there was nothing wrong with that. But had she ever seen him boldly grin? Tepid smiles of assurance or pleasure, yes. But what of outright joy?

Her mother's hand pressed against her wrist as Flora finished braiding her hair. Flora lifted her gaze to Mother's reflection, finding her observing her in concern. It was only then that Flora realized she'd stopped paying attention to Mother's words some time before.

"Is something wrong, dear?"

"Of course, not," Flora replied with forced equanimity. "I was merely woolgathering."

Mother arched her eyebrows in gentle reproach, obviously not believing her. "Is it your sisters? You'll recall we said you needn't watch them so closely."

Flora concentrated on tying the bow at the end of her mother's braid.

"I realize Mabel can be trying." Mother sighed, pouring lotion from a bottle into her hands. "We shouldn't allow her to get away with as much as we do. She thinks I don't know, but I'm quite aware that she does a poor job of assisting me in dressing so that I'll not ask for her help. However, that doesn't mean I should give in to her machinations. That's not fair to you. Or Alice," she added as an afterthought.

"I hate to speak poorly of my sister . . ." Flora hesitated briefly before stating emphatically. "But she's the *sneakiest* person I know."

"Yes, well, she's not as clever as she thinks."

Flora wasn't exactly certain what to make of this somewhat

oblique statement or the severe expression that accompanied it, but her mother was rising to her feet.

"Have patience a little longer," she told Flora, clasping her arms at the elbows. "We'll be home in Winnipeg in a week to ten days, and you and Crawford can begin planning your lives together once again."

Flora's answering smile felt tight. Nearly as tight as the band of dread that seemed to wrap around her chest at the prospect. But she said nothing to her mother. Instead, making her way to her own cabin, wondering what kind of terrible person she was to feel thus, and how on earth she could make it go away. When she opened her door to find Mabel already inside, sitting on Alice's bed to remove her shoes, her heart leaped in relief that her youngest sister was not being escorted about the ship by Mr. Kinsey.

"You're not remaining out?" Flora asked in genuine surprise.

"Not with nothing to do," Mabel groused, dropping one shoe to the floor with a thump. "The men all hared off to the Smoking Room as soon as the band finished, and most of the women dispersed as well."

That she was thinking of someone in particular was evident, and Flora realized she'd forgotten to ask Mabel to introduce her to Miss Young.

Flora drifted toward the table at the center of the room, spying the first-class passenger list—copies of which were always delivered to the cabins on the first evening at sea so that passengers could locate any friends on board. She idly flipped through the pages. "What about Alice?"

"I believe she went for a stroll with Mr. Sloper up on deck." Mabel scowled. "At least, I presume that's why she came to fetch her coat. She was in too much of a hurry to answer my questions."

Flora frowned, wondering if the night air was good for Alice's health. Flora dropped the passenger list and crossed to the dressing table, reaching up to unclasp her diamond-and-opal flowered pin from the center of her bodice. Alice was old enough to mind herself. It was past time Flora trusted her to do so. Trusted her not to do anything foolhardy.

However, when Alice crept in after eleven on stockinged feet, Flora was forced to consider revising this sentiment.

# CHAPTER 13

❧

*Friday, April 12, 1912*

It hadn't been easy to rise at the crack of dawn, especially after indulging in the *Titanic*'s excellent selection of whiskey and cigars and a few rounds of cards in the Smoking Room, but Chess had managed it. Barely. Though he blamed the indulgences for his stiff joints and slower than normal reactions while joining Charlie Fortune and his friend for a game of squash. Not that they hindered him much. He still could have single-handedly thrashed both men without the racquet professional's help.

Fortunately, Charlie and Davidson were good sports. In the past, he'd had men challenge him to a match, thinking they could best him, and then grow snarling and spiteful when they could not. This forced Chess to take on the tiring task of soothing their ruffled feathers by downplaying his ability, lest his image as the charming ne'er-do-well be damaged. But Charlie seemed thrilled to have been bested so soundly and Davidson accepted it with a smile.

At one point during their match, Chess thought he'd caught sight of a woman in periwinkle watching from the spectators' gallery, but the next time he looked, she was gone. She'd been too far away for him to tell who she was, and she just as easily might have been Davidson's wife or another curious female, but

Chess liked to think it was Flora Fortune, irresistibly drawn to watch him play. It certainly made him exert a bit more effort than he'd needed to.

After a dip in the saltwater pool to soothe his sore muscles, Chess ordered a tomato omelet and smoked salmon for breakfast. He knew he would need to increase his training soon if he was going to be ready for his first tournament, and that also meant regulating his diet.

"No sirloin steak or sausage this morning?" Karl asked as he settled down at the table across from him, his blond hair still damp from his ablutions. "Don't tell me you've begun to get in fighting shape already?"

"You'd best start monitoring your intake as well, old man, if you don't want me to trounce you like I did last year," Chess quipped between sips of coffee.

"I don't seem to recall any trouncing." Karl grinned. "You're not starting to become senile now in your advanced age?"

Chess arched an eyebrow at his friend witheringly, as he was only two years older. He then plucked a bright red strawberry from the dish at the center of the table, marveling at it slightly, before popping it into his mouth. "Fancy? Strawberries in the middle of the ocean in April."

"I just heard Lady Duff-Gordon make a similar remark," Karl said, reaching out to take one for himself. "Is there nothing the *Titanic* doesn't have in her larders?"

Chess waited for Karl to finish ordering his breakfast from the steward before asking, "How fares the incomparable Miss Newsom?"

"Very well," he replied. "Not a touch of *mal de mer*. Unlike that Swiss family on B-Deck which hasn't been so lucky."

Chess made no comment on this, preferring another topic of conversation while he finished his omelet. The electric lights glinted off the crystal and silverware, and the hum of conversation was more muted than the evening before, as breakfast was a relaxed meal, with passengers coming and going as they pleased. Charlie and Mr. Fortune were seated at their assigned table, but he'd yet to see any of the Fortune ladies make an appearance.

"What of Miss Fortune?" Karl queried, failing to hide his smile behind his coffee cup. "How fares she?"

"Still engaged, if that's what you're asking," he answered dampeningly as he took another bite of salmon.

"Ah." Karl sank back in his chair. "She's resisting your wiles, then."

Chess's brow furrowed in irritation. "I haven't been using my 'wiles,' as you call them."

"But you will."

Chess didn't know how to respond to the calm certainty of this statement. Truth be told, he didn't know exactly how he felt about Miss Fortune. She was lovely, yes. Intelligent. Funny. He doubted most people referred to her as such, but she had a sly wit he found delightful. She also wasn't willing to play anyone's fool, and he liked that about her. Respected it.

"I can tell she intrigues you," Karl continued. He leaned forward, lowering his voice. "Just . . . don't hurt her. Miss Newsom likes her sisters, and I imagine she'd like Miss Fortune as well."

Chess scowled, feeling a bit affronted his friend felt he needed to issue this warning. "Do you truly think so little of me?"

"No. But she's not some jaded widow or a New York debutante looking for a flirtation." Both of whom were his forte.

"I'm well aware."

Karl held up his hands briefly, signaling his acquiesce. "I just wanted to be sure."

Chess was still annoyed with his friend when he set off on the tour of the ship, but Charlie's enthusiasm and Thomas Andrews's unfailing good cheer proved impossible to resist. There were simply too many fascinating things to see, and both Charlie and Mr. Fortune asked astute questions.

Astute questions that Chess soon discovered weren't limited

to the ship or their host. He didn't know if Mr. Fortune vetted all his acquaintances so assiduously or if he was being given special consideration, but he'd never felt so skillfully interrogated. Given Karl's warning, he had to wonder whether Mr. Fortune had also noted his interest in his daughter. Perhaps he wasn't being as circumspect as he'd thought. Whatever the case, he couldn't decide whether Mr. Fortune ultimately approved or disapproved of him, and he found, to his surprise, that he cared what the wily Canadian thought. Chess took it as a good sign that Mr. Fortune invited him to join him for a drink that evening.

One thing that was crystal clear to Chess was how knowledgeable Mr. Andrews was about his ship, and how hard he was working while the passengers were at their leisure. Andrews was supposed to be part of a nine-man "guarantee group" sent by the shipbuilder to address any problems that arose on the *Titanic* during her maiden voyage, but as far as he could tell, Andrews was the man everyone went to. During their tour, he was stopped numerous times to answer questions or direct men on how to fix an issue. Apparently, there were problems with the heating in some areas of the ship, and the faucets in the second-class lavatories had proved perplexing. All the while, Andrews was settling little quarrels between members of the staff or accepting hearty handshakes of congratulations from passengers. Chess wondered how the man wasn't dead on his feet, but Andrews still had a smile for everyone. It was impossible not to admire him and his magnificent ship.

Chess was contemplating these matters as he stepped off the lift on C-Deck and rounded the corner toward his room when he heard a voice coming from one of the narrow corridors off to the right. It was a woman's voice, pitched high, as if speaking to a child. A governess perhaps, or a nanny?

He stumbled to a stop at the sight of a woman on her knees, leaning forward toward something. The first thing that was apparent was that this was not some sort of servant. Not judging from the fabric and quality of the garment. The second was that she must require some sort of aid, for a lady would never kneel on the floor in a public area. Especially not with her bottom in the air. And a very fine bottom it was, he couldn't help but notice.

He ventured slowly toward her, uncertain how to make his presence known without embarrassing her.

"Oh, no, no, no. Don't fight me, you poor thing," she crooned. "I'm trying to help you."

It was then that Chess realized he knew exactly who she was. He battled his amusement at finding her in such a predicament. For Miss Fortune would never risk looking like a fool for just anyone. Though it turned out that this "anyone" was, in fact, not a child, but a cat. It gave a plaintive meow. One to which Miss Fortune responded with soothing sounds.

Chess cleared his throat. "One can't help but notice, Miss Fortune, that you might be in need of some assistance."

"Not me," she replied, barely sparing a glance over her shoulder at him. "But this feline. She's somehow gotten her claw snagged on something peeking out of the slats of this locker. The poor dear can't get free."

Evidently, Miss Fortune was an animal lover or just inordinately fond of cats, for she'd not exhibited even a flicker of mortification at being found in such a compromising position, and by *him* of all people. Her attention was focused solely on freeing the feline.

"Perhaps if you shifted to the side, I could help with that."

She wriggled to the right, and he dropped to his knees beside her, removing his pocketknife, which he opened with a snick. Miss Fortune carefully grasped the tangled tabby cat's paw in one hand while attempting to calm her with the other. For a moment after catching sight of him, the feline attempted to retreat, but she seemed to recognize they were trying to help her. That, or Miss Fortune's voice was simply mesmerizing. Hearing her speak in such soothing, melodious tones, he gave it even odds.

Once the cat quieted, Miss Fortune looked into Chess's eyes. "Do you think something can be done?"

At such a close proximity, he could see a ring of deep cobalt blue surrounding her pupils and flecks of silver at the edges of her irises. Her face was open and trusting, pleading for his help, and he suddenly realized he would do just about anything to give it.

"Hold her steady. I'm going to cut this string so that at least she's free from the locker. But I don't want to slice her in the process." He learned forward, gritting his teeth as he slid the knife through the strands of white thread. At one point the cat's claws scratched him, but he ignored it, continuing to extract her from the tangle.

When at last she was free, the cat reared backward, but Miss Fortune was there cradling her, crooning to her once again as she began to slide the snarl of thread from her claw. "There we go. There we go. Just a little more. We've got it!" She grinned, scratching the cat behind her ears. "Yes, now. That's much better."

Chess expected the cat to race off now that it had its freedom, but apparently it was smarter than that. Had Miss Fortune been stroking his back and clasping him to her breast like the feline, he would have stayed exactly where he was as well.

Slowly, Miss Fortune rose to her feet, holding the cat almost like a baby as she scratched under her chin. "Thank you," she said as he stood to join her. She stared up at him sweetly. "If you hadn't come along, I'm not sure what I would have done."

"You would have found a way to free her. I have every confidence in that. But it might not have been as pleasant." He lifted his hand to pet the cat, but then realized there was blood on it.

"Then I'm doubly glad—oh!" She grabbed his hand. "You've hurt yourself." She'd removed her gloves, and he liked the feel of her warm skin against his.

"It's merely a scratch," he assured her, stanching the bleeding with his handkerchief.

"Well, be sure to wash it well. Who knows where and what Miss Puss has gotten into." She lowered her gaze to observe the cat's belly. "Or rather Mrs. Puss. This cat has dropped a litter of kittens recently." She moved out into the larger corridor, glancing about her before turning her steps toward the bow. "If I'm not mistaken, there's a stewardess cabin . . . yes!" Her footsteps hastened as she caught sight of a woman in her distinctive white uniform emerging from an interior cabin ahead of them. "Excuse me!" Miss Fortune called. "Miss Bennett!"

The woman with light brown hair and a sharp chin turned to look at them and smiled. "Miss Fortune, what can I—oh! Have you found Jenny? Jim—the ship's scullion—has been looking for her. He was worried something had happened to her. She hasn't injured herself, has she?" she asked, reaching out to rub the cat's ears.

"No, but she got herself tangled in some wire," Miss Fortune explained. "We managed to free her. But am I right?" Her face tightened with concern. "Has Jenny recently given birth?"

"Aye. Dropped a litter just a few days before our departure. Jim's been looking after them all, as Jenny adores him. I think because he's always in such a good humor, even though he's terribly overworked. He's a big fellow, but one of the kindest you'll ever meet."

"Are the kittens near the galley, then?" Miss Fortune asked, cutting off this speech.

"Oh, aye. But Jenny knows how to find her way there. She roams free, doing her job hunting for mice." Her eyes twinkled in amusement. "Likely knows the ship better than even Mr. Andrews by now. Though . . ." She paused. "She doesn't usually venture into the passenger areas." She shrugged. "No matter. Just set her down and she'll be off."

But Miss Fortune was clearly reluctant to do that. "Oh, well, I suppose, I wanted to be *sure* she's not injured. Or her kittens." She nibbled her bottom lip quite endearingly. "Please, I know it's highly irregular, and rather intrusive, but . . . I need to see for myself that she's well and truly all right. *Could* you show us where they're nested?"

Bennett seemed torn. Such a request was certainly unusual,

and normally passengers wouldn't be allowed in the crew areas because they wouldn't wish to be. But she plainly liked Miss Fortune, and what's more, she liked Jenny. Bennett gave the cat one last look before turning to see if they were alone. Then she nodded. "Come with me. But I can't take you into the third-class areas, or they'll have my hide for contaminating the quarantine," she added over her shoulder as she hustled them down the corridor.

"I understand," Miss Fortune assured her, still cradling Jenny.

Bennett paused near midship, peering fore and then aft before leading them into an interior cabin that appeared to be some sort of pantry. Inside was a staircase they took downward, emerging in a much larger pantry, bustling with staff preparing the ship's lunch. Several members of the crew turned to look at them curiously, but most were too busy to pay them much heed. The air was thick with the smells of cooking and steam from the rows of hot presses. The walls were lined with shelves containing stacks of the Royal Crown Derby china on which they dined, and hanging above were racks of crystal glassware. The space was almost unbearably warm, and Chess felt a pulse of empathy for the chaps forced to work there day after day, meal after meal.

They rounded a corner and passed through a door into the scullery—another stuffy room, though at least the space was illuminated by two portholes. Jenny's beloved scullion, Jim, was not present, but the cat leaped from Miss Fortune's arms and padded toward one corner, where half a dozen kittens were curled up in a mound of blankets. They cried softly for their mother until she settled down among them and flopped to the side so that they could suckle.

Miss Fortune leaned forward to watch, her face pink and her eyes shining with delight. She stood in a beam of sunlight, which brought out glints of copper in her brown hair, and Chess didn't think he'd ever seen anything more beautiful in all his life.

It shifted something within him, making him lighter and somehow more grounded than he'd ever recalled being. It was similar to what he felt stepping on a tennis court just before the start of a match. The smell of the grass, the crisp wind combing through his hair, the give of the lawn beneath his feet, the anticipation in his muscles as he waited for his opponent to serve. And yet this was different. This was *more*. It hollowed him out and also filled him until he feared he couldn't contain it all.

Flora looked up at him then, sharing her joy, pouring it into him in a way he hadn't even known he needed. "Aren't they adorable?"

He found it difficult to speak. "Yes." He cleared his throat, moving a step closer. "Yes, they are."

It was hard to tell where one wiggling gray-and-brown ball of fur began and another ended as they clambered to be fed. All the while, Jenny lay there contentedly, her eyes closed to slits, as a soft, rumbling purr issued from her throat.

"As you can see, they're all well," Bennett muttered anxiously behind them.

"Yes. Yes, they are." Flora straightened and turned toward her, evidently also sensing the stewardess's impatience that they return to their own domain. "Thank you."

"O' course, miss," she answered with a tight smile.

"Back the way we came?" Chess queried.

Once again, Bennett led the way, surprising a young maid in the maids' and butlers' pantry on the deck above. Once they'd emerged in the corridor, the stewardess hurried off to her duties, leaving Chess and Flora staring at each other. For perhaps the first time in his life, he felt irrationally tongue-tied, and scolded himself for his ridiculousness. She was the same woman he'd teased the night before. The same woman he'd helped rescue a cat not a quarter of an hour earlier. If he didn't say something soon, she would think he'd turned soft in the head.

His gaze dipped to the square neckline of her gown. "You've something . . ." He gestured vaguely, and she looked down and gave a light laugh.

"Apparently Jenny was marking me," she jested as she brushed the cat hair from her bodice. It was then that Chess realized she was wearing periwinkle. His lips curled upward at the discovery, a feeling of triumph surging through his veins.

So she *had* come to watch him play her brother at squash that morning. Though he guessed she'd never admit it if he asked. It didn't matter. Not now that he knew it.

But evidently he hadn't done a good job at masking his enjoyment of this fact, for she tilted her head, eyeing him askance.

"What?" she demanded.

He shook his head.

"No, seriously. What are you thinking?" She flushed, wrinkling her nose. "I suppose my behavior earlier wasn't quite dignified—"

He cut her off by lightly touching her arm. "I thought it was better than dignified. It was heroic."

She blushed even brighter before scoffing. "Heroic?"

"Not many ladies of my acquaintance would risk their clothing, let alone their dignity, to save a trapped animal. At most, they might have summoned a staff member to see to the matter. But you couldn't leave the creature alone like that, could you?"

She shook her head.

"I think that speaks far more to your character than you realize."

Her eyes shimmered with some depth of emotion as she peered up at him. One that almost made him forget himself and their surroundings and pull her into his arms. But then she lowered her gaze, breaking the spell.

They could hear voices approaching and she turned her head to the side to listen. "I should go," she said, backing up a step. "My mother . . ." She couldn't seem to finish the sentence, but she didn't really need to. He recognized this for the retreat it was.

"Of course," he reassured her.

She pivoted to go but then paused, turning back. "Not every gentleman would have behaved as you did. And I . . ." She looked away shyly. "I thought it rather heroic, too." With one last glance in his direction, she hastened down the hall.

# CHAPTER 14

༄

*Friday, April 12, 1912—10:05 a.m.*

Alice spent most of the late morning strolling on the Promenade
Deck with Mrs. Brown and her more petite but equally gregarious friend, Mrs. René Harris.

"Her husband owns the Hudson Theatre in New York,"
Mrs. Brown declared, leaving Alice slightly awed and a little trep-
idatious. She wasn't certain her mother would approve of her so-
cializing with theater people, but she had to admit to a thrill of
excitement at meeting someone so interesting.

"I am not accustomed to so much sitting," Mrs. Brown confided, adjusting her marvelous broad-brimmed hat with feathers
as they circled the ship. "And a sedentary existence combined
with all that rich food is not good for the constitution."

"Speak for yourself," Mrs. Harris retorted with a throaty laugh.
"But I do take your point." She sighed. "What I wouldn't do for
a canter through Central Park at the moment. But only if I could
be right back here on the *Titanic* after. Isn't she a beaut?"

Alice took this question to be rhetorical but had to agree. She
was a beautiful ship.

The sea that day seemed a bit choppier, but one could tell
only by looking over the side of the ship at the water. The
weather remained calm and favorable, but clouds were gathering

in the west, making Alice wonder if there would be rain showers later.

"Tell me about yourself, Miss Fortune," Mrs. Harris demanded, sporting her own grand hat. This one was adorned with tulle and flowers. "May . . . that's Mrs. Futrelle. She said you're from somewhere up in Canada?"

"Winnipeg. But I'm afraid there's nothing really interesting about me," she demurred. "I would much rather hear about you and your husband's theater. What an exciting life you must lead!"

"It certainly has its perks. But it's not without its challenges." She shared a sardonic look with Mrs. Brown. "The Folies Bergère Theater Harry opened last year in New York . . . An incarnation of the Paris cabaret," she explained to Alice. "Has not panned out. My boy lost a considerable amount on that venture." She flipped her hand as if to brush it away. "But such is life. And Harry has just signed a contract to produce his first motion picture."

"Now, that's where the money's at," Mrs. Brown enthused. "It won't be long until there's a cinema in every town in America. And Canada, too," she added with a look at Alice.

"But, please, Miss Fortune. I do not believe your life can truly be so dull. Did you not just finish your grand tour? Harry and I recently visited Italy, Egypt, and Morocco."

This was a topic Alice was enthusiastic about, and they spent a lap of the ship comparing the sites they'd visited, the food they'd eaten, and the clothes they'd purchased in Paris.

She paused as they passed the aft railing a second time, looking out over the Second-Class Promenade and then the Well Deck below. Both bustled with passengers from the other classes attempting to get some exercise. On the Second-Class Promenade, two adorable little girls with large bows in their hair jumped over the quoit board, utilizing it in some sort of makeshift game of hopscotch. They appeared to be about the same age as the boy they'd passed earlier pulling a toy ox, and she imagined he would have enjoyed playing with them, if only they'd been in the same class.

At the stairs leading down into the Well Deck, a woman stood with a man who had climbed the steps from third class to speak with her over the low gate separating the two classes. They appeared quite familiar with each other, and Alice found herself wondering how they were acquainted. Friends? Neighbors? Something more?

She watched them for some time while Mrs. Brown and Mrs. Harris chatted and found herself growing melancholy. She thought she'd hidden it well until Mrs. Brown spoke.

"Why the long face, dear?"

"I wager I know."

Alice turned to look into Mrs. Harris's empathetic gaze.

"You're missing your beau, aren't you."

Alice smiled sadly. "Terribly."

Mrs. Harris moved closer. "Absence is often the hardest thing. Why, I remember how utterly useless I was at my job at a Manhattan law firm after I met Harry. I'm surprised they didn't fire me before I quit to marry him." She chuckled. "Truth be told, even now I still miss my boy when he's not underfoot. Which is why I butt my nose into every little part of his enterprise, just so I can be near him. He tolerates me."

"Utter nonsense," Mrs. Brown declared. "That man knows how lost he would be without you. Why, he's always saying how if anything happened to him, you could pick up the reins. He knows your worth, my girl." She nodded her chin decisively. "He's a good one."

Alice considered asking her about Mr. Brown and whether she missed him, but then decided against it. If she didn't mention him herself, then it might not be the happiest of topics. After all, for every marriage like the Harrises' there was another where the two parties were just as eager to escape each other.

Alice hoped she and Holden would never grow tired of each other. Just the thought of it made her ache.

Mrs. Brown linked her arm with hers. "My best advice is to begin as you intend to go on. It may cause some chafing early on, but at least then you'll both know where you're at. Men adapt more easily when they're young," she added with a pat to her hand.

Begin as she intended to go on? Alice didn't know what to do with this advice, when what she wished to do was to continue traveling and exploring and having adventures.

It wasn't long before they heard the faint sound of music drifting through the air, and they made their way inside and up the stairs to the First-Class Entrance on the Boat Deck. There, under the frosted glass dome, the band had set up around the piano. Alice tipped her head back and closed her eyes. If she listened closely during a lull between ragtime tunes, she thought she could hear the glass beads hanging from the light fixture at the dome's center making a soft tinkling sound, owing to the almost imperceptible vibrations of the ship.

William Sloper appeared then, claiming the seat next to her on one of the settees. "You were missed last night," he murmured, never removing his eyes from the band. "We had an immensely good time. Nothing untoward, as I promised. Though it would have been even better had you been there."

Alice felt torn again about her decision not to join Mr. Sloper and a few of his friends and acquaintances in Thomas Cardeza's suite. As Mrs. Brown had mentioned the day before, Mr. Cardeza had put the extra space in his deluxe suite on B-Deck to good use by hosting poker games on the private promenade.

"What of his mother?" she whispered. "I would have thought she would object." After all, Charlotte Cardeza was a notorious dragon, and Alice couldn't imagine she approved.

"She retired early, and her bedchamber is on the opposite side of the suite. I suspect she heard nary a peep. He's hosting another game tonight."

Alice turned to look at William, warring with herself. William had said nothing untoward had happened. At least, nothing more untoward than poker, whiskey, and tobacco. Alice *wanted* to go. She wanted to experience at least *one* more adventure before their journey ended.

"Harris was there." William slid his gaze toward Mrs. Harris, who sat in a chair nearby, making his meaning clear. "Said he was going to invite his wife to join us. Apparently, Mrs. Harris is quite the card sharp."

Alice sneaked a look at the woman in question, finding her absorbed in the band. Yes, Mrs. Harris was a theater person, and so perhaps not quite respectable in her mother's eyes, but still— someone else she knew would be there. And that someone else was a woman.

"I'll think about it," she whispered. But by the time the band had finished and the ship had tested its whistles on the three working funnels, signaling it was noon, she'd already made up her mind.

"Excuse me!" Mabel declared in affront as she was nearly mown down by a young man racing past her on the Grand Staircase.

"Sorry!" he called behind him.

Mabel scowled at his retreating back and huffed in annoyance as two more gentlemen skirted past her. What on earth had gotten into them?

It wasn't until she reached C-Deck and saw the crowd of men gathered around the notice board outside the Purser's Office that she remembered this was where the ship's run would be posted after it was calculated every day around noon. So it was the winner of the previous evening's betting pool concerning the mileage the *Titanic* had covered since noon the previous day that they were so obsessed with.

"Four hundred eighty-four nautical miles! That's better than the *Olympic*'s tally on the first day of her maiden voyage."

"Bested her by more than fifty miles."

"Aye, and only twenty of the *Titanic*'s twenty-nine boilers are lit."

"I heard they're lighting more."

Mabel rolled her eyes. If this was what they were going to be subjected to for the remainder of the voyage, then she was afraid she might resort to taking an auger to her eardrums.

Once inside her cabin, she didn't bother to climb up into her own bunk but flopped back on Alice's bed, draping her hand over her eyes. She knew she was being overdramatic but she didn't care. Nothing was going her way.

Miss Young had been closeted with Mrs. White all morning when she had most needed to talk to her. Mabel was still unable to locate Mrs. Candee. And her parents had not taken the bait when she'd introduced them to Dr. Leader and Mrs. Swift the previous evening, asking about the places from which they hailed, of all things, and not the fact that Dr. Leader was a *female* physician.

What's worse, following their dinner conversation, she'd suddenly had the suspicion that they were trying to pair her with *Mr. Kinsey*. Which was utter nonsense! Anyone with eyes could tell he was interested in Flora, not *her*. But Flora was engaged to Crawfy, so in her parents' minds, that was that.

Mabel frowned. Flora would never be happy if she married Crawfy Campbell. Mabel had been certain of it before, and after seeing the way Flora and Mr. Kinsey giggled together the previous evening, she was even more convinced. Now, if only Flora could see it.

As if on cue, Flora entered their cabin. A frown marred her brow. "Have you seen Alice?"

"Not since she was playing Sleeping Beauty," Mabel responded blithely, sitting upright. "Why?"

"You were already snoring—"

"I don't snore!" Mabel protested.

"But she crept in carrying her shoes at half past eleven and had the devil of a time wriggling out of her gown and corset instead of waking us to help her undress."

"You were watching her struggle!" Mabel gasped at the deviousness. "But half past eleven. That's not very late."

"It is for her! It is when most of the public rooms close at eleven."

Mabel pushed to her feet. "It's almost time for lunch. I'm sure we'll find Alice in the Dining Saloon." She paused next to her sister, picking what appeared to be a clump of fur from the Valencia lace along her collar. "What's that?"

Flora plucked it from her fingers and turned away, but not before Mabel caught sight of her high color. "Just a bit of cat fur."

"You were petting a cat?" Mabel asked in confusion.

"Shall we?" Flora said, hastening through the door.

When they reached the Reception Room, they spied Alice standing before the hunting tapestry as she chatted with Mr. Sloper and several of his friends, including Mr. Kinsey.

"How was your squash match with Charlie this morning?" Mabel asked the tennis star.

"I enjoyed myself," he replied, rolling one of his shoulders. "It felt good to swing a racquet again after a few weeks' hiatus."

"He trounced us," Charlie announced with far too much cheer. "You should have been there."

"Yes, it was quite invigorating," Mr. Kinsey drawled, locking gazes with Flora. He was clearly communicating something to her. Something she seemed determined not to understand.

Arching her chin slightly, Flora instead turned to the man Mr. Kinsey had been speaking with before they approached. "Mr. Cardeza, do you also play?"

"No, no. Tennis is not for me," he replied.

Scrutinizing his pasty skin, Mabel could well believe it. With his medium stature, neatly combed brown hair, and spectacles, he presented an unassuming picture for a dragon's son.

"I understand you're staying in one of the parlor suites," Mabel remarked, her curiosity getting the better of her. "I hear they're the most sumptuous rooms afloat."

"It is quite handsome. If you'd like to see it, I'm—"

"Flora! Mabel! There you are," Alice exclaimed, interrupting Mr. Cardeza. She gave a breathless laugh. "I can't believe I slept so late this morning."

Mabel eyed her sister suspiciously, for she knew Alice had seen them approach. It was almost as if Alice hadn't wanted Mr. Cardeza to finish what seemed to be an invitation, but that didn't make sense. Surely Alice would wish to see the suite as well.

Before she could probe deeper, the bugler began to play and the double doors to the Dining Saloon were thrown open for lunch.

The meal passed with little incident aside from the family's usual exchanges of good-natured teasing. However, following lunch, when Mabel tried to convince her sisters to stroll with her, they made it clear they had other plans.

"I'm on my way to the Reading and Writing Room," Flora informed her, striding toward the lifts. "I have a number of letters to write."

Mabel wrinkled her nose in distaste. "Don't be a spoilsport, Flora. You've got the rest of your life to sit in your fusty old parlor and write letters."

When this failed to move her, Mabel spun about to appeal to Alice, but she was now nowhere to be seen.

"But it's such a lovely day," she tried again, scrambling to catch up with Flora. "Why would you wish to remain indoors?"

"Last I looked, it was drizzling."

Mabel followed her sister up to the A-Deck, stepping out onto the promenade to see that her sister was correct. Specks of rain splattered the glass windows. Though it wasn't coming down hard, and with the forward portion of the promenade being enclosed, a stroll wasn't out of the question. However, Flora had already disappeared into the Reading and Writing Room, putting a punctuation mark on their discussion.

The last thing Mabel wanted was to be cooped up in a room filled with the sounds of pens scratching. Instead, she went to the Lounge to pick out a book from its shelves—something delightfully frivolous—and settled into one of the deckchairs lining the enclosed promenade. A steward helped her to wrap herself in a warm rug and fetched her a cup of hot bouillon, and soon she was immersed in the world of the Paris opera, where a phantom haunted its halls.

She wasn't certain how long she'd sat there, barely moving except for the flip of a page or a sip of bouillon, when the clink of something hitting the deck to her right brought her out of her reverie.

"My apologies," the woman seated next to her said, leaning over to right the mug she'd knocked over. "I didn't mean to disturb you." She smiled and nodded at Mabel's book. "You were quite absorbed in that."

Mabel tilted it so that she could see the cover.

"Ah, now I understand. I, too, am an admirer of Leroux." The petite woman was swathed in stylish black velvet and ermine with a chic hat perched on her head. "Have you gotten to the part where the Angel of Music is unmasked?"

"No! Don't tell me," Mabel protested.

"Oh, I won't," she promised. "But you must tell me when you do. It is wonderfully chilling," she said, and shivered.

Mabel laughed. "I will. But what are you reading?"

The woman looked about as if to see who was listening, intriguing Mabel. Then she removed the cloth she held over her lap to show her a book with the name Elinor Glyn boldly splashed across the cover. Glyn was Lady Duff-Gordon's sister. The one who wrote bawdy fiction.

Mabel gasped, sitting forward in her seat. "I have been dying to read that!"

The woman quickly covered it again, with a twinkle in her eyes at Mabel's reaction.

"Well, perhaps not *dying*," Mabel revised, tempering her words. "But eager." She didn't add the fact that she hadn't been able to locate a copy in Winnipeg because Glyn's books had been banned.

"It's been helping to keep me distracted," she confided, the sparkle in her eyes dimming. "My son was injured in an airplane crash, you see, and I'm hurrying home to be with him."

"Oh, my goodness! Was he badly hurt?" Mabel queried. An airplane crash! Why, she hadn't even known anyone who had flown in one of those machines, let alone crashed in one.

"Well, his telegram was decidedly short on details, but I've been assured he's not in danger of succumbing to his wounds, thank heavens. But I know I won't truly rest until I've seen him for myself."

"I can imagine. My mother is always saying that young men are inexorably imprudent and reckless, and that we must forgive them for it. I'm Mabel Fortune, by the way," she added, extending her hand to the woman.

"Pleased to meet you, Miss Fortune. I'm Helen Churchill Candee."

Mabel was hard-pressed not to behave imprudently and reckless herself by hurling herself at Mrs. Candee now that she'd finally found her. "But you are an author as well!" she exclaimed.

She flushed. "You've read that, have you? Well, I'm simply glad my meager efforts helped to secure Oklahoma statehood."

Mabel stared at Mrs. Candee in incomprehension for several seconds before realizing she was speaking of *An Oklahoma Romance*, a fiction novel Mrs. Candee had written. "Of course, but you also wrote *How Women May Earn a Living*," Mabel clarified.

Mrs. Candee pressed a hand to her chest and gave a light laugh. "Oh, yes. I see." She raised her hand to an acquaintance passing by who tipped his hat to her. "Are you pursuing a career, then?"

"I hope to," Mabel admitted candidly. "I want to convince my father to allow me to attend university, but thus far all of my attempts have failed miserably."

Mrs. Candee sized her up with one swift glance. "He expects you to marry well."

"Yes! And thinks attending university will ruin my chances to do so." Mabel sat back with a scoff. "Not that *I* care if it does, but from all the evidence I've been able to gather, this is patently false. Dr. Leader and Mrs. Swift, and any number of university-educated women I've met, have wed successful and respectable men."

"They married successful, respectable men certainly," Mrs. Candee said. "But they were men of a different class in their way of thinking. One more equable and broad-minded." At Mabel's blank look, she added, "Men who are not necessarily of the stripe your father has in mind for you."

Mabel tipped her head back against her deck chair and stared at Mrs. Candee.

"I take it this is not something you've taken into consideration before?"

"No," Mabel responded faintly.

"I empathize with you, Miss Fortune. I truly do. It is a precarious situation we live in when women are expected to be entirely dependent on a man, and men are supposed to bear the weight of all that dependence unaided."

There was a sorrow-filled, almost wistful quality to Mrs. Candee's tone, and, gazing at her profile, Mabel wondered if Mrs. Candee was thinking of her own disastrous marriage to a husband who was rumored to have been shockingly abusive. If so, Mabel marveled at her ability to feel any empathy for him.

"So what should we do?" she asked.

"We do what we *can* do, Miss Fortune. Fight to change it. In whatever way we can."

"The vote?"

"Among other things." She stared very directly at Mabel. "You must understand, Miss Fortune, that if you are to pursue a career, this is merely the first of many hurdles you will face. Are you prepared to face them? Are you prepared to defy failure? For failure is not usually the fault of a poorly chosen occupation or a lack of talent, but the lack of perseverance and the will to forge your own success."

Mabel considered her words, feeling them settle in her stomach. They fluttered like butterflies, nervous to take flight, uncertain whether they were even capable.

"Do you have the will to forge your own success?" Mrs. Candee asked her pointedly.

Did she? It was a question worth considering. If convincing her father was but the first obstacle, did she have the will, the desire to face more?

Mabel felt the answer stir within her. "Yes," she declared succinctly. "Yes, I do."

Mrs. Candee's lips curled into a smile before she peered at the watch pinned to her coat and began to gather her things. "I'm afraid I have another engagement, but I would very much enjoy speaking with you more. Would you care to join me for tea with some friends later in the Café Parisien?"

Mabel eagerly accepted, hugging her book close to her chest as she watched the other woman walk away. The *Titanic* might be racing across the Atlantic at ever increasing speeds, but she still had four days to figure out how to change her destiny.

# CHAPTER 15

❧❧❧

*Friday, April 12, 1912—7:00 p.m.*

"Miss Fortune."

At the sound of Mr. Andrews's voice, Flora paused in her descent of the Grand Staircase and turned to greet him with a smile.

His genial gaze dipped to take in her cream-corded silk dinner gown covered with chiffon and gold lace. "But, my, you look lovely this evening," he declared, adjusting the cuff of his dark evening coat.

"Thank you," she replied, raising her voice slightly over the din of conversation filling the Reception Room below. "And I must also thank you for the tour you gave my father and brother this morning. Charlie has been unable to talk of anything else. You've made quite the impression."

Mr. Andrews offered her his arm. "'Twas my pleasure. The lad has a good mind. I'm sure he'll make a success of whatever he puts it to."

"Tommy," a man at the bottom of the stairs near the candelabra hailed him before turning to address her. "And I believe this is one of the Misses Fortune."

Flora recognized him as the ship's distinguished surgeon, Dr. O'Loughlin. Pleasantly round with graying hair and an impressive mustache, he seemed to be a popular figure among the passengers and staff. He had been conversing with a dark-haired stewardess whom Mr. Andrews greeted by the name of Miss Sloan.

"I'm the eldest, Flora," she told the doctor, offering him her hand.

"Ah, the eldest and the finest, no doubt." He winked.

"Now, why do I suspect you would tell all my sisters the same," Flora bantered in return.

Miss Sloan grinned. "Aye, she's taken your measure."

"That she has," he agreed in the same lilting Irish brogue as his other companions. Flora began to feel her Canadian accent was rather flat in comparison.

"All of us stewardesses have long marveled at the fact that the dear old doctor has managed to remain a bachelor," Miss Sloan leaned over to confide.

"And I keep tellin' 'em. Sure, haven't I worn all the knees out of my trousers proposing to ladies, and sure, they won't have anything to do with me at all."

This was obviously a familiar jest and Flora smiled appreciatively. Even though he'd undoubtedly heard the witticism before, Mr. Andrews grinned as well, but there was an underlying sadness to it. Flora wasn't the only one to notice.

"Well, Tommy, it seems to me that the *Titanic* is an unmitigated success," Dr. O'Loughlin declared. "I've heard nothing but compliments from the passengers and crew alike."

"Aye," Miss Sloan agreed. "She's a beauty. And the changes you made to the staff quarters for us are perfection."

"I'm well pleased," Mr. Andrews replied, but then sighed. "The only thing I do not like is that it is taking me farther away from home every hour. I've written to my wife twice a day since we left, but of course, I'll have to wait to post those letters until we reach New York." He tugged at the sleeves of his shirt and coat again—a nervous habit, it seemed. "I wish my wife hadn't been feeling unwell when I left. And my daughter Elizabeth, too. My father was also quite ill." He sighed. "Though I know my being there would not make any of them better."

"Aye, and that's the truth," Dr. O'Loughlin assured him. "You told me their physicians are looking after them. They're in good hands, to be sure."

Mr. Andrews peered absently toward the crowd now beginning to stream into the Dining Saloon. "I just hope they know I would be with them if I could."

Flora pressed her hand gently to his forearm where it was linked with hers, touched by his worry. "They know," she stated with quiet certainty.

His gaze dipped to meet hers and he nodded before turning to address the stewardess with a fond smile. "Carry on, Miss Sloan. And convey to the other stewards and stewardesses what a fine job they are doing."

Her face warmed as if he were the sun. "I will, Mr. Andrews." She bobbed a brief curtsy before hurrying off.

Flora found herself with not one, but two escorts into dinner, as Dr. O'Loughlin moved to her other side. She enjoyed their genial conversation, allowing herself to relax and silence her ongoing concerns. But the instant her eyes lifted to meet Chess Kinsey's across the room, any illusion of sangfroid fled along with her usual poise. She'd done her best to avoid him all afternoon, hoping distance would temper her impression of the man. Yet here she was, still baffled by how one glimpse of his amber eyes could make her chest feel tied up in knots.

The trouble was something had changed between them that morning. He'd been so *kind*. He hadn't scoffed at her determination to rescue the ship's cat or at her insistence that she see Jenny safely back to her kittens. Instead, he'd aided and abetted her. Things she could never imagine Crawford doing, let alone his exerting the effort to understand why she needed to do so. Had her fiancé found her in such a compromising position, not only would he have probably scolded her, but also accused her of having lost her wits.

But Chess had *laughed*. And perhaps even more astonishing,

he'd treated her as if her actions were not only natural but endearing.

It was uncomfortable to find herself comparing Crawford to another man and realizing he didn't measure up. And what's more, not in qualities that were superficial and fleeting, such as good looks or charm, but attributes she deemed essential—compassion, tolerance, patience.

So she supposed it wasn't any wonder why her feelings toward Mr. Kinsey had grown rather warmer than the chill disapproval she'd initially held toward him, and far more complicated.

Just as well that the only chair left at her family's table forced her to sit with her back toward Mr. Kinsey and his companion, Mr. Behr. If nothing else, it would prevent her from sneaking glances at him throughout the evening.

Mr. Andrews and the surgeon exchanged a few words with her family before continuing to their own places at the chief purser's table, leaving the Fortunes to enjoy their meal. Her family had great praise for the Consommé Sévigné, lobster Newburg, mushroom vol-au-vent, and Surrey capon, but Flora found herself too unsettled to manage more than a few bites of any of the courses. Even the pineapple royale couldn't tempt her.

"You've been awfully quiet this evening," her father said as she pushed her dessert about her plate. "Not developing a case of *mal de mer*, are you?"

"No, Father. Just tired, I think."

His dark eyes seemed to see more than she wished. He swiped his napkin over his mouth, ruffling his mustache. "It will be good to be home, won't it? I suspect this trip has given you a new perspective on matters. We've done and seen many things." He sat back, turning his head to survey the throng of first-class diners before meeting her gaze again squarely. "But I trust you'll remember that flash isn't substance, and you'll see that my judgment is still sound."

Flora swallowed the stickiness that had gathered at the back of her throat, knowing perfectly well what he meant. He was no fool. "Yes, Father."

He reached out to pat her hand in approval. "Good girl. Your mother and I know we can always count on your good sense."

Guilt lanced through her, but she forced herself to smile. In the past, she would have been pleased by his praise, but now it settled like a cold lump in her breast.

After dinner, as the family made its way out to the Reception Room to listen to the band following dinner, as had become their custom, Flora tried to shrink back into her role of the dutiful daughter. She even allowed herself to be seated between Mother and Mrs. Hays, who were certain to squelch any frivolous discussion. But her sisters seemed to have other ideas.

"Flora, Mr. Sloper and Mr. Kinsey have invited us all to go for a stroll on deck," Mabel declared, having bounded over to the settee with Alice in tow. Her eyes were bright, and her cheeks flushed with excitement. "Please, say you'll come with us. We shall make a party of it," she finished, smiling at the two gentlemen.

Flora's heart kicked in her chest as she locked eyes with Mr. Kinsey. He appeared as affable and coolly composed as ever, but she also thought she detected a certain reserve. One that, perhaps, he'd adopted for the matrons seated beside her.

"Don't you think Flora should join us, Mother?" Mabel cajoled. "As a chaperone," she added, with a smirk at Flora.

"Yes, of course Flora must go with you," Mother replied.

Flora felt a prick of irritation at being trapped like this.

"Be sure to bundle up." Mother called after them.

"We'll meet you next to the lifts on C-Deck," Alice informed the men as they trailed behind them up the stairs.

Having fetched their coats and hats in short order, they arrived at the lifts to find Mr. Kinsey already waiting for them. Flora fussed with the collar of her ermine-lined coat and readjusted the angle of her green velvet cap, avoiding his eye, while he and her sisters decided to take the lift up to A-Deck, where Mr. Sloper's cabin and the promenade were located, instead of waiting for him to come to them.

In the shuffle, as they all crowded into the lift along with another couple, Flora found herself standing directly in front of Mr. Kinsey. Despite the layers of silk and wool between them, she swore she could feel the heat of him and the taut underlying strength of his form. She was vividly reminded of her reaction to his play on the Squash Court that morning, when she'd sneaked into the spectators' gallery to watch. The sight of him lunging to and fro—bending and twisting and swinging—the lines of his muscles evident despite being covered practically from head to toe in crisp white cotton, had made her flush with a sharp yearning.

A similar yearning unfurled inside her now, making her pulse throb and her breath lodge in her chest. The air around her seemed to be filled with the scent of his cologne. Either his body or hers swayed, bringing them infinitesimally closer, and she closed her eyes, fighting the urge to lean back against him. Someone might have spoken to her, but it was naught but a faint hum in her ears for her entire being seemed to be focused on the man behind her.

When the lift reached A-Deck and the gates clattered open for them to step out, Flora had to force her feet to move, lest she make a complete cake of herself by continuing to stand there dumbfounded. Even so, her disorientation hadn't gone unnoticed, for Mr. Kinsey reached out to grip her elbow, making the skin there pebble at his touch. Before she knew it, her arm was linked with his and they were following a chattering Mr. Sloper and her sisters out onto the promenade.

The night air was cool against her cheeks and almost piercing with clarity as it filled her lungs. The overcast skies from earlier that day had drifted away to reveal a star-strewn sky. Beyond the glass of the enclosure, they twinkled like bright gems scattered across a swath of midnight velvet.

Neither Flora nor Mr. Kinsey spoke as they turned their feet toward the bow of the ship, strolling over the sleek decking. But as the silence stretched, Flora began to fret over what she should say. It might have helped if Alice and Mr. Sloper had not adopted a pace far faster than the leisurely stroll they'd proposed, for then Flora and Mr. Kinsey might have benefited from their lively chatter to cover any awkwardness. But Alice and Mr. Sloper seemed oblivious to their speed and the steadily widening gap between the two couples.

Conversely, Mabel appeared restless, stopping periodically to gaze out over the water or to examine something along the side of the ship. Between Mabel's dawdling and Alice and Mr. Sloper's haste, Flora found herself virtually alone with Mr. Kinsey. Or as near to alone as a couple could possibly be on deck where others periodically strolled by.

"Your family has expectations for you."

Flora turned from her scrutiny of Mabel to look up at Mr. Kinsey, though his gaze remained trained ahead.

"Expectations for your future," he clarified.

"Yes," she said, jarred and confused by this opening remark. "Doesn't your family have expectations for you?"

His mouth twisted. "Not really. Or rather, I suppose you could say they expect me to do nothing."

Despite his mocking tone, Flora sensed the pain this admission caused him. Particularly when he grimaced as if he wished he could recall the words. "Nothing? But I thought you were an attorney for your family's company?"

"I am. But essentially for appearances' sake." His mouth clamped into a tight line for a brief moment before he added. "They assign me only the most mundane of tasks." It was difficult to make out his expression in the alternating light and shadow of the dim overhead deck lamps. "I'm a Kinsey and a second son. We're rascals and ne'er-do-wells, just as you suspected. Not good for much more than being charming dinner companions."

Flora frowned, uncertain why he was telling her this. "But that's not true."

"Isn't it?" The harshness of his tone took her aback.

"You are a brilliant tennis player," she exclaimed. "By all reports, one of the best in America, if not the world."

"That's simply because I'm a natural."

"Are you going to try to tell me you don't train and practice? That you don't do it far harder and more often than you lead others to believe?"

He didn't deny this but instead shifted tactics. "Yes, but tennis is relatively useless. After all, I can't play forever. My body won't be able to keep up."

But she had already taken his measure and she knew this was merely another insecurity he'd kept well hidden.

"But I imagine you've already given some thought to what you'll do after you retire," she coaxed, gentling her voice. "I imagine you've given it a great deal of thought, though you're hesitant to admit it."

They had rounded the corner at the forward end of the promenade, and he brought her to a stop, turning her so that he could look into her eyes. "How do you know me so well?" His voice was frayed and torn, like a thread ready to snap.

There was starlight in his eyes and something more. Something warm and melting and yet bracing like the cold air filling her lungs. He'd looked at her like this once before, down in the scullery when they'd taken Jenny back to her kittens, but this time it was even more intent. For several seconds, it robbed her of words and wits, and made her long for things that couldn't be.

She knew what he was about to do. Just as she knew she would have allowed it, but for the sudden appearance of another couple rounding the corner of the promenade as they had a minute before. And so the quavering moment ended not with an embrace, but with him smoothly pivoting them so that they could resume their stroll.

Her blood still pounding in her ears, she looked about, realizing her sisters were gone. At some point, they'd slipped away—Alice on Mr. Sloper's arm and Mabel in a solo pursuit. Some chaperone she had turned out to be.

The truth was, she was the one who needed a minder. Because she'd nearly kissed a man who was not her fiancé. And, worse still, she actually felt disappointed she hadn't.

# CHAPTER 16

Chess knew the exact moment Flora realized her sisters had disappeared.

He'd noticed them melting away, one by one, some moments before. He'd recognized the sheer contrivance of it. What he couldn't deduce was whether it had been for their own benefit or for his and Flora's. Perhaps both. After all, Alice and Sloper had been conspiring about something, and the youngest sister, Mabel, simply had that look of mischief about her.

Whatever the case, Chess didn't say anything. Not when their maneuvering had left him exactly where he wanted to be—alone with Flora.

And then he had to go and do such a doltish thing as to start talking about expectations and his ne'er-do-well existence. If he'd *wanted* to push her away, he couldn't have said anything more calculated to do so.

But instead she'd done the most astonishing thing. She didn't look at him with disgust. She didn't run. Instead, she'd countered his arguments and sought to reassure him, to bolster him, even. She'd read between the lines, and over and around them in a way no one had bothered to before.

It made him want to tell her about the investments he kept private from his family, the ones that had garnered him enough wealth to step out of his family's shadow and refuse the extravagant stipend he was allotted as a second son if he chose. It made him want to tell her that he *had* thought of his future after tennis. About his tentative plans to start a business manufacturing and selling sporting goods—making them more accessible and affordable to a larger number of consumers.

He'd visited the neighborhoods where children played baseball in the streets with little better than sticks and rocks. He'd seen the battered and deflated balls and rickety rackets missing half their strings. He'd ensured that better equipment anonymously made it into those kids' hands, but he could only help those he was aware of, and there were far more beyond his reach. But if the goods were cheaper and easier to purchase, perhaps more families would be able to acquire them. It made good altruistic sense. And it made good business sense as well.

However, he'd never shared any of this with anyone beyond his private attorney and financial adviser, because he'd known what his family would say. They would laugh or sneer or merely shake their heads. Even most of his friends would ask why he would wish to bother when he could float through life as he was.

Only Flora expected more, and he liked that. He *liked* that she had expectations of him, and that she could see there was more to him than the roguish guise his family had forced him to adopt. The faith and trust reflected in her blue-gray eyes were intoxicating. So intoxicating he thought he just might be willing to do anything to keep it.

So when she dipped her head, hastening her steps down the promenade, he felt a surge of alarm that he'd done just the opposite.

"We . . . we should return inside," she stammered. "I need to find my sisters."

"I'm sure they can look after themselves." When she didn't respond, he added, "Sloper would never attempt anything untoward, if that's why you're concerned."

"No, but I'm meant to be their chaperone, and I haven't done a very good job." Her face lifted briefly to his, revealing bright eyes and pink cheeks, before her gaze skittered away. "If something should happen . . ." She shook her head. "Mother and Father would be terribly disappointed."

He sensed then what had truly unsettled her. It wasn't so much her sisters' absence but her attraction to him. She strove to hide it, but their awareness of each other was keen. It crackled in the air between them and hummed under his skin.

He slowed their steps. "Nothing is going to happen to your sisters. Not on the *Titanic*. But I don't know if I can say the same for you."

Her gaze collided with his.

"That you won't allow it to happen."

"I . . . I don't know what you mean."

Her pupils were large pools in the dim light, and her lips moist, and it took everything within Chess not to pull her into his arms. For he knew if he did so, he risked her slapping his face and never letting him near her again. That was the *last* thing he wanted. Not when he'd just realized what he *did* want.

Her. All of her. Forever. This Crawford Campbell fellow be damned.

The chap had been foolish enough to let her go, and Chess was going to find a way to make that separation permanent. If they'd already been married, then it would have been different. But they weren't, and to Chess's way of thinking, that meant Flora was still fair game.

Chess could feel her attraction to him. If he played his hand right, he just might be able to win hers. And if he did, he would spend the rest of his life making sure she never regretted it.

But for now, retreat was the better part of valor. He withdrew half a step away from her. "I see. My misunderstanding, then."

If such a thing were possible, she appeared even more flustered as she struggled to form a response, and in the end simply nodded.

He crooked his elbow, offering it to her. "Let's find your sisters."

He left Flora near the Forward Grand Staircase, where she insisted on continuing the search for her sisters herself and turned down the corridor toward the Smoking Room. The best of the numbers from the range of mileage estimates for the next day's run would undoubtedly already be taken, but there might be a few decent wagers to be made. In any case, he was due to meet Mr. Fortune for a drink, and he strongly suspected the man did not like to be kept waiting.

As he passed through the Lounge, he removed his overcoat, draping it over his arm, and reached up to slick back his sun-bleached brown hair. Pushing through the door, he was immediately surrounded by a haze of smoke and the low hum of masculine voices. Paneled as it was in mahogany inlaid with mother-of-pearl, one would have expected the room to be dim and brooding, but the backlit, hand-painted stained-glass windows inset along the inner walls offered the illusion of daylight and the coal-burning fireplace gave off a cheery glow.

Chess allowed his gaze to skim over the occupants in dark leather club chairs, searching for his quarry, and found him staring up at the painting hanging over the mantel. He'd overheard the artist Frank Millet and the president's military aide, Archie Butt, discussing the piece by Norman Wilkinson the previous evening; otherwise, he wouldn't have known that the painting was called *Plymouth Harbour*, or exactly what it was supposed to depict. But then again, art had never been his forte. He wondered if Mr. Fortune was of a similar mindset. His slightly disapproving frown made him suspect so.

Mr. Fortune turned as Chess approached, offering him his hand. "Finished your stroll with my daughters, have you? I was beginning to think their charms had distracted you."

"While they are undoubtedly charming," he began, draping his coat over one of the empty chairs before claiming the other, "I assure you I hadn't forgotten our arrangement." He lifted his hand, signaling to a passing steward, who he trusted would bring his usual. He tipped them well enough for them to remember.

Mr. Fortune appeared to be nursing a pint of stout, which he lifted to take a healthy draft before returning it to the green baize tabletop. A bit of foam clung to his mustache. "Aye, I suppose it wouldn't do to rush off and risk insulting them."

"I find it's best to never risk insulting a lady," Chess said, leaning forward slightly to confide in him.

The balding man chuckled. "Aye, isn't that the truth. I've four daughters, mind you, and I'll tell you, no one holds a grudge longer or fiercer than a young lady." He pointed his finger in emphasis. "Remember that."

"I will."

"And my Mabel . . ." He folded his hands over his chest. "Her memory is lengthy. No doubt, the liveliest of the bunch." There was a glint of fondness in his dark eyes as he shook his head. "Headstrong as the day is long. But she's forthright and honest. You'll always know where you stand with her." He sighed. "I suppose you could say she's the most like me. Had she been a boy, she would have been a force to be reckoned with."

Chess lifted the glass of whiskey neat that the steward had brought him and downed a finger's worth, enjoying its burn as it slid down his throat. It also allowed him a moment to take a measure of the other man before responding. For Chess hadn't thought he'd given *anyone* the impression that he was interested in the youngest Fortune daughter.

"Each of your daughters is uniquely intelligent and dynamic. Alice, for instance, seems quite adventurous."

"Alice?" Mr. Fortune remarked in surprise. "Oh, no, no. You've got that wrong. Ever since a young age, her health has been delicate. Lung issues. And while I admit she's rallied quite admirably for our tour, she'll always be somewhat fragile. Her fiancé, Holden Allen, understands that. A sweeter, more biddable girl you'll never meet."

Chess was hard-pressed not to frown, for this had not been his impression of Alice Fortune. Yes, she presented a picture of sweetness and biddability, but underneath she seemed as determined as Mabel to do what she wanted to do. He knew Alice had been speaking to Sloper about the poker games Thomas Cardeza hosted in his private suite. In fact, Chess strongly suspected that was where the pair had sneaked off to while he had been distracting Flora.

Mr. Fortune's conviction in Alice's timidity made Chess wonder if he genuinely knew any of his daughters.

"And Flora?"

Mr. Fortune's gaze sharpened, telling Chess he wasn't oblivious to his interest in his second daughter. "Flora is a sensible and dependable girl. Never given her mother or me a moment's grief. She understands her commandments and follows them to the letter."

In particular, *honor thy father and mother*, Chess felt certain he was implying.

Mr. Fortune sank back in satisfaction. "Crawford Campbell will make her an admirable husband, and I'm sure they'll have a comfortable life."

But that didn't mean a happy one. He was forced to bite his tongue lest he lash out with these very words. The way Mr. Fortune spoke about his second daughter made her sound deathly dull—a mindless drone to do her father's and then her husband's bidding—and Flora was so much more. She was witty and wise, sensitive and compassionate, and so deeply kind.

Truth be told, she did everything deeply. Her elegant, restrained exterior was but a gilded surface she'd donned to conceal the truth. For underneath she *thought* deeply, she *felt* deeply, she *loved* deeply. She needed a husband who understood that, who cherished it.

But this was not the time or place to try to enlighten her father. Chess might be known for his fierce tennis serves, but he also understood the strategic benefits of a good volley. How wearing an opponent out made it far more difficult for them to stretch to the corner or counteract the sidespin he put on the ball. How a diabolical backhand could win a match as surely as an ace.

After all, he hadn't become a ranked tennis player merely on the strength of his service.

Chess enjoyed another sip of his whiskey and settled in for a long chat. "So tell me how you came to own the land encompassing Winnipeg's main thoroughfare. Did you really arrive in Manitoba with barely a penny to your name?"

"Aye, well it was more like a quarter," Mr. Fortune began with false modesty as he launched into his tale.

# CHAPTER 17

✦

*Saturday, April 13, 1912*

Mabel nodded her thanks to the steward as he set a cup of coffee before her in the D-Deck Reception Room. She knew she was early, but she was too excited to do anything else. Not when Miss Young, or rather Marie, as she'd asked Mabel to call her, might arrive early as well.

When Marie had coaxed the details of her conundrum out of her earlier that morning, she'd convinced Mabel that what was missing from her strategy to persuade her father to allow her to attend university was a well-reasoned written argument and evidence that she had thoughtfully weighed all aspects of her decision. Marie had contended that her father, like most men, was more apt to be swayed by reason and logic, so Mabel must tailor her approach as such. What's more, Marie had agreed to support her in this effort by helping her craft just such a proposal.

After months of fruitless circling, Mabel felt heady with the surge of renewed hope. In a few hours' time, Mabel would have an ironclad strategy to win Father over to her way of thinking. And to ensure it, she'd invited Mrs. Candee and Dr. Leader to join them. After all, four heads were better than two, especially when they belonged to such intelligent and accomplished women.

Mabel smiled into her cup of coffee and squared the stack of

White Star stationery she'd brought, eagerly anticipating their conversation as the sounds of those still enjoying lunch filtered through with the opening and shutting of the doors to the adjoining Dining Saloon. From where she was seated at a table on the port side near the bow, all was relatively quiet, and she ruminated on Mrs. Candee's suggestion that she pursue law. She'd said that there was a need for more women with legal training to help further the cause of women's suffrage everywhere, and while Mabel had no intention of telling her father that, this avenue certainly piqued her own interest.

Her pleasant contemplations were soon disrupted by the prattling voice of a man. She struggled to hide her irritation as he and his companion claimed chairs just two tables away from hers in the large and otherwise nearly unoccupied room. Could they not have chosen seats elsewhere?

But then she realized she knew them. The man in uniform with the white beard was the ship's captain, and the tall, lanky chattering fellow was Mr. Ismay, the managing director of the White Star Line. Like every other gentleman on board, they appeared to be discussing the ship's daily run. Having heard enough talk of it during lunch, Mabel glowered into her cup of coffee, attempting to ignore them. But Ismay was far too earnest about the success of the ship, and his voice easily carried.

"Five hundred nineteen nautical miles," he enthused. "Average speed of twenty-point-nine-one knots. By Jove! Better than the *Olympic* on her maiden voyage." He sighed in satisfaction. "We made a better run today than we did yesterday, and we'll make an even better run tomorrow, wouldn't you say?"

To this, either the captain nodded or Ismay rushed on without awaiting a response. As far as she could tell, he was doing all the talking.

"Things are working smoothly. The machinery is bearing the test. The boilers are standing up to the pressure of full-steam quite nicely, and more are being lit. You intend to test all twenty-nine eventually, didn't you say? Revolutions are increasing on the reciprocating engines. At this rate, we will beat the *Olympic* and get in to New York on Tuesday!"

Mabel had given up any effort not to eavesdrop by this point. It would have been impossible not to. And perhaps now she might have something interesting to contribute to the next conversation she was subjected to about *Titanic*'s mighty attributes. But this last statement startled her. If the ship reached New York on Tuesday, then she would have one less full day at sea. One less day to garner advice and craft a successful argument.

Could the director be right? He seemed well-informed, and he was certainly in a position to know. The captain had thus far not said anything, but he also hadn't disputed Ismay's assertions.

She shifted slightly in the guise of examining something on the hem of her mulberry pongee skirt trimmed with brown, wanting to get a surreptitious look at Captain Smith's face. From what she could see out of the corner of her eye, his posture was relaxed and his features unruffled by his companion's enthusiasm, which was difficult to deny. Such was Ismay's excitement that he kept repeating himself. The captain let him ramble, apparently enjoying his ease.

Sometime later, Ismay finally seemed to talk himself out, urging the captain to his feet. "We will get somebody and go down to the Squash Courts."

Marie appeared shortly thereafter with a bright smile and a breathless apology for being late.

A few minutes later, Mrs. Candee joined them as well, along with three of the men from the coterie that had sprung up around the lovely divorcee. The first was Mr. Woolner, a tall, debonair Englishman; the second, a Mr. Björnström-Steffansson, the son of a Swedish pulp baron; and the third, Edward Colley, a merry Irishman with a booming laugh. The six of them formed a lively party—one to which others seemed to gravitate, coming and going throughout the afternoon.

It was impossible not to note the remarkable sense of camaraderie among all the passengers. And Mabel found it difficult not to be drawn into the bonhomie, lulled into believing, at least for a time, that her troubles beyond the ship did not exist. But as the band began to set up in the opposite corner of the room before teatime, and her companions slowly drifted away, she realized with dismay that she'd whiled away the entire afternoon and made almost no progress on her plans to persuade her father.

"Come to my cabin tomorrow morning. We'll work on it then," Marie assured her.

She gave Mabel's shoulder a squeeze and bustled off toward the Forward Grand Staircase just in time to miss Alice as she sat down across from her sister.

"Who was that?" she demanded brusquely.

"Miss Young," Mabel answered, studying the snide twist to her sister's lips. "What's got your knickers in a bunch? Did Flora confront you about your retiring to our cabin so late last night?"

Alice scowled. "That's vulgar. And no. She's too busy taking tea with Mr. Kinsey, Mr. Behr, and Miss Newsom in the Café Parisien."

"Is she really?" Mabel replied with furtive delight.

"I can't help but feel that Flora is revealing an appallingly fickle nature previously unbeknownst to us all," Alice groused.

"What on earth are you talking about?"

"She's only known Mr. Kinsey for three days and she already seems ready to throw over Mr. Campbell for him. I thought she was more loyal than that."

"Have you gone balmy? This is what we wanted."

"It's what *you* wanted," she accused. "While I can't help but think of poor Crawford."

"Yes, poor Crawfy, who has only bothered to write our sister one letter in the over three months we've been away," Mabel retorted. "Who has never made Flora genuinely smile. I'm sure he'll be heartbroken and not simply wounded in his pride."

"You've never liked him," she muttered.

"Yes, that's well established." Mabel frowned at her normally cheerful and good-natured sister. "I don't know what's troubling you, but you're confusing your feelings for Holden and his for you with Flora's relationship with Crawford. They're not the same."

Mabel waited for Alice to respond, but she just continued to glare across the room at the far corner. With a shake of her head, Mabel rose from her chair to find more pleasant company.

"Miss Newsom is delightful," Flora declared as she exited the Café Parisien.

"Karl certainly seems to think so," Chess quipped.

She turned to him laughingly, knowing full well he was happy for his friend even if masculine stoicism forbade him from saying so. His attire today was a bit bolder, sporting as he was a blue serge suit and a brightly patterned tie, but also somehow fitting, given the Continental flare of the ersatz sidewalk café built along the starboard side of the À la Carte Restaurant. The coffee was strong, the sandwiches were elegant, and the pastries were served from a circular, tiered buffet by waiters who spoke only French. They were even suitably stuffy.

"Do you think he'll propose?" she asked, taking more time than was strictly necessary to adjust her gray suede gloves. But then she'd not been anticipating the pang such a question had caused her.

"If he can screw up the courage."

She took his proffered arm, and allowed him to lead her toward the Aft Grand Staircase. Though not as grand as the Forward Grand Staircase, it was still richly carved and paneled, the circular mirrors lining the walls of the Reception Room outside the restaurant showcasing it in their reflection.

"Is the prospect truly so daunting?" she teased, having always imagined the matter was fairly straightforward for gentlemen. After all, they weren't forced to sit around, waiting for someone to take an interest.

"It can be," Chess replied. "Even if one is relatively certain of the woman's favor, a chap can never be absolutely sure. In that instant, the cards are entirely in her hands."

Flora couldn't withhold her scoff of derision.

He turned to her in surprise. "You disagree? Do you think a gentleman is never rebuffed?"

"Oh, for certain he is. But it's entirely the gentleman's choice whether to even *attempt* it. Any young lady making such overtures would be seen as vulgar and forward. Sometimes even too coquettish a smile is enough to see one snubbed."

As they reached the A-Deck, he turned their steps toward the doors leading out to the promenade, where a steady stream of passengers could be seen strolling in the hour before the sounding of the bugle to tell them it was time to dress for dinner. It was the most fashionable time to see and be seen other than at dinner, when the sky, deepening toward twilight, was painted in a palette of mauves, oranges, and purples. As they inserted themselves in the flow of passengers, Flora recognized the couple before them as the Astors, for few men were as tall or lanky as the colonel. He was leading a scraggly dog on a leash, while Mrs. Astor walked beside him, a pretty ermine cap perched on her head.

Flora lowered her voice to barely a murmur so as not to be overheard. "Even when a woman has reached that moment when she supposedly holds the fate of the gentleman in her hands. Even then her control may be far less than you think. For society has expectations, and fathers have great influence."

She could feel Chess's dark eyes intently upon her, but she didn't dare turn to meet his gaze. All she could focus on was the weight of her revelation, the way it pressed down on her chest, and the cool air stinging her heated cheeks.

"Then the world is foolish."

Surprised by the intensity of his deep voice, she turned to look at him, finding his amber eyes bright with conviction.

"For she deserves nothing less than to be absolutely persuaded of his adoration and devotion. To be certain it is one that echoes her own." His voice dropped to a whisper, his eyes drifting over her features. "Because she's too remarkable not to be told every day how extraordinary she is."

Awareness of him tingled across every nerve, particularly in the places his gaze touched. Warmth pooled deep within her, and she found she needed to remind herself to breathe. It was all she could do to keep her feet moving forward, let alone form a response.

And then the opportunity was stolen from her by the booming drawl of Colonel Gracie. "Miss Fortune," he cried.

She blinked as he strode forward to address her. "I do declare, it is good to see you." He glanced over his shoulder. "I was just remarking to Mr. and Mrs. Straus what a fine trio of young ladies you and your sisters are. Why, Miss Alice was obliging enough to keep me company for an hour this afternoon."

Flora suppressed a grimace on her sister's behalf. For all that Colonel Gracie meant well, an hour of his rambling on about his treatise on Chickamauga, among other things, could not have been easy to endure. She turned to greet the Strauses, who also must deserve their names writ in the annals of saintliness. This wasn't the first time she'd spotted them in Colonel Gracie's company, specifically the kindly Mr. Straus, the co-owner of Macy's department store.

But more often she'd seen the older couple strolling arm in arm about the decks of the *Titanic*, their heads bent close together. Truth be told, they seemed inseparable. So content were they with each other that she'd overheard several of the passengers referring to them as Darby and Joan from the old poem. The sight of them always drew a smile to her lips, and now was no different, despite the tumult of emotions still humming through her veins from Chess's professions.

"How is your heart?" Their second day aboard ship, Flora had discovered the stout and elegant Mrs. Straus struggling to climb the stairs, her hand pressed to her chest. Flora had helped her back to her cabin, where the matron's maid took control of the situation. "I trust it's better now that you've settled into the voyage."

"Oh, yes, my dear. Much better," she assured her. Her cheery face was wreathed by a cloud of dark hair streaked with gray. "'Tis only a nervous complaint." She turned to her husband with his well-trimmed white beard, patting his arm where it linked with hers. "Nothing to be concerned about."

But Flora could tell that Mr. Straus was concerned anyway. It was reflected in his dark eyes behind his round spectacles and the quiet affection of his presence.

"And who is *your* young beau?" Colonel Gracie interjected. "I don't believe I've had the pleasure."

Chess's pointed stare practically dared her to deny it as his lips twisted with his usual wry humor.

"This is Mr. Chess Kinsey," she replied. "You might know him from—"

"Tennis," Colonel Gracie finished for her, offering Chess his hand. "I'd heard there were a number of players aboard. Headed home for the season?"

"Yes, among other things."

"Good man! Do you predict a good one? I've heard tell of an up-and-comer from California who's supposed to have a serve to rival your own."

Flora felt a touch to her elbow and allowed Mrs. Straus to draw her a short distance away from the men.

"Your sister appeared to be nursing an aching head earlier," she said softly. "And I hope her time above decks didn't make it worse." The twinkle in the older woman's eyes as they cut toward Gracie left Flora in little doubt as to what she was talking about. "If she has need, I have some powders that should help. Just send word and I'll be sure to get them to her."

"Thank you. That's very kind," Flora said, wondering if she should look for Alice. She hadn't seen her since lunch, after which she'd hared off to who knows where.

Part of her felt that any headache would be just deserts for whatever Alice had been doing that had caused her to retire so late. Flora had been able to smell the cigarette smoke wafting from her clothes and hair as she entered their cabin. And if there had been cigarettes, then there had undoubtedly been liquor. They tended to go hand in hand.

But Alice was also her little sister, and her health was delicate. Or at least, it had been. The very fact that she'd upended her normal schedule the past two nights—retiring late and sleeping longer into the morning—troubled Flora. She feared it was only a matter of time before these changes began to take their toll on Alice's previously fragile constitution.

"You look after them, don't you?" Mrs. Straus remarked before clarifying. "Your sisters and brother. And mother and father, too."

"Yes, I suppose I do," she admitted.

"You're a good girl. We all need looking after sometimes. Even parents." She peered fondly at Mr. Straus. "And husbands."

"How long have the two of you been married?" Flora asked, pressing her mauve velvet hat with ostrich feathers to her head as a gust of wind tugged at the pins holding it in place.

"Forty years. And you know"—she clutched the chinchilla stole draped around her shoulders tighter around her throat and leaned in as if confiding a secret—"we have never been separated for a single day or night. Whither he goes, I go," she added in satisfaction. "How long have your parents been married?"

Flora tipped her head back, calculating. "Almost thirty-six years, I believe."

She nodded as if this confirmed something. "If you want my advice, Miss Fortune, find a man who is kind. A man who warms you from the inside when he looks at you." She turned toward her husband, who was looking at her that very way even as Colonel Gracie continued to pontificate. "A man you cannot bear to be parted from. And then cleave to him." She tightened her hand into a fist for emphasis.

Flora's gaze shifted to Chess, finding he was watching her. A secret smile played over his lips, perhaps meant to confirm what she already suspected about Colonel Gracie dominating the men's conversation, and it landed in her chest like a heated brick, its warmth spreading outward.

She blinked in befuddlement as Mrs. Straus patted her arm, reclaiming her attention.

"You won't regret it," she told her before returning to her husband's side.

Blankly staring at the space where the woman had just stood, Flora tried to come to terms with this revelation. The Strauses had been married for forty years. Her parents for thirty-six. Where would she be thirty-five or forty years hence? Who would be beside her?

She tried to imagine Crawford in that place, but even conjuring the memory of his face was difficult, let alone the notion of him at her side. The Strauses had never been separated for a single day or night, yet Crawford had allowed her to leave him for more than one hundred. No, they weren't married yet, but if not for the grand tour, they would have been. Had he even *thought* of her every day? His lack of letters would seem to indicate he did not. And if he looked at her with any sort of affection, it certainly didn't warm her from the inside. Not beyond the barest twinge of regard.

But Chess? She braced herself before daring to meet his eye. The gleam there did all sorts of things to her inside. She already found herself anticipating when next she would see him, and yet they were nothing to each other, really. Just fellow passengers on a ship steaming across the Atlantic. But the idea of waking up five days hence and never seeing him again left her feeling cold and bereft. The notion of flinging herself into the frigid sea held greater appeal.

"Colonel," Mrs. Straus stated, interrupting him with a contrite smile. "Let's allow these young people to resume their stroll, shall we?"

"Oh! Oh, yes, of course," Colonel Gracie agreed, tipping his hat to Flora. "Another time."

They carried on their separate ways, with Flora still musing over Mrs. Straus's words.

"What are you thinking?" Chess ventured to ask after several moments of silence. "Colonel Gracie didn't steal your tongue, did he?"

She laughed softly. "No. Just . . . Mrs. Straus told me they'd been married forty years."

"Quite an achievement," he agreed, darting a glance behind them to catch another glimpse of them. "And they still seem to like each other. An even greater one. They seem well suited," he added when she failed to expound on her thoughts.

"They do. Though I suspect some of that contentment is by choice," she dared to suggest, curious what he would say. "There are bound to be moments when one could just as easily choose the opposite. To pursue the shiny bauble rather than cherish the pearl in one's hand."

He stared down at their feet for several moments as they walked, and she was beginning to believe he didn't have a response to this when he finally spoke. "My grandparents were married for forty-*eight* years. And I think they were as much in love on the day my grandfather died as the day they met. My grandmother told me once that marriage wasn't a single big decision but a million tiny ones sprinkled throughout your lifetime." He turned to look at her. "That of all of humanity's failings, the worst is the fact that love and happiness, if left untended, can shrivel and die."

"She sounds like a wise woman," Flora said softly.

The skin across his cheekbones tightened. "She was." He swallowed. "She died last year."

Flora reached out to thread her arm through his, leaning into him briefly in what comfort she could offer.

They finished the rest of their stroll in silence as she ruminated on what had been said.

She was still ruminating on it when she returned to her stateroom to dress for dinner and found Alice already there, slumped on the edge of her bunk.

"No Mabel?" she asked.

Alice gestured listlessly toward the interior door. "Mother summoned her to help her dress."

"Ah. Then I suppose we'd best check that her buttons are done up straight before we go into dinner."

Alice offered her a weak smile.

Flora sank down beside her, pressing her wrist to her forehead. "Are you feeling well, dearest?"

"I'm well enough."

"Are you certain? Because Mrs. Straus offered one of her headache powders . . ."

"I said, I'm well," she snapped. Her blue eyes blazed at her. "Besides, don't tell me you don't think I *deserve* the discomfort."

Flora felt a pulse of guilt for having nursed that very thought.

Alice turned her back to her. "Will you please unfasten this dress."

Flora did as requested, her fingers dancing over the tiny shell buttons. Given Alice's foul mood and her aching head—no matter how she denied it—she probably should have left matters well enough alone, but her curiosity soon got the better of her. "Incidentally, what *were* you doing out so late?"

When Alice refused to respond, Flora struggled to tamp down her frustration. "I'm worried about you. It isn't like you to be so secretive or to retire so late. And now your health is suffering and—"

"I told you, I'm well!" She pulled away from Flora, tugging the bodice of her dress down while some of the fastenings were still in place. Flora heard a seam pop. "And I'm not being secretive."

"Then why won't you tell me where you were?"

"Because you're not my keeper, Flora. Mother told you your chaperoning duties were at an end."

"They won't be if I tell her you've been sneaking in after midnight reeking of cigarettes."

Alice narrowed her eyes. "You wouldn't dare."

Flora surged to her feet, moving several steps toward the interior door, but before she could touch it, it opened to admit Mabel.

She shut it quickly, pressing her back to it. "Lower your voices or Father is going to hear you."

"Perhaps we should let him," Flora threatened even as she spoke in a more modulated register.

Alice arched her chin in challenge. "Perhaps we should. After all, if anyone is being secretive, it's *you*!"

"Me?"

"Spending all your time with Chess Kinsey. Drinking tea. Going on long walks."

Flora's cheeks burned at the implication.

"For all we know, he's been pulling you into dark corners."

"I don't know what you're implying, but we're merely friends."

Alice stepped closer. "Are you?"

"Alice," Mabel warned, as Flora spluttered, "Yes! I'm engaged to Crawford."

Alice scoffed. "Well, you certainly don't act like it."

Flora felt as if she'd been slapped.

"Your loyalty is supposed to be to *him*," Alice persisted. "Not some man you've only just met. What could you possibly know about Mr. Kinsey in the matter of just a few days?"

She was right. She *did* barely know him. But what did she really know about Crawford even after being courted by and engaged to him for nearly a year? He never shared anything significant with her. Not like Chess. To be brutally honest, she suspected that Chess had revealed more of himself to her in just three days than Crawford might in a lifetime.

"Alice, stop!" Mabel barked.

She rounded on her. "No. I know you don't like Crawfy, but Flora agreed to marry him."

"But Flora isn't happy with Crawford. The dud has hardly been in contact with her."

Flora's chest tightened with the knowledge that her sister was aware of this. That not only had she noticed but that she'd pitied her for it.

"But Chess makes her *smile*. He makes her *laugh*. And he's not even backed her into a corner and kissed her senseless." Mabel turned to spear Flora with her gaze. "He hasn't, has he?"

"No!"

One corner of Mabel's mouth quirked. "More's the pity."

"Mabel!"

"So he's not a cad," she concluded her argument.

"It's still disloyal," Alice charged, tugging at the ribbons of her stays. "Father and Mother trust you. They would be horrified to see how you're abusing it."

Each word smarted, doubly so because they were accusations Flora had already leveled against herself. Which also gave her the clarity to see what Alice refused to. "It sounds to me like you could just as easily be scolding yourself."

Alice's head snapped up so that she could glare at her, telling Flora she'd hit the nail on the head.

A loud rap sounded on the door, startling them all. "Girls!" their father's voice boomed.

They exchanged wide-eyed looks.

"Stop squabbling," he ordered. "Your mother and I aren't about to postpone our dinners because the three of you can't get along. Finish dressing and meet us in the saloon."

They each breathed a sigh of relief, for if that was his response, then he couldn't have overheard anything of import. Even so, they clamped their mouths shut, contenting themselves with scowls and sharply tugged fastenings in the place of words.

# CHAPTER 18

❧

*Sunday, April 14, 1912*

Sunday dawned bright and sunny—a picturesque morning in most respects save for the wind. It lifted Chess's tousled hair and cooled the sweat on his brow as he leaned against the rail of the Boat Deck, still dressed in his tennis whites, to soak in the sunrise glistening and sparkling off the sea.

After indulging Colonel Gracie—whose mouth proved faster than his racquet—in a match on the Squash Court, he'd spent the better part of an hour practicing his own serve and return. He'd considered visiting the swimming pool but found Gracie already holding court there and didn't have the patience for any more of the man's talk of Civil War battles or questions about Miss Fortune.

While she hadn't precisely ignored him the previous evening, it was clear that Flora had been conflicted. Obviously, someone had said something to her. Someone in her family, most likely. Perhaps even her father. Chess had thought he'd made some progress with the man over drinks Friday evening, but Mr. Fortune was not a fellow to be easily swayed. It would take time to bring him around, especially when his mind was already made up. Time was something Chess didn't have.

And the *Titanic* was speeding up. There were rumors she

would reach New York by Tuesday evening instead of Wednesday. A fact he did not relish, as the other gentlemen seemed to. With the additional boilers lit, and with the calm seas, the ship's run posted at noon was certain to be even faster than it had been the day before. Unless they encountered poor weather, he couldn't see the captain lowering the speed. Not when, by all accounts, she was performing beautifully.

Given all these factors, the betting had been rather frantic in the Smoking Room following dinner the previous evening. Flora had claimed fatigue, retiring to her stateroom shortly after the meal ended, so he'd taken himself off to the male bastion. However, he'd quickly grown tired of all the boasting and rampant speculation. It also didn't help that Quigg Baxter had cornered him and continued to extol the virtues of the mistress he'd secreted aboard the ship, despite Chess's determined efforts to turn the conversation to hockey. Once he'd escaped, he'd considered retiring himself, or going in search of Karl, but his friend was surely in the company of the lovely Miss Newsom, and he didn't want to bungle Karl's efforts there.

Then he'd recalled the private poker games Thomas Cardeza had been hosting. The one Sloper had been trying to convince Alice Fortune to attend. Chess had wondered if she was there, and whether she would be able to give him any insights into the shadows he'd seen in Flora's eyes when he spoke to her after dinner. But his arrival in the B-Deck parlor suite seemed only to prompt Alice to flee, leaving him none the wiser about Flora's state of mind.

The sweat having now cooled on his skin, he felt the chill of the morning air and was turning to go when a pair of voices drew his attention toward the Officers' Promenade. Stepping away from the rail, he could just barely see the two men beyond the lifeboats blocking his view. They seemed to be sharing information as they changed watches.

"Did they manage to fix the wireless?"

"Aye, just before five," the second man replied. "Though all told, it was down for nearly six hours. They're gonna have a devil of a time dealing with the backlog, and what's more, on no sleep."

The first man grunted in commiseration.

"I'd steer clear of the Marconi Room for the day if I were you. Warn the others."

Chess had considered sending a marconigram to his staff in New York, alerting them he might be arriving a day early, but upon hearing this he decided the matter could wait.

He moved toward the First-Class Entrance just as another man was exiting, lifting the collar of his coat around his neck against the cold. From his ruthlessly slick-backed hair and pronounced jaw, Chess recognized him as Harry Widener, bibliophile and son of Philadelphia businessman George Widener. His rare book collection included a Shakespeare Folio and a Gutenberg Bible, among other things, and some nights past, Chess had learned that Harry was carrying home a second edition of Bacon's *Essays*. The way he'd waxed eloquent about it, Chess had to wonder if he was sleeping with it in his bed.

"Kinsey!" Harry declared upon seeing him. "Just the man I've been looking for."

Chess's eyebrows arched. Although he and Harry were cordially acquainted, he wouldn't have particularly considered him a friend. He was a Yale man, after all, and Harry had attended Harvard.

"Mother and Father are hosting a dinner party in the Restaurant tonight," he informed him. "It's to be in honor of the captain, and they've invited a slew of important friends. I'm not included. Not that I care to be. So I wondered if you might join me at our own table. I spoke to Behr, but he said he's otherwise engaged."

As invitations went, it certainly wasn't the most enticing. But, given Flora's awkwardness over dinner the previous evening, there was some appeal in not being forced to dine with her seated just thirty feet away. Especially if she intended to brush him off in favor of her fiancé. Besides which, he'd yet to dine in the much-lauded Restaurant, and if he was to do so, Sunday would be the evening to do it.

"I would be pleased to," he told Harry.

"Excellent. Seven o'clock?"

Chess agreed and then excused himself before he started shivering.

# CHAPTER 19

❦

Normally Alice found Sunday-morning services to be peaceful and reflective, but not this morning. Not when she and Flora had not spoken since their bitter quarrel the previous evening. Even now, her older sister stood at the opposite end of their family's row of chairs, cradling a hymnal while the captain led them in a somewhat plodding rendition of "O God, Our Help in Ages Past."

The captain's gold-trimmed blue uniform had been given a bit of extra attention, as had the appearances of most of those present, including her brother Charlie. His shoes shined with such a brilliant gleam that Alice was sure she could see her reflection in them. She found her gaze drawn to them time and time again, as well as to the sumptuously carved oak sideboard and piano behind the captain at the center of the First-Class Dining Saloon. Anywhere but toward Flora or Mr. Kinsey in the row adjacent.

For Mr. Kinsey knew her secret. He'd seen her in Mr. Cardeza's parlor the previous evening. And while it seemed he'd not yet divulged this to anyone, she couldn't help but fret that he would. Particularly when the service ended and he made a beeline toward the Fortunes.

"Good morning, Kinsey," Charlie hailed him first. "Already been to the Squash Racquet Court?"

"I have," Mr. Kinsey replied, shaking her brother's hand.

They exchanged a few more pleasantries before he turned to acknowledge her. "Miss Alice."

She could tell by the look in his eyes that he was thinking of the poker game, but he didn't betray her.

Alice flushed guiltily anyway.

She excused herself and drifted toward the beautiful upright piano, murmuring greetings to those she passed. The pianist who had vacated its stool nodded to her politely before slipping away. She reached out to trail her fingers across the ivory keys, peering surreptitiously over her shoulder as Mr. Kinsey finished shaking hands with Father and turned to Mabel.

Mother's lips pursed at her grinning youngest daughter, who must have said something cheeky to Mr. Kinsey. Then the man turned to address Flora, whom Alice had never seen looking more miserable in all her life. Flora could barely meet his eyes, but when she did, her gaze was so imploring that it pierced Alice's heart. Turning away, she sank down on the bench, tugging off her gloves, and began to play at first a run of scales and then a series of chords, letting her fingers wander where they would. Anything to distract her from what was happening behind her.

Because Flora was in love with Mr. Kinsey. This much was obvious to Alice, even if Flora didn't yet realize it or, perhaps more accurately, she didn't want to acknowledge it. Alice knew because her sister's emotions echoed her own.

Alice closed her eyes, pushing aside her sudden yearning for her fiancé, Holden, and transitioned into a piece by Mozart as the rest of the passengers departed and the stewards began rearranging the chairs and preparing the tables for luncheon. But her harsh words from the previous evening echoed in her ears, haunting her even as she sought to escape them. She'd been so terribly cruel and unfair to Flora, lashing out because of her own worry and discontent. At least her sister had meant well with her own prodding about Alice's incongruous behavior. She couldn't say the same.

Alice wouldn't have blamed Flora if she'd decided to wash her hands of her. But Alice had risen this morning to find that her sister had still propped the small leather valise and her portable writing desk in front of the outer cabin door in order to alert her if Alice took to sleepwalking in the middle of the night. Flora had done this despite Alice's retiring long after her. She didn't know many people who would go to such trouble to care for someone who had just treated them so shabbily.

She sighed. An apology was in order. And though Mr. Kinsey might very well keep the matter to himself, she realized she should tell Flora about the private poker games, too.

Maybe just not yet. Not until the game Mrs. Harris—the theater manager's wife to whom Mrs. Brown had introduced her— had invited her to take part in that very afternoon was over.

Mrs. Harris had promised that this game would be quite exclusive, so Alice didn't have to worry about some of the questionable behavior that had occurred on previous nights. Plus, they needed her to round out their number in order to keep any of the professional gamblers on board from inserting themselves into the game. She could hardly back out now. Or so she told herself.

As the reverberations of the last chord faded away, the thuds, scrapes, and clinks of the stewards' efforts reasserted themselves into her consciousness. She lifted her fingers from the piano keys and let out the breath she'd been holding, knowing she couldn't stall any longer. It was time to find Flora.

Swiveling on the bench, she began to rise, only to be arrested by the sight of her sister.

"That was lovely," Flora told her as she pushed away from the partitioning wall where she'd been standing. She worried her hands before her. "Sonata number eight, correct?"

"Yes, the second movement," she replied, coming to her feet.

Flora glanced toward the door. "They've canceled the lifeboat drill. Something about the winds being too strong."

Alice nodded, unsure what to say, and fell into step with her sister as she turned toward the exit, allowing the stewards to finish their work. The Reception Room was all but deserted, and as the door closed behind them, Flora cleared her throat as if to speak.

Alice reached out to grip her hands, halting her. "I'm sorry, Flora. I shouldn't have said the things I did. It was wrong of me."

"No, I'm the one who should apologize," Flora countered. "You were merely reminding me of my commitments."

Alice shook her head. "No, I was lashing out because I feel so out of sorts. We've been traveling so long, and it's all been so *wonderful*. But I miss Holden. And I don't know what to expect when we return." She stared forlornly at their joined hands. "I fear I've changed. That he won't recognize me."

"Oh, darling," Flora crooned, pulling her into her arms. "Holden *loves* you. Haven't his letters made that clear?" She pulled back so that she could look into her face. "And as for your fear that you've changed, of course, you have! We *all* have. Considering the journey we've taken, it would be impossible for us *not* to." Flora smiled consolingly. "But Holden will understand that."

If only it were so simple. But Flora hadn't read all of Holden's words. All his hopes and plans for their future. A future Alice wasn't sure she wanted anymore. How could she tell him that?

"Regardless," Alice said, hoping to turn the conversation away from herself. "I shouldn't have reproached you so that I could feel better about Holden. You haven't been disloyal."

"Haven't I?" Flora's eyes were troubled, her irises a stormy tinge of gray.

"I know you, Flora. You are the most steadfast, sensible woman alive. If your heart was claimed by Crawford, if it had *ever* been, you wouldn't have allowed yourself to be charmed by somebody else." She paused, hesitant to add the rest, but she also recognized that what her sister needed right now was brutal honesty. "To fall in love with them."

Flora's eyes widened with shock and alarm. "I'm not—"

"You are," Alice interrupted, refusing to allow her to hide from the truth. "You are," she repeated more gently as Flora's mouth worked, still trying to formulate a response. "And you've never loved Crawford."

Flora's eyes lowered as if in shame.

"There's no cause for recrimination. You didn't lie to Crawford or pretend your feelings were engaged. He offered for you freely without false pretenses." Alice tilted her head. "He didn't tell you that he loved you, did he?"

Flora's mouth twisted. "No."

Alice nodded. She'd expected as much. Crawford didn't seem like a man in love. "You were willing to accept his proposal because he was a respectable man who would be able to provide you a comfortable life, and because Father and Mother promoted the match. However, the situation has changed." She arched her eyebrows, daring her to contradict her.

"Mother must have given you the same speech she gave me. About how an engagement is a time for a couple to get to know each other more intimately in order to decide whether they are genuinely suited before their vows are spoken."

Flora stared at her in bewilderment.

"Well, it's true." She reached out to smooth the embroidery on the sleeve of her sister's gown. "You've not yet committed to him. There's still time to change your mind."

"But what about Crawford? What about Father and Mother?"

Alice threaded her arm through Flora's, guiding her toward the stairs. "Crawford may be disappointed at first. He might have his pride wounded. But do you think he wants to marry a woman who's in love with someone else?"

Flora appeared struck by this.

"On a related note, doesn't *he* deserve the chance to find love or at least contentment with someone?" Alice waited a moment for this to sink in before addressing the other. "As for Father and Mother . . ." She exhaled heavily. "I know you pride yourself on being dutiful, on always doing the right thing. But what if the right thing is contrary to your being dutiful?"

Flora's voice stretched thin with distress. "But what if I'm not certain what the right thing is?"

Alice met her gaze levelly. "I think you do."

Flora halted, squeezing her eyes shut. "I'm afraid I'm wrong. I'm afraid Father and Mother . . ." She broke off as if unable to speak the words aloud.

"They won't hurt you. You know that. Or even cut you off. Not unless you intend to run off with Mr. Kinsey without the benefit of wedlock."

Flora scowled at her.

Alice supposed that was the type of thing Mabel would usually suggest, not her, but she was still puzzled. "They might disapprove." Something flickered across Flora's features. "That's it, isn't it? You fear their disapproval? But why?" She was baffled. "I know it's uncomfortable, but surely not terrifying. It's not as if they're going to stop loving you."

But Flora blanched, and Alice suddenly realized her sister didn't believe this. She didn't believe that their parents would love her if she disappointed them. Perhaps she didn't believe anyone would.

Impulsively, Alice threw her arms around her sister, wondering when Flora had started to think this. Alice didn't remember much about her childhood before she fell ill, but her earliest memories of Flora were of her caring for others. Reading to Alice while Mother was busy elsewhere or minding Mabel and Charlie so that Mother could tend to Alice. They'd had nurses and governesses, but somehow Flora always seemed to be charged with someone's care. Or perhaps she'd taken it on willingly because otherwise she would be alone and ignored.

Flora stiffened, at first resisting Alice's embrace, but then she softened, a sigh escaping from her lungs. "I know you're just trying to help," she said, misunderstanding the reason for the hug. "If Crawford were here, maybe it would all be easier. Or if I were certain of Chess's intentions." She shook herself, pulling away. "But enough of me. What about you? What can I do to help?"

She scrutinized her more closely. "Or is that why you've been talking to Mr. Sloper so much?"

This was not the direction Alice wanted their conversation to turn, but once the question was asked, she couldn't ignore it. Or pretend that Mr. Sloper was her confidant.

"No. He simply provides a welcome distraction. Sometimes occupation is good for the mind."

"You aren't still concerned about the fortune that man gave you in Cairo, are you?" Flora asked, her mind leaping somewhere Alice hadn't expected.

"Maybe a little," she hedged when, truth be told, it had barely crossed her mind.

"I'm sure I'll feel better once we reach New York," she concluded before glancing about her. "But I can't say the same for Mabel."

Flora took the bait. "Why do you say that?"

"Because she seems determined about something, but thus far she's been thwarted."

Flora considered this before responding. "Do you know what that something is?"

"No. And she seems anxious that we don't find out."

A slight furrow formed between her sister's brows. One that Alice almost felt remorseful for causing. But if Flora was busy watching Mabel, then she couldn't keep track of Alice, too. Not if they weren't in the same place. And she strongly doubted Mabel's secret involved poker.

# CHAPTER 20

❧❧❧

*Sunday, April 14, 1912—1:15 p.m.*

"Any plans for the afternoon?"

Mabel paused with her bite of roast duckling partway to her mouth, turning to meet Flora's eye. "Not currently." Ever since she'd arrived at their table for lunch, her sister had been acting strangely, insisting on sitting next to Mabel and peppering her with questions whenever the conversation lagged. Which mercifully hadn't been often.

Like every other male in the room, Charlie was enamored with the impressive speed of the *Titanic*'s run since noon the previous day. Mabel had heard the statistics—546 nautical miles, with an average speed of 22.06 knots—but she'd done her best to ignore the rest.

"I thought I might enjoy reading and a cup of tea by that cozy fire in the Lounge," Flora announced to no one in particular, before turning to Mabel. "Care to join me?"

"Speaking of the Lounge," Father suddenly remarked, saving her from having to respond, "I was introduced to Isidor Straus and his wife there a short time ago. He's co-owner of Macy's department store."

"They're a delightful couple, don't you think?" Flora replied. "They dote on each other so." She turned to Mother. "I suspect you would like Mrs. Straus very much."

"Hmm, yes," Father said, regrasping the reins of the conversation. "We walked to the Purser's Office together as we both had marconigrams to send. Apparently, one of their sons is traveling to Europe on the *Amerika* and they hoped to transmit a wireless message to him and his family while the two ships were in range of each other."

"Oh, how lovely," Mother said. "And yours? Was it a business matter?"

Father adjusted his coat across his barrel chest. "Just wiring the Belmont Hotel in New York to reserve our rooms for our arrival Wednesday."

"At the speed we're going, the *Titanic* should arrive in New York on Tuesday," Charlie piped up to say.

"Ah, my boy, but if we do, we won't reach the pier until late in the evening, and it's company policy to permit passengers to remain on board and wait to disembark after breakfast."

This was clearly something Charlie hadn't known—Mabel, either—but it made a great deal of sense.

"At any rate, as I was saying"—Father's mustache fairly bristled, revealing his impatience with their interruptions—"I was chatting with the Strauses when they mentioned that they'd met you yesterday, Flora." He turned toward her pointedly. "You and Mr. Kinsey." The last word was slightly clipped.

Flora's complexion paled, but otherwise she hid her reaction well behind a drink of her wine. "Yes, Father. Miss Newsom invited me to take tea with her and Mr. Behr and Mr. Kinsey, and then we decided to stroll on the Promenade."

"Mrs. Straus didn't mention Miss Newsom or Mr. Behr."

"Really? That's curious?" Alice contributed, her eyes on her plate as she forked a bite of creamed peas and potatoes. "I saw them all entering the Café Parisien together."

What was curious was that she was covering for Flora after expressing her disapproval of their little tea party to Mabel just the day before. Evidently, her sisters had resolved their differences.

"I met Miss Newsom's mother and stepfather yesterday," Mother said. "Mr. and Mrs. Beckwith from Ohio." She pressed a hand to the pearls draped around her neck. "Miss Newsom is a charming girl. Though I don't think her parents are as enthused by a match with Mr. Behr as she is?"

"Why?" Flora said in surprise.

Mother shrugged. "I didn't pry. But it seems one of their reasons for traveling to Europe was to separate them." Her eyes flicked briefly toward Mabel, perhaps recalling they'd had similar intentions in regard to Mabel and Harrison Driscoll. "But Mr. Behr seems to have followed them."

Flora frowned. "I was under the impression he'd had business in Europe."

Mother picked up her fork. "I'm only repeating what I heard."

"You must be relieved Harrison didn't follow me." Mabel couldn't help but needle her mother.

"Oh, we had no fear of that, dear. He couldn't afford it."

Mabel felt the sting of those waspish words. She might have only been pretending to be enamored of Harrison, but she still felt affronted on his behalf. Though she couldn't deny that what Mother had said was true. He could barely afford a train ticket to Winnipeg, let alone a European grand tour.

"Father couldn't afford it at Harrison's age, either," she retorted instead, reminding her parents that neither of them had come from money. A fact her father was proud of. He loved to talk about how he'd built a fortune to match his name, from nothing but a few pennies, a lot of hard work, and a bit of luck.

"As I've said before," Father reminded her sharply, "once Mr. Driscoll has made his first million, he'll be free to pay his addresses to my daughter. But until then, he'll not lay a finger on you or your inheritance."

"If you've no other plans, you girls might pay Mr. Ross a visit," Mother suggested, redirecting the conversation as their plates were cleared away by their table steward in preparation for the next course. "I believe he's feeling a bit neglected."

"Then perhaps I'll postpone my reading so we can visit him after lunch," Flora promised.

Mabel wanted to tell her to speak for herself, but contrary to popular belief, she knew when it was best to keep her mouth shut. Especially now, when she needed to remain on Father's good side and her comments about Harrison had already aggravated him.

After all, the ship was speeding up, and all too soon they would be arriving in New York, and Father would no longer be distracted by the *Titanic's* immensity and luxury. She strongly felt that if there was any time to convince him to allow her to attend university, it would have to be now.

To that end, as her family rose from their table, Mabel hurried in her blue serge hobble skirt to be at her father's side. "Father," she stated politely, ignoring the pulse hammering in her throat, "might I have a moment of your time?"

He peered at her with a sideways glance, never breaking his stride as they passed through the doors into the Reception Room. "Later."

"But, sir . . ."

"Later, Mabel," he retorted more brusquely.

Her steps faltered and her hands clenched at her sides as he charged on ahead. Everyone trailing behind them swerved around her, leaving her feeling rather like a rock in the middle of a stream, always stuck in the same place while everything else moved on. Only Flora paused to wait for her.

"You don't have to come, you know. Not if you don't want to." Her gaze was kind but searching, trying to ferret out the reason for Mabel's frustration. "I'll make your excuses."

"No, I'll come," she declared, realizing she was speaking of their visit to Mr. Ross. If nothing else, doing so would at least help put her in Flora's good graces. "You shouldn't have to go alone."

Though nonchalantly spoken, her words achieved their intended results when Flora turned to search for their siblings.

A small furrow formed in Flora's brow. "I'd hoped at least Alice would join us."

"Apparently she had other plans."

The furrow deepened.

For all of Mabel's reticence about joining Flora in her visit to Mr. Ross's cabin, she proved decidedly good at cheering him up. Flora stood near the door, smiling as Mabel told him about an incident that had occurred over dinner the previous evening. Her sister was prone to exaggeration, which often aggravated Flora, but in this instance, she had to admit, it was put to good use.

Mr. Ross seemed to have improved since her last visit. Swathed in a thick robe, he sat upright on a settee with a cup of tea at his elbow. His cheeks had even regained a healthy flush. Or perhaps that was simply the amusement Mabel caused him. Either way, Flora was glad of it.

"She's quite the ham, isn't she?" Mr. Beattie quipped at her side.

"You have no idea," Flora said with a low chuckle. "It's good to see Mr. Ross up and about, if confined to his cabin." She turned to study the neat and dapper man. "But what of you and Mr. McCaffry?"

"It's true, we've both done our best to keep Mr. Ross company, but we've spent a fair share of our time in the Smoking Room and Lounge as well." He turned a gentle smile on her. "Have no worries, Miss Fortune. We've not been neglected."

Their attention was recaptured by Mabel and her exuberant antics. Flora had missed part of what her sister had been saying, but she was quite certain a monkey was not on board the *Titanic*, regardless of what Mabel might be implying. Mr. Ross tipped his head back to laugh—a deep, merry sound in the small space. Being an interior cabin, it boasted no windows, but Flora had learned that Mr. Sloper's stateroom was next door, and from time to time Mr. Ross joined him there to enjoy the sunshine spilling through the large A-Deck windows.

"I hear you have an admirer."

Flora turned to find Mr. Beattie's eyebrows raised and one corner of his lips quirked upward. "Let me guess? Mr. Sloper has been gossiping."

"Of course, he has. He's as bad as a woman." He held up his hands to fend off Flora, chuckling. "*Most* women."

"Thank you," she replied primly, turning pointedly back toward Mabel, but Mr. Beattie was not so swiftly deterred.

"So, it's true, then?"

She crossed her arms, refusing to look at him. But his decisive rejoinder ruined that resolve.

"Good! It's about time someone showed sense. The fact is, Crawford Campbell won you too easily."

She flushed.

"I know your father pressed you to accept his suit." He tilted his head toward her. "For reasons of his own, I might add. And you are dutiful to a fault. But Campbell deserves to face a bit of competition." His voice turned wry. "Maybe then he'll at least expend more than the minimum effort."

"And if he doesn't?"

His eyes answered before his mouth. "Then cut him loose." His gaze narrowed shrewdly. "Or have you already decided to do so?"

"I haven't decided anything," she protested. Then for the sake of honesty, she added, "But I admit, Mr. Kinsey does make me ponder it."

Mr. Beattie's voice was solemn. "Given the kind of woman you are, Miss Fortune, that says a lot."

Flora fell silent, considering his response.

She was still considering it sometime later when she found herself standing next to the Forward Grand Staircase. She wasn't sure how long she'd been hovering there, but when she lifted her gaze toward the landing, she saw Chess descending toward her. The sun-faded locks in his brown hair appeared even more bleached in the light filtering through the frosted glass dome overhead, and his amber eyes seemed to glow. But it was the gentle curl to his lips, the private little smile for her alone, that reached inside her and turned her heart over in her chest.

Alice had been right. She *was* in love with him. Or at least, far closer to it than she'd ever been with Crawford—or any other man, for that matter. It was a somewhat discomposing revelation. So much so that all she could do was stand there dumbly as he moved toward her.

"Am I allowed to approach?" he asked as he drew near.

She nodded, still having trouble finding her voice. "Of course," she finally managed to say.

He tilted his head, searching her features. "Except . . . there's no 'of course' about it, is there?"

That he was referring to her behavior last night was obvious. She had been rather hot and cold in turns throughout the crossing, uncertain of herself and her feelings, trying to be loyal to Crawford and not wanting to disappoint her parents. But all that struggle had been for naught. Because the brutal truth was, she'd fallen for Chess anyway.

"Will you walk with me?" he asked, even though she hadn't spoken, and she nodded.

They collected their coats and hats, meeting once again in the A-Deck Reception Room, where they paused so that Chess could pull on his gloves. Mr. Ismay, the managing director of the White Star Line, stood off to the side, speaking to two men who appeared to be a father and son.

"Nothing to be concerned about," he told them as they perused a piece of paper. "It *is* the north Atlantic, after all. There's bound to be ice. But I doubt we'll reach any of it until about nine o'clock tonight."

The father passed the missive—which she thought must be a telegram—back to Ismay, who pocketed it. "Will this affect the *Titanic*'s speed?"

"I doubt it. Two more boilers were opened up today, in order to attempt a full-steam run tomorrow. As long as weather allows, of course. Andrews is quite confident in her."

His gloves now on, Chess guided her through the door to the Promenade.

"I suspect that will help you in your wager on the ship's run this evening?" she teased him.

"*If* I place a bet," he replied. "I didn't last night."

Flora shivered in the cool air, adjusting her green velvet hat. "I see you're not addicted to games of chance, then."

"No." He chuckled humorlessly. "That is one vice that the men in my family do not share. And probably why we've managed to hold on to our wealth for so long." A stiff blast of wind suddenly struck them, stinging her face. She shifted closer to Chess, shrinking away from the cold.

"It *is* noticeably cooler, isn't it?" he said. "That ice warning Ismay showed the Thayers makes sense now. Let's turn and walk away from the open aft Promenade. At least the enclosed portion should offer us some protection from these bitter winds."

She readily agreed but hesitated briefly to watch a seaman drop a line over the open side of the deck.

"He's checking the water temperature," Chess explained.

Despite the chill, there were still many passengers strolling along the enclosed Promenade. They passed the beautiful film actress Dorothy Gibson, who—Flora was pleased to note—did not turn Chess's head as she did many of the gentlemen nearby. Some distance ahead of them, she could also see the Strauses walking arm in arm, as they always did. She wondered if they were talking about their son, to whom they'd recently sent a marconigram.

Whatever it was they were discussing, Flora was struck by the deep contentment that existed between them. Each leaned slightly toward the other, as if looking for support to stay upright. Or perhaps it was a sort of gravitational pull they felt to be near one another. This was a marriage to be emulated. Much as with her parents' union, there was a sense of love and care and trust evident in every look, every interaction. It wasn't loud or demonstrable, but quiet and tender.

"You're deep in thought," Chess remarked. His eyes invited her to confide in him, but he didn't pry.

"I'm struggling with something," she admitted, knowing she owed him some sort of explanation for her behavior. "Something bewildering. Something I didn't expect."

"I understand," he replied, lifting his opposite hand to rub the back of his neck in an uncharacteristic display of insecurity. "To tell you the truth, I've been feeling much the same. Bewildered. Unprepared. I expected to return to New York in mid-April, to my office at my family's company, and to begin preparations for my first tennis tournament in a little over a month. Just as I have for the last six years without alteration." He paused, as if gathering himself. "But then I met you." He turned his head to meet her gaze.

Her heart fluttered in her chest. If she could capture the glint she saw in his eyes and bottle it as an elixir, she thought she could live off that alone for the rest of her life. "I guess this hasn't been easy for either of us." She'd meant her words in jest, but when their eyes met again and held, his were gratifyingly earnest.

"On the contrary. Being with you, getting to know you . . . it's been the easiest thing in the world."

Flora gripped his arm more tightly, feeling so buoyed by his words that she feared the wind whipping about the decks of the ship would carry her aloft. She didn't care that her heart was in her eyes, or that the pulse fluttering at her throat must tell him exactly how he affected her. She only cared that the blood pumping through her veins fizzled like champagne and that whatever he read in her expression had made him grin just as broadly as she.

# CHAPTER 21

*Sunday, April 14, 1912—4:00 p.m.*

Though she knew it was decidedly juvenile, Alice couldn't suppress a giggle as she leaned forward to rake in a pile of chips. She'd never known until that moment just how much fun winning could be. No wonder the men retired to the Smoking Room every night to indulge in such games of chance.

Even now, of the eight players seated at the table, only two were women. René Harris sat to her right, puffing on a cigarette. René's husband, Harry, the theater-owner, sat on his wife's other side. He was a congenial, soft-spoken man. One who clearly adored his more brash wife, who called him "my boy." The other players included Jacques Futrelle, the mystery writer, their host Thomas Cardeza, and three other men Alice had just been introduced to.

Mr. Cardeza said very little during the game, preferring to concentrate on his cards through his round gold-framed spectacles. But the others were more lighthearted, chatting and jesting between bids. Truth be told, several of them seemed rather taken with Alice. A fact she wasn't above exploiting. René, of course, recognized this almost immediately, observing the proceedings with a secretive little smile. She was undoubtedly using it to her benefit as well, for she was ahead by no small amount.

Invariably the talk soon turned to the *Titanic*'s speed. All of the men present had taken part in the betting over the ship's daily runs, and their anticipation for that night's bidding was high. Having had her first taste of gambling, Alice couldn't help but think it sounded fun.

"It's only too bad the ladies aren't allowed to wager," she lamented, scrutinizing the latest hand of cards she'd been dealt. Seated as they were around the wicker table on the Cardezas' private promenade, she was glad for her fur-lined coat, which protected her from the chill of the afternoon. She tugged the collar up higher as a stray draft snuck down the back of her neck. It might have been warmer to play inside, but then the haze of cigarette smoke would have become unbearable.

"Too right," René concurred before flashing a cheeky smile. "Though it would no doubt cause heart palpitations in some of the matrons."

"I would be more than happy to place a bet on your behalf, Miss Fortune," Mr. Futrelle declared in his customary drawl.

"I was just about to offer the same thing," a young gentleman groused, plainly disgruntled that the other man had beaten him to the punch.

Alice smiled gratefully at the young man before turning to Mr. Futrelle. "I will accept your offer and hopefully have winnings to reward your kindness with."

But as the afternoon wore on, the pile of chips she'd planned to place her bet with dwindled. Her early success had evidently gone to her head, just as Mrs. Harris and Mr. Sloper had warned her not to let it do. She'd forgotten that poker was as much a game of luck as skill, and instead of using sober judgment, she began to panic. Particularly when her winnings dipped below her initial buy-in, and then even lower into the funds she'd filched from Flora's stash of pin money.

Alice had told herself she was merely borrowing it. That there was nowhere for Flora to spend it on board the *Titanic* anyway. Not unless she intended to buy a silly trinket souvenir from the Barber Shop. Alice had even assuaged her conscience by promising she'd put back more money than she'd originally taken. That, in actuality, she was doing her sister a favor. But as she watched her chips continue to dwindle, a sick feeling filled her stomach. One that she knew wasn't caused by the cigarettes.

She considered using one of the short lulls between hands to dash back to her stateroom for more money, but she'd already used everything she possessed. She would have taken Mabel's pin money when she borrowed Flora's, except she knew Mabel had already spent it. As far as Charlie's pocket money went, Alice had no idea where he kept it, and she didn't dare enter her parents' cabin to search for anything.

In the end, she was forced to admit she might only have been saved from losing everything by the blast of the bugler summoning everyone to dress for dinner. Especially since she was holding a rotten hand and hadn't had the sense to fold.

She worried her bottom lip as she gathered up her meager dispensation, warring with herself about what she should do next.

For a fraction of a second, she considered letting the blame shift to Mabel, as it inevitably would. Mabel was notorious for spending her pin money before she'd even received it. As a consequence, she was always begging her siblings to loan her more. She would naturally be the first suspect.

But Alice quickly discarded this notion. It would only be compounding a deception with one even worse. However, there was still the betting pool for the ship's run. If she could win, she would be able to replace all of Flora's money, with her sister none the wiser that she'd taken it.

But if Alice didn't win . . . Her stomach dipped alarmingly. She would lose it all.

"Miss Fortune," Mr. Futrelle murmured, rounding the table to stand next to her chair. "Did you still wish for me to place a bet for you?"

It was on the tip of her tongue to decline, but the fear of discovery, of having to explain everything to her older sister, proved greater than her sense. As did the tempting possibility—no matter how minuscule—of coming out ahead.

"Yes," she declared, rising to her feet to pass him the money. "Five hundred seventy-five nautical miles. Try to get a bid as close to that as possible."

He nodded, stuffing the blunt into the pocket of his perpetually rumpled suit. "I shall do my best."

Mabel was about to do something foolish. She knew she was letting her impatience get the best of her, and yet she couldn't stop herself.

Her footsteps padded down the steps toward D-Deck, where she could hear the band playing for teatime. It was more crowded than usual. All the public rooms were, owing to the tremendous cold on deck, but it was easy to spot her father's balding head, nonetheless, standing near the tapestry.

As she bore down on him, she knew she wasn't comporting herself with the ladylike grace her mother expected of her, but she was determined to speak her piece, and she refused to be put off again. Only when she was standing directly before him did she rein herself in, folding her hands demurely in front of herself as she waited for her father to finish what he was saying to the gentleman beside him and acknowledge her. She was at least relieved to see that he was in a better mood than he'd been in at lunch. He even chuckled before turning toward her.

"Father, may I speak to you?"

A tiny furrow formed in Father's forehead, but he nodded and led her toward the door to the Dining Saloon, holding it open for her to pass through. One of the dining stewards cast an aggrieved look in their direction before resuming his work to prepare the tables for dinner.

"All right, then, Mabel," he declared, crossing his arms over his barrel chest. "What did you wish to say?"

Inhaling a calming breath, she opened her mouth to begin, only to be cut off brusquely.

"This isn't about Mr. Driscoll, is it? For I've already made my feelings clear."

"No, this isn't about Harrison," she replied, unable to resist using his first name to irritate her father, despite the fact she desperately wanted him to be amenable. "But it is about my future. I want you to consider allowing me to attend university," she said, maintaining as even a tone as possible. "To study the law."

"There's no need for you to learn such things. Not when your place will be at home."

Her hands clenched at her sides as she struggled to restrain her temper, determined to plead her case. "There are agencies where women and children are in need of legal counsel. Agencies where I could be useful."

"You can be useful at home. And those women and children can just as easily get their legal counsel from men."

"Perhaps, but they're more comfortable with women. And few men wish to take on their cases."

Her father scowled, and she realized that she might have unwittingly revealed too much. After all, she knew his views on suffrage and divorce. So she pressed on before he could speak.

"There are dozens of respectable ladies on this very ship who have university educations and careers. Doctors and lawyers and writers. And lest you fear further education will render me unmarriageable, most of those women went on to wed highly respected men."

"Mabel . . ." Her father turned away with an exasperated sigh. "I have already introduced you to a great number of highly respected men. Rendering your attaining a career entirely unnecessary."

Mabel nearly stamped her foot. "You're not listening to me."

"I am," he stated harshly. "Oh, I am," he scoffed. "But your place is at home. Not at a university or in an office . . . or in a suffrage march." He bit off the last, daring her to deny her beliefs on that subject. "And I'll not hear another word on the matter."

A bleakness stole over her, hollowing her to the bone. This

was it, then. Her father would never relent. She would be forced to remain at home until she married. Until she turned as compliant as Flora, willing to wed a man as dull as ditchwater. Anger burned through her, swift and furious, forming a haze over her vision.

"Then you leave me no choice but to marry Harrison," she informed him in a voice that came deep from the fire inside her.

Father's face flushed red and the vein in his temple began to throb. "I won't give my consent. And without my consent, neither of you will receive a penny of your dowry or inheritance."

"It doesn't matter. Harrison will allow me to attend university."

"He can't afford it!"

"We'll make do," she replied, taking perverse pleasure in hearing him roar while she kept her tone low.

"How? Money doesn't grow on trees, my girl."

"That won't be any of your concern, now, will it?"

"It will when your children come along and there's not enough food for their bellies."

She began to turn away. "You needn't worry. We won't come begging. You can save your *charity* for home." With this parting shot of sarcasm, knowing he would connect it to a verse he often quoted from 1 Timothy, Mabel strode from the room.

Her fury propelled her across the Reception Room and up the stairs, but some steps short of their cabin door it burned itself out, leaving behind nothing but a raw ache. Stumbling through the door, she was relieved to find it empty. Sinking down on one of the chairs, she stared blankly at the floral arrangement on the table before her, asking the daisies and chrysanthemums blearily, "What have I done?" Her only answer was the fall of a single white petal, an echo of the tear spilling from the corner of her eye. The first of many.

Despite the bitter cold that afternoon, Flora and Chess spent most of their time on deck, strolling, or seated in loungers with warm rugs draped over their laps. The truth was, Flora barely felt the chill, so warm was she simply from the pleasure of being with him. She had no doubt that, like Chess, her cheeks and the tip of her nose were red, but she didn't care.

Through the long afternoon, they circled the ship, but all too soon the sun began to dip toward the horizon and the decks started to clear. It was only a matter of time before the bugler announced it was time to dress for dinner, yet still they walked, determined to enjoy every last moment. Flora wished it would never end.

As they neared the Aft Staircase entrance, they spied two women seated on a pair of steamer chairs. She didn't recognize either of them, but Chess did.

"The woman on the left, that's Mrs. Thayer," he leaned in to say. "And the woman in black on the right, that's Mrs. Ryerson. She lost her son, quite tragically, to an automobile accident, and is headed home along with her husband and the rest of her children to plan his funeral."

"Oh, how terrible!" Flora gasped. "No wonder I haven't seen her about. They must be sequestering themselves in mourning."

Which made Mr. Ismay's abrupt intrusion all the more bumbling. The White Star director seemed to appear almost from nowhere and plunked down in a steamer chair next to them, adjusting the lapels of his dark blue suit. "I hope you are comfortable."

Mrs. Ryerson appeared taken aback and needed a moment to gather herself before answering. "Yes. Thank you again for offering us the use of that additional stateroom and a personal steward. They have proved a boon to our family during this time."

"Of course. If there's anything else I can do . . ."

Mrs. Ryerson thanked him again politely, but it was obvious that what she wished most was for him to leave her alone with her friend. Unfortunately, the man was rather notorious for misreading social cues.

After moving a few steps onward, Chess maneuvered Flora toward the railing so that they could peer out over the water. The sun sparkled off the sea, leaving a glittering trail like diamonds leading westward, as if to lure the ship onward.

Mr. Ismay asked Mrs. Ryerson and Mrs. Thayer a number of questions, which the ladies answered civilly, but the entire conversation was decidedly stilted. It seemed to Flora that Mr. Ismay was deeply affected by Mrs. Ryerson's loss and sincerely eager to help. He simply didn't understand how best to express himself.

Flora winced as he veered to a wildly different topic. "Well, we are in among the icebergs."

She imagined the ladies' expressions were bewildered, but it was Ismay she took note of as he searched his pockets before triumphantly producing a paper. He held the document out so that they could read it but retained possession of it. Flora wondered if it was the same telegram he'd shown Mr. Thayer and his son earlier that afternoon.

"We are not going very fast. Twenty or twenty-one knots," Ismay stated. "But we are going to start up some new boilers this evening."

Chess frowned, and Flora had to concur with his disapproval. Telling passengers that the ship was among icebergs and in the next breath that it would be speeding up hardly seemed fitting or reassuring.

Fortunately for everyone, a pair of gentlemen were approaching from the aft promenade, causing Ismay to push to his feet. He offered a hastily worded farewell and disappeared through the door from which he'd come before the two women's husbands joined them.

"That man is a menace," Chess declared softly after the Thayers and Ryersons departed, though it was said with pity rather than scorn. "How is the mention of icebergs supposed to console a grieving mother?" One who had three more children on board the ship with her.

Flora frowned out at the water. There was nothing as far as the eye could see—no icebergs *or* ships—but that didn't mean there weren't any lurking beyond the horizon. She assumed a ship wouldn't send out an ice warning to her fellow liners if there wasn't some genuine reason for caution. "Should we be worried?"

"I imagine the captain and crew are taking it all as seriously as they should. After all, they steam this route westward across the Atlantic approximately twice a month the year round. They must know what they're doing."

"I suppose so." After all, Ismay might be managing director, but he was not a sailor or a member of the crew. Though she couldn't help but wonder why he'd been in possession of that telegram with the iceberg warning. Shouldn't it have been with the captain?

Chess wrapped his arm around her, drawing her closer. "Besides, I know you've already heard all the statistics from Charlie." His dark eyes twinkled down at her. "You've heard of the watertight compartments. And Andrews told us himself that the ship could break into three separate pieces and each part could still stay afloat. I would say that makes the claims of practical unsinkability pretty valid."

She exhaled, consoled by this logic. "You're right. To tell you the truth, most of the time I almost forget we're at sea. The ship is so stable." She turned to stare out at the deepening colors of the opalescent sky juxtaposed against the water. "Except moments like now. Isn't it beautiful?"

"Yes."

But when she turned her head, it was to find him gazing at her, not at the sunset.

"Yes, *she* is," he murmured.

The way he looked at her made her heart surge inside her chest and her nerves thrum underneath her skin. Intellectually, she knew the feeling for what it was—desire—but she'd never felt it to this degree. Never had it been directed back at her along with a heady mixture of admiration and tenderness.

They were alone on the Promenade Deck but exposed to the sight of anyone who might round the corner farther along or exit the Aft Staircase door. Yet she couldn't summon the will to care or to pull away, putting the proper amount of space between them. She'd wondered what it would feel like to have his arm around her, and it was delightful. She'd wondered what it would be like to be so close to him, and it was exhilarating! Now she wondered what it would be like to be kissed.

He leaned closer, and her eyes dipped to his mouth before feathering shut as his lips met hers. Dimly she was aware of a roaring in her ears and the scent of his sandalwood cologne, but the rest of her being was concentrated on the feel of his mouth, warm and sure, moving against hers and the tea-and-peppermint taste of him as he deepened their kiss. His jaw was dusted with the barest hint of dark stubble, which lightly abraded the sensitive skin around her lips. A sensation she found far more pleasurable than she would have ever expected.

Her hands gripped the lapels of his coat, worried she might dissolve into a quivering pile of custard if she didn't anchor herself to him. Likewise, he tightened his grip around her waist, pressing her flush against the long length of him so that she could feel the firmness of his muscles, even through their layers of clothing.

It might have been seconds or minutes that they stood locked in their embrace, their mouths melding as one, but the joy and revelation and fervor of it were utterly dashed by the cold bucket of water that was her mother's voice.

"Flora Ethel Fortune, for shame!"

# CHAPTER 22

꧁ ꧂

Flora gave a strangled gasp, ending what had been, without question, the most remarkable kiss of Chess's life. Remarkable because of how desperately he'd wanted it, he wanted *her*, all of her—her body, her spirit, and her heart. He'd never felt this way before. It was intoxicating and discombobulating and utterly wonderful.

Except when Flora looked as she did now. As if her entire world were imploding around her and there was nothing she could do about it. It pricked his heart and his pride, but it also made him want to gather her against his chest and shield her from the shrapnel, no matter the pain and injury it caused him.

"Unhand her this instant," Mrs. Fortune demanded, trembling with fury.

Still, he didn't instantly obey, instead waiting for Flora to look at him, to assure him that she had her footing. The way she backed up several steps when he let go lodged a splinter in his heart.

"Come with me *now*, Flora," Mrs. Fortune demanded, the brilliant earrings dangling from each side of her head, swaying with her vehemence.

He didn't stop Flora. Not when he knew he was in the wrong. He shouldn't have kissed her. Especially not somewhere they might be seen, exposing her to a scandal. But he sure as hell didn't regret it. He made sure she knew that, meeting her stare with steady assurance, trying to ease her distress. He would make this right. He would seek out her father as soon as possible. It was what he'd intended to do anyway, but now the matter was far more urgent.

"I will speak with Mr. Fortune privately," he said.

"You may try," Mrs. Fortune snapped, her gaze raking over him from head to toe as if he were muck found at the bottom of her shoe. "But it will be of no avail. Flora is already engaged. *Now*, Flora!"

Flora did as she was told, but not without peering over her shoulder at him one last time, her heart in her eyes.

Chess clenched his fists. He would speak to her father to see what could be done, and just how high the barriers were in his way. But first there was dinner to get through. Mr. Fortune was undoubtedly already dressing for dinner, and intercepting him before he reached the saloon could prove difficult. If the man would even speak to him while he was intent on escorting his family to their evening meal, where all the eyes of society would be on them.

Chess bit off a curse.

For he'd just remembered that he'd agreed to dine with Harry Widener in the Restaurant. Flora would think he'd abandoned her. With one last look toward the sun as it sank below the horizon, as shadows began stealing over the *Titanic*'s decks, he charged toward the door. He would have to find a way to remedy that.

# CHAPTER 23

Mother didn't speak. She wouldn't. Not until they reached their cabins. But once inside with the door shut, her words erupted from her mouth as if from a geyser. Flora had but a moment to realize Mabel was also there, and she looked as if she'd been crying, before Mother rounded on her.

"For shame, Flora! That I should live to see the day when one of my daughters behaved so disgracefully. And *you* of all of them." She flung her arm toward her youngest daughter. "I might have expected something like this from Mabel. But not you, Flora." She turned away, holding up her hand. "*Och*, I can't even look at you." The roots of Mother's Scottish heritage always found their way to her tongue whenever her emotions were high.

"I'm sorry, Mother," Flora began, ignoring Mabel's questioning look.

"Do you know what sort of scandal you're courting?" Mother demanded to know. "You might have been seen by anyone. Your reputation, *and your sisters'*"—she flung her arm toward Mabel again—"would be in tatters."

"Leave me out of this," Mabel snapped.

"Hush!" Mother ordered. "I don't need your cheek." She narrowed her eyes. "I heard about your threats to your father. Blackmail, more like. And I'll not have it. Any of it! It appears we've been too soft with all of you. You've become spoiled, thinking you can do as you please, marry whom you please, obey when you wish. No more! You'll honor your father and mother, and you'll mind your place, as the good Lord demands it."

The door opened then to admit Alice. Her eyes widened, and her cheeks flushed with such palpable guilt that Flora could only wonder what *this* sister had been up to. Apparently, they were all keeping secrets.

Mother's gaze swung to Alice. Her nostrils flared, clearly catching the same scent Flora had, just before her face wrinkled in disgust. "And just where have you been that you come in here smelling like a brothel?"

Flora flinched. Suggesting she smelled like a brothel was harsh, though Alice *did* smell like a gentlemen's smoking room. However, she would never have been allowed in that chamber on this ship.

When Alice made no response other than to stare pale-faced at her, Mother moved a step closer, sniffing in disdain. "Is this Mr. Sloper's doing?"

Alice's lips parted as if she meant to say something, but no sound emerged.

Mother whirled away, clutching her temples. "I knew this trip would bring us grief. I told him and I told him. But did your father listen to me? Of course, not." She whirled back to rake her furious glare over them all. "We must dress for dinner, but do not think for a moment that this discussion is over. Not for any of you." She arched her chin, summoning her iciest composure. "Wear your new Worth gowns. It is Sunday. Everyone will be dressed in their finest. We will all descend together." Her eyes swung to Flora. "And you will stay away from that man. Do I make myself clear?"

"But, Mother . . . ," Flora tried again.

She threw up a hand, refusing to listen as she strode toward the interior door. "Mabel, you will help me," she ordered without looking back.

Mabel flung a helpless look at her sisters before trailing after their mother.

Flora wanted to stamp her foot and howl in frustration. If Mother would just let her explain!

The door shut with a click, and Flora and Alice turned to look at each other. Obviously, there was more to Alice's furtive activities than she'd told her, but Flora found she couldn't summon the will to question her. Besides, who was she to cast stones? Instead, she urged her to turn around.

"Let's get you out of your tea gown so you have time to wash up. A bit of lavender mist in your hair also wouldn't be remiss."

Mother had been correct. It seemed all the ladies had dug into their wardrobes and trunks to unearth their recently purchased Parisian gowns and collected their flashiest jewels from the purser's safe. Perhaps it was those diamonds and rubies draped around so many women's necks and wrists, reflecting off the crystal and silverware, or the sense of camaraderie that seemed to fill the air. Whatever the case, the Dining Saloon seemed to sparkle even more brilliantly to Alice's eyes than on previous evenings. There was a happy smile or at least a smirk of contentment to be found on practically every face.

Every face, except the Fortunes', that was. But it was impossible even for them to remain immune to the bonhomie surrounding them for long.

Rather than settle immediately at their tables, passengers seemed to linger, talking to one another, even crossing the room to greet a friend. Women laughed with vivacious abandon and the men surveyed those around them with approving glints in their eyes. The pompadours were larger, the grins wider, and the excitement palpable. She could almost feel it in the pulse of the ship.

Or perhaps that was simply the revolutions increasing as they connected more boilers to the engines. Either way, Alice knew she couldn't be the only one of her sisters relieved by its softening effect on their parents. They were still angry, but it had lowered to a simmer.

Though it wouldn't remain so for long if Flora didn't stop sneaking glances toward Mr. Kinsey's empty table.

Alice moved to her sister's side, draping an arm about her waist in both solidarity and warning. "Have you ever seen so many diamonds," she murmured to distract her.

"They must have emptied half the vaults in Europe," Mabel quipped from her other side. "And many of the wealthiest passengers aren't even here. They must be dining in the Restaurant." She scoffed. "Look at Zette Douglas."

The woman in question had entered on her brother Quigg Baxter's arm and was being escorted to their table. Flora stiffened slightly, perhaps a silent reaction to the woman's gauche appearance, for she wore a diamond tiara in her hair. While fashionable a year or two earlier, it was now considered vulgar for anyone but royalty to wear such a headpiece.

"Perhaps she doesn't know," Alice suggested, wanting to give her the benefit of the doubt.

"She should," Mabel retorted.

"Miss Fortune."

Flora's muscles hardened almost to stone at the sound of the deep voice. Disengaging from Alice, she turned to greet the grinning face of Mr. Behr—Mr. Kinsey's friend, tennis rival, and tablemate.

"Miss Alice. Miss Mabel," Mr. Behr continued as both sisters turned to him as well. "You all look lovely this evening."

"Thank you," Flora replied woodenly. "I do hope Miss Newsom is well."

"Oh, yes, indeed." He nodded in the direction of her table. "What a merry evening this is. Though it appears I am to dine alone. Mr. Kinsey is engaged to dine in the Restaurant with Harry Widener, lucky chap. The fellow asked him this morning."

Ah, so that was his game. Mr. Kinsey had undoubtedly put him up to it. To ensure Flora wouldn't worry that he was avoiding her or Father. He was also perhaps reminding Mr. Fortune—who was bound to overhear—that Chess Kinsey was not a nobody.

The Wideners were a very prominent and wealthy family, and for their son and heir to invite Mr. Kinsey to dine was a mark of distinction.

Alice hid a smile, finding herself even more fond of Mr. Kinsey than she'd been before.

Mr. Behr peered at the tables around them. "But it seems I won't be the only one."

He was correct. There were more than a few tables missing their usual occupants. Even the chief purser's table, where Thomas Andrews was sitting, was absent a few members, including Dr. O'Loughlin, who must still have been seeing to Mrs. Harris. Alice hoped he could make the dear lady comfortable after her terrible fall earlier.

Alice had been at René Harris's side when she'd slipped on a bit of dampness while descending the Grand Staircase after their poker game in Mr. Cardeza's suite. She'd taken a tumble and broken her arm. Though the plucky dame had striven to hide it, it had been obvious she'd been in a great deal of pain, but Alice trusted Dr. O'Loughlin had been able to give her something to ease it.

One woman at the chief purser's table wore a beautiful white lace gown with an ermine stole draped around her shoulders, and she was far from being the only lady dressed in this manner. The bitter cold outside had penetrated the ship, prompting many of the women to don warm wraps over their evening gowns. The Fortune women were heartier than that, having endured enough Winnipeg winters to make them more immune to such drafts and chills. Even so, Alice found herself wishing she'd draped a light shawl over her blush pink gown.

"One of the officers told me the temperatures tonight are expected to dip below thirty degrees Fahrenheit," Charlie told them as he sampled the plover eggs with caviar. He waited to swallow before continuing. "Add in the wind generated by the ship steaming forward through the atmosphere, and the crew anticipates a disagreeable night, indeed, above decks."

"Poor fellows," Flora said, eschewing the plover eggs for an oyster.

"Maybe you should offer them the use of your buffalo coat, Father," Charlie teased.

Father made a sound between a harrumph and a chuckle even as Mother protested. "Oh, please, do not pull that ratty old thing out of your trunk."

"I told you that coat would come in handy," he declared, ignoring her. "It always does."

"Perhaps," Mother conceded. "But *you* have no reason to be above decks in the freezing cold. And much as the crew might be grateful for it, I doubt they would be allowed to wear something that was not issued as part of their uniform."

"You are simply determined to see it kept stored away," Father retorted with a hitch at the corner of his mouth.

Alice smiled at her parents' playful banter, heartened by it. But Flora proved even more daring.

"I have always admired the easy affection you share," she said. "The teasing and camaraderie. It comforted me as a child and struck me as something to aspire to as I grew."

The table fell silent, none of them oblivious to her reason for making this statement.

"Aye, but it's something that must be worked at," Father warned. "Nothing in life worth having is kept that way without nurturing, my girl."

"I do not doubt your wisdom," Flora replied carefully, gazing at the vase of daffodils at the center of the table. "But if there is not already some warmth of feeling, if there is only cold obligation and duty, what is there to cherish and nurture?"

None of the siblings spoke, tensely anticipating their parents' response.

Unfortunately, they were interrupted by the arrival of their steward, who set their soup—Consommé Olga or cream of barley—before them and asked their preference between filets mignons Lili, chicken Lyonnaise, or vegetable marrow farci for a later course. By the time he had finished, they were confronted with yet another distraction.

Mrs. Allison from Montreal had brought her daughter, Lorraine, into the saloon to see how beautiful everything was, and perhaps justifiably to show off the adorable toddler. The little girl greeted Mother and Father charmingly before moving on to the occupants of Mr. and Mrs. Allison's table. A few other people came forward to speak to the little girl as she made the return trip back to the Reception Room and her nanny, including Mr. Andrews.

"His daughter is about the same age," Flora said softly as they watched him bend over to speak to her. There was an ache in her voice. "He has been missing her terribly."

Returning to their plates, they were engulfed by the sumptuousness of the dinner. All of their meals on the *Titanic* had been lavish and delicious, but Sunday's dinner was by far the grandest. Poached salmon in a mousseline sauce; lamb, duckling, and sirloin with green peas and Parmentier potatoes flavored with rosemary; punch romaine as a palate cleanser; roast squab; asparagus vinaigrette salad; pâté de foie gras; and an elegant selection of desserts for their tenth and final course, including Waldorf pudding, peaches in Chartreuse jelly, chocolate éclairs, and French ice cream. Alice tried to limit herself to but a few bites of each or else she would burst out of her corset.

Which provided a convenient excuse when, at the end of the meal, they drifted out to the Reception Room to the strains of something from *Madama Butterfly* by Puccini being played by the band. Alice grasped her mother's elbow lightly. "May we be excused to our cabin for a moment?" she said, trusting Mother would infer the reason for Alice's request.

"Of course, dear," she replied distractedly as she returned to her conversation with Mrs. Hays.

Alice didn't waste a moment before linking her arms through Flora's and Mabel's and towing them toward the staircase. "We all need the retiring room," she insisted when her younger sister began to protest. Just to be contrary, no doubt.

# CHAPTER 24

꧁❦꧂

For many, dining in the À la Carte Restaurant might prove a highlight of their voyage aboard the *Titanic*, but for Chess it was an exercise in frustration. He didn't want to be seated in the graceful establishment astern of the Aft Grand Staircase. Not when Flora was in the Dining Saloon. But one did not simply cancel on a Widener. A fact that he hoped Karl had impressed upon the Fortunes, to Chess's advantage.

Fortunately, Harry proved a better conversationalist than Chess remembered. He refrained from droning on about the minutiae of his rare book collection and instead focused on their fellow diners. Indeed, it was difficult to ignore the number of prominent society figures surrounding them.

Figures who looked perfectly at home among the walls and fluted columns paneled in walnut, and the gilded and carved moldings and ornamentations. Louis XVI chairs were positioned around tables of various sizes, supporting vases of roses giving off their sweet fragrance and small lamps casting a warm glow across the tablecloth. The pink carpet wasn't particularly to Chess's taste, but he couldn't deny the quality. The windows were also a welcome change from the backlit portholes of the Saloon, allowing diners to peer out at the starry sky.

Harry, being better informed than Chess, pointed out the Duff-Gordons. Chess was aware that Lady Duff-Gordon was also the fashion designer Lucile, who had recently created quite a stir with her garments among his mother and her friends in New York, but he was more interested in Sir Cosmo. The man was a noted fencer, after all, having won a silver medal in the team épée event at the Olympics. Harry also nodded toward a nearby alcove, where Edgar Meyer sat with his wife, Leila, dressed in mourning for Leila's father—Andrew Saks, founder of the Manhattan department store carrying his name.

But by far the most interesting table was the one hosted by Harry's parents. Much of the party was concealed in an alcove near the door, but one end of the table extended beyond the privacy screen. Captain Smith, in whose honor the dinner party was being given, was one of the guests seated at this near end of the table. As Harry had hinted, the rather exclusive guest list included the Thayers, William and Lucille Carter, and Major Archibald Butt. They were loud and boisterous, all but drowning out the strains of Tchaikovsky played by the trio positioned in the small reception room outside the restaurant.

It seemed to Chess that Mr. Ismay—dining with Dr. O'Loughlin at a table at the center of the room—kept looking longingly toward Wideners' party. A number of other diners might have felt the same way. The party was certainly difficult to ignore and kept them all entertained.

However, Chess was already counting the minutes until he could politely excuse himself and seek out either Flora or her father. The lobster, caviar, hothouse grapes, and peaches were undoubtedly delicious, but he barely tasted them.

Though there was a bit of excitement when Henry B. Harris, the Broadway producer, and his wife appeared.

"Took a tumble down the stairs, I heard," Harry explained as a round of applause went up for Mrs. Harris, who entered with her arm nestled in a sling. Obviously, Harry hadn't been the only one to learn of the incident, but that didn't surprise Chess. On board a ship, gossip traveled quickly.

The thought made Chess go cold as Ismay and Dr. O'Loughlin stood to greet the Harrises. If someone had seen Chess kissing Flora—someone other than Mrs. Fortune, that is—then that gossip would also have already made the rounds, and it would be Flora who would bear the brunt of the scandal.

He felt anew the urgent need to make things right. And the sooner the better.

As if conjured by his thoughts, he heard the name Fortune mentioned, and looked about in alarm.

"Yes, Miss Fortune was such a boon to me," Mrs. Harris was saying. "She comforted me while my Harry went in search of you, Dr. O'Loughlin. Oh, but hasn't Dr. Frauenthal done a marvelous job. What Providence we had to have such a specialist on board."

Harry Widener was now watching him with interest. "I'd heard you were spending a great deal of time with one of the Miss Fortunes, but I didn't know what to make of it." He sipped from his glass of brandy. "So, it's true, then?"

Chess watched idlily as the Harrises joined the mystery novelist Jacques Futrelle and his wife at their table, trying not to reveal the anxiety such an ambiguous question had caused him. "I suppose it depends on what you've heard."

"That you're thinking of settling down." Harry watched him closely. "Maybe even retiring from tennis."

"I'm playing my best tennis ever. Why would I be considering retirement?"

Harry shrugged. "It's simply something I heard." He paused, waiting for Chess to continue, and then prodded. "And Miss Fortune?"

Chess turned to gaze out at the black night, resplendent with stars. "She's quite special, I'll tell you that. Quite special indeed."

# CHAPTER 25

❦

"All right, out with it," Alice declared as she closed the door behind them, obviously expecting them to spill their secrets.

Mabel crossed her arms and leaned back against the wardrobe. As far as she was concerned, she would listen to their confidences and even offer her opinion, but she wasn't going to share a drop of hers. Not when it would only bring her more grief.

When neither she nor Flora were forthcoming, Alice darted a glance at Mabel's mulish expression before addressing their older sister. "What happened, Flora? Did Mother catch you and Mr. Kinsey . . ." Color tinted her cheeks as she left the sentence dangling.

"She caught us embracing." Flora paused, worrying the chain of her necklace. "On the Promenade Deck."

Alice gasped even as Mabel grinned. "That must have been some kiss."

Both her sisters turned to stare at her.

"To make Flora forget herself and where she was," Mabel clarified. "Normally she has the senses of a cat."

"Well, I didn't this time," Flora replied with a humorless laugh.

"I bet it was worth it."

Flora didn't respond, instead crossing toward the porthole to pull aside the drapes and peer out into the chilly night.

Alice scowled. "Does he mean to marry you?"

"He said he intends to speak with Father."

"Well, then, everything will turn out fine." The false cheeriness of Alice's voice grated on Mabel's ears. "Mother and Father might be angry now, but they'll forgive you once you're wed."

Flora pressed her hand against the cool glass of the porthole. It would leave smudges—something Flora *hated*—but she did it anyway. "Mother told him not to bother. That I'm already engaged."

This was more than Mabel could bear. She'd already been told the path she wanted for her life was unacceptable. Flora couldn't be denied her happiness, too.

"Then run away with him."

Flora pivoted to gape at her.

"Elope," Mabel persisted. "You said he wants to marry you. And I know you want to marry him. So when the ship docks in New York, leave with him. He and his family are wealthy, aren't they?"

"Yes, very wealthy, from what I understand," Flora answered slowly.

"Then, you have no need of Father's money. And, knowing you, you still have half the pin money Father gave each of us before we departed on our grand tour." She flung her arm out toward the dressing table drawer where Flora had stashed it.

Alice stepped forward anxiously. "Now, wait just a moment. Let's not be hasty. An elopement would be a *terrific* scandal. Wouldn't it be enough to merely *threaten* it should Father refuse to accept Mr. Kinsey's suit?"

"Perhaps," Flora conceded. "Though I pray it doesn't come to that. I don't *want* to have to resort to such extreme measures. I just want them to listen to me!"

"As do we all," Mabel muttered bitterly, and then regretted it as her sisters' attentions swung to her.

"We haven't much time," Flora said. "But what did Mother mean when she said *you'd* made threats to Father?"

It was Mabel's turn to avoid her sisters' probing looks, turning toward the mirror to adjust the pearl-encrusted comb in her hair. "It's none of your concern."

"It isn't to do with Harrison Driscoll, is it?" Alice asked. "Mabel, you know that man is only interested in your dowry."

"No, it's not about Driscoll," Flora said with a quiet certainty that rattled Mabel, causing her to lift her eyes to meet her sister's bright blue-gray ones in the reflection of the mirror. "I'm not sure you're truly even smitten with the man. But there *is* something you want. Something Father has denied you."

Mabel stood stiffly, battling the urge to do exactly what she'd told herself she wouldn't.

"What I don't understand is why you won't tell us." There was hurt mixed with the bewilderment in Flora's voice. "Maybe we can help."

"You can't," she stated harshly. "At least . . . not yet."

If Flora were to wed Mr. Kinsey, then perhaps Mr. Kinsey would be open-minded enough to pay for Mabel's education. She knew better than to ask Crawfy or Holden. They were much too traditional and far too deep under Father's thumb. But Mr. Kinsey didn't strike her as the type of man to be controlled by his father-in-law. Perhaps that was exactly the problem.

"We should return to the Palm Court," Alice said, interrupting their exchange. "Before Mother comes looking for us and confines us to our cabin for the remainder of the night."

"Just a moment." Flora stepped around her, pushing shut the door her sister had begun to open.

Alice turned to her in surprise.

"*You* still haven't explained yourself. Why do your clothes smell so strongly of cigarettes? Why have you been retiring so late?"

"We're out of time," Alice protested, looking like a cornered hare.

But Flora kept her hand firmly planted on the door over Alice's head. "Then I suggest you quit stalling."

Alice frowned, crossing her arms over her chest. "I . . . I attended a few private parties. With Mr. Sloper. And others."

"Mrs. Harris?"

"There's nothing untoward about them," Alice stammered. "Except the smoking. Which I didn't partake in! And . . . and a bit of drinking."

"And where were these parties hosted?"

"Private suites," Alice replied obliquely.

However, Flora had evidently grown tired of interrogating her. "Well, Mother and Father are bound to find out, so you'd best tell them yourself."

Alice's face crumpled with hurt.

"*I'm* not going to tell them," Flora snapped in annoyance before tossing a look at Mabel. "Though I can't speak for Mabel."

"You won't, will you?" Alice pleaded.

"No," Mabel grumbled. "But Flora's right. One way or another, they'll find out. It would be better if they learned it from you."

Alice nodded, though Mabel doubted she would follow their advice. Had their situation been reversed, she wouldn't have. She would have bided her time, waiting to see if her transgression was discovered. After all, what had honest communication ever gotten her, but a firm denial and a door shut in her face.

Mother swept her gaze over her daughters suspiciously when they returned to the Reception Room but resumed her conversation with the lady next to her. This should have relieved Alice, but she couldn't shake her feeling of dread. That their adventure was nearly at an end. That her parents would discover she'd attended Mr. Cardeza's poker parties. That Flora would realize she'd stolen all her pin money.

A quick sweep of the room as the violin and piano played the opening bars to one of Dvořák's *Humoresques* told her that Mr. Futrelle wasn't there, and neither was Father. With any luck, Mr. Futrelle would be in the Smoking Room, securing her the perfect bid, and Father would be amicable to Mr. Kinsey's suit. For that must be where Mr. Kinsey was as well.

While Flora accepted a steaming cup of coffee from one of the stewards and joined their mother, perhaps hoping to get somewhat back into her good graces, and Mabel gravitated toward Mrs. Candee and her merry coterie of gentlemen, Alice found herself unable to remain still. Much like pretty Dorothy Gibson, the film star, who kept peppering the band with requests for dance music as she clicked her satin heels and waved her arms to the beat. Except Alice merely wandered, exchanging a brief word here and there with another passenger.

She had paused to listen to a lively number from Franz Lehár's operetta, *Die lustige Witwe*, when she was distracted by the laughter of two couples passing around a little book. It appeared to belong to the woman in the squirrel coat, whom Alice recognized, with a jolt, as Lady Duff-Gordon, the fashion designer. The handsome man beside her with the trim mustache must be her husband.

The other couple were not much older than Alice, and while the woman seemed to have taken some care with her answers in the "confessions" book, the man seemed to view it all as a bit of a lark. "Likes," he murmured. "Well, let's see . . . a stout lager, a good ski slope, and my beautiful wife." His wife simpered as he continued. "Abominations . . . a rain delay, a soggy sandwich, and a rutted road."

"Edgar," his wife scolded even as Sir Cosmo chuckled.

"What's next? Madnesses?" He gave a bark of laughter. "Well, I only have one. To live!" he stated with a grand flourish.

Alice felt a chill breeze blow across the back of her neck, raising the fine hairs there, and turned to discover from where it had come. There were stray drafts all over the ship, courtesy of the bitter cold outside, but no one else nearby seemed affected. Certainly not the two couples who continued to jest over their answers.

That's when she spied Mrs. Margaret Brown seated near one corner, bundled up in furs.

"You look chilled to the bone, my dear," Mrs. Brown declared as she approached. "Come sit beside me and we shall set you right."

A haze of French perfume surrounded the Denver socialite as Alice sank down beside her, feeling like a tufted titmouse come to rest in the fur they filched to make their nests. But then the thought of filching made Alice wince.

"Are you quite all right, Miss Fortune?" Mrs. Brown asked with concern, pressing a hand to Alice's forehead. "You look a bit piqued, but you don't feel warm. In fact, you feel cold. These dresses . . . they may be lovely, but they don't do a thing to protect young ladies from the cold."

"I think I'm simply tired," she replied meekly. "It's been a long day."

Mrs. Brown didn't appear convinced. "You've the look of a woman with a dark secret."

Alice stilled. "Why do you say that?"

"It's merely an observation, dear. But should you need to unburden yourself." She tapped the side of her head. "I've a good ear."

That might be so, but she also had a loud mouth. But Alice supposed that didn't mean Mrs. Brown couldn't be counted upon to be discreet. She didn't seem the catty sort.

"Have you ever done something . . . ," she began hesitantly, "something that shocks even you . . . something you didn't truly want to, except . . ." She broke off, shaking her head, and then tried a different tack. "*Is* honesty always the best policy?"

Mrs. Brown appeared to give this due consideration. "Well, that depends. If you think your sister looks like a gargoyle in the new gown she happens to adore, then no. Telling her would just be cruel. But if the truth stirs an ache in you, if it makes your stomach cramp or your heart pound or your palms sweat . . ."

Alice felt all those things. At that very moment, in fact.

"Then yes. Honesty is best. For *your* good, if not theirs." Mrs. Brown turned to meet her gaze. "Don't ever be afraid to speak the truth, Miss Fortune. Not when it needs to be said."

Alice's pulse beat in her ears as she recognized the wisdom of what she must do. With her parents. With Flora. And with Holden. Though none of the confessions would be easy. Particularly the last.

When the band began playing its final number for the evening— a song from *The Tales of Hoffmann* by Offenbach—Mother beckoned to Alice and her sisters. Apparently, they were to be kept under tight supervision, not allowed to wander at their own whims. For her part, this didn't matter, but poor Flora. Her sister turned her head slowly to the left, then the right, clearly searching for Mr. Kinsey. They all knew he must be meeting with Father. Perhaps at that very moment. Yet she was being forced to retire before learning the answer to her fate.

Alice knew that if she were in Flora's shoes, she would be frantic with worry. While Flora was undeniably more stalwart than she, it still simply wasn't to be borne! Not if there was something Alice could do about it.

# CHAPTER 26

❧❦❧

Chess wasn't surprised when he reached the Smoking Room before Mr. Fortune. He'd expected he might be forced to cool his heels. So he claimed a table far from the fireplace, where he knew the bidding on the next day's run would take place, and ordered a Rob Roy as he settled in with a few newspapers to wait. He declined a request to play bridge, and several acquaintances stopped to speak with him, but he made it clear that he wasn't eager for company. They quickly took the hint and moved on.

By all rights, Mr. Fortune might have kept Chess waiting for hours to punish him for his infraction, but Flora's father strode into the room at about half past eight, appearing ready to do battle. Had he a sword strapped to his back like his ancestors of old, Mr. Fortune no doubt would have removed it from its scabbard, at the very least, as a threat. Quickly spotting Chess, Mr. Fortune made no bones about his intentions, sinking down into the chair next to his. "I'll hear you out, Kinsey, but only out of courtesy to your family's business reputation. *You* are already on thin ice."

"Thank you, sir."

He chomped down on a cigar he'd pulled from his pocket, turning his head to allow the steward who had approached to light it before ordering a whiskey for himself. It was then that Chess noticed the two men approaching with grim expressions. They pulled out the other chairs at the table and sat without preamble. Reinforcements then . . . should Chess's words not prove amenable. Though, truth be told, neither man seemed like the type of chap he'd want at his back during a fight. They looked like bankers or businessmen, resembling each other closely enough with their balding heads and light mustaches that they might have been brothers.

Fortune didn't bother introducing them. "Now, what do you have to say for yourself," he demanded, glaring at him through the haze of his cigar smoke.

"Thank you for agreeing to speak with me," Chess began carefully. "I realize, in regard to my behavior this afternoon, that I was completely in the wrong." He spread his hands palms out. "All I can say is that I was overcome, and I allowed my feelings for Miss Fortune to get the better of my judgment."

This was not something that was easy to admit, particularly not in front of a table full of relative strangers, but at least one of the other chaps seemed to soften at this admission.

"I want to make it right," he continued. "And not simply because my actions were untoward, but because I have become quite enamored of your daughter, sir. I would very much like her to do me the honor of becoming my wife."

Fortune did not intend to make this easy. He inhaled from his cigar, stewing over Chess's response as he slowly exhaled. "You are aware she's already engaged."

"I am," he conceded.

"Yet you chose to pursue her anyway."

"I did."

"Why?" Fortune leaned forward intently. "One would think an honorable man would know not to poach in another man's territory."

Chess didn't appreciate Fortune's wording, but he understood his intent. "Because Miss Fortune is too extraordinary."

Fortune sank back at this pronouncement, and Chess noted the second man's stern expression ease a bit.

"And she is not yet bound to Mr. Campbell," he pointed out. "Had she already been wed, I would never have pursued her. Indeed, when we first met, I didn't intend for this to happen. But she is too remarkable to be ignored. I do not think I could have resisted her had I tried."

Fortune's drink arrived, and he took a healthy swallow, glancing toward the raised voices of those making their bids before replying. "All that may be true." His gaze flicked up and down over Chess contemptuously. "But why on earth should I favor your suit over Campbell's?"

In spite of their brief time together, Chess had taken Mark Fortune's measure. His own hardscrabble upbringing had made him determined never to see his children face the same. And yet, being a self-made man, he still placed a great deal of value on the meaning of hard work. It was why, despite the large inheritance he would receive, his eldest son had been sent to British Columbia to make his own way, in a manner of speaking. Likewise, he wanted his daughters to marry respectable, upstanding men from good families, but he also wanted to know that those men had worked for what they'd achieved, not merely had their wealth handed to them.

In many ways, this was the opposite of the Kinseys, for whom labor was anathema, something to be avoided at all costs. Especially if one was a second son. As such, Chess had to throw out every preconceived notion of who he needed to present himself to be beyond the respectability of his family name. Fortune wouldn't care about his family's wealth. But he *would* care about Chess's.

He straightened. "Because I am not just an idle tennis star who has been granted all his accolades. I trained hard to achieve them. I didn't just stumble my way into being an attorney in my family's company, I placed second in my class at Yale. And my wealth doesn't come solely from my family, but a sizable stock portfolio I manage on my own." When he named the details and amount, he was rather satisfied by the way Fortune's eyebrows shot upward, though they quickly crashed again in doubt. "All of this is verifiable," Chess added before Fortune could question it.

"Which you will, of course, wish to do once we reach New York. I will instruct my advisers to speak freely with you and answer any queries you might have."

Fortune sat back, continuing to puff on his cigar. Chess had plainly surprised him and hopefully shaken his mistaken perception of who Chess was. Just because he'd inherited a great deal of wealth didn't mean he had rested on his laurels.

"What of your future?" Fortune posited. "You can't intend to play tennis forever. What then?"

Chess had known this question was coming, but it irked him all the same. As if being an attorney and managing his stocks were not employment enough. "I've a mind to start a sports equipment manufacturing company," he said. "One that can supply sporting goods at a cheaper cost to a greater swath of the population."

This captured Fortune's attention, and Chess felt a swift sense of elation, knowing he as good as had him.

Fortune leaned forward, gritting the cigar between his teeth as he spoke. "How would you go about doing it?"

# CHAPTER 27

❦

*Sunday, April 14, 1912—10:15 p.m.*

Flora pushed up from her bed, tugging on the tasseled belt of her wrapper and flinging it aside to reveal her coral-pink silk-and-chiffon gown underneath. "You'll cover for me?" she asked her sisters anxiously as she pulled on her heavy wool coat trimmed in ermine.

"Yes," Alice replied. A glitter of excitement showed in her eyes as she hurried across the room to begin stuffing items under Flora's covers to make it look as if she lay asleep.

Mabel moved to help her. "Just be careful." She grasped Flora's arm to halt her as she turned to go. "And don't get caught. Otherwise, it will be our hides, too."

Flora nodded. Even though it seemed certain now that her father wasn't coming to inform her of her fate—despite the fact she'd waited for what had felt like an eternity since he'd returned to his adjoining cabin—there were other potential pitfalls that might snare her. Namely, her brother Charlie, who had yet to retire. She had to take care, for all their sakes.

She strode toward the door, only to turn back once more to drop a swift kiss on each of their cheeks. "Thank you."

A suspicious brightness lit Alice's eyes as she shooed her on. "Go. Go!"

Flora inched the door open, peering out to be sure the passage was empty before slipping out. At the junction with the main corridor, she looked left and then right before hurrying toward the staircase and lifts, praying Charlie didn't choose this minute of all minutes to return to C-Deck, for there was nowhere for her to hide.

She'd decided that if Chess was still awake, he would be somewhere on A-Deck. If he'd retired . . . well, that didn't bear thinking about. Not yet. Her cheeks flamed at the very thought of knocking on his cabin door. If she could even find it.

She hastened upward, scouring the stairs for familiar faces, particularly, for ladies in whom her mother might have confided about her daughters' misbehavior. While there were still many people about at this hour, she found no one to alarm her. At the door to the Reading and Writing Room, she paused only briefly, already deducing Chess wouldn't be inside, and then turned toward the Lounge. It was the one place where he most likely would have settled to wait for her. If he was waiting for her at all. She took a swift breath, squashing the worry before it could plant roots, and pushed open the door.

She spotted him almost immediately, seated in an alcove, far from the gathering of people clustered around the warmth of the fireplace. His head was bowed over a book, but he looked up as she approached, and the gleam in his eyes made her stumble.

"I knew you would come," he stated simply, closing his book as she stopped before him.

She looked down to see that it was a copy of Ernest Shackleton's *The Heart of the Antarctic*—the very same book they'd discussed only a few short days before. "I knew you would be waiting for me." She sank down beside him on the green velvet settee. "Looking at icebergs?" she murmured somewhat inanely, not having the foggiest idea what to say in such a situation.

"Anything to stop me from staring at the door."

She wanted to touch him, to clasp his hand, but they were in a public room, surrounded by dozens of people.

As if reminded of the same thing, Chess pushed to his feet. "Come with me."

Flora followed as Chess returned his book to the library steward, before guiding her toward the door leading aft. She spied Mr. Sloper's blond head at a table with another man, the film actress, Dorothy Gibson, and her mother. They were playing cards while Miss Gibson and Mr. Sloper flirted. Flora couldn't withhold a reluctant grin. The man truly was incorrigible.

Chess began to button his wool overcoat as they hastened down the corridor, leaving no doubt as to their destination, and Flora tugged her fur collar up higher around her neck. Even so, she wasn't prepared for the full force of the cold as they stepped out on deck. Yet the wind was incredibly calm—the only breeze being the one that was generated from them moving forward—and the sea was as still as a mountain glade. If she were to toss a rock into it, she would be able to watch its ripples expand outward forever.

And the stars! Flora had never seen them shine so brilliantly. There was no moon, no light to compete with their glow. And glow they did. Right down across the water, touching the horizon. It was so clear that the stars even appeared to have a texture, standing out from the firmament like jewels spangled across a bodice.

Flora's heart caught in her throat at the utter beauty of it all, making her temporarily forget everything but the sheer delight of being here to witness such a sight. She exhaled in wonder, her breath fogging in the air. Chess's hand gripped hers, sharing in this moment, in the pureness of its joy.

A shiver worked through her frame, and Chess drew her away from the rail and into the shelter and shadow created by an alcove. He wrapped his arms around her, sharing his heat. From somewhere below, she could hear faint strains of music.

"What did Father say?" she finally dared to ask.

She couldn't see his eyes—it was too dark—but she could feel the rumble of his voice in his chest beneath her hand and feel its warm exhalation against the skin below her ear. "That if my finances prove to be as I've claimed, and once you've severed things properly with Campbell, then I may ask for your hand in marriage."

Flora gasped as her heart burst with light. "Truly?" She gripped his shoulders. "Are you telling me true?"

He chuckled, and she could hear that his happiness echoed her own. "Yes. Yes, I'm telling you true."

"Oh, Chess," she exhaled just before his mouth met her own, and an entirely new and different shiver worked through her frame.

When he lifted his mouth, it was to press his forehead against hers. "Will you?" he asked, his breathing ragged. "Will you marry me, then, Flora? I know it's wrong to ask you now, but I can't help myself. I need to know. Will you make me the happiest of men?"

"Yes, Chess. Yes, I will."

He kissed her again, pressing her back against the wall and doing all sorts of wondrous things with his tongue and lips and teeth. When finally he pulled back, it was with a muttered curse. Both of them knew they could go no further, no matter how much they longed it. He backed away a step, allowing cold air to rush between them. A fact she immediately regretted, though she knew better than to urge him back.

"I . . . I should return to my cabin before I'm missed," she finally managed to stammer as she clung to the wall at her back. Part of her suspected it was the only reason her legs hadn't given out.

"Yes, of course," Chess replied, turning to look behind them. "Perhaps along the promenade, even though it's cold."

"There's less a chance of being seen," she agreed.

"Yes." There was a sheepish note to his voice.

"Soon we'll no longer have to worry about that," she assured him, linking her arm through his.

"Soon we won't have to worry about a lot of things," he replied. "Including stopping ourselves."

Flora flushed with heat upon hearing the timbre of his voice, knowing precisely what he meant.

They strolled in silence, and while she couldn't read his thoughts, she liked to think they were similar to her own. That they had found each other. That they were to have the chance of a life together. That there was nothing that could tear them apart now. So buoyant was she that she was quite certain she was nearly skipping. The smile Chess flashed her as they approached the doors to the Forward Grand Staircase confirmed it.

He pressed a swift kiss to her lips before urging her toward the entrance. "Go! Before I refuse to ever let you out of my sight again and cause a *real* scandal."

She laughed before whispering. "Good night!"

He lifted his hand in farewell as she disappeared inside.

# CHAPTER 28

❧❧❧

Chess was quite certain there was a rather large and rather ridiculous-looking grin plastered to his face, but he didn't care. He'd won Flora. What's more, he'd done so by convincing her father of the worthiness of his suit, so no scandal need ensue. They would be wed with the full approval of her family. And his. That went without saying. They would simply be pleased he was taking a wife of good family. The rest wouldn't matter a fig.

Yes, she would have to break the news to Crawford Campbell, no easy task. But once that was done, there would be no impediment. Nothing else between them.

Chess turned to stroll back down the promenade, barely feeling the cold, such was his elation. He tipped his head back and closed his eyes. Or perhaps it was the memory of that kiss and the urgent little sounds Flora had made at the back of her throat that warmed him. He groaned, knowing that at another time, in another setting, he might not have found it so easy to stop himself. Not when she'd been urging him on. They would need to be stricter about their chaperonage from here on out.

He inhaled a deep breath, hoping to clear his head, and caught a whiff of a damp, penetrating odor he couldn't identify at first. It wasn't altogether appealing. In fact, it smelled clammy.

That's when he realized what it was. Something he'd only ever read about until now. They said icebergs had a smell, and this must be it.

He moved toward the rail, peering out over the starlit sea. It still made his heart clutch at its beauty, but there were no icebergs in sight, and in the clear night air he could see quite an astonishing distance. Or he supposed, it was nearly clear. When he looked up at the lights along the promenade's ceiling, he could see little wisps of mist clinging to them in a prism of colors before disappearing.

Pushing away from the rail, he continued down the promenade. Stuffing his hands in his pockets and hunching his shoulders against the cold, he wondered briefly if the clarity of the night and the calmness of the sea helped or hindered the lookouts.

Stepping through the door into the Aft Grand Staircase entrance, he shook himself, as if to dislodge the chill and crossed the few steps to the Smoking Room. It was as busy as ever, with nearly every table occupied, though it must be after eleven. He saw William Carter, Major Butt, Harry Widener, Mr. Thayer, and Frank Millet, among others.

One of the men who had accompanied Mr. Fortune to his interrogation earlier in the evening hailed him from across the room, and Chess made his way over to him.

"Come join us now that you're to be an honorary one of us," the fellow declared, grinning, before offering him his hand. "I'm Beattie, by the way. And this other ferocious chap is McCaffry."

Chess shook the second man's hand. "You're not related, then."

"No," McCaffry said, with a chuckle. "Though we get asked that a lot. But we *are* from Winnipeg, and fond of the Fortune sisters."

"Especially Flora," Beattie added, holding up his finger. "A finer woman you'll not meet. And don't you forget it."

Chess lifted his hands in defeat. "I won't."

"Good. Then what's your libation of choice?"

They were joined for a time by Major Peuchen from Toronto, a gregarious fellow, but around half past eleven, he departed. At such a late hour, they all should have been making their way back to their cabins, but many seemed intent on enjoying another cigar, another drink, or another hand of cards until midnight, when the lights were turned out.

At about twenty to twelve, as Chess himself was considering retiring, a sudden jolt startled them. It wasn't a shock, exactly, but sort of an abrupt deceleration. It rattled the chandeliers overhead. However, what made him and everyone else stand up in alarm was the wrenching motion to the entire room.

"What the bloody hell was that?" someone exclaimed, and then everyone started talking at once.

Chess didn't bother with words, but instead followed the same instinct several of the other fellows seemed to have. He turned to race through the revolving doors leading into the portside Verandah Café. They skirted the white wicker tables and chairs and emerged through the sliding glass door onto the Promenade Deck. At first, he wasn't certain what they were looking for.

That was, until someone shouted, "An iceberg just passed astern!"

"Ground against the starboard side," a second man said. "Nothing to worry about."

Almost as soon as the words were spoken, a disconcerting silence fell as everyone struggled to understand. It was the engines, Chess realized with a queer feeling in his gut. They'd stopped.

"Merely a formality," an older fellow said. "She's *Titanic*, for goodness' sakes."

The others nodded and agreed, shrugging as they returned to the Smoking Room and their drinks. Chess remained a moment longer, feeling distinctly uneasy. For certain, the *Titanic* was the safest ship afloat. At most, she'd probably dented her hull. But he struggled to brush his worry aside.

Following the others inside, he found everyone's spirits as high as ever. Though there was *some* grumbling about the ship's loss of speed and what that might mean for the next day's run tally.

"Oh, shut your gob," one man barked, evidently tired of listening to his friend's bellyaching. "The captain will start her back up soon enough."

"It really was an iceberg," a man burst through the door to inform them. "There's ice on the Fore Well Deck."

A nattily dressed fellow lifted his glass. "Run along and fetch me a block, then. I could use some in this."

This earned him a hearty round of laughter. One that ended in cheers as the engines were restarted.

"See, I told you," the surly man remarked. "I expect the iceberg scratched off some of the ship's new paint, and the captain doesn't like to go on until she's painted up again."

This quip was met with more general amusement. But even as Chess sat back down at the table with Beattie and McCaffry, he could feel that the vibrations weren't as vivid as before. If they were moving forward, it was at a slower pace.

# CHAPTER 29

❧

*Sunday, April 14, 1912—11:40 p.m.*

Mabel and her sisters had fallen silent some minutes earlier, having exhausted their excited chatter over Flora's future. The lights had been turned off, and Mabel's eyes had adjusted to the darkness, allowing her to make out the molding at the edge of the ceiling above her bunk. She heard the rustle of sheets as Flora shifted in her bed across the room and the soft exhalation of Alice's breath below. That they were both thinking of their fiancés—or, in Flora's case, soon-to-be fiancé—was obvious. If Mabel had felt the same way about someone as they did about Holden and Chess, then she would likely be thinking of him, too.

Instead, she was recalling her argument with Father. She couldn't help but replay the words they'd said to each other, despite the deep ache they caused her. Round and round they repeated in her head, and if she closed her eyes, she could see Father's scornful glare.

Though she would rather die than admit it aloud, the disdain her father held for her, for the way she wished to live her life, cut her to the quick. She'd heard her family accuse her often enough of being selfish and spoiled, but she'd always thought that was just a familiar insult for them to fling. That deep down they knew her better than that. But her father's contempt had made it clear that wasn't true. He didn't care for any of the things she did or any of the things she wanted. If anything, he despised them.

She wanted to believe her sisters were different, that they would understand, but their eagerness to settle into the roles prescribed for them made her fear that was purely wishful thinking.

She fisted her hands in the blankets pulled up to her chin, fighting the urge to cry. A battle she was losing when she felt a sharp lurch. She blinked up at the ceiling, wondering at first if she'd imagined it, but then came the sound of faint metallic scraping and a shudder.

All three sisters bolted upright in bed.

"What on earth . . . ?" Alice murmured as they all sat immobile, listening to figure out where the sound was coming from.

Flora leaned forward, tugging aside the curtains covering the porthole just in time to see the shadow of something pass beyond the window.

"What was that?" Mabel demanded to know as she threw back her blanket to scramble down from her bunk.

Flora was now pressed to the outer wall, her face against the glass to try to see better. "I don't know. Another ship maybe or . . . an iceberg. That must be it."

"Did we hit it?" Alice wanted to know.

Their inner door burst open to reveal Charlie's silhouette backlit from some light source in the other room. "Did you hear that?"

"Yes," Mabel replied. "We think it was an iceberg."

"Truly?" He crossed the room toward Flora's bed, where she was still peering out the porthole.

Flora sat back, allowing him to look, though the iceberg must have long passed from view. "Did it wake Father and Mother?"

"I knocked on their door," Charlie answered distractedly. "But Father told me it was nothing and to go back to bed."

"Well, it certainly wasn't nothing," Alice retorted in a strangled voice.

"Yes, but you know Father." Charlie arched his neck as far as he could to see whatever might be there and then reared back. "I'm going on deck to see what's happened."

"I'll come, too," Alice told him as he began to retreat across the room.

"We'll all go," Flora announced with a glance in Mabel's direction.

"All right," Charlie agreed. "But hurry!"

It was while they were throwing on their coats over their nightclothes and wrappers that Alice paused in donning her slippers to ask. "Do you hear that?"

Both Mabel and Flora froze.

"Hear what?" Mabel asked, and then it struck her. She didn't hear anything. The throb of the engines that they'd become so accustomed to was missing. Only in the awful silence that had descended did she recognize its absence.

This, more than the small tremor, made her heart lurch.

"It's probably just a precaution," Flora told them as she buttoned her coat. "They'll have to repair any small damage, after all." She didn't sound in the least worried, and Mabel began to wonder if her reason for going up on deck was to see Mr. Kinsey rather than out of genuine concern or curiosity.

Whatever the case, Charlie returned to urge them along, and soon all four of them were tumbling out the door. It was impossible not to feel a small illicit thrill as they hurried along the corridor together like a group of miscreants.

It reminded Mabel sharply of Hogmanay some years past, when they had stayed up to watch the clock turn over to midnight and the new year. Someone had suggested, as a lark, that they should build a snowman at half past twelve in the morning. Their parents had long been in bed, so the siblings had snuck outdoors to perform this task. Which had then dissolved into a snowball fight and a sledding party. As loud as they'd been, and as damp as their outerwear was still steaming next to the hearth the next morning, Mabel was quite certain their parents had known. But they'd never said a word. Not even when they were all nodding over their hymnals in church, struggling to stay awake.

She wasn't so certain their parents would view tonight's foray as indulgently, but that didn't keep them from going. And they were far from the only curious passengers. Multiple doors opened along the corridor, so that people could confer with one another and ask the stewards what was going on. No one seemed overly concerned. If anything, they were disgruntled.

"The ship probably dropped a propeller," one man grumbled before telling his wife to go back to bed.

Mabel overheard one steward suggest the ship had sliced a whale in half. She considered correcting him, but instead hastened after her siblings. Maybe the object Flora had seen out the porthole *had* been a whale. Or half of one.

But when they reached the forward Promenade Deck, it was all too obvious that Flora had been correct. The Well Deck below was strewn with clumps of ice, which must have been wrenched from the iceberg during the collision. It dusted the deck beneath the railing where they stood, and Charlie stooped to gather it up, pressing it into a ball he showed them.

The air was bitter cold, slicing Mabel to the bone, but also moving. The engines must have restarted, carrying them forward in the water. A fact that seemed to calm the nerves of those who were present. That and the appearance of Mr. Andrews, who paused beside the Fortunes to gaze out over the Well Deck.

"What's happened?" one woman asked him. "Is there cause for concern?"

"Be easy. It will be all right," he assured them all, lifting his hands to stay their questions. "You're absolutely safe. We have everything under control." Several more pressed him with queries, all of which he answered politely, but succinctly, before moving on.

Flora hunched deeper inside her coat and stamped her feet. "Well, it's not entirely unexpected. They had iceberg warnings, after all. Though it would have been nice if they could have avoided hitting one." She looked about her. "But I suppose they are monstrous things at times, aren't they?"

"They had iceberg warnings?" Alice queried.

Flora nodded. "I guess I didn't tell you. I overheard Mr. Ismay showing one to some passengers."

Mabel was puzzled. "Yet they continued to increase her speed?"

She shrugged. "They thought they could maneuver around them."

This seemed to Mabel to be faulty logic, but then all the men on board seemed to be unnaturally obsessed with speed. Including Charlie.

"There are many who would say that the quicker you can get through the ice field, the safer you'll be," Charlie pointed out.

"Unless you hit something," Mabel retorted.

Alice linked her arm with hers. "Don't be cross, Mabel." She smiled, clearly having recovered from the initial shock. Her nose wrinkled with mischief. "Shall we have a snowball fight?"

"Only if I can join in."

Flora's pulse leapt at the sound of Chess's voice. She'd wondered if he would join them. Had even hoped he would. But she'd known he might have already retired, and with his cabin somewhere portside aft, he might not have noticed the collision with the iceberg on the starboard side. It had sounded minor enough to her ears and she'd seen the actual iceberg glide past.

She couldn't halt the broad grin that split her face as she turned to greet him and was warmed by his answering smile. Though it dimmed slightly at the sight of all the ice scattered below.

He stepped up next to her to peer over the rail. "I knew we hit an iceberg. It jarred us in the Smoking Room quite soundly. But it looks like the starboard bow took most of the impact."

"Andrews told us there's no cause for concern," Charlie informed him blithely.

"Yes, but that's what he would tell us regardless," Chess answered.

Flora turned to look up at his features, but they appeared as unruffled as always.

"They certainly don't seem alarmed," he added, gesturing to the men in the Well Deck below who were making a game of kicking the ice about.

Someone from farther along the promenade yelled down to them, asking the men from third class to toss up a chunk of ice. Several of them gathered up snowballs in response, hurling the projectiles up at their laughing counterparts in first class.

Under the cover of these antics, Chess reached out to take her hand in his. He squeezed it—in comfort, in solidarity—she wasn't entirely sure, but she was glad of it anyway. When Mr. Behr and Miss Newsom joined them, he was forced to release her, and her fingers suddenly felt cold and bereft.

"So it's true?" Mr. Behr demanded to know. "We hit an iceberg."

"I'm afraid so," Chess replied.

"But Mr. Andrews told us to be easy," Alice chimed in to say, perhaps as much struck by the paleness of Miss Newsom's face as Flora was. "They have everything well in hand."

However, the moment the words were out of Alice's mouth, the breeze began to die away, and the comforting vibrations Flora had felt below her feet were stilled again. At first, no one dared to speak, as if trying to pretend for the person beside them that nothing was wrong. People simply watched the lopsided snowball fight, the shouts and laughter of its players winging into the starry night.

As usual, Mabel was the first to find her tongue. "Why do you think they stopped the engines again?"

"Repairs, no doubt," Charlie replied.

Chess agreed. "Depending on the location of the damage, a proper repair might require the ship to remain stationary."

It all sounded perfectly reasonable, but Flora felt the first ink-lings of sincere doubt shake her confidence. Inklings that these words were meant to placate them.

"Does it . . . ," Mr. Behr began tentatively, staring straight ahead. "Does it feel as if the ship is listing slightly to starboard?" Though his voice had been even, she could see the strain in his eyes when he darted a glance at Chess. Whether this was be-cause Mr. Behr wanted Chess to confirm or deny his suspicions, she couldn't tell, she was only glad her sisters farther away hadn't heard him.

"Perhaps slightly," Chess agreed, and Flora concentrated, try-ing to sense whatever it was that they were feeling.

Just then, a tremendous howl split the night sky, making them all cower, covering their ears.

"What the devil?" she shouted, uncertain she could even be heard above the deafening roar. It seemed to echo about inside her skull.

"It's the funnels blowing off their steam," Chess leaned over to yell in her ear. "The steam is no longer feeding into the en-gines, and the pressure in the boilers has to go somewhere. So the safety valves have been triggered, allowing the steam to es-cape up the pipes in the funnels."

She looked blindly upward, but the ceiling of the promenade obscured any sight of the offending smokestacks. "How long is this going to go on?" she hollered back.

"Well, she built up a full head of steam from twenty-four or more boilers. So, I imagine quite some time."

She pointed back down the promenade, urging the others to follow.

They weren't the only ones escaping the racket and the cold. Many of the others who had come out to the promenade to see what had happened were also retreating to the interior. Once in-side, the noise lessened, but by no means disappeared. So loud was it, Flora suspected it could be heard throughout the entire ship.

A large crowd was gathering in the A-Deck Reception Room

beneath the magnificent wrought-iron-and-white-glass dome and up in the Boat Deck entrance. Stewards moved among the milling throng, calling out words of reassurance and attempting to coax them back to their staterooms.

"Now, how am I supposed to sleep with all this commotion going on?" one gentleman in a bright purple banyan and plaid pajama pants demanded to know. "It sounds like a thousand railway engines thundering through a culvert."

Flora was struck by the rather comic sight of many of her fellow passengers. Normally primped, pressed, and squeezed into corsets and the latest Paris fashions, matrons and gentlemen alike milled about in various stages of undress, wearing a hodgepodge of dressing gowns, fur coats, and slippers, with their hair unbound, tumbling down their backs.

But all amusement fled at the appearance of Mr. Sloper, whose brow was scored with worry. "You've heard, then? About the iceberg? I saw it from the promenade. It was a great monstrous thing. Are they still telling people to return to their staterooms?"

"Yes. Why? What is it?" Flora asked.

Mr. Sloper was rarely serious, but he was deathly earnest now. His gaze swung to Alice. "Because they're uncovering the lifeboats."

Alice knew precisely why William's eyes had sought hers out as he made this pronouncement. She knew it but shied away from it, not wanting to give the thought even the barest consideration. The very notion made her go cold.

"Merely a precaution, I'm sure," Mr. Kinsey proposed, though the way he looked at Flora told her he was more concerned by this development than he wished them to know.

"Yes," Mr. Behr agreed, his thoughts clearly also on the woman he favored as he peered sideways at Miss Newsom. "There must be a procedure they're supposed to follow in the event of an incident at sea. Likely something written up by the head office for liability purposes."

Miss Newsom nodded as if this made complete sense, and Alice supposed it did. But deep inside she wasn't convinced.

"We should make sure your parents are aware of what's going on," Mr. Behr suggested, and the pair headed off toward the staircase.

"Perhaps we should also check on our parents," Alice ventured, hugging her coat tightly around her. She wanted to change into some warmer clothes and put her hair up, too, though she didn't say this aloud, since many of the people around her seemed to be treating this like a farce. They laughed and jested and asked the stewards to bring them drinks.

Which made the ferocious scowl of the man who suddenly appeared behind them all the more alarming.

"What is it, Dodge?" William asked, evidently acquainted with the man.

"Stokers. I saw two stokers on deck." His dark eyes beneath heavy black brows dipped to Alice, and then he drew William aside, muttering something in his ear. Whatever he said made William's back straighten and his head lift like prey scenting danger.

"What? What did he say?" Alice demanded as Dodge moved on. If the other man had seen two stokers, then they must have come from the boiler rooms deep within the ship. Normally, they weren't allowed in the passenger areas, so their presence on deck was cause enough for alarm. But there had to be more to it for it to have unsettled William.

To her everlasting irritation, he ignored her, instead latching onto Mr. Kinsey's arm and whispering in his ear. Alice narrowed her eyes at the men, trying to read from Mr. Kinsey's expression what William might be saying, but Mr. Kinsey proved to possess a superb poker face. She was about to stamp her foot and demand that they tell the rest of them what they were muttering when a woman in a bright kimono rushed up to Mabel.

"Miss Fortune, how glad I am to have found you," she gasped. "Have they explained what's happened? I know we've hit an iceberg. Or"—she glanced over her shoulder—"I've just learned it. But how serious is it?"

Upon her arrival, Mabel's posture had turned rigid, but she softened under the woman's appeal. "I don't know, Miss Young. The stewards have been urging everyone to remain calm and return to their cabins."

Miss Young's eyes searched Mabel's. "But you think there's more to it."

"I . . . I'm uncertain," Mabel admitted.

This seemed enough of a confirmation to Miss Young. "I saw Mr. Andrews below. He told us not to worry, but he was moving rather quickly down the stairs, intent on something."

"Probably inspecting the ship for damage," Charlie offered. Andrews was the ship's architect, after all. He knew the *Titanic* better than anyone.

Miss Young leaned in, lowering her voice so that she could barely be heard above the rumble of other voices and the steam still blowing off above. "And I overheard a man saying that . . . that the Squash Racquet Court is flooding."

This jarred Alice, for the court was only a few decks below their cabin, and if it was flooding, then the hole must be serious, indeed. However, one single hole should be of little danger to the *Titanic*. Though it might prevent them from traveling on to New York. They might have to wait to be transported to another steamer or towed into port. Perhaps this was the whispered warning the Dodge fellow had given to William.

"I promised to keep Miss Gibson apprised," William said before rushing off, leaving Alice to scowl after him.

This seemed to also recall Miss Young to her obligations. "And I should return to Mrs. White. She'll be beside herself with worry and trying to rise from bed on her injured ankle if I don't stop her." She grasped hold of Mabel's hand and squeezed. "Thank you."

"Of course," Mabel said as her friend hurried away.

Alice turned to scrutinize Mr. Kinsey, wondering if she might convince him to tell her what William had confided in him, but the firm resolve in his dark eyes told her not to. "I think we should all return below to dress more warmly."

"Why?" Flora asked. "Mr. Andrews and the crew evidently have matters well in hand. Shouldn't we simply do as we're told and go back to bed?"

Alice frowned, unable to tell whether her older sister actually believed this or if she was simply determined to put on a brave face.

Mr. Kinsey took hold of Flora's hands. "I don't think it would be a bad idea to be prepared. Just in case."

Flora's gaze turned pensive, sensing as Alice did that he wasn't telling them everything.

He squeezed her fingers. "You wished to inform your parents what's happened anyway. So why don't you let your father decide."

His voice was too bright now, something Flora also noted with suspicion, but she reluctantly agreed. "If we return, we'll meet back here?"

"Yes," he promised, and Flora turned as if to shepherd her sisters back down to their cabin, but then wavered. "What of Mr. Ross?" She looked at each of her siblings in turn. "He and Mr. Beattie and Mr. McCaffry should be informed."

Alice hadn't even given their Winnipegger travel companions a thought, but Flora was right. Being ill, Mr. Ross might not even be aware what was going on.

"I'll tell them," Mr. Kinsey volunteered. "I'm acquainted with Beattie and McCaffry, and I'm sure they can point me in Mr. Ross's direction."

"A-10," she told him, even as it was evident that she was wondering, as Alice did, how they had met. Perhaps that was a silly question, considering that all the men seemed to congregate in the Smoking Room whenever they politely could. Mrs. Harris had jested this was their way of preventing the vapors from prolonged exposure to females. A quip that had made Mr. Harris chuckle but the other males within hearing distance scowl.

"Mrs. Harris!" Alice suddenly gasped, startling the others. "Oh, I do hope someone has informed her and her husband. She's the one who broke her arm earlier this evening during a fall down the stairs," she reminded them. She'd done so as they were leaving Mr. Cardeza's poker game.

Alice realized that her chances of winning the day's run had been utterly dashed. Even if the ship was able to begin steaming toward New York again, it would take precious hours if not days to regain her speed and momentum. The most she could hope for was that the contest would be scratched and all of the bidders' money would be returned. That was about a quarter of what she'd taken, but at least it would be *something*.

"Charlie," Mr. Kinsey called after them. "A moment."

Alice looked over her shoulder, suspecting he was about to relay to her brother what William had told him, so that their father could also be informed. A sour feeling filled her stomach, for she felt certain it could be nothing good.

# CHAPTER 30

❧

*Monday, April 15, 1912—12:10 a.m.*

As Charlie hastened after his sisters, Chess felt a strange yawning sensation fill his chest watching them turn to descend the stairs. Part of him felt panicked at the thought of them—of Flora—leaving his sight, but he had several tasks to complete and could do them far more quickly without them in tow. He headed off toward the bow, intent on locating Mr. Ross. Beattie and McCaffry were aware of the iceberg and had almost certainly already alerted their friend, but for Flora's sake, he would make sure of it.

Chess knew that Mr. Ross was ill, so it might take him a considerable amount of time to dress and make his way above deck. If the worst should happen, the fellow should at least be given a fighting chance.

Chess was no expert, but he'd spent enough time sailing to know that the reports he was hearing and his own observations were not adding up to any encouraging result. Both he and Karl had noted the slight list toward the starboard bow. That, coupled with the report of the squash court filling with water, might not have been overly concerning, but Dr. Dodge's testimony from the stokers that water was pouring into the stokeholds below was too much to ignore.

Whatever the truth about the state of the *Titanic*'s seaworthiness, he suspected they would find out soon enough. The captain had undoubtedly ordered the carpenter to sound the ship, and Andrews would be doing his own inspection. It was only a matter of time before a conclusion was made and instructions were given.

With any luck, another ship would reach them before it became necessary to put people out into the lifeboats to transfer them. All the better if they could wait until daylight. Dangling over the side of a massive ship in a tiny boat would be alarming enough without having to do so during the pitch-black night. Their saving grace was that at least the seas were calm. He only prayed they remained that way.

He found A-10 on the port side with relative ease and discovered its occupant already standing, or rather leaning in the doorway in his plaid pajamas. He might have been a good-looking fellow if not for the sickly cast of his features.

"I say, do you know what's going on?" the chap demanded.

"You must be Ross," Chess said. "Miss Fortune sent me. I'm afraid we've hit an iceberg. You'd better dress as warmly as you can and come out to the Boat Deck."

"An iceberg? Is that all?" Ross scoffed, turning back to his bed. "I'm sick. It will take more than an iceberg to get me off this ship."

"You may have no choice," he warned.

Ross waved his hand at him in dismissal.

Chess hesitated. After all, he couldn't force the man to dress and come with him. If Ross chose to remain here, that was his own affair. In truth, it might even be for the best. It would probably be hours before the ship foundered—*if* she foundered, and standing or sitting above deck in the freezing cold couldn't be good for the fellow.

"So be it." His duty to Flora discharged, he nodded his head and turned to go. If he saw Beattie or McCaffry, he would let them know their friend was still below. They could tend to the chap. Chess needed to see to Flora and her family.

He returned the way he'd come, briefly exchanging information with those he passed. No one seemed alarmed, least of all the stewards and stewardesses, who were run off their feet from calls from the passengers wanting news. And all the while, overhead, the funnels continued to blow off steam, a shrill tenor accompaniment to all their thoughts and movements.

As Chess neared the Reception Room, the sound increased in the large, open, dome-topped space. There were lines of people waiting to use the lifts, so he moved toward the stairs. A group of gentlemen, including Colonel Gracie, clustered to one side of the foot of the staircase. They appeared to be examining a round, flat piece of ice and jesting that someone should take it home as a souvenir.

"Kinsey, have a look at this," Gracie said with a chuckle as Chess hurried past.

"Yes, I've seen," he answered without stopping. "The Well Deck is covered with it."

He plunged down the steps, nearly stumbling in his haste, but caught himself on the rail in time. Once he had his feet beneath him again, he moved more slowly. It certainly wouldn't do to take a tumble now and break a limb.

The situation on B-Deck and then C was much the same. Lines of people were waiting for the lifts, and even more were milling about, uncertain of what to do but with little sense of urgency. Lower in the ship, the noise from the funnels was more muted, offering not only a welcome respite but also a lulling sense of security. At this level, one might have feasibly slept through the collision and the ensuing racket unless awakened by the absence of the engines' vibrations. It was a somewhat alarming thought, but surely the stewards would eventually be sent through the entire ship to knock on every door and rouse its occupants. Time enough yet for that.

Trusting that Charlie had made the situation plain to his father, Chess set off down the long corridor to his own cabin. There he pulled on an extra pair of woolen socks and discarded his evening coat for a warm woolen jumper. He stuffed a bit of cash into his overcoat pocket, his grandfather's pocket watch, and a pair of apples. With one last look around at his opulent surroundings, he closed the door, hoping his premonition was wrong and he would be returning in a few hours' time for some much-needed rest.

A few feet along the corridor, he met a fellow pounding on someone's door. "Henry, open up!" he yelled through the wood, loud enough to wake everyone in the neighboring cabins. "This is serious! I heard the captain telling Colonel Astor to get his wife up. That we might have to take to the boats." He looked up as Chess walked past, offering him a pained smile before resuming his pounding. "Brother, please! This is no small matter."

It came as something of a relief to Chess that he wasn't the only one concerned, but if what that fellow had said was true, if the captain had said those words to Colonel Astor, then it meant the situation might be even more serious than he'd assumed. He scowled. Either way, he was determined to be ready, and that Flora and her family would be, as well.

At the base of the Forward Staircase, he hesitated, wondering if he should go to their cabin to prod them along. But they might already be up on A-Deck, waiting for him to return. Electing to stick to the plan, he began to climb, only to have his stomach pitch at the realization that there was now a definite list to starboard. It had been less noticeable in the corridor, but on the stairs it was impossible to miss. If the list was increasing this quickly, that was not a good sign.

Chess took a firm grip on the rail and utilized all his tennis training to propel himself up the stairs as quickly as possible. He needed to find Flora.

# CHAPTER 31

❦

Mabel didn't know exactly what her brother had said to their father. All the men seemed intent on keeping the severity of the situation from the women, as if they couldn't handle the truth. But whatever it was had convinced him that they should all dress in their warmest clothes and go up on deck.

"Is this truly necessary," Flora grumbled to herself as she sorted through the clothing scattered across her bed before sitting down to begin tugging on a warmer pair of stockings. "Everyone knows the *Titanic* can't sink. So, what are we going to do? Traipse about in the cold for no good reason?"

"No good reason?" Alice paused while pulling on a woolen cardigan to protest. "She struck an iceberg!"

Flora shrugged as if this were an everyday occurrence, and Alice drew breath to object again, but Mabel gripped her arm, stopping her. She shook her head.

It seemed perfectly obvious to her that Flora was keenly aware of the potential gravity of the incident. She simply didn't want to acknowledge it, and this bluster was her way of coping. Mabel didn't know why Alice couldn't see this.

For her part, Mabel didn't know what to think. Half an hour earlier, she was lying in bed, ruing her fate, and now she was dressing to go up on deck in the bitter cold of night with her family, preparing to possibly abandon the ship. Everything seemed oddly dreamlike as she debated with herself whether to wear this dress or that hat. And what of her jewelry? Did she take it? Leave it behind?

Alice answered that question by stuffing it all into the pockets of her coat. So Mabel did likewise. Then Father was pounding on their door, telling them to hurry up.

As Mabel had expected, Flora was the last to finish, being hustled out the door by their father himself. He wore his moth-eaten buffalo coat—the one they'd all teased him about. Mabel could only imagine how absurdly pleased he was by the fact that it had proved a useful item to pack, after all.

Mother, on the other hand, eyed it with pinch-lipped disfavor. Or perhaps that was simply her displeasure at having been roused from bed at such an hour. Mother hated to be rushed or to have her routine interrupted in any way, and while appearing elegant as ever, bundled in her dark moleskin coat and hat, she was clearly frazzled.

Despite the wait, Mother insisted they take the lift, and stood griping and commiserating with the other men and women irritated to be woken in the middle of the night by such nonsense. Her remarks only served to irritate Father, but honestly, it was his own fault for not sharing with them all that he knew.

Once back on A-Deck, they discovered the Reception Room to be even more crowded than before. Some had gone below to dress more warmly, as they had, while others were still wearing their pajamas with kimonos or coats thrown over them.

"Where is Kinsey?" Father demanded to know.

"I don't know, Father," Flora replied calmly. "He had to return to his own cabin and ensure Mr. Ross had been roused. But he promised he would meet us back here as quickly as he could, and I'm certain he will."

Their father gave a harrumph, which could have indicated any number of things, and Mabel was not in the mood to translate. Not when she was searching the crowd for her friends—chiefly Marie Young and her injured companion, Mrs. White, as well as Mrs. Candee and her coterie. She thought she spotted Dr. Leader and Mrs. Swift across the room. Strains of music drifted down the corridor leading aft, suggesting the band had begun to play in the Lounge. Although intended to keep them all calm, no doubt, the jaunty notes of Joplin's tune "Pleasant Moments" only served to add to the strange otherworldly atmosphere. Mabel was tempted to pinch herself just to be sure she really was awake.

The door to the Promenade Deck opened behind them as a number of ladies and gentlemen entered, causing the sound of the funnels blowing off to swell.

"Mr. Beattie," Alice called out, recognizing him among their number.

He changed direction toward them.

"What is the matter? You look very grave."

Beattie's eyes swept over the group, including Major Peuchen, who at some point had joined them. "Why, the order for life belts and boats."

Mabel suspected many of them felt as stunned as she did, for no one spoke for a moment. Despite all their precautions, she'd never actually believed they would truly be getting into the lifeboats.

Peuchen, still in evening dress, was the first to find his voice. "Will you tell Mr. Ross?"

"Mr. Kinsey has already gone to do so," Flora informed them. "Though he didn't know about the life belts and boats at the time."

Beattie nodded. "I'll go and see Ross, just to be sure." His mouth flattened. "He's not going to like this order."

After Beattie and Peuchen rushed off, the Fortune family huddled together.

"We shall have to go back for our life belts," Father said. "Or at least someone will."

"I'll go," Charlie offered.

"I'll come with you," Flora chimed in, adjusting her gloves. "You can't carry six of them."

The pair hurried off, and Father lifted his gaze to the Grand

Staircase, which led up to the Boat Deck. Mabel recognized the look in his eyes. She'd seen it many times, including the afternoon before. It was one of dogged resolve.

"Come," he urged them. "I want to see the situation for myself."

"But we told Mr. Kinsey we'd meet him here," Alice protested.

"We'll return," Father replied indifferently. "Or Kinsey can come find us."

Though she knew it was wrong to do so, Alice couldn't help cursing her father, at least in her mind. They'd promised Mr. Kinsey they would meet him on the starboard side of the A-Deck Reception Room. That was also where Flora and Charlie would expect to find them when they returned with all their life belts. Why must they go up to the Boat Deck now to investigate?

As they climbed, Alice discovered there were as many people gathered in the Boat Deck Entrance Hall at the top of the staircase beneath the Art Nouveau frosted dome as below, perched on settees and clustered together in groups, trying to stay warm. When they passed through the doors and out into the night, she was struck by two forces: the biting cold that nipped at the exposed skin of her face, and the wailing of the funnels. Without any walls standing between them and the sound of the escaping steam, the racket rendered communication nearly impossible.

They could see crewmen now, calmly moving about as they uncovered and cleared the lifeboats on the forward part of the ship, following the orders of a grim-faced officer. As of yet, there were not a great deal of passengers on deck, but then they'd been sent below for their life belts. The boat nearest where they stood was being connected to the davits arching overhead, in preparation for loading.

Alice eyed the modest craft—so small and diminutive compared with the enormous *Titanic*. She suddenly remembered the words of the fortune teller in Egypt. *I see you adrift on the ocean in an open boat.* Panic began to build inside her.

As if sensing her distress, Mabel squeezed her hand where she still clutched it and leaned over to yell in her ear. "Just breathe. In and out."

She closed her eyes, realizing the edges of her vision had grown a bit fuzzy, and tried to obey.

"This is just a precaution," Mabel continued. "Following protocol, remember?"

But was it? She'd doubted it when Mr. Kinsey first offered the explanation, and she still did.

Father yelled something at them, but she didn't quite catch what he'd said. Mabel gripped her hand tighter and towed her along beside her. Blinking open her eyes, Alice fastened her gaze on her parents' backs. They stepped through a doorway and into the relative warmth of the Gymnasium.

Alice inhaled, her lungs better able to work without the scream of the funnels piercing her skull so sharply. A number of others were also gathered there, entertaining themselves on the equipment. She remembered how just a few short days ago she and her siblings had done the same. A pair of men sat at the rowing machine, while one lady was riding a stationary bike, and another perched on the electric camel. The large map on the wall showed the *Titanic* perched in the middle of the Atlantic with naught but a vast ocean of blue surrounding the ship. She turned her head away, not wanting to focus on that.

"Perhaps we should return to the Reception Room . . . to wait for instructions," Mother suggested, her face blanched.

Father moved toward one of the large arched windows to look out at the progress on deck. He rubbed his fingers over his mustache. "Yes," he finally murmured. "At least it will be warmer there."

They followed their father, but rather than stopping in the Reception Room, he veered toward the long corridor that led to the Lounge, where the band was playing. Mabel tugged on his sleeve. "Shouldn't we wait here for Flora and Charlie?"

"Your mother needs to sit," he snapped. "They can find us."

She frowned at his back as they hurried away.

"One of us could wait here for them," Alice suggested uncertainly.

The sisters turned to survey the growing crowd. Some now wore their life belts, while others merely draped them around their necks or over their arms. There was a great deal of jesting about how strange they looked. Alice spied several women still in their glittering evening gowns, while others hadn't bothered to change out of their nightclothes. The stewards and even the chief purser's urgings that they go below to dress warmly and fetch their life belts seemed to have little effect on some, while others reluctantly turned to obey.

"Come on," Mabel grumbled, pulling Alice through the throng toward their parents, who were already halfway to the Lounge.

# CHAPTER 32

"Charlie, slow down!" Flora hollered at her brother, who paused on the landing below. "I can't move that fast," she told him crossly, squeezing close to the railing to pass a trio of ladies climbing toward her side by side rather than in single file. They glared at her as if *she* were the one in the wrong.

Once she caught up to him, she latched onto his arm. "Rushing about wildly will not help anyone," she scolded him.

However, Charlie didn't appear in the least affected. "I'm not rushing," he retorted. "You're merely slow!" He looked pointedly at her skirt. "Or your dress is hindering you."

She arched her eyebrows. "Yes, let's just see how fast *you* can run down a flight of stairs in a gown without tripping."

He flashed her a grin. "I'd rather not."

As they turned the corner to descend toward C-Deck, they met a man hurtling up toward them, taking the steps three at a time. It wasn't until he brushed past them that Flora realized it was Mr. Andrews. But when she called his name, he didn't stop or even acknowledge her, disappearing around the bend toward the next flight. For a man who was infallibly amiable and polite, a man who always had a smile for everyone, this was startling, to say the least.

She turned to look at Charlie. He appeared equally taken aback.

"He looked worried," he said.

Mr. Andrews knew the ship better than anyone. If he was worried . . . The thought left her with a horrible, indescribable feeling in the pit of her stomach.

On C-Deck, they discovered dozens of men and women crowded around the window to the Purser's Enquiry Office, insisting their valuables stored in the safes be returned to them. Next to the noticeboard, a woman stood weeping while a man tried to calm her by explaining that they wouldn't sink, but even if they did, they'd sighted seven ships that day. He pointed at the bulletins. One of them would come to assist them. It wasn't until Flora and Charlie had hurried past that she realized the man and woman were the Futrelles.

On their corridor, they found their Irish steward with the gap between his front teeth knocking on doors to rouse people. "The captain says that all passengers are to dress themselves warmly, bring their life preservers, and go up to the top deck," Ryan told them when they reached his side. He scrutinized their attire. "I see you're already halfway there."

"We've come back for our life belts," Flora replied.

He nodded. "Let me know if you need help retrieving them from the tops of the wardrobes."

She remembered the way Mabel had teased the steward about the necessity for life belts on an unsinkable ship and swallowed.

In the end, even with her height, Flora had to rely on Charlie to fetch the life belts. They easily found six, plus an extra, which Flora decided they would take for Chess, just in case. Just before leaving, she went to the sink and filled a cup to drink deeply, thinking of what Shackleton and other explorers had written about the agonies of thirst. "You should drink, too," she told Charlie, feeling a sudden panic seize her that it might be a long time before any of them were able to have water again.

Charlie gathered a few blankets to take with them and, with their seven life belts, they returned to the corridor to find a gentleman in his bathrobe arguing with their steward.

"This is absurd!" he protested. "My wife can't stand around in the cold."

"I understand your frustration, sir. But it is a rule of the Board of Trade—"

"The Board of Trade be damned. You can't sink this ship. No matter what we've struck. She is good for eight to ten hours at least. Long after the sun rises." He slammed his door in Ryan's face, and Flora watched as the steward slowly clenched and unclenched his fingers, plainly battling his irritation.

"Ah, good, you've found the life belts," he said, turning to them. "Do you know how they fasten?" He took the blanket from her and tucked it under his arm before draping one of the white life belts over her head and beginning to tie it around her torso.

Despite his cheery expression and bravado, she could tell he was far from sanguine. "Please, tell me," she begged. "Is it truly serious? Is there really any danger?"

"Danger, miss? Why, it's a rule of the Board of Trade," he said, resuming the same speech he'd been about to give the other man, as if reading it from a script. "That even in the threat of danger, life belts be donned by the passengers. *Not* that I think this ship can sink. She's an unsinkable ship. Everybody knows that." His gaze lifted from the straps to meet hers. "But if she does go down, I'm sure we can cheat the drink for about forty-eight hours. There," he declared with one last tug. "Now, you can help your family with theirs." He grasped her arm somewhat impulsively, staring at her earnestly. "Make sure they wear them, miss. And follow the captain's orders."

She nodded, having trouble finding her voice. "I will. But what about you?"

"Oh, don't worry about me, miss. I can look after myself."

Charlie gripped her elbow, urging her forward.

The life belt proved cumbersome and not altogether comfortable, and her brother wasn't making any allowances for it. She began to perspire beneath her heavy wool-and-fur coat as she struggled to keep up with him. There appeared to be as many people going down as up, and half of those ascending had no life belts with them.

As she brushed past a woman on B-Deck, she heard a yip and a whine and realized the object she was clutching wasn't a baby but a small dog. A Pomeranian, if she wasn't mistaken. In all this mayhem, the pets must be as terrified as the children.

Her heart stuttered as she suddenly thought of Jenny, the ship's cat, and all her kittens. What would become of them? Hadn't the stewardess said a scullion looked after them? A big, quiet fellow whom Jenny adored. Maybe he would get them out.

She paused in the middle of the stairs, turning to peer over the railing back down toward the decks below.

"Miss?" someone behind her protested, pushing against her back and forcing her to begin climbing upward again. All she could do was say a silent prayer for the felines and their keeper.

"Where are they?" Flora asked in bewilderment when they reached A-Deck and saw no sign of their family or Chess.

"Perhaps they went up on deck, like the captain ordered."

"And didn't wait for us?" Her vexation only increased at having to tote her objects up another flight of stairs while wearing her bulky life belt, but at least once they passed through the doors onto the Boat Deck, she was no longer warm. With the funnels roaring, it was virtually impossible to communicate more than a word or two. She saw that the officers tasked with preparing the boat immediately in front of the entrance to the Forward Grand Staircase were resorting to hand gestures and taps on the shoulder. They were working quite efficiently, in fact, and appeared nearly ready to begin loading. A crowd had gathered before the boat, waiting for the order.

Not wanting to be swept toward the bow and the other lifeboats currently being readied, Flora and Charlie headed aft, searching for their parents, sisters, and Chess. Charlie popped his head into the Gymnasium, but then retreated, shaking his head.

Where were they? In the dim lighting, they couldn't see far.

Perhaps they'd missed them? Or maybe they'd gone to the port side of the ship?

They were about to return to the Entrance Hall to cross to the doors leading to the port side when Flora caught sight of Chess standing at the rear of the milling throng. Arched up on his toes, he appeared to be searching the faces of the passengers before him. Flora opened her mouth to shout his name, but then realized the wail of the funnels would drown her out. So instead she plunged forward.

# CHAPTER 33

❧❀❧

Chess had waited for some minutes for the Fortunes to return to the A-Deck Reception Room, but when they didn't appear, he began to suspect Mr. Fortune had already hustled them on deck. If he'd learned anything over the past few days, it was that his future father-in-law was not the most patient of men.

Then Chess had done the same dunderheaded thing he'd accused Mr. Fortune of, and bounded out onto the Promenade Deck, wasting precious seconds searching there before realizing they would more likely have gone up to the Boat Deck. Since he'd now learned that the mail room was flooded and that by all reports water was spilling over into the adjacent cabins with frightening speed, he was even more anxious to see Flora and her family claim seats on one of the lifeboats, just in case, God forbid, the worst happened.

He arrived on deck to find one of the officers—a bluff Scottish fellow—attempting to load the first boat. "'Tis just a precaution," he kept saying with a smile of encouragement. "'Twas perfectly safe," he would add, "as the sea was calm, and it probably wouldna be long before they were brought back on the ship." But while people would approach the boat, most balked at the point of boarding, unwilling to trade the security of the *Titanic* for a rickety little boat out in the great wide ocean.

Eventually, a few boarded, and then a few more—men included, for many of the women would not go without them. The film star, Dorothy Gibson, climbed in, clinging to William Sloper's hand and wailing something about a little gray automobile. A woman in only her bathrobe, slippers, and a steamer cap was then assisted over the gap into the boat. Once all the women and children nearby who were willing to board were loaded, a few groups of men were allowed in, even as their friends yelled at them in jocular voices not to go.

"Chess!"

When he turned and saw Flora, he was so relieved that he pulled her into his arms, ignoring the bulk of the life belt between them as well as her brother.

She cupped her hands around her mouth to yell into his ear. "Have you seen the rest of my family?"

"Maybe they're inside," he yelled back, pointing toward the door. "The Lounge. But there's room in this boat. Why don't you go? Charlie and I will find the rest of your family."

She reared back accusingly, almost as if he'd bitten her. "Sloper is on board."

Her eyes slid toward the boat dangling over the side of the ship, still only about half-full, and then she shook her head stubbornly. "Not without my family."

He stifled a sigh, having already suspected this would be her answer. In any case, it was already too late. Murdoch was instructing the crewmen that had been assigned to the lifeboat to row away a short distance from the ship once they reached the water and stand by the gangway. Then he gave the order to the crewmen manning the davits to lower away. Chess wondered if Murdoch had ordered them to row to the gangway because they intended to load more passengers from the hatches below. This would explain why the craft was half-empty. Then the davits would have less weight to support, and the third class wouldn't have to be herded up to the Boat Deck.

Chess, Charlie, and Flora watched as the boat dropped out of sight, dangling above the sea sixty feet below, then began making their way toward the entrance foyer. Chess stopped short at the sight of Karl standing with Miss Newsom and her parents. As Charlie rushed ahead toward the Lounge, Chess pressed his hand to his friend's shoulder. "Are you trying for the next one?" he yelled into Karl's ear.

Karl nodded. "You?"

"We have to find her family."

His gaze flicked toward where Flora hovered beside him.

"Have the women ask. Then they'll let you in," Chess told him.

Karl acknowledged this information with a dip of his head and then offered Chess his hand. The two shook firmly—a gesture they had exchanged perhaps hundreds of times, including across the tennis court as rivals, but never with the significance it had in that moment.

Karl urged his party toward the boat, where Chess's advice seemed unnecessary. Mr. Ismay himself, in his dressing gown and slippers, coaxed them all to get in. Mr. Andrews was there, too, lending a hand in the loading and trying to persuade the women it was safe.

It was a confusing process, as some of the men were allowed to board without protest, while others were told, "Women and children first." Upon hearing this, Lady Duff-Gordon refused to board, striding off in a huff, which Chess suspected was meant to mask her fear. Though, it seemed, if she'd waited just a moment longer, her husband might have been allowed to accompany her.

There was a commotion near the side of the ship, and Chess turned in time to see two men leap from the railing into the boat Karl had boarded as it began to descend. The passengers surrounding it gasped in shock and alarm. Chess could only hope the men hadn't caused any injuries or, worse, overset the boat. But the tall officer directing the lowering process seemed more angry than concerned. "I will stop that," he shouted loud enough to be heard over the escaping steam. "I will go down and get my gun."

It was a stark reminder that in such situations the officers were charged with maintaining discipline by any means necessary.

He heard a pop like distant gunfire and then saw a white streak arching overhead. A rocket detonated some seven hundred feet in the air, the explosion momentarily lighting up the entire deck in a dazzling flash like the sizzle of a photographer's flash powder, throwing white stars out into the dark sea.

In the blue-white light, Chess caught his first clear view of Flora's face since she'd arrived on deck. Her brow was tight with strain and her eyes bright with fear. Everyone knew what rockets at sea meant. They were a distress call. And a serious one, at that.

As the shower of illumination dissipated, he gave in to impulse, pulling Flora close and pressing his lips to hers. Her breath was warm in the chill air, the skin of her nose and cheek cold, but she kissed him back as eagerly as he had kissed her. When he pulled away, darkness again wrapped the ship, leaving only the dim glow of the deck lights.

"Let's go find your family."

# CHAPTER 34

Mabel possessed a keen appreciation for the absurd, but the scene playing out before her was beyond her ability to perceive.

The orchestra—some in blue uniform coats and some in white jackets—were set up in one corner of the Lounge playing ragtime tunes and waltzes, apparently anything with a lively beat. Currently, the notes of "Oh, You Beautiful Doll" wafted overhead as stewards circulated, serving cocoa, coffee, and brandy. One would have imagined they were at some sort of party, a mad masquerade where those in silk negligees and kimonos lingered beside others in full evening dress or a fellow at his country estate preparing to join a shooting party.

But beneath the chatter and laughter and faux bonhomie ran an undercurrent of fear. It made tempers flare and annoyance spike.

When a passenger arrived with his dog clutched in his arms as one would a baby and began making extravagant demands, no one was in the mood to accommodate him. A woman in a sleek sealskin coat who had arrived in a bit of a tizzy, declaring everything a farce, actually went so far as to tell the man with the dog to "shove off," earning herself a smattering of applause.

Mabel hovered behind the settee where her parents and Alice were perched near the electric fireplace. Mother sat with her shoulders hunched, seeming as chilled as ever. From here they had a clear view of the door, so they could spot Charlie and Flora the moment they arrived.

Alice perked up as a woman entered carrying two life belts, dressed elegantly in a black velvet suit with white silk lapels, a sable fur draped over her shoulders, beckoning her closer and introductions were swiftly made.

"What a night!" Mrs. Brown declared, allowing her sable fur to droop. "I could scarcely believe it when my steward told me to dress and come up on deck. But now they appear to be making us wait."

A woman wrapped in chinchilla sidled closer, leaning in to speak directly in Mrs. Brown's face. "Didn't I tell you something was going to happen?" she declared almost triumphantly, before carrying on, her maid trailing after her.

"Yes, Emma. Yes, you did," Mrs. Brown responded before rolling her eyes. "She's only reminded me every time she's seen me. Though I suppose it's because of her benighted premonition that I put this in my pocket for luck."

She removed a small turquoise object, opening her hand so that they could see it. Mabel realized it was a tomb figure from Egypt. A merchant in Cairo had tried to sell them one, purporting they brought good fortune.

"You'd be better served to put your faith in the Lord, Mrs. Brown, than such idolatry," Father replied sternly.

But Mrs. Brown remained unruffled. "Yes, I know. Truth be told, I simply wanted a souvenir, and a pretty one it is."

Mabel noted how Alice's hands had tightened in her lap, the knuckles showing white, and wondered if Mrs. Brown's talk of Cario and fortunes had made her think of that soothsayer. None of them had given the man's words much consideration, but it was impossible not to feel at least a little unnerved by them now.

"Good evening, ladies. Or is it morning?" The steward who appeared before them proclaimed with false cheer. "Captain's orders are for everyone to put on a life belt. I see you have yours," he said to Mrs. Brown, before removing one that was draped over his arm and dropping it over Mabel's head. "Try this on for size." He chuckled, beginning to fasten it. "It's the very latest fashion. All the stylish people are wearing them."

"Oh, but our brother and sister have gone to fetch ours from our cabin," she protested.

"No matter. They're all the same. Simply leave any extras draped over this settee for others to claim." Finishing with one last tug, he moved on to Mrs. Brown. "Shall I help you with yours, madam?"

Mabel stared down at the offensive-looking drab white garment, suddenly feeling marked and exposed, and less sangfroid than she had a moment before. Even the music seemed to take on a groggy tinge, as if the tuning on some of the instruments was too flat. She gripped the back of the settee lest she topple over.

Then Charlie burst through the door. "Here you are," he declared, quite unnecessarily as he hastened toward them. "We couldn't find you!" He thrust a life belt into each of their parents' and Alice's hands, and upon discovering Mabel already outfitted, pulled the last one over his head. "We also brought blankets, thinking we might need them."

Mother accepted this last offering with more verve. "Thank you, dear. That was very thoughtful. But where is your sister?"

Charlie looked behind him, as if surprised Flora wasn't with him. "We must have gotten separated on the Boat Deck. They're already loading and launching the boats."

This last statement struck Mabel in the chest.

"Into the water?" Alice asked faintly.

"Just as a precaution. They're sending the women and children, and some of the men, off in the lifeboats until the ship can be properly inspected, and then they'll bring everyone back on board. Board of Trade regulations and such. I heard one gentleman say that an officer had told him the Marconi operators have been exchanging wireless messages with several ships nearby who are ready and able to come assist should it be needed."

This, at least, was reassuring news. Surely if the *Titanic* was sinking, they would already be steaming to their rescue.

"Is Flora waiting for us on deck?" Mother asked, sounding as if that were the last place she wished to be.

"She and Kinsey and I were all headed to the Lounge together." Charlie turned to look toward the door again. "So they should be along shortly."

The band broke off, and voices began hushing one another as a steward stepped forward, trying to gain everyone's attention. "Women and children will kindly proceed to the Boat Deck," he pronounced in a booming voice, before reiterating, "women and children only." With a nod to the musicians, he turned to go.

Before they could put bow to string, Mabel noted the sudden silence. "Listen!"

The others paused to do so, and Alice's eyes widened. "The steam stopped blowing off."

"Finally!" Father exploded. "It was about to drive me mad."

At that moment, Flora and Mr. Kinsey stumbled through the door. "They've already launched two boats," she told them. "And they're loading a third. I saw Mrs. Hays and her daughter, Orian, being hustled into it, along with Vera Dick and a few others." She looked at Alice. "Mr. Sloper left in the first boat."

"They're firing rockets," Mr. Kinsey pronounced solemnly to their father.

This seemed to contradict what Charlie had just told them. She turned to eye her younger brother suspiciously. Had he been trying to reassure them by lying? If so, he'd done so unabashedly, for he didn't even flush under her scrutiny.

"Then let's get these ladies on deck," Father said, pushing to his feet.

"I'll not leave you," Mother protested, clutching his arm as she joined him. Her face was as white as a sheet.

He patted her hand. "And perhaps you won't need to. If Mr. Sloper was allowed to go, then they're allowing some gentlemen to board."

But Mabel knew that voice. Mother would know it, too. Father was placating her. However, Mother simply clutched his arm more tightly, playing along with the fiction.

They made their way along the corridor, through the Reception Room, and up the Grand Staircase to the Boat Deck entrance, where a steward was directing women to the port side and men to the starboard, but Father, Charlie, and Mr. Kinsey ignored this directive and remained with them. They pushed their way through the exit onto the crowded deck, discovering the boat directly in front of them nearly loaded.

There was a point of light coming from the boat, and Mabel thought at first it was a lantern, but it was too small and swung about with too great a frequency to be such a thing. It puzzled her at first until she realized what it was—an electric light affixed into the handle of a walking stick. Mrs. White owned such a device. Marie had described it to her.

Arching up onto her toes, she could, indeed, spy the imperious woman seated in the bow of the boat, gesturing with her opera cane as if she intended to instruct the crewmen on their jobs. A fact that at least one of the officers did not appreciate. He turned his head aside, blinking as if something were in his eyes and then snapped at another crew member. "Tell her to switch it off or I'll throw the damn thing overboard."

Without the roar of the steam escaping the funnels, Mabel could hear the officers' voices quite clearly, along with the subtle creaks and groans of the ship in the cold. Mabel tipped her head backward, marveling at the clarity of the stars overhead, and then at her ability to pay them the smallest heed given the events unfolding before her. As she stood squarely facing the port side of the ship, she could feel the deck slanting toward the bow, so that her right foot bore slightly more of her weight. Yet some of the people before her seemed oblivious.

Several women got to the point of climbing into the boat, only to turn back, refusing to leave their husbands. First it was a pair of young ladies who appeared to be almost newlyweds, and then an older woman, who went as far as stepping onto the gunwales before passing her fur coat to another woman in the boat and retreating. Mabel realized this last woman was Mrs. Straus. She clung to her husband, who was demanding to know why she had not gone.

"We have lived together for many years," she told him. "Where you go, I go!"

An officer tried to convince her to reconsider, but she shook her head. "I will not be separated from my husband. As we have lived, so we will die, together."

Mabel flinched, glancing anxiously toward where her mother gripped her father's arm.

The officer in charge stepped back, giving the order for the boat to be lowered. Mabel spied a number of familiar faces seated within, including those of the Countess of Rothes, her cousin, and the pretty Spanish bride wailing almost inconsolably for her husband, who was still on deck. Among the passengers were also Dr. Leader, Mrs. Swift, and Marie Young perched beside Mrs. White. She felt a sharp pulse of anxiety for them but also relief that they had made it on board.

As the boat began its descent, Captain Smith himself picked up a basket that appeared to hold bread and passed it across. "There is a light out there," he told the crewman in charge of the craft. "Take the women to it and hurry back as speedily as possible."

This caused a surge of hope in more than Mabel's breast as they all turned their heads, straining to see in the direction the captain had pointed. True to his word, there *was* a light—faint, but noticeable. It must be another ship. The Marconi operators must be communicating with it, just as Charlie had said. She turned to him and impulsively hugged him from the side.

A rocket burst overhead, drawing their gazes upward to watch the falling white stars, and she found herself praying. Praying that they would all be saved, that they would all be preserved. If so, she promised she would stop all her petty rebellions and find a way to come to terms with her father.

It all seemed so absurdly insignificant now.

Alice's eyes widened as a commotion farther along the deck drew her attention. A mass of men had emerged onto the Boat Deck. Their faces were streaked with grime and soot, their eyes rimmed in red, and they each appeared to be carrying their dunnage bags.

Stokers.

Though she'd never seen one before, she was quite certain that's who they were, and that their presence on deck was not only unprecedented but alarming.

One of the officers stepped forward, shouting, and ordering them back below. They all turned and silently complied.

Alice scrambled to process what this meant. Had they been flooded out of their quarters? Would they be allowed to come back on deck later? Would there be enough boats for them as well as for all the passengers? She had absolutely no idea.

She allowed herself to be carried along with the crowd of passengers gathering before the next lifeboat as the officers began loading it. Mrs. Candee was handed in by Mr. Woolner, stumbling as she stepped down into it. Several of the wives who had previously balked at entering the boat that had just been lowered were helped over the side of this one. One boarded only after her husband reminded her of their one-year-old daughter back home.

Alice could tell that her mother was nervous, and she and her sisters all hesitated to step forward to board until she did. Father would expect them to care for Mother. But what if she backed out as Mrs. Straus had?

"Excuse me, please," said a voice behind her. "*Excusez-moi, s'il vous plaît.*" She shifted to allow a young man carrying a white-haired woman to pass. It was Quigg Baxter from Montreal, cradling his mother while his sister Zette trailed behind them.

The officers took great care, helping the Baxter women into the boat and settling them comfortably.

Quigg then retreated through the crowd, only to reappear with another woman on his arm. She was quite beautiful and wore a long woolen motor coat over naught but a pair of slippers. When Quigg tried to hand her up into the boat, she began to protest. "I will not go without you," she pleaded in French, and when that had no effect. "My jewels! I must get them from my cabin."

Mrs. Brown, who had also been standing nearby, stepped forward. "I'm afraid you really must board, my dear. It's merely a precaution."

Between her and Quigg, they finally convinced the young woman to board, and Quigg proceeded to introduce the bemused woman to his equally perplexed mother and sister. "Look after her," he instructed his mother, as if it were the most natural thing in the world. Reaching into his coat, he produced a silver flask and took a long drink before passing it over to his mother. "You'll need this to keep warm out on the open sea."

"Is this brandy?" his mother demanded in outrage. "What have I told you about drinking?"

But Quigg cut her off with unruffled composure. "Are you comfortable, Maman?" He blew her a kiss. "Goodbye. Good hope to you and the others."

"Unhand me!"

Alice turned to see Mrs. Brown being lifted by a seaman and dropped into the boat, too, to her great indignation. One look at Mother's face told her there would be no hope of getting her into that boat now, and Alice silently cursed the sailor. The order was given to lower away, and Alice stepped up to the rail to peer over as it inched downward. Too late, she realized this was a bad idea, for her mother and sisters joined her.

It seemed tremendously dark out there, far beyond the reach of the ship's lights. From this height they couldn't even see the water below, so the little boat seemed to be dropping away into nothingness. Alice's stomach lurched and a wave of fear rolled up inside her.

It didn't help that the crew appeared to be struggling with the falls. The occupants had to reach out to push away from the *Titanic*'s hull. When one end of the boat suddenly pitched lower than the other, it threatened to capsize them all into the icy sea fathoms below. Fortunately, the officers soon righted her, but the crewman in charge of the boat yelled up that he had no seaman to help him row.

"Any seaman there?" the officer on deck yelled, turning to look about him.

When no one answered, Major Peuchen stepped forward. "Can I be of any assistance?"

The officer looked him over. "Are you a seaman?"

"I am a yachtsman, and can handle a boat with an average man, if I can be of any use to you."

"Better go down below and break a window to reach the boat," Captain Smith, standing nearby, suggested.

But the other officer seemed to have a different opinion. "If you're seaman enough to get out on those falls and down into the boat, then you may go ahead."

Even though Major Peuchen was not a young man, he gamely grabbed hold of a loose rope dangling from the davit arm and swung himself out over the ship. They watched with bated breath as he scrabbled down perhaps thirty feet of rope and dropped into the boat. Alice laughed in delighted relief and turned to share it with her sisters, only to discover that Mother had retreated from the rail.

"I'm not going without you. I'm not going without you," she kept repeating to Father despite his protestations.

Father gathered her close, retreating toward the door. "Give us a moment."

As they disappeared inside, Alice realized she could hear music again, but much closer. It was coming from just inside the

First-Class Entrance under the glass dome. It was disorienting to hear a Schubert waltz, as if one part of her brain were trying to tell her everything was all right while the other was communicating that it clearly was not.

All four Fortune siblings and Mr. Kinsey turned to look at one another, uncertain of what to do. They couldn't leave the ship without Mother. It was out of the question. But what if Father couldn't convince her?

They watched as the ship's officers and most of the crewmen still on deck moved aft, toward the lifeboats there. Another boat still dangled from its davits next to the one still being lowered, but the empty vessel appeared to have been dropped to the level of the A-Deck promenade and then abandoned.

"They forgot the forward promenade is enclosed," Charlie deduced as they peered over the side of the ship at it. "They must be having trouble opening the windows."

In the meantime, they'd elected to load the other boats still at Boat Deck level.

"Should we wait here or move aft so we can claim seats in those boats when Mother returns?" Mabel asked.

"I don't know," Alice admitted, noting that Flora and Mr. Kinsey had their heads together, murmuring animatedly about something. "What do you think, Flora?"

Flora looked up, all but ignoring her question. "We're going over to the starboard side to see if we might have a better chance there. The officer loading the boats on that side was not being so stringent about only allowing women and children. If Mother won't go without Father, then perhaps if they'll let Father and Charlie board . . ." She didn't finish the sentence and didn't need to. Alice understood her meaning. Just as she didn't need to explain when she turned to peer up at Mr. Kinsey with both hope and terror in her eyes.

"Go," she replied. "But hurry! We'll wait here."

Mr. Kinsey gripped Flora's hand, and they made their way inside to cross to the starboard side of the ship.

Shouts came from the aft of the ship, and Alice turned to see a large mass of people gathering there. While matters had been progressing relatively calmly and orderly before, there was now a growing frenzy in everyone's voices and movements. Another rocket flashed overhead. Her words caught in her throat when the illumination revealed just how much lower the bow was than it had been when the last rocket exploded.

"I'll . . . I'll go see what the situation with the aft boats is," she stammered, finding herself anxious to move away from the water slowly crawling higher along the bow, even though that meant temporarily leaving her brother and sister behind.

"I'll go with you," Charlie offered.

Mabel nodded. "I'll wait here for the others."

Alice tucked her hand in her pocket, feeling the jewelry she'd stowed there. A swift look down the deck told her it was even more crowded than before. "But first, take these," she told her brother, passing over the trinkets. "For safekeeping."

He accepted them without argument, not needing to be told why she was giving them to him.

"Mine, too," Mabel said.

With their jewelry secured in his pockets, Charlie took hold of Alice's arm to guide her down the deck, where it seemed they were loading the aft-most boats first. Clusters of people—many of them men—gathered around them all, jostling for position. Yet there were still some wives as reluctant to leave their husbands as Mother had been. In some instances, the husbands and seamen had to work together to tear the women away from their spouses and force them into the boats. "Go, Lotty!" one man shouted. "For God's sake, be brave and go. I'll get a seat in another boat."

It was increasingly clear just how anxious the officers and crewmen were becoming to fill the boats and get them away.

They were less inclined to listen to anyone's objections, instead forcing them into the boat despite their wishes. Children were even snatched off the deck and out of mothers' arms and passed over the side to be looked after by strangers. "Stand back!" they ordered. "Stand back and let the women get into the boats."

The farthest aft boat began to lower away, much fuller than the previous boats they'd seen lowered, and just a short time later the boat next to it was ready to descend. One of the younger officers, a Welsh fellow who, while boyish in appearance, possessed a keen sense of authority, had taken control of the loading, and he kept having to yell at men who jumped in ahead of some of the women. "Get out and be a man! We have women and children to save."

Finally, he'd had enough. Pulling his revolver from his pocket, he fired it into the air, making people gasp in alarm. "Stand back! I say, stand back! The next man who puts his foot in this boat, I will shoot him down like a dog."

Several more women were loaded, and then the young officer stepped into the boat and gave the order for it to lower away. Some moments after it dipped out of sight, they heard three more gunshots, though they weren't close enough to see what had happened.

Alice turned to her brother with wide eyes. She hoped Flora and Chess had found the loading process to be calmer on the starboard side, but, regardless, they were running out of time and boats. Whereas earlier, there seemed to be more than enough of both, now there was far too little. Everything had compressed and turned in on itself.

"Let's return to Mabel," Charlie suggested, draping a protective arm around her.

They kept close together, squeezing between the people crowded around the next boat in line as it loaded. Some of the passengers' eyes looked wild, and there was a great deal more pushing and shoving than before. So much so that one stewardess was bumped over the ship's edge, mercifully landing in a lifeboat.

Once past, Alice and Charlie hurried toward the bow of the ship, now having to mind their steps because of the increasing slant, but Mabel still stood alone. Where were the others?

# CHAPTER 35

❧✦❧

Flora and Chess hurried through the door on the starboard side—the jaunty strains of "Alexander's Ragtime Band" echoing after them—to discover with a lurch in her heart that all the forward boats were gone. Even worse, as they neared the Bridge, they could see water beginning to creep over the forecastle.

"Dear God in heaven," Flora murmured at the sight, fully comprehending for the first time that the *Titanic* and everyone on board were in mortal danger.

Chess gripped her hand and towed her after him toward the aft deck.

Her legs burned as they raced along the tilting deck, and her breath escaped in puffs in the cold air. All four of the aft lifeboats were filling fast with passengers. However, the last three boats had been lowered to the level of the open A-Deck promenade below and were being loaded there. The only remaining boat on their level would soon be sent away, so if they had any hope of boarding one of these boats, it would be from those at the deck below.

A swift survey of the occupants of the boat before them showed there were a smattering of men seated with the women. Mrs. Futrelle waved to Flora from her bench, and the Scottish officer turned to look at her. "Come on, then, lass," he urged her. "There's room."

Flora shook her head and backed away, but Chess prevented her.

"You should go."

She glared at him, her heart pounding wildly in her chest. "Not without my mother and sisters."

When it seemed he would protest further, she dodged around him, marching back toward the First-Class Entrance. His arm grasped hers from behind and she began to fight, afraid he intended to force her into the boat.

"Wait, Flora," he pleaded. "I merely meant to tell you there's a shortcut to the other side."

She stopped struggling, her breath leaving her in a ragged exhale, and peered up into his shadowed eyes, grateful she wouldn't yet have to say goodbye. He took her arm, steering toward a narrow passage which cut between the raised roof over the Smoking Room and the dome over the rear First-Class Entrance. As they neared the opposite end of the passageway, another rocket burst in the sky above, revealing a pile of luggage they diverted around. She heard some of the passengers imploring the officers to allow them to take their bags, but they were each denied, and the suitcases tossed in the growing heap.

A few men stood off to the side, jesting about their hysterics over their pitiful baggage until someone snapped at them to shut up. "It's all the possessions they have in the world, and they've not the funds to replace them. You'd be begging to keep them, too."

The calmness and order which had reigned on the starboard side had disintegrated into madness here as they struggled to get the next boat away while the previous boat was tangled in its falls.

Flora firmly believed their best chance was to go down to the A-Deck promenade where the last three aft starboard boats were loading. There, they might at least have a chance of the men joining them. She intended to tell her family exactly this, but when they arrived, Father had already decided on another plan.

"You, your sisters, and your mother will get in this boat. Number ten, the officer told me."

Flora's chest flooded with panic. "Father, there are three boats on the other side."

"We need only one."

"Yes, but they are letting the men in."

"Ahead of the women?" he asked incredulously.

"If there are no women nearby. Or if the women insist they must come."

He gestured broadly with his hands. "Then they should send some of these women over there."

"But they aren't and there are empty seats. Why should you not go?" She looked at Charlie and then Chess, their visages swimming before her eyes. "Why should you not all go?"

"Flora, pull yourself together and listen to yourself," Father barked. "I will not take a seat which should belong to a woman. I will not dishonor myself in such a manner. And neither will your brother or Mr. Kinsey."

Flora straightened her backbone, her stubbornness rearing its ugly head. "Then I won't go either."

"Now, see here," Father began, but she was already backing away, holding her hands before her.

"I won't. I won't." She turned to flee as he reached for her, dashing up the deck toward the First-Class Entrance.

"Flora!" he shouted, followed by another cry from one of her sisters, but she ignored them, darting around a couple.

This was all nonsense anyway. None of this could be happening. Not truly. It must be a dream. A very bad dream. Likely brought on by talk of her sister's fortune. Soon she'd wake up safe in her bed and have a good laugh at the preposterousness of it all.

Why the band was even playing "The Glow-Worm" as if to mock her as she hurtled through the door and down the Grand Staircase. They wouldn't have chosen such a lively tune at a moment like this if there was actually something to be feared. If it was anything more than her fevered imagination. Even the way her feet fumbled on the stairs, as if the angle of the steps, the very laws of physics were different here, convinced her this could not be real.

But then why was she still running when she could hear Chess calling her name? Why was her skin slick with sweat and her throat dry and her stomach heaving? Why was her heart beating so hard and her breath sawing in and out of her chest so fast that she was beginning to see white spots at the corners of her vision? Yet she couldn't stop running, she wouldn't stop running. Because if she did . . . if she did . . .

It might all be true.

"Flora!" Mabel yelled, but Flora was off like a shot, her skirts crumpled in her fists. Mabel turned to follow, but Chess reached out a hand to stop her.

"I'll go," he told them with a sideways hop. "Just get them seats on that boat," he directed Father. Then he was off, too, his long strides eating up the expanse of the deck.

"Of all the times to behave so foolishly," Father pronounced gruffly, pounding the rail as he turned to stare out over the dark water drawing ever closer. "I don't understand what has gotten into her."

"She's terrified," Mabel said. She looked up as another rocket burst, waiting until the white stars raining down had reached the water to continue. "And I can't say I blame her."

They heard the captain's voice coming from the direction of the bow. "How many of the crew are in that boat? Get out of there, every man of you!" He must have been using a megaphone. It was the only way the sound could have reached them when they couldn't even see the captain from their vantage.

Mabel turned toward where the next aft boat had been lowering, creaking on its davits, but the officer that had overseen its loading was no longer there. They'd assumed he would move on to number ten next, but where had he gone? The other officer had moved forward to start filling the smaller boat near the Bridge, but now the second man was gone as well.

"Perhaps we should try for that forward-most boat?" she suggested as Charlie strode off a short distance in that direction, apparently trying to find out what was going on.

"Dashing about will do us no good," Father stated firmly. "We stay here. They'll have to fill this one soon, and then we'll be ready."

"Mrs. Allison," Mother gasped as a woman dragging a little girl behind her rushed past with a man trailing in their wake.

Mrs. Allison halted midstride. "Mrs. Fortune! Have you seen my baby?" She grasped Mother's sleeve, still gripping the little girl's hand with her other. "Have you seen Trevor? His nanny took off with him and we can't find him. Oh, that thoughtless woman!"

She was hysterical. Her little girl—the same little girl she'd brought down to the Dining Saloon just hours before so she could show her how pretty everything was—looked on with large, frightened eyes, a doll clutched under her arm.

Mr. Allison tried to calm his wife, but she shook him off.

"Mrs. Allison, surely your maid has already taken him into one of the boats," Mother said.

"But why didn't she wait for us? Why didn't she let us know?"

Mabel's gaze dropped to the terrified little girl, listening to everything being said. She was only two or three, and entirely reliant on her parents. Mabel remembered seeing her in the Verandah Café. She'd sat with her legs swinging, eager to play with the other children, but even more eager for her mother's approval. Could she even swim?

"My sister Flora said she saw your nanny board one of the boats on the starboard side with your baby," Mabel stated, before she could think better of it.

"She did?" Mrs. Allison's hand released Mother's sleeve to grasp Mabel's. "She knows what Miss Cheaver looks like? What Trevor looks like? Where is she? Your sister." Her eyes darted around the members of their party until they landed on Alice, who shook her head.

"Not here at the moment," Mabel demurred. "But she *told* me she saw the Allisons' nanny and their baby."

This was a blatant lie, but one she felt no qualms in telling. Not when this woman was out of her mind, and her daughter was about to pay the price for it. If she thought she could have gotten away with it, she would have told Mrs. Allison *she'd* been the one to see her nanny board with Trevor, but she had been afraid her family would contradict her. Flora, on the other hand, had been on the starboard deck twice without any other witnesses except Chess.

But apparently this wasn't enough for Mrs. Allison. "I need to see him for myself," she declared, beginning to pull her daughter away.

"But they've already gone," Mabel insisted. "They're far from the ship by now."

"At least, leave your darling girl with us while you look," Mother suggested. "It's Lorraine, isn't it?" she asked the child, who stared back at her with wide eyes. "We'll keep her safe for you, and you'll be able to search faster."

"Yes, think of the child, Allison," Father chimed in to say to the girl's father.

"I *am* thinking of the child," Mrs. Allison shrieked. "Lorraine is staying with me." Then she strode off before they could stop her, the girl running alongside her. Mr. Allison trotted after them.

"We can't just let her go," Mabel protested. "All the boats are nearly gone."

Father wrapped his arm around her, pulling her close to his side.

"You did your best, Mabes." His use of his pet name for her caught her so off guard that she turned her face into his chest, inhaling the moldering scent of buffalo fur. "All we can do is pray they find their son and his nanny."

So her father knew she'd been lying, and yet he didn't scold her. That was perhaps a first. And possibly a last. Mabel was on the verge of sobbing. Only the sound of a Scottish officer's stern voice kept her from crumpling.

"You and you," he shouted to two seamen. "Get this boat off her chocks."

Despite the frenzied nature of the work and the crush of desperate passengers filling the deck, the officer worked with calm precision, his face a pale mask of determination. If not for the glimpse of the revolver he clutched in his hand hidden in the folds of his long coat, Mabel might have believed him entirely unfazed by the events unfolding.

Once the boat was swung out and level with the deck, they began boarding. Except Flora still hadn't returned. But if they waited for her, there might not be seats left for any of them.

A whistle blew toward the bow, and the captain's voice rang out from his megaphone again. "Bring those boats back, they are only half filled! Go round to the starboard side to the gangway doors."

With those words, Father's decision was made. He grasped Mabel with one hand and Mother with the other and towed them toward the Scottish officer. "I've three ladies here!"

Mabel glanced over her shoulder to see Alice trailing behind them with Charlie.

The Scottish officer gestured the three women forward, but Father and Charlie were kept from getting too close to the boat.

"I won't leave you," Mother told Father tearily.

He clutched her shoulders. "Yes, you will. Your girls need you, remember. I love you, Mary." He pressed a forceful kiss to her temple and then turned her firmly toward the lifeboat. "Now, go!"

As Mother staggered forward, accepting the Scottish officer's assistance, Father hugged Mabel once more. "Mabes, I love you," he said into her ear, offering her a smile and a wink as he pulled back. "Don't worry, my dear, your mother will take care of you. I'll find Flora, and we'll be on the next boat."

Mabel's hand was gripped by the officer, and she was drawn to the rail.

At some point during the evening, the tilt Mr. Kinsey and Mr. Behr had noticed shortly after the collision with the iceberg had apparently shifted to port. For now, the list was so pronounced that there was a two-and-a-half-foot gap between the ship's hull and the lifeboat. Her heart surged into her throat as she was told to leap across it.

She looked at the officer as if he'd lost his mind.

"You'll have to do it, lass. Your mam made it, and you will, too." He nodded toward the fellow standing in the bow of the boat. "Seaman Evans will catch ye."

"Aye, lass. Come on!" the seaman yelled in encouragement.

There was nothing for it. She jumped. The cold air rushed past her cheeks as she hurtled through the air and then landed with a thud, the seaman's hands gripping her tightly. She gasped in relief, nearly toppling backward until he righted her. Pressing a hand to her back, he pointed her toward the other seaman, who was helping her mother onto a bench.

Many of the boats they had watched leave might have only been half-full, but that was not to be the case with this one. It being the last boat on the port side, the officers seemed intent on filling it to capacity, and as quickly as possible. One crew member dressed all in white—perhaps a baker—kept returning to the side of the ship with children in his arms, and hurling them across to Evans, who blessedly caught them. It might have been shocking if not for the urgency they all now felt to save as many people as possible. Having allowed Alice to sit next to Mother, Mabel gathered several of these children close to her side, trying to comfort them as best she could and hoping their mothers would soon follow.

As one unfortunate woman in a black dress was attempting to make the leap, her heel snagged on the edge of the deck, and she plummeted through the gap with a scream that rent the trembling night air. Mabel cringed, bracing for the worst for the woman, but fortuitously someone on A-Deck below reached out and caught her, hauling her back aboard the ship. A few minutes later she made the attempt to cross the gap again and was successful.

The boat was filling fast, yet still there was no sign of Flora. Fearing she'd missed her in her distraction settling the women and children around her, she turned to look at Alice, whose arm was draped around their mother's huddled form. Before she could even speak, Alice shook her head in the negative.

Of all the times for Flora to turn truculent. Where had she run to? Had Chess been able to catch her? Flora was more clever than most people gave her credit for. If she didn't want to be found, Mabel imagined she could manage it. But then that would defeat the purpose of her revolt, would it not?

No, Flora wouldn't be cowering. She might have, for a moment, lost herself in blind panic, but she would have righted herself again. She would have gone to the starboard side to try to secure places for them all on one of the boats there, and Chess must be trying to convince her to board a boat there. That made sense. That made perfect sense.

Still, when the officer pronounced the boat full and ordered it lowered away, Mabel nearly screamed at him to stop, to wait for her sister. But there were almost sixty women and children crowded in the seats around her. There was no room for Flora, and, besides, what right did she have to risk their lives for hers?

Mabel turned blindly toward the rail as the craft began its descent by fits and jerks. Father and Charlie stood watching, smiling and waving as if sending them off on an afternoon jaunt. Just over their shoulders, she spied Mr. Beattie and Mr. McCaffry, both men as calm and cheerful as the rest of the husbands and fathers lining the railing of the ship to see the boats away.

It was all Mabel could do not to begin blubbering at the sight. Father and Charlie had told them they would catch another boat, but it was crystal clear now that was impossible. Just as it was apparent that the ship that the captain had told some of the boats to row toward—the one whose light could be sighted in the distance—was not coming to help them. Or if it was, that it wouldn't arrive in time.

As they continued their descent, she strained to keep Father and Charlie in her sight. Her last glimpse of them was bathed in the blue-white light of an exploding distress rocket, their expressions as genial as ever. Behind her, Mother gave a trembling sob.

However, the excitement in their little boat was not yet over. As they lowered past A-Deck, first one man and then another jumped over the side of the ship and into their vessel, landing on one woman who shrieked in outrage. They both swiftly dropped out of sight, likely rolling beneath the benches in fear they would be ejected from the boat. But there were few seamen in their craft, and they were occupied with lowering the falls. Not only did they have to contend with the *Titanic*'s port list, but also the fact she was quite alarmingly down at the bow, complicating matters.

The nearer they drew to the water—passing alternatingly through light and shadow as they lowered past each deck of portholes illuminated from within—the more obvious this became. When the boat finally landed on the water with a bone-jarring thump, the seamen struggled to release the falls. She didn't know what the trouble was, whether the ropes were tangled or the mechanism was broken, but their efforts weren't helped by the splashes of people jumping or falling into the frigid water all around them from the decks above, or the unnerved ramblings of one of the other crewmen. "Hurry up! The boilers may explode at any moment."

This possibility was something Mabel hadn't considered. Neither had most of the other women in the boat if their sudden cries of alarm were anything to judge by.

"Shut it!" one of the seamen snapped at him. "We're workin' as fast as we can."

"Well, work faster!" the fellow barked.

Once the boat was free, the oars were pulled out and they began to row away from the ship at a somewhat beleaguered pace, for already there was another problem. There weren't enough seamen in the boat to manage the oars and the tiller. A pair of women volunteered to help.

"I can row," Mabel said, speaking up. "I'll take my turn when you need relief," she told them. Several other women, including Alice, chimed in to say the same.

There was another boat just ahead of them, closer to the bow, and it was rowing about, picking up some of those who had jumped from the ship and were now treading in the icy water. But weighted down as they were at full capacity, the crew members of Boat 10 hauled hard on the oars, ordering the women rowing to do the same. There were frantic murmurings about the suction the ship might create as she sank. A factor that, judging from their straining muscles and chalk-white faces, the sailors took seriously.

# CHAPTER 36

❧

*B loody hell*, Chess swore to himself. *She's fast.*

Flora darted down the steps and across the Entrance Hall still filled with people. Why were they not trying for the boats? She raced down the corridor and passed the Reading and Writing Room to the Lounge. Here she struggled with the door, buying him a few precious seconds. But she still managed to dash across the Lounge and skirt through the opposite door before he could stop her. At the revolving door into the corridor that led to the Aft Staircase and the Smoking Room, Chess saw his chance.

She plunged inside, pushing the door on its axis, but before the glass in front of her could reach the opening, he stopped it with the hard plant of his foot against the rear divider of the next section, effectively trapping her inside. Such was her momentum, that she ricocheted off the pane of glass and staggered backward. When she turned toward him, her eyes were wide with incomprehension, the pupils nearly swallowing the irises.

"No!" she gasped, stumbling toward the glass closer to him. "Let me . . . go."

She was struggling to catch her breath and so, lest she lose consciousness, he released his foot, pushing the door forward.

She tumbled out, catching herself from falling at the last moment with a hand to the floor. But before she could take more than two steps, he wrapped an arm around her from behind and hauled her back against him.

"No," she protested again, gasping for air. Her skin was pale.

"You have to slow your breathing, Flora," he told her calmly as he propped her up against the wall. "Or you're going to faint."

"Can't," she panted, closing her eyes.

"Flora, look at me," he urged, cradling the back of her neck with one hand and her face with the other. He wished he could get closer, but her life belt and the one still draped over his arm prevented him. "Flora."

Her eyes opened to slits. "Purse your lips. Draw your air in and exhale through that. Yes, like that. Very good," he coaxed, kneading the back of her neck with his fingers. "You're going to be all right. Everything is going to be all right."

"No, it's not."

Though he was tempted to lie to her, he could tell by the sharp glitter in her eyes that it was not going to help. For the truth was staring them both in the face. The deck beneath their feet felt strange. The list to starboard earlier had since straightened and then shifted heavily to port. The Forward Well Deck would soon be awash—if it wasn't already. The *Titanic* was dying quickly, and there were not enough lifeboats for everyone. Not even close to enough.

So knowing this might be the last moment he ever had alone with her, he instead opted for the truth.

"No, it's not. You're right, Flora."

Her breathing hitched and then slowed a fraction as her eyes focused on him.

"I . . . I don't know what's going to happen." He closed his eyes, pressing his forehead against hers for a moment before lifting it so that he could gaze into her beautiful blue-gray eyes. "The only thing I know is that I love you, Flora." His voice cracked, but he kept going, cradling her jaw between his hands. "I love you and I need you to keep trying."

Her eyes were awash with tears. "I need you to keep trying, too."

"Oh, I haven't given up," he assured her as he scrambled to

memorize every curve and line of her features. Every fragrant note of her scent. "But you're not giving me a chance to save my own life."

She recoiled as he spoke the harsh words. "I . . . I'm trying to save you and Father and Charlie. To find a boat . . ."

He shook his head, cutting her off.

"I won't . . . *we* won't take a seat in a lifeboat which should belong to a woman. Please, don't ask us to dishonor ourselves that way?"

Her face fell and he could hear the hitch in her breath as she struggled not to sob. "But how"—she hiccuped—"how will you survive?"

"You must trust to Providence and to me." He stared down at her intently. "I promise you I will commit every last ounce of my will to surviving. But I can't do that if I'm also trying to save you. I *need* you to get in that lifeboat with your mother and your sisters. I *need* to know that you're safe."

"And Father and Charlie?"

"I will do what I can for them. But none of us will have a chance of surviving if you stay. We will be too preoccupied with saving you."

Tears spilled from the corners of her eyes, and he swiped them away from her cheeks, wishing it was in his power to spare her this, to spare them all. But while it was sometimes jested that his serves were fast enough to cheat time, the fact was his time was running out. Even now, he felt it running through his fingers.

"Are you ready to board now?" he asked.

She nodded.

Pressing his mouth to hers, he sealed their promises with a swift kiss. Then he gripped her hand and pulled her toward the Aft Grand Staircase.

Except he'd forgotten the Aft Staircase didn't continue up to the Boat Deck. He glanced around. There must be a staff staircase located somewhere close. But was it behind a door? And which one? He began to pull Flora back in the direction they'd come, but she resisted.

"Is that Mr. Andrews?" she asked, instead tugging him toward the entrance to the Smoking Room, which had been left propped open.

He was surprised to see the ship's architect standing on the opposite side of the chamber, facing the hearth. A fire burned merrily in its grate, and the tables were still littered with detritus from earlier that night—tumblers half-filled with liquor, cigars moldering where they rested in ashtrays, hands of cards merely turned over where the players had previously sat.

Andrews was gazing up at the painting hung over the fireplace, his arms folded across his chest. His face was one of a man who was heartbroken. Chess wondered if Andrews was thinking of his wife and daughter back in Belfast, whom he'd spoken of so often and so lovingly, longing to return to them. Or if he was thinking of his ship—the *Titanic*—his greatest triumph, and how it was inexorably sinking into the depths of the frigid north Atlantic with so many souls still aboard, including himself.

"Mr. Andrews."

Chess then realized they weren't entirely alone in the room with the ship's designer. There was also a steward.

The steward lifted the life belt resting on a table nearby. "Aren't you going to have a try for it?"

But Andrews simply continued to stare at the ship depicted in Plymouth Harbour, like a man paralyzed.

The steward turned then, catching sight of them. "You need to get to the boats!"

"Where are the nearest stairs to the Boat Deck?" Chess asked.

"Follow me."

Chess took hold of Flora's hand, towing her toward the door as the steward hurried along the corridor down which they'd come. He paused about halfway down the passage and pushed open a door leading out onto the port-side promenade.

"Immediately to the right, there's a set of stairs."

"Thank you," Chess told him, bundling Flora out the door. He thought the man meant to follow them, but the door shut between them and the steward. Perhaps he was going to try once more to prod Andrews out of his stupor.

They hustled up the stairs, emerging near the spot where the Fortune family had been waiting for Lifeboat 10. But while there were still plenty of people rushing to and fro, clustered along the railing looking out to the darkened sea, the boat had gone! He spied Mr. Fortune and Charlie at the rail at about the same time they spotted them and hurried over. They drew Flora into their arms, reproving and consoling her by turns, while he scoured the length of the deck. There had to be another boat. There had to be.

There! Near the bow. There was a flurry of activity.

"This way!" He grasped Flora's hand again, pulling her toward the bow, mindful of the increased slope of the deck downward. They passed a fellow strolling about the deck in his stocking feet whom Mr. Fortune called out to.

"Molson, what the devil are you doing? Where are your shoes?"

"Took them off," the fellow replied, falling in step with Mr. Fortune. "They'll only hinder me while I swim. This isn't my first shipwreck, you know. Swam to safety once in the Gulf of St. Lawrence, and I figure a three- or four-mile swim will see me safely to that ship a point and a half off the port bow everyone keeps seeing the lights for. I'll send her for the rest of you," he declared, slapping Mr. Fortune audibly on the back before he peeled away, presumably to dive over the rail.

"Bloody fool," Mr. Fortune declared, and Chess was inclined to agree. If Molson made it more than a mile before his muscles seized up from the cold, that would be a miraculous feat.

As they neared the Bridge, Chess could see the crew working to get a collapsible of the Engelhardt variety hooked up to the falls. The davits were being cranked back in from having previously lowered a boat, and the canvas sides of the collapsible had to be raised.

A group of men which included Chief Purser McElroy and Dr. O'Loughlin, stood nearby. They were soon joined by another man who had come dashing up a forward set of stairs from the Promenade Deck below and then bent forward at the waist to catch his breath.

"Hello, Lights! Are you warm enough?" one of the men teased him.

The panting man looked down at himself, realizing, to the others amusement, that he presented quite a sight. Even though the air temperature was frigid, he stood before them coatless and bathed in perspiration, wearing only a pair of pants and a sweater, with the hem and collar of his pajamas poking out from underneath. The officer gave a good-natured chuckle before offering each of the men a brief handshake and moving on to help ready the collapsible.

Chess decided this was the man he would trust to get Flora safely away from the ship. So they stuck close by even as they could see the water creeping ever closer. It was already crawling up the stairs just abaft the Bridge toward A-Deck, and it would only be a matter of minutes before it reached the Boat Deck.

# CHAPTER 37

⌒⌘⌒

Alice wanted to scream at her mother to stop making those keening noises of distress. Alice understood she was cold and frightened, that her mind was fragmented with anguish, but so was hers. Every single one of them in their boat was suffering the same agony.

But Alice didn't say anything. She didn't speak. She didn't move. She simply sat stiffly in her seat, staring at Mabel's coat in front of her and rubbing small circles on Mother's back as she ordered herself not to think, not to feel. Just to be.

For when she thought, when she felt, she remembered.

She commanded herself to empty her mind. To ignore the cold and darkness and fear bombarding her senses.

But she couldn't close her eyes. She couldn't close her eyes, because when she did, she saw Charlie's boyish grin as she'd told him to look after Father. She saw Father preening in his matted buffalo coat. She saw Flora smoothing Alice's hair back from her brow with a gentle smile. She saw Mr. Beattie, Mr. McCaffry, and Mr. Ross. She saw their cheery steward, and Mr. Futrelle with his rumpled coat, and Mr. Harris with his ever-doting grin for his wife.

She couldn't close her eyes, but she also couldn't bear to look at anything around her. Because when she gazed out across the sea toward the *Titanic*, she noted another of its portholes had slipped beneath the water's glassy surface. Or she saw the figures rushing along its decks like ants over a log. Or she recoiled at the sight of another body hurtling into the ocean from too great a height.

When she turned the other way, she found herself combing the darkness for the ship the captain had pointed out earlier. The light he'd told the other lifeboat to row toward and then return. But there was no light. There was no boat. Only a black void filled with twinkling stars.

So to maintain her sanity, she stared at Mabel's back. Stared at it until she went cross-eyed, and then stared some more.

At some point, she didn't know when, the music echoing across the water shifted. It changed from the jaunty ragtime tunes Mabel was so fond of and the waltzes Alice could play along with, moving her fingers over imaginary piano keys, to the hymns they sang each Sunday. Familiar verses and stanzas that sprang to mind without conscious thought.

Alice found herself murmuring the lyrics to herself, winging them upward in a frenzied prayer that until that moment she'd been unable to form words to offer. She begged and exhorted and pleaded, her stomach threatening to expel its contents and her chest tight with dread.

Her disordered mind berated her, insisting she might have done something more useful like Mabel warming and comforting the children on either side of her. She might have consoled the woman clutching an infant to her chest and fretting about the whereabouts of her two-year-old son who had become separated from them. Or spoken up to ask if there was an extra blanket for the woman shivering in little more than a night gown. Or offered to take the oar from one of the women who must be tiring.

But all she could do was stare at Mabel's back and pray. Thoughts more than declarations. Feelings more than words. The fragile soul of her humanity crying out to a creator too immense to fathom for a miracle.

And then a sharp crack split the still night air, as loud as a clap of thunder reverberating off a mountain, and twice as terrifying.

Flora knew she'd agreed to board a lifeboat without Chess and Father and Charlie. She'd even accepted the reasons why. But when the time came, when the officer the other men had called "Lights" called out for women and children to step forward, her legs refused to do so.

"Flora, you must go," Father insisted, wrapping her in one last hug. He smelled of buffalo and fear. "Please, I need you to look after your mother and sisters," he murmured in her ear. "They need you."

Charlie's arms enveloped her next. "Don't fret, Flora. We'll be on just the next boat." The words fell flat, for they all knew the likelihood of that, but Flora offered him a pained smile anyway.

She saw the look Father and Chess exchanged. The one that told her Chess would force her into the boat by any means necessary if she didn't go willingly. He gripped her hand, leading her toward the line of crewmen that now cordoned off the corner of the Boat Deck where the lifeboat was hanging on the davits to prevent men from passing through. The officer had already threatened violence with his pistol in order to clear a group of men who had rushed to fill it just moments before.

When they reached the line, Chess pulled her into his arms. He clutched her as tightly to him as her life belt allowed and pressed his mouth to her temple. "Don't you ever forget how extraordinary you are, Flora Fortune," he declared in a trembling voice before pushing her through the cordon of men who separated to let her pass.

She stumbled forward, and by the time she righted herself, he was already backing away, his gaze still locked with hers as he was swallowed up by the crowd. The officer gripped her shaking hand and guided her toward the boat, helping her to clamber over the bulwark into the vessel. It wasn't until her knees hit the back of the bench and she sat down with a thump that she realized tears were streaming down her face.

"Please, catch my wife," she heard a voice cry. "Be careful. She has a broken arm."

She looked about her blindly as a woman was set beside her, her arm cradled in a sling. Seeing the brackets of pain at the corners of her mouth, Flora came to herself with a start and reached out to situate her more comfortably. Several more women were handed into the boat as the sound of crewmen shouting rose above the tumult. "Are there any more women? Are there any more women?"

Flora felt a surge of hope that all the women had boarded, and that the men could now join them without dishonor, but one by one more women continued to trickle in. Worse still, the list to port was so alarming that Flora feared the ship would topple over onto its side.

"All male passengers to the starboard side to straighten her up!" the officer in charge ordered.

It took everything within her not to shriek "No!" as more women were settled around her, some of them holding children. A father from second class passed over his two young sons, wrapped warmly in blankets. The youngest was swaddled so snuggly, his coverings resembled a papoose. The moment of their parting was so heart-wrenching, the father's trust in this boatload of strangers so poignant, that Flora temporarily forgot her own pain as she and the other women took the tender children into their care.

Then she heard a voice she'd thought never to hear again ringing out from the deck. "Ladies, you *must* get in at once. There isn't a moment to lose," Mr. Andrews ordered sternly, having roused from his stunned immobility earlier in the Smoking Room. "You cannot pick and choose your boat. Do not hesitate. Get in, get in!"

The sight and sound of him recovered from his moment of weakness and now on deck trying to do whatever he could to save others brought a lump to her throat. One last woman was helped over the side of the boat even as the scene on deck grew ever more frenzied. A surge of passengers—mostly men, from what she could see—had to be held back by the cordon of crewmen while two senior officers conferred. The chief officer appeared to be ordering "Lights" into the boat, but with great determination he planted his feet back on the deck. Instead, a steward clambered over the side and they began to lower.

"Harry!" the woman with the broken arm shouted as her husband threw a blanket down to her.

"Goodbye, sweetheart!"

Next to him, several gentlemen lined the rails, including the president's adviser, Archie Butt, and the artist Frank Millet. Flora was very much struck by their composure.

At the edge of the group of men hovered the Strauses, and Flora realized with a jolt that Mrs. Straus had held fast to her pronouncement. She would not leave her husband. There they stood, arms wrapped around each other, bidding them adieu. "God go with you," Mrs. Straus called out.

As they reached the level of A-Deck, the lowering suddenly halted as the seamen struggled with the forward fall. Two men perched on the rail at the open end of the Forward Promenade decided to take advantage of this momentary pause, leaping out toward the boat. It was no small jump, as the list had caused the collapsible to swing out almost half a dozen feet from the side of the ship. The first man made it into the bow, falling head over heels, but the second man's leap was too shallow. He landed on the gunwale. His life belt cushioned him but also caused him to rebound and almost fall into the water. At the last moment, he caught himself, and they pulled him on board, even as his feet dangled over the side into the icy water.

Flora was shocked to discover that the bow had sunk so low in the water that their drop from the Boat Deck to the sea was no more than fifteen feet. She remembered the evening when she'd watched an emergency cutter being swung out from these very davits to dangle over the side of the ship. Then the sea had seemed fathoms below. Now, in the darkness, they could still see the people above them on deck. Though she didn't spy Chess or Father or Charlie. They must have retreated to the other side of the ship as ordered.

The collapsible touched down and began to pull away from the *Titanic* just as the water inching upward reached the ceiling of the Forward A-Deck Promenade. Meanwhile, all around them deck chairs were raining down, presumably thrown into the water so that the people who had not made it into the lifeboats would have something to cling to. Except some of them were hurled awfully close to their position, making it even more imperative that they get away from the ship quickly. But as the oarsmen began to turn the collapsible, one of them cried out, having noticed something in the water. It was a swimmer moving toward them. They reached out to haul him aboard.

The fellow was shaking from head to toe and a woman behind Flora tossed a fur wrap over him. "Jane," he said.

She gasped. "My God, it's my husband, Frederick!"

A pulse of jealousy, hot and sharp, surged through Flora at this discovery. What she wouldn't give for their situations to be reversed. To find that it was Chess or Father or Charlie they'd pulled into the boat, not this fellow named Frederick.

He grasped his wife's hand, pulling himself up onto the bench beside her before addressing the crew. "Let me take an oar. It will help warm me."

They obliged, and soon all the oarsmen were determinedly pulling, anxious to get away from the ship. Flora kept her eyes on the *Titanic*. All along the waterline, water flooded through open portholes and windows, filling cabins still illuminated by electric lights. It made the sea surrounding the ship gleam with a preternatural glow. As if the ocean itself, or even the very gates of the underworld, were opening to devour the ship.

# CHAPTER 38

❧❀❧

Chess felt an odd sort of detachment settle over him. Flora was safe. The fear that had clutched his chest, robbing him of breath, seemed to have been all for her, and in its place a numbness began to take hold. One that made him feel as if he'd stepped outside himself to watch a theatrical production unfold, albeit one that bordered on the unbelievable.

He'd obeyed the officer's directive to move to the starboard side along with Mr. Fortune and Charlie, finding it still crowded with people—most of them men, but also some women.

The last boat had already left the starboard side, so now the passengers were scrambling up the sloping deck toward the stern, hoping to put as much distance as possible between themselves and the encroaching water. The musicians had emerged from the Forward Grand Staircase entrance and stood together near the door, still wielding their instruments as they set bows to strings to play the strains of a hymn. "Jerusalem" or "Land of Hope and Glory," he thought.

Out over the water, he could see the lights from some of the lifeboats. Most seemed tremendously far away—just pricks of light on the horizon—while overhead the plethora of stars continued to twinkle in the heavens.

Had it truly been only hours before that he'd stood here with Flora in his arms and marveled at the beauty of the sky? What he wouldn't give to return to that moment, to capture it forever.

"Shouldn't we move toward the stern, too?" Charlie asked, stepping up to the bulwark next to him. "Shouldn't we follow?"

Chess could sense the younger man's agitation, his restless uncertainty. Ostensibly, that would seem the wisest thing to do, but he wasn't so certain. While remaining on board the ship and out of the freezing water seemed like the shrewdest option, he also knew that the last rush was the most dangerous.

A deck chair suddenly sailed over the side of the ship to his left, shattering the calm surface of the water where it shimmered with phosphorescence. He looked over to see a man dressed in white hurling another one over the rail, with a stack of several more waiting. They bobbed back to the surface as they landed, and Chess perceived they would work as makeshift life preservers—something for those without life belts to hold on to.

Realizing he'd yet to don his own life belt, Chess pulled the one draped over his arm over his head and decided that if this was to be it, then he would rather do something useful in his last moments than stand about sulking and raging.

"Come on," he urged Charlie and Mr. Fortune, weaving his way through the fleeing passengers toward the stacks of chairs leaning against the far wall, intent on dragging them over to the railing to help pitch them overboard, and was nearly tripped up by a pack of yapping dogs that came stampeding down the deck. Evidently someone had released the canines from the kennel—an act of compassion, no doubt, meant to give them at least a fighting chance for survival. The last of the group was a bulldog, who paused to bark and spin in a circle, as if he thought this was all some sort of game, before lumbering after the others. Chess didn't know why that, of all things, should suddenly threaten to break him, but it did.

Glancing around himself uncertainly, he caught sight of a number of men scrambling over the roof of the Officers' Quarters. They were wrangling with the bulk of another collapsible—possibly two.

Chess changed course, gesturing to Charlie and Mr. Fortune to follow.

He clambered up to the roof, throwing himself into the task of assisting the officers and crewmen struggling to shift the crafts from their secured locations.

"Of all the foolish, idiotic places to store a lifeboat," one of the men was cursing.

A debate was raging over how best to get them down from the roof and into the davits to be loaded. Those on the starboard side were attempting to prop up oars to slide the collapsible down at an angle, while those on the port side were merely going to attempt to lift it. Seeing they needed more muscle, he scrambled toward the port side of the roof, catching sight of Mr. Beattie and Mr. McCaffry lending their aid with the starboard boat.

By now, they were racing the rising sea, and every second counted. The lights flickered and dimmed, only to brighten again, though not at the same intensity. The officer nicknamed "Lights" was in charge of the port-side efforts, calmly directing them in what to do as they slowly maneuvered the heavy, unwieldly craft toward the edge of the roof.

At one point, Lights exclaimed to one of the crewmen in surprise, "Hemming, why haven't you gone yet?"

"Oh, plenty of time yet, sir," the fellow responded cheerily, raising a macabrely amused grin to Chess's cheeks. Plenty of time, indeed.

As they neared the lip, Chess looked up to see Mr. Andrews striding toward the Bridge, a life belt in his arms. Chess was glad that the ship's architect's life hadn't ended alone in despair inside the Smoking Room. He watched as Andrews paused to speak to the captain, who a short time later, raised his megaphone to his mouth. "Abandon ship!" he called. "Every man for himself!"

Chess didn't know if it was the unfortunate timing of this pronouncement or the flurry of people that suddenly emerged on the deck through the Grand Staircase entrance—some of them women and children—or even the unexpected lurch of the ship that brought water up over the rail onto the port-side deck. All he knew was that the collapsible slipped from his and the other men's grasps and crashed onto the deck below—upside down. The sea was now sloshing up the forward hatchway and sending waves streaming along the decking.

In the fray he'd lost sight of Mr. Fortune and Charlie, for his only thought at that moment was to right the collapsible and help these newly surfaced women and children into it. He leaped down onto the deck, icy water splashing halfway up his legs and filling his shoes. Even as he bent to lend his back to the effort, *Titanic*'s bow took a small but definite plunge.

The dip knocked him off his feet, and a wave washed him toward the side. Only by grabbing onto one of the davits was he able to swing himself back on deck. The Boat Deck seemed to lift slightly just before the ship appeared to right herself. Chess stood gripping the bulwark, cold sea water dripping from his hair into his eyes as he tried to reconcile what was happening.

For a brief but faulty moment he thought the *Titanic* might actually remain afloat as it was. But then reason reasserted itself. He took a step toward the still overturned collapsible just as the ship plunged again. A wave swept aft over the Boat Deck, throwing him into the sea.

# CHAPTER 39

❧

Mabel watched the *Titanic*'s stern rise out of the water and her bow sink below the waves. The lights continued to blaze along her decks and through the windows and portholes, while the notes of a familiar hymn carried to them across the still air. They lodged in her heart like a splinter.

The night seemed to split open as a series of roars echoed over the water.

"It's the boilers," someone whispered. "They're exploding."

The ship continued to creak and growl as its downward angle increased. Suddenly, it plunged several feet, then paused, balanced as if on a knife's edge. Mabel found herself holding her breath, uncertain what would happen next. A trembling exhale passed her lips, her warm breath turning to fog in the cold night air as to her horror, the *Titanic*'s stern resumed its ascent with even greater speed, and the bow sank deeper.

The music abruptly stopped midverse, and the screams and cries of those thrashing and churning in the water seemed to amplify in comparison. She wrapped her arms more tightly around the children seated on either side of her, cradling their heads close to her chest in hopes of dampening the horrific sounds. Their little bodies trembled in the cold, but neither cried. Perhaps the moment was too immense for their minds to process. Or so she hoped.

With a wrenching groan, the forward funnel slowly toppled,

slamming down into the water where Mabel could imagine people had been swimming. She flinched as it landed in a shower of
sparks and a plume of black smoke.

The ship seemed to glow with a dull red haze as the stern continued to rise, lifting the enormous propellers out of the water.
Its lights flickered, and then from somewhere deep within, a
tremendous noise rumbled through the air, building in intensity
as it crashed and crackled and rumbled. As if every object inside
the *Titanic*, from the Royal Crown Derby china down to the engines, had slipped from the shelves and broken loose from the
fastenings to plummet down toward the bow.

The lights guttered once more, then the ship went dark. Only
a single light positioned on some sort of masthead gleamed on
through the night. Which did nothing to quell the terror that suddenly gripped every breast, as if with one collective breath everyone still aboard the ship shrieked. A shriek Mabel felt in the
marrow of her bones.

With the loss of the lights, it was more difficult to see what
was happening, but she could tell that the stern was still rising.
Until, with one great crack, loud enough to rend the heavens,
the *Titanic* seemed to split in two near its center, and the middle
section crumpled into nothingness. The stern fell backward,
dropping back toward the sea to settle more or less level with
the water. The force of the descent dislodged the third and
fourth funnel and sent them hurtling into the sea—one forward
and the other back.

For one heartrending moment it seemed that the claim about
the *Titanic*'s ability to be sliced into separate and distinct pieces
and still remain afloat appeared as if it might be true. That the
stern of the ship would remain afloat, and all those still aboard
her would be safe. If the power of Mabel's will had been enough,
it would have stayed buoyant.

But again the stern started to rise higher and higher, then
twist, as if some enormous sea creature beneath the waves intended to wield her like a baseball bat. Her propellers sparkled

in the starlight as they pointed up toward the heavens, with the stern nearly vertical, and she began to sink, plunging downward ever faster, with barely a ripple outward.

The people still clinging to her decks were helpless against such a force, and those watching from the lifeboats could do nothing but witness the horror. Mabel's entire body shuddered as the *Titanic* slipped beneath the waves.

# CHAPTER 40

❧

A Frenchwoman's wail pierced the darkness, but Alice found she couldn't make a sound. Whatever breath she possessed had been expelled from her lungs the moment the *Titanic* disappeared, and she suddenly felt quite certain she would never draw another.

Then a sound reached her ears that she would never ever, even to her dying day, be able to forget. It wrenched and tore at her very soul and hovered over them all like a great swarm of locusts, devouring everything in sight. All light. All peace. All hope.

Dear God in Heaven. They were dying. All these people thrashing about in the water were dying. And Charlie or Flora or Father or Mr. Kinsey could be among them.

"We have to go back," she squeaked, finding that, after all, she *could* draw breath. "We have to go back," she repeated more loudly.

"Yes!" another woman chimed in to say.

"But they'll swamp us," someone else protested.

"We have to *try*," another woman countered.

"Ladies, we're filled to capacity," one of the seamen said. "We *can't* take on any more. But some of the other boats will have room," he assured them. "They'll go back."

But would they? Alice strained to hear the splash of oars returning to the wreck, but all she could hear were the desperate cries of those in the water, frantically struggling. A woman near the bow of the boat tried to sing, and others joined in around her, murmuring the words to "O God, Our Help in Ages Past," but their voices were weak, and though Alice tried, she couldn't summon enough will to join them. Not when she also wanted them to be quiet so that she could listen for other boats.

"We should shout," one of the crewmen suggested. "It will warm us and help us to keep our bearings."

This was obviously a lie. A ploy, however well meaning, to block out the feverish moans and howls of those in the water. Although a few tried, most of them couldn't manage it. It was their punishment, their penance for finding a seat in the lifeboats when so many others had not.

Alice squeezed her eyes shut and tipped her head back as tears slipped down her cheeks. She silently screamed her despair to God, repeating her loved ones' names over and over again.

But giving in to despair would help no one, least of all herself. Their situation was still precarious. The sea might be calm now, but if it turned choppy or the wind began to pick up, they could find themselves in a serious predicament.

A ship had been sighted off the port bow, but every trace of it had since disappeared. Which made her wonder if any of the officers' assurances that a distress call had been sent out on the wireless and that ships were racing to their rescue was even true. Even if they were, how far away were these ships? Would they have to wait for hours—for days, even—to be rescued?

When she blinked open her eyes, she discovered she was staring up at the night sky, strewn with stars. It was a strange dichotomy, these serene and brilliant heavens and the cold and ruthless sea where so many fought for their lives.

Suddenly a shooting star streaked across the sky, and as she waited, another and another. While in Egypt, one of their guides had told her that when you saw a shooting star, it was the departed soul of someone you loved sending you a message in the night sky. Similarly, their grandmother had always said it was an indication that another soul had made its way home to heaven to be with its Savior. With so much suffering occurring nearby, it was impossible not to wonder.

She turned to adjust the blankets over her shivering mother. "They might have made it onto another boat," she told her. "Don't give up hope."

Mother didn't respond, and there was little else Alice could do for her. So she turned to the crew members who were debating what to do.

"Perhaps if we could transfer some of our passengers to another boat, we could go back for more," one of the men was saying.

The other agreed. "I saw a green light off in that direction," he said, pointing. "One of the officers must have brought a box of flares into their boat with them. But we don't have enough rowers."

It had since been discovered that the fireman allowed into the boat couldn't pull an oar, and neither could the steward. The two seamen in charge had tasked the steward with controlling the tiller so that they could both row, but that still left them short, even with the women who had volunteered earlier.

"I can row," Alice piped up to say. "Our father taught us— both my sister and me." Odd to think that this of all things might turn out to be the most useful skill he'd ever passed on to them. "To our brothers' chagrin, since we can outrow them."

"All right," the crewman agreed. "We'll see about that."

Flora rocked back and forth with the little fellow swaddled in her lap, singing gently but determinedly, though the child made nary a whimper. He merely stared up at her and around at the other people surrounding them in the boat as if only mildly curious about the precarious situation he'd found himself in. All the same, she kept singing and rocking, ostensibly for the child, but in truth, as much for herself. To soothe the icy fear trickling through her veins for Chess, Father, and Charlie. To drown out the nightmare-inducing cries of those struggling in the water.

And then to distract herself from the eerie silence that began to fall as those same voices died away.

They were all doing what they could for one another, even the crewmen and the male volunteers who were straining at the oars in the collapsible craft. It seemed they were not as easy to manage as those in a normal boat. That, or it was because they had but one true seaman, along with a steward, a man who claimed he designed yachts and had rowed for Yale, and a few other inexperienced individuals. As close as they were to where the ship had gone down, an attempt was made to go back for the survivors, but the boat seemed to be drifting farther away rather than nearer, and the men had since given up.

For a brief moment after the *Titanic* had disappeared beneath the flat surface of the sea, she'd sworn she'd seen Charlie. He was flailing his arms and calling to her, his life belt keeping him afloat. But she blinked her eyes, and he was gone.

She knew it was impossible that she could have seen him. The darkness was so thick, she couldn't even make out the features of the person seated next to her let alone someone in the water hundreds of feet away. But that didn't quiet her disordered thoughts.

She wasn't the only one who swore she saw loved ones among the tangled wreckage of chairs and cushions and scum of cork. Nor was she the only one trying to distract herself with singing or chatter. One woman prattled on incessantly about everything and nothing, to no one in particular.

Flora didn't know what would become of them and preferred not to contemplate it. Not while there was this curly-haired tike to comfort. Not when she felt as if she were standing at the edge of a dock, staring down into . . . nay, *leaning out over* a rippling sea of darkness and despair. One small nudge, and she would topple into it.

"Hoy!" A voice suddenly pierced the night. "Is there another boat over there?"

"Aye!" the seaman in charge called back.

"Who's in charge?"

"Quartermaster Bright, sir." He clearly recognized the other voice was one of authority.

"Aye, then, Bright. It's Lowe. Consider yourself under my orders. Row yourself over to me."

This they did to the best of their ability while word spread around the boat that the man who'd called to them was Fifth Officer Lowe. That he'd see them to safety. Periodically they heard him hailing other boats with the same message, and it soon became apparent he intended to create his own little flotilla.

"If the boats are tied together, then a passing steamer will see us more easily as one large object," he explained as ropes were thrown out to secure the boats gathering around his. "How many seamen are present?"

The crew members responded from each of the various boats. As far as Flora could tell, there seemed to be four lifeboats in total plus Officer Lowe's. She also learned she was in the boat they were calling Collapsible D.

"All right, then," Lowe declared. "We're going to distribute the passengers in my boat among yours, and then you seamen will come into my boat so we can go over into the wreckage and pick up anyone still alive."

This took some time to do, as there were thirty-three passengers to be transferred. While they waited for this to be done, some of the occupants of the other boats began calling out to each other, trying to locate lost loved ones. Flora didn't know what boat number her sisters and mother had climbed into. Or if she'd been told, she couldn't recall.

But when a timid voice suddenly spoke up to ask if there were any Fortunes present, Flora's heart leaped in relief.

"Alice, is that you?" she called back. "It's Flora."

"Flora! Oh, thank heavens!" she replied. "Mother, did you hear that? Flora is in one of the other boats."

"Is Mabel there with you also?" Flora asked.

"Yes. We're having quite the picnic," Mabel quipped. "You should be sorry you're missing it."

Flora laughed at the horrible jest, simply glad to know her sisters and mother were safe.

"Are you, indeed, the elder Miss Fortune?" the woman beside her with the broken arm queried. "Miss Alice's sister."

"I am," Flora answered in surprise.

"Oh, tell her Mrs. Harris is with you. She will want to know," she insisted before crying out herself. "Alice. Miss Fortune. It's René Harris. I'm here as well."

"Oh, wonderful," Alice said.

"Seated by your sister, of all people, and didn't even know it."

"Yes? How extraordinary."

There was a strange note in Alice's voice, but Flora hadn't long to contemplate it, for she was soon distracted by Mr. Lowe's colorful language. He was interspersing his commands with curses as he tried to redistribute all the passengers as swiftly as possible so that he could return to the wreckage. Flora couldn't blame him, considering the near silence now coming from those in the water—they were running out of time to save anyone.

"Jump, God d*** you, jump," he ordered one woman who was dithering over taking her next step. He eventually ended up virtually flinging her into the other vessel, to be caught by the seaman there. Then he turned to a woman with a shawl draped over her face who in her haste stumbled to make the crossing. Flora attributed this to a desire not to also be tossed bodily, but Lowe was more suspicious. He yanked the shawl off her head to reveal that the woman was actually a man attempting to disguise himself. Lowe made a low sound of disgust, then grabbed hold of the fellow, hurling him into the other boat.

All told, Flora's boat received about twelve new occupants, and twenty-one others were scattered among the other three. The seamen then clambered aboard Lowe's boat and set off into the wreckage after Lowe ordered those remaining boats in the flotilla to lie on their oars and stay together.

So much time had passed, Flora feared it would all be for naught, but maybe some of the survivors had managed to climb onto the wreckage or keep themselves warm by swimming about. It seemed possible.

One little girl had become separated from her mother during the transfers and some time had to be spent consoling her. When finally she'd calmed enough for others to try to communicate over her screams, Alice ventured to ask the question Flora had been bracing for.

"Father and Charlie . . . and Chess," she added as an afterthought. One Flora didn't fault her for, though his name caused a pang in her chest. "Are they with you?"

"No," was the only reply she could manage, unable to offer false assurances.

The fear that had gripped Mabel's heart had eased a fraction at the sound of Flora's voice. At least she had made it off the ship. At least she was safe.

As for the others . . . she would not think of them yet. Not when Officer Lowe might return with them, having plucked them from the icy water and cursed at them not to die on him now.

A reluctant grin quirked the corners of her lips at the thought. She'd decided she rather liked the blasphemous fifth officer. After all, he was only saying the things she was already thinking, and at least he was straightforward and honest.

Their boat had met with Lowe's a short time before the others had arrived, so she'd had more exposure to his rough attempts to comfort the sobbing women around him. To hear him beg. "Please, don't cry." And then threaten. "You'll have something else to do than cry. Some of you will have to handle the oars." And then remonstrate. "For God's sake, stop crying. If I had not the responsibility of looking after you, I would put a bullet through my brain." But her favorite remark had been when he'd recommended, "I think the best thing for you women to do is to take a nap." That one had made her want to howl with laughter. Which simply proved how barmy she'd become.

If nothing else, listening to Officer Lowe's cursing had temporarily distracted them from their misery. The cold and darkness and ominous silence tore at Mabel's nerves now that she'd been ordered not to row and the children she'd previously looked after were being cared for by others. There was nothing to do but wait. But wait for what? And for how long?

The woman who had been crushed by one of the men leaping into their boat from A-Deck had suffered injuries to her leg and ankle. Her daughter tended to her as best she could in between issuing complaints about the conditions in the boat and her affront at the man who had injured her mother. While Mabel empathized, she was also glad for the large man's presence. They had already been short several oarsmen, and now that Seamen Buley and Evans had gone off with Lowe, if they didn't return, they would be down two more. They could use the fellow's strong back.

A gentle breeze began to pick up, at first only ruffling the hairs poking out from beneath her fur steamer cap. But then the previously tranquil sea developed a slight swell, knocking the hulls of the boats against each other. In response to this, the ropes were slackened, and the flotilla began to drift apart. Mabel, Alice, and the others in their boat lowered their oars, trying to keep themselves as close to the others as possible, but this was no easy feat. Periodically they caught sight of the green flares in the distance that they'd learned were likely being fired by an officer in one of the other boats, attempting to signal to any vessels coming to their rescue. But they were too far away, and the strength of their rowers was limited.

Peering out across the black sea, Mabel became conscious of a horizon to her left. It was naught but a smudge of gray, but it gradually turned to orange. Even more exciting than the first signs of dawn was the dim light. One that was not a star or a green flare or the rising sun. She wasn't alone in noticing it. Others perked up, only to slump in disappointment a few moments later as it disappeared. But it returned, growing brighter, followed by a second light, and then a green sidelight.

Some in the boat cheered. Some sobbed. Mabel gripped her oar tighter and urged the others to row.

# CHAPTER 41

❧

Flora soon also found herself in possession of an oar. Having passed the small curly-haired child to another woman, she'd taken a seat next to the yacht builder named Hoyt, whom they'd dragged from the water earlier, to help pull the oar while Quartermaster Bright and another fellow strained at the other. They were not a cohesive team, and Hoyt's shivering at times hindered efforts more than he helped, but she did her best to compensate for it and ignore the chattering of his teeth. Regardless, there was no doubt they were struggling to make any progress. She hoped her sisters were in better hands as their flotilla drifted apart.

As dawn broke over the horizon, Flora felt some sense of relief. After all, it was easier to be hopeful in the light of day than in the gloom of night. Particularly if one could see the other lifeboats, and not just the occasional green flare wielded by one of the surviving officers.

Flora blamed it on their exhaustion, because it took some time before anyone recognized what the lights appearing on the horizon meant. A ship! A large one, hopefully steaming to their rescue. Even so, the ship was still so far off, and they would still have to row to meet her when she stopped.

But as the sky continued to lighten and the wind picked up, she caught sight of another lifeboat far closer. It had been rigged with its sail and was cruising along at quite a clip. As she watched, it veered toward them, evidently noticing their struggle.

"Ahoy! Who's in charge here?" It was Officer Lowe again, come to the rescue.

"Quartermaster Bright, sir."

"Oh, yes. And you've only the one seaman? We'll give you a tow."

Flora sighed in relief, but it was short-lived. She'd just recalled that Lowe's boat had been the one to sail back to the wreckage looking for survivors. Scrutinizing the number of passengers aboard his vessel, it didn't appear there were many. Worse still, the crew's faces were a testament to the awful sights they'd witnessed. Some of their bleak eyes were red rimmed, and all of them were pale, their mouths set in grim lines that refused to speak except in the barest syllables as they rigged up the tow line.

It didn't take long to deduce that Chess, Father, and Charlie were not among the occupants, and with this discovery Flora's heart all but gave out. It was good that she was no longer expected to row. Not when what she really wanted to do was crumple into a ball at the bottom of the boat and cry.

The ship in the distance fired off a signal rocket, and its faint sound as it burst reached them over the wind now rushing past as Lowe again let out the sails on his boat and towed them along. But Flora didn't even look up to acknowledge it. It was all she could do to give the older curly-haired boy a nod of thanks as he offered her one of the cookies Mr. Woolner had been feeding him. Considering the manner in which the boy had been greedily consuming them, this was, indeed, an act of kindness. One she could not repay with discourtesy, so she brought the cracker to her lips to nibble, only lowering it when he looked away, for it tasted like ashes. Mr. Woolner flashed her a grimace of understanding, but she turned away, unable to stifle her anger at the unfairness that *he* should survive when those she loved had not.

The sky was growing brighter now, quickly, and all around them in the water they could see icebergs—some small, others enormous. Flora gaped at the massive berg with two peaks that appeared to be at least two-hundred-feet tall. Was that the iceberg the *Titanic* had struck? There were so many. It could have been any one of them.

A sudden shout drew their attention toward a group of people who appeared to be standing on top of the water, as if part of a biblical miracle.

"Are they balancing on a sheet of ice?" one man asked.

As they drew nearer, Flora could see that the dozen survivors were precariously perched on a collapsible boat much like their own, but the sides had fallen in and the bottom was inundated with water. Lowe carefully maneuvered his boat closer, but when just a hundred or so feet away, startled them all by firing four or five gunshots into the water. The children in Collapsible D began to sob.

"Now, see here," Lowe shouted to the people in the floundering collapsible. "You must not rush the boat. We'll transfer you one at a time at my direction."

After closing the gap between the two crafts, they slowly began the process, for the occupants of the swamped collapsible could not move any faster. First came the only female, a small, black-haired woman dressed in brown, who promptly crumpled into the bottom of Lifeboat 14, where the seamen covered her with blankets and worked to warm her. Some of the survivors were so frostbitten in their legs from standing practically knee-deep in the icy water that the seamen had to bodily lift them into the boat. One fellow was unconscious.

The survivors explained that they'd gone down with the ship but managed to swim over to this collapsible—one of two that the remaining officers had been attempting to launch when they ran out of time. Hope surged sharply inside Flora's chest. Her boat had not been the last to leave the ship, then. There had been two more. If these people had made it onto this raft, then perhaps Chess, Father, and Charlie had made it onto the other.

"Who are they?" Lowe asked, pointing to the bottom of the swamped collapsible.

"Died in the night," one man answered for them all.

"Are you certain?"

They assured him they were, but Officer Lowe leaned over the boat to check each body carefully anyway. Flora happened to be at a vantage to see that the first was a crewman in uniform, while the other two were men in evening dress. She gasped and then turned away as she caught a glimpse of the third man's face. It was Thomson Beattie.

She closed her eyes, grieving for her friend, and offered up a prayer for his soul. For all their souls. Those lost to the deep and those left to live on.

When Lowe covered Mr. Beattie's and the other two men's faces with life belts and then set the craft adrift, she opened her mouth to protest, but then realized it would do them no good. They were dead, and the two vessels containing the living were already crowded. The three bodies could be recovered later.

The sun had since breached the horizon, tinting the ice around them with shades of mauve and coral. In another lifetime it might have been a magnificent sight, but Flora could only appreciate their deadliness. She thought of Shackleton's book and how she and Chess had admired it. How she'd found him in the Lounge just seven or eight hours earlier studying the pictures of the icebergs. Dear God, what a fool she'd been not to understand how danger and beauty could lurk hand in hand.

One child who had slept through much of the excitement of the night woke, stirring in his nanny's arms. He rubbed his eyes and turned to look about him in wonder. "Look at the beautiful North Pole with no Santa Claus on it!"

Several of the other passengers chuckled, but Flora's heart ached all the more for his innocence, and the realization that so many of these children's naivetes had been utterly shattered. And they were the lucky ones.

Almost there. Almost there.

Alice repeated the words in her head as she heaved on her oar.

For hours they'd been rowing, watching as the sun climbed higher in the sky and boat after boat reached the steamer before them. It seemed at times they would never reach her. But little by little, the ship had grown larger in her field of vision until now the vessel was towering over them. Not as high as the *Titanic* had towered, but at least this ship was still afloat. That was all that mattered.

The ship had four masts but just a single funnel, and now that they were close enough, she could read the word *Carpathia* painted across her bow. Alice didn't care what her name was, merely that she was here to rescue them, and that at least this portion of her nightmare would be over.

Her hands were badly blistered, and at some point she realized that her lips were bleeding. The cold and salty spray of the sea had made her lips so chapped, they'd cracked. Each dart of her tongue across them stung, and yet she couldn't help it. At least the sting told her she was alive.

A look about her showed that their boat wasn't the last to arrive, but nearly. A second boat was approaching the ship alongside them, while another heavily loaded vessel lagged even farther behind. If there were any other lifeboats left, then they'd drifted far beyond the wreckage or capsized. Given the choppy waves they were now fighting through, the latter was not a remote possibility.

She supposed another boat might be hiding behind one of the icebergs dotting the sea around them. One of the occupants in her boat who was not manning the oars had claimed she could see at least twenty icebergs, ranging in size from small to mountainous. Other than the passing thought that they looked like giant opals, Alice had been too preoccupied to pay them much mind.

The large fellow beside her—the one who had leaped into their boat as it was lowering, whom she'd since learned was named Neshan—seemed to be of the same mind, for he grunted every time someone remarked on them. He didn't seem to understand much English or speak it except to proclaim his nationality as Armenian, but he clearly recognized the word *iceberg*. Mabel had been paired on the opposite side of the boat with the other jumper who had hidden in the bottom of the boat, a Japanese gentleman, while the steward—a fellow with the misfortune of sharing the same name as notorious Scottish criminal William Burke—controlled the tiller.

Finally, they drew alongside and several sailors from the *Carpathia* clambered down a ladder into the boat to secure her to the ship just below an open gangway. Then, one by one, they were helped up to the ship. The children were hauled up first inside canvas bags, then the lady who had been injured when Neshan leaped into the boat. The rest of the women followed. Many were too cold and unsteady to climb the short Jacob's ladder, so they were pulled up in a bosun's chair.

This was not the case with Alice or Mabel. If anything, they were overheated from their exertions with the oars. But they *were* exhausted. Even so, Mabel managed to scramble up the ladder to be there when Mother was pulled up in the bosun's chair, and Alice climbed up after.

Once on deck, she took two steps forward and nearly crumpled to her knees simply from the feel of more or less solid ground beneath her feet after such a harrowing night. Two crewmen grasped her arms, helping her forward until she had her feet squarely under her again. Stewards wrapped them in blankets and gave them cups of warmed brandy even as they took their names and class and asked if any of them needed immediate medical attention. Then they were shepherded down a corridor deeper into the ship.

Everything was so eerily calm after all the dreadfulness that had come before that Alice found it difficult to order her thoughts. The things that had happened, the things she had seen . . . everything seemed beyond her ability to reason. Given their silence, she assumed Mother and Mabel were struggling in much the same way.

When they rounded a corner and Alice was suddenly enveloped in a pair of arms, she was too stunned to react. Until she realized it was Flora. Her arms seemed to lift and tighten of their own accord. It was over all too swiftly, and Flora turned to embrace Mabel and, lastly, Mother, who held on to her for a very long time.

When Mother finally allowed Flora to step back, her face was a rictus of forlorn hope. "Charlie? Your father?"

Flora could only shake her head. "But there are boats still arriving. We picked up more than a dozen people who managed to survive the sinking. Perhaps some of the other boats have as well."

From the almost feverish gleam in Flora's eyes, it was clear she recognized what a long shot this was. That she was trying to convince herself as much as them. But given Mother's fragile state, given her *own*, Alice was grateful for any reason to keep hoping as long as possible.

The steward led them to the crowded dining saloon, where coffee, hot soup, and sandwiches were waiting. Mother gripped Flora's hand, refusing to let her go even to fetch her some food, so Alice brought it to her. When she returned, Flora told them how she had reached the *Carpathia*.

"If Officer Lowe had not taken us in tow, I'm quite sure we would still be out there. Even so, we only made it to the ship about an hour ago."

"He behaved quite admirably tonight, didn't he?" Mabel remarked.

"He did," Flora agreed.

"Aside from his shocking language," Mother said, staring down into her bowl of soup as she stirred her spoon round and round.

Flora reached over to slide the sandwich on Mother's plate closer to her, urging her to eat. "I can't fault him for that, given the extreme strain he was under." Her head lowered, her voice turning solemn. "You should have heard the way Officer Lowe called encouraging words back to us, especially toward the end." She huddled deeper into the blanket draped over her shoulders. "I suspect he prevented more than a few of us from sinking entirely into despair." Her gaze lifted to Alice. "Mrs. Harris has declared herself half in love with him."

"He is rather attractive," Mabel piped up to say. "Tall and slender and sinewy. I noted his cap kept tilting to one side, and you know that means he's got a streak of mischief in him."

Mother looked up from her soup to scowl at them. "I hardly think this is an appropriate topic of discussion, particularly given our current circumstances."

Maybe not, but it had made Alice feel better, and it had pulled Mother from her fretful preoccupation over the fate of Father and Charlie. Until all the boats were in and they knew if other ships had picked up any survivors, they couldn't know for certain what had happened to them.

Her eyes shifted to Flora.

Or Chess.

Dwelling on it constantly would only make them ill.

Mabel shrugged one shoulder, cradling her steaming cup of coffee between her hands. "I didn't mind the way he cursed, either."

Alice was hard-pressed not to laugh at this last outlandish remark, knowing full well what her younger sister was doing. It worked, too. For Mother huffed in aggravation before finally lifting a bite of soup to her mouth. Alice offered Mabel a grateful smile, and she dipped her head minutely.

"Speaking of Mrs. Harris . . ." Flora turned to survey the room. "Where is she?"

"Maybe she went up on deck to watch the boats come in," Mabel suggested. Scouring the occupants for her dear boy— Mr. Harris.

Flora conceded this. "That's where I was when I saw the pair of you pulling at the oars." She stared pointedly at their hands. "You should let Dr. McGee take a look." Lifting her hands, she revealed bandages covering her own blisters. Father's insistence that all his daughters learn to row properly had proved more valuable than he could possibly have known.

Alice winced as she took another spoonful of soup. "Perhaps he has something for our lips as well."

They approached the doctor stationed in one corner of the Dining Saloon with medical supplies as soon as they were finished, hoping that they would be able to convince Mother to let the man take a look at her, too. This was easier said than done, but the compassionate man grasped the situation immediately and managed to coax her into at least allowing him to check her vital signs and examine her extremities for frostbite.

"Are you all family?" he asked as he assessed one of Mother's hands and then the other.

"Yes," Flora said.

"And . . . are you all accounted for?"

It fell to Flora again to make their response. The lump in Alice's throat was too big to speak.

"We're still waiting for news of our Father and younger brother and . . ." Flora's voice broke off, either unable to say Chess's name or unsure whether to mention him in front of Mother.

The doctor searched her eyes for a moment before taking in Alice and Mabel, and then their mother, whom he studied for a long time in concern. "I believe I can arrange a cabin for you, where you can stay together."

"That is extraordinarily kind of you," Flora said. "I understand that accommodations are going to prove very tight."

He nodded, his concerned gaze returning to Mother. "If you will give me just a few moments."

"I heard there are not enough cabins or even enough berths for all of the survivors," Flora told them as Dr. McGee went to speak to a steward. "Some of *Carpathia*'s passengers and crew are generously giving up their own beds and bunking with others. I even heard the captain has offered his cabin to Mrs. Astor and a few other ladies. But there will still be many who are forced to sleep in the public rooms and corridors, wherever they can find space. To be offered a private cabin is an incredible privilege."

They had just come from the most lavish ship in the world, where their family had not only one private cabin but three, as well as a private bath, now they were all simply grateful to be alive.

"I am needed on deck," Dr. McGee informed them before slapping the steward beside him on the back. "But Burnley, here, will show you to the cabin, and I will come by to check on you this afternoon."

Flora guided Mother in the direction the steward led them, but her eyes followed the surgeon, clearly wondering, like Alice, why he was needed on deck. Had another boat arrived? One whose passengers were in a sorrier state than the others?

Alice didn't want to go to this cabin they were being led to. She wanted to go up on deck, and so did Flora. She could tell. But it would be the height of discourtesy to reject the cabin being offered to them. Even more alarming, Mother was in a state of near collapse. This was as obvious to Alice as it had been to Dr. McGee, and the reason he'd offered them a private cabin in the first place. They needed to see her settled before venturing up on deck.

The cabin they were shown to was by no means large, but for their purposes it was more than ample. They persuaded Mother to rest, removing her shoes and coat and smoothing her brow. But the moment Flora mentioned going to search out the latest news, she bolted upright, her eyes bright with fear. Only after Flora promised not to leave her side did she agree to lie down again.

Alice could sense the turmoil in her sister. Flora was desperate for information. But after being separated from her all night, Mother attached great significance to Flora's presence.

"We'll go," Alice said.

Flora's mouth was clamped tight in frustration and worry, but she nodded.

"I'll return with any news I can," Alice added, knowing it was unnecessary, but the stark dread in Flora's eyes was too great to be ignored. There was also something to be said for the fact she *had* panicked and run when they were supposed to board the lifeboats together. "Just don't leave Mother."

"I won't."

# CHAPTER 42

⌒⋆⌒

Mabel knew that for as long as she lived, even if it was to the ancient age of one hundred, she would never experience a day more fraught with sorrow.

She and Alice arrived on deck to find survivors lining the rails, frantically scanning the horizon for more boats. The two boats that followed theirs had unloaded, and now the sea was dotted solely with icebergs and wreckage. Deck chairs, life belts, silk-covered cushions and pillows, wooden splinters, the front of a piano, a striped barber's pole, and even a woman's fur hat suspended on a slat of white enameled wood were strewn across a sea carpeted with yellow scum and streams of granular reddish-brown cork. But there were no bodies.

Mabel didn't know what to make of this or how to feel. Did that mean there were more survivors than they'd believed, picked up by other boats? Or had the deceased been carried off by the wind and currents? Maybe the life belts had failed, and they'd sunk to the bottom of the ocean. She wanted to howl in frustration, but she was also glad not to be surrounded by a floating graveyard. She feared many of the passengers, including her, would never have recovered from such a sight.

She and Alice circulated among the survivors, finding some friends while others were missing. Dr. Leader, Mrs. Swift, Mrs. Margaret Brown, Mr. Sloper, Mrs. Candee, Mr. Woolner, and

Marie Young—who hugged her tightly—were all accounted for. But while Mrs. Futrelle and Mrs. Harris were present, their husbands were missing. As were countless other acquaintances, including Mr. Beattie, Mr. McCaffry, and Mr. Ross; the Strauses; the Allisons and little Lorraine; and dear Mr. Andrews. Worse still, none of them had any news to share about Father or Charlie or Chess.

A coldness gripped Mabel's heart as the truth began to sink in. And then it was confirmed. Second Officer Lightoller had stayed aboard the *Titanic* until the very end, going down with the ship. Yet he'd managed to climb aboard one of the collapsible boats and save himself. He knew exactly how many boats the *Titanic* had been carrying and how many were launched. He had also been the last person to board the *Carpathia* from the last lifeboat, which had arrived a short time ago, so he was able to confirm that all the boats were now accounted for.

As word of his assertion spread, there were those who protested, still clinging to a false hope that their loved ones might have survived the icy water to be picked up by another ship. Given the fact that nearly all the people rescued from the water had been taken down to the *Carpathia*'s hospital to be treated for various injuries and frostbite, Mabel knew full well that they were deluding themselves.

"We . . . we should tell Mother and Flora," Alice murmured, barely able to speak through the tears slipping down her cheeks. All around them, people were quietly weeping, their fortitude shattered. There were no great screams or cries of anguish, just stunned sobs, hoarse moans, and faces pinched with grief.

Mabel nodded. "You go."

Alice looked at her in disbelief.

"I . . . I want to search the dining saloons and hospitals. Just . . . just to be sure."

"Yes, I suppose that makes sense," she said softly, swiping at her cheeks. She clasped Mabel's arm. "Don't be long."

Mabel turned away, lest Alice see the single tear she dashed away from the corner of her eye. She couldn't give in to tears just now. She wouldn't!

She exhaled a long, trembling breath, nearly breaking her oath. Then, with renewed purpose, she whirled away from the sight of the *Carpathia*'s crew loading some of the *Titanic*'s lifeboats onto its forecastle and strode off to find the Dining Saloon. In the end, she only had to follow the flow of first-class passengers who were already being herded in that direction for some purpose. She soon found out.

Circling the edges of the room, she allowed her gaze to dwell on the faces of each and every individual, searching for Father's and Charlie's beloved features, or Chess's handsome ones. Until Mrs. Harris suddenly exclaimed, "Please don't!" to a group of musicians who had gathered near the piano. It took Mabel several moments to grasp why Mrs. Harris had objected to their playing music. Only when an Episcopalian clergyman had begun to read the service for the burial of the dead from the Book of Common Prayer did she recognize that they'd intended to perform a funerary hymn.

Mabel stood there stunned, unprepared for the enforced finality of the moment. She knew it was meant to provide comfort to those who were grieving, but for those who hadn't even overcome the shock of it, let alone accepted it, the act felt merciless. She wasn't ready. She wasn't even remotely ready. Had she been able to escape, she would have, but she was now hemmed in on all sides. Even so, as the air in the room seemed to grow thinner, she considered pushing and shoving her way out.

A minister from Baltimore ended the impromptu service with a prayer of thanksgiving for the living, and this, at least, was something Mabel could grasp. She *was* grateful to be alive. She was grateful her mother and sisters had survived. But . . . her father . . . and Charlie . . .

She hiccupped on a sob. Her father had always understood her need to question. Had seemed to encourage it. Until those questions drove her to want to attend university. But now he was gone, and there would be no opportunity to challenge that stance. There would be no questions at all. No strong-armed hugs. No winter sleigh rides with just the two of them when the others thought it too cold. No one to call her Mabes.

And Charlie . . . poor, eager, noble, ingenuous, sometimes exasperating, but always well-meaning Charlie. He was so young! Just nineteen. Had he ever kissed a girl? Or smoked a cigar? He'd had so much of life ahead of him!

She was weeping in earnest now and could not stop. But she was in good company. Others were softly weeping, their sobbing muted. They were simply all too exhausted, and their voices too hoarse from the long, cold night on the sea to do more.

As soon as the service ended and she was able to push her way through the crowd without making a scene, Mabel did so. She considered returning to the cabin assigned to them. She wanted nothing more than to lie down and sleep. Besides, Mother and her sisters must be wondering where she was. But she had one more place to check before being able to extinguish all hope.

The hospital.

When Mabel came tumbling through the cabin door, both Flora and Alice hushed her with a scowl. They'd just gotten Mother to sleep. She'd been distraught at the news of Father's and Charlie's deaths. Though with the aid of a healthy dose of brandy, they'd been able to calm her enough to convince her to lie quietly, eventually finding solace in slumber.

As such, this was the first moment Flora had been able to sit with her *own* anguish. The first time she'd been able to stare into the face of her loss and the lashing pain and yawning emptiness it carried with it.

Until in stumbled Mabel, her eyes lit with an unholy excitement that curdled Flora's blood. How could her lips even form a smile in a moment like this? How could they even contemplate it? Where had she been, anyway? Avoiding duty and unpleasantness, as always. Leaving it all to Flora and Alice.

Flora's anger and indignation roared to life, unwilling to be quelled in the face of her unfathomable sorrow. Just as she was about to speak, Mabel made her heart stop.

"Chess is here! He's alive!"

For a long moment, Flora couldn't form a thought. She could only sit there, staring at her sister suspended in time, waiting for her heart to beat again.

"Where?" Alice asked for her.

"In the hospital. He's injured. I don't know how severely."

"He must have gone down with the ship like some of the others we heard about." Alice clasped her hands over her mouth at the horror of it before turning to Flora, who had still not spoken.

Both her sisters moved toward her in alarm, pressing hands to her shoulders.

"Breathe, Flora," Mabel urged.

After several shallow gulps she managed to find her voice. "Is it . . . is it really true?"

Mabel lowered to her knees to look up at her, clasping one of her hands. "Yes, Flora. I saw him with my own eyes."

Tears seeped from the corners of Flora's eyes and a tremulous smile formed on her lips. Could it really be? Chess was alive! She closed her eyes, letting the tears fall faster. Thank God! *Thank God!*

But then they snapped open as she thought of Father and Charlie, still lost to the depths. Her heart sank like a stone. How could she feel joy knowing that?

Alice knelt to take hold of her other hand. "It's all right to feel happy." Her cheeks were also streaked with tears as she flashed her a grin. "I'm happy, too. For you. It is possible to feel both joy and grief."

She was right. On the one hand she wanted to sink to her knees and never rise, and on the other she wanted to leap and dance and twirl. But while her sisters understood, would their mother?

She looked at Mother asleep in the bottom berth, her back

turned to them and her white hair splayed across the pillow. Mother was so fragile right now, and Father had charged her to look after her.

Alice squeezed her hand. "Go to him. We'll look after Mother."

"He's injured, Flora," Mabel said. "He needs you."

This galvanized her. She pushed to her feet, pulling her sisters up with her. She embraced them each in turn, whispering simple words of affection into their hair cascading in snarls down to their waists. They smelled of the cold and the sea.

It took Flora some time to find the hospital, having to pause and backtrack multiple times as she'd forgotten to ask Mabel for directions. When she finally found it, she stood gasping against the doorframe as her eyes scoured the room's occupants.

"Are you in need of help, miss?" a steward in a white uniform coat asked her.

"No. Just . . . looking for someone." She pressed a hand to her chest, gathering her composure. "I was told he was here."

He nodded in understanding. Presumably she wasn't the only woman who'd come dashing in here in such a state. "What's his name?"

"Chess . . . or rather, Chester Kinsey."

"Just a moment."

He crossed the room and passed behind a white curtain. Flora leaned to the side and arched onto her toes, trying to catch a glimpse of whoever might be inside, but the drapery was kept discreetly shut. A few minutes later a man came striding out.

"I understand you're looking for Mr. Kinsey," he asked in a low voice.

"Yes. Is he here?"

"He was," he confirmed. "I imagine he's on deck now, exercising, as I instructed him to."

"Thank you," she said, and turned to go.

"He needs to keep moving as much as possible, miss," he called after her. "It's the only way he might save them."

She didn't understand what the doctor meant, and she didn't stop to ask, being too anxious to simply find Chess.

Once on deck she hurried along the promenades, searching for his familiar long-legged form. She was momentarily distracted by the sight of the massive ice field spread out for miles toward the horizon. Icebergs dotted its expanse like tall towers or yachts at full sail, but the sheets of ice were such that in places it seemed one could walk across them as on land. They caught the morning sun, nearly burning her eyes with their intensity as the *Carpathia* made its way around the perimeter.

She even ventured onto the decks reserved for third class, where, due to the quarantine restrictions, she normally wouldn't have been allowed. But given the fact that all the classes had already been thrown together in the lifeboats, the crew's enforcement of such rules had slackened.

Everywhere—no matter the class—silent misery was written on every face. Many were without proper clothes, having escaped in little more than pajamas or hastily donned garments. Some didn't even have shoes. Only the blankets thrown over their shoulders kept them from freezing in the icy air.

She circled the ship twice, growing more and more agitated with each passing moment. Finally, she stopped in the middle of the Boat Deck, spinning around as her eyes scrutinized everyone within sight, and wondering if he might have returned to the hospital. What if there had been some sort of mix-up, or she was hallucinating?

Then she spied him emerging through one of the doors. Her heart fluttered wildly like a caged bird as he staggered forward, moving stiffly. His clothes were matted, and his face was shadowed with stubble, but he was alive.

She stumbled toward him one step and then another. And then she was running, hurtling in his direction. He looked up and saw her, bracing his legs just as she flung herself into his arms. He lurched backward, colliding with the wall behind him as he wrapped his arms around her and buried his face in her hair.

She sobbed aloud, adding the salt of her tears to that of the ocean already encrusting his coat. "I thought I'd lost you," she repeated over and over until he tipped her face up to press his lips to hers, the bristles around his mouth lightly abrading her skin. His hands raked through her hair, pulling the tangled strands away from her features as their mouths parted so that they could look at each other.

Her face was a blotchy, tear-streaked mess, she was certain, but the gleam in his eyes told her he didn't care. There were lines wrought across his countenance that told a harrowing tale. She smoothed her hands over the skin now drawn so tautly over his bones that they seemed to protrude and leave his eyes sunken and shadowed. Pain bracketed his mouth.

A smattering of applause broke out near them, and Flora flushed as she stepped back from Chess to receive a few hearty congratulations. Others merely smiled. But Flora also sensed the sadness behind some of the felicitations. Their wish for their own happy ending.

"Mabel saw you in the hospital," Flora explained to Chess, noting his gritted teeth as he pushed away from the wall. "Do you need to sit?"

He took a firm grip of her hand. "Actually, I need to walk." He lifted her hand, scrutinizing the bandages.

"Blisters," she replied in answer to his unspoken question. He hobbled forward a few steps before his gait straightened to a degree and she recalled what the doctor had said. That Chess needed to keep moving as much as possible. Though she still didn't understand. "But if you're in pain, shouldn't you be resting."

"It's frostbite," he pronounced. "Dr. Blackmarr suggested amputation."

# CHAPTER 43

❧

Chess had never felt so much pain in all his life. Each step made him want to grind his teeth down to nubs. He imagined it might feel the same if dozens of silver toothpicks had been plunged into his flesh. Yet within the ache there was also an odd numbness— a sensation that while some parts of his legs hurt acutely, other parts were dead. However, sitting still almost made it worse. At least while he moved the pain had purpose.

When they'd reached the *Carpathia*, he'd managed to climb up the rope ladder onto the ship, even though his legs felt frozen. But then most of his body had felt numb with cold. He'd downed the tumbler of brandy a steward had handed him and asked after Flora and the Fortunes. Once he'd learned that all four women were safely on board, he'd shuffled off to one of the ship's galleys and managed to eat a bowl of soup and some warm bread before climbing into a warm space behind one of the stoves. He'd curled up in several blankets before allowing his exhaustion to carry him into oblivion. Meanwhile, the cook had thrown his drenched clothes into an oven to dry out.

He'd believed he was well enough, but when he woke an hour later, the pain and deadness had intensified. So he'd taken himself off to the hospital, where Dr. Blackmarr, a passenger assisting the ship's surgeons, had diagnosed frostbite. Chess had not been prepared when the doctor had advised that amputation might be necessary, or for his almost cheery assertion that the operation could be performed on board the ship.

The thought of losing his legs horrified him. He would never walk, or run, or play tennis again. Never dance with Flora. And what of the logistics of a whole host of other things? No. He balked at the very idea.

The doctor had replied that he had one other option. That if Chess exercised his legs almost continuously, there was a possibility he might be able to save them. Chess had latched onto this alternative and vowed to stride up and down the decks and corridors of the ship day and night until they reached port. But first he wanted a hot bath.

Somewhat revived, he'd gotten dressed again in his dry, albeit salt-stained clothes and gone above deck to begin his exertions. He'd made inquiries about the whereabouts of Flora and her family, and a steward had promised to find out for him, but she had found him first.

When he'd looked up to see her running toward him, her copper-brown hair flying out behind her, the sight was like the sun emerging after weeks—no, *years*—of endless, dreary winter. Had he been able to, he would have run to her also, but it took all his will for his legs not to give out when she'd slammed into him. Thank heaven the wall had been at his back.

Even in all the hours of bleak desperation after he was swept from the deck of the *Titanic*, when exhaustion and bone-chilling cold had racked his body and he'd feared he couldn't endure even another minute, he'd never felt so close to weeping as he did in that moment that he clung to Flora. All the terror of what he'd seen and endured came burbling to the surface, along with his remembered dread of what she might have been going through. Even secure in a lifeboat, that didn't mean she was safe. There were dozens of things he could imagine happening to her, starting with them capsizing.

But here she was in his arms. Her heart beating next to his. Her scent in his nostrils. Her mouth lifting eagerly to meet his.

Had they not been on deck surrounded by witnesses, and had his legs not ached like the devil, he was quite certain their embrace would not have ended there.

Now strolling, or rather hobbling hand in hand with her, he told himself to be circumspect with the truth, but he discovered that was impossible with her. Maybe it was because he was still too bleary-eyed or because shared tragedy had torn down his normal barriers. He suspected it had more to do with it being her— gazing up at him with compassion and understanding in her blue-gray eyes, gripping his arm and resting her head on his shoulder both in comfort and solidarity.

"You were in the water a long time, then?" she said when he'd finished explaining Dr. Blackmarr's diagnosis. "What happened?"

Chess exhaled a long breath, intending to explain briefly. But it all came pouring out.

He'd been trying to help right the collapsible after it had fallen from the roof of the Officers' Quarters, landing on the deck upside down with a crash, when a wave had swept him over the side of the ship. The freezing water had driven the air from his lungs, and it was all he could do to fight the instinct to breathe in before he surfaced. Thank heavens for his life belt, for if he'd not been wearing it, he wasn't certain he would have ever found his way.

He emerged facing the ship, sucking in great gulping breaths as the water below him rumbled and thundered with muted eruptions. Then the first funnel fell with a terrifying groan, crushing the people in its path. The wave it created spun him outward, but the wake from the second funnel falling pulled him under, sending him tumbling through the water yet again and pelting him with small pieces of debris, which accounted for many of the cuts and bruises all over his body.

His energy was all but spent as he fought his way to the surface for a second time, but by Providence, he emerged next to the overturned collapsible. Several men were already on top of it, including Second Officer Lightoller, who had dived from the

Bridge as it was going under. Chess had tried to pull himself on board but struggled to do more than heave his torso up over the side of the cork fender, hanging on for dear life as he shivered and tried to catch his breath.

The *Titanic*'s stern continued to rise slowly into the air just fifty or sixty yards away as people desperately clung to her. The sea around the ship was already littered with debris and thrashing swimmers. He watched as the ship broke in half with a great rending crack just in front of the third funnel and the stern dropped back to a horizontal position, only to rise again to near perpendicular. It balanced there for a number of seconds before sinking with a loud hissing sound and disappearing beneath the water.

The sights and sounds he had heard during the minutes following the sinking would haunt him for the rest of his life. Somehow, he managed to pull himself farther onto Collapsible B, and it was a good thing, too. Because the boat rapidly filled, and swimmers who then came alongside could merely cling to the edge, gradually freezing to death in the water. Others grabbed onto deck chairs and other flotsam, even a wardrobe floating nearby. However, most of the people were left to flail in the icy water, which soon took its toll.

Tightly packed in with the others on the boat, Chess hunched in on himself, trying to conserve as much body heat as possible. He'd begun to lose sensation in his feet, but he didn't know how much of that was because of the awkward manner in which he was perched with a man seated on them or because the water kept washing over and submerging them. A fellow he was seated next to named Bride, who he learned was one of the Marconi operators, was in much the same situation. On his other side was Jack Thayer, who at seventeen proved to be just as plucky in the end as the stokers and other fellows on the boat.

For a time, they thought they needed only to wait for the other lifeboats to return. Chess knew many of them had left the *Titanic* half-full. But after a time, they realized that was not going to happen. Surrounded by the desperate cries of those in the water—screams they knew the people in the other boats must have heard—it seemed unfathomable that they didn't return.

And then it was all but too late. At least for those who had not reached the collapsible. The silence that fell as, one by one, the swimmers around them took their last breaths was almost more unbearable than their moans. But soon they had more pressing concerns.

Most of the occupants of Collapsible B were now standing, trying to keep as much of their bodies out of the cold water as possible and make room for others. At thirty-one, they'd reached the maximum capacity, though there were still people in the water nearby asking to be brought aboard. When someone would die and fall off the raft, someone else would clamber on board to take their place. Chess watched it happen so many times that he discovered, to his horror, that he was becoming inured to it.

Just as horrifying a discovery was the fact that the boat was sinking lower and lower under their weight. To keep other swimmers from trying to force their way on board, some of the men were using oars and planks of wood to push them away and row the collapsible farther from them in the water. One swimmer was even clubbed in the head with an oar. All Chess could do was maintain his grasp on Jack Thayer, who was kneeling on the hull and struggling to stay aboard while another fellow gripped Chess's other side. It was a precarious balance. Even more so for the men standing.

Someone near the bow swore he saw Captain Smith in the water nearby, but few of them paid heed. Officer Lightoller certainly didn't. When he discovered the wireless operator Bride was among them, Lightoller plied him with questions about the distress calls he and his colleague had been able to send. Bride told them several ships had responded, but *Carpathia* was the nearest, and it had been three hours away. This cheered many of the men's spirits, giving some of them the energy to reorganize themselves in the boat according to Lightoller's instructions, standing in two rows, facing forward, as they held on to each other's life belts. Then he had them lean in accordance with the direction of the waves that had begun to kick up, trying to keep the overturned collapsible level to maintain its buoyancy. This was no easy task, and even those who were unable to stand tried to help.

Lightoller also convinced them to yell together, attempting to hail any boat that might be close by. But their shouts of "Boat ahoy!" went unanswered, and they soon gave up in order to preserve their strength. In any case, the growing swell was causing more air to seep out from underneath the boat, and it required all their concentration to work together to keep it afloat.

As the situation grew more and more desperate, one crew member asked, "Don't the rest of you think we ought to pray?" A poll was quickly taken of everyone's faiths, and it was decided the Lord's Prayer would be best. Then the fellow led them in its recitation.

Though Chess was a member of Trinity Church in Manhattan and considered himself a believer, he'd never felt particularly devout. But in the dark of that bleak and endless night, he discovered he had more faith than he'd ever realized. He prayed as fervently as he could while laboring to keep Bride's head above the sloshing waves, reaching into the depths of himself. When they fell silent, he felt a peace he could only describe as divine. Whatever came next, he was ready.

He was seated too low in the boat to be of much use searching the horizon for the lights of any ships. They'd been fooled too many times already by the green flares Lightoller believed an officer in another boat was sending up. But as dawn cast a pale wash over the sky, someone spotted a cluster of lifeboats nearby. Lightoller managed to find his whistle and blew two sharp blasts. "Come over and take us off!" he cried.

Two of those boats came to their rescue, though they nearly capsized them in the process. Each precarious leap of one man into the other boats threatened to dislodge the rest of them. Chess eventually made his way into Lifeboat 12, his legs prickling as if needles were being jabbed into them. There they huddled under steamer blankets, trying desperately to get warm as Lightoller took command of the boat and plied the tiller. The craft was heavily weighed down, but at least not sinking like their abandoned collapsible. They were the last to reach the *Carpathia*.

Neither Chess nor Flora spoke for a long time after he finished his recitation, and he could guess where her thoughts had gone.

"I'm sorry about your father and brother," he murmured. "They were right behind me on the roof of the Officers' Quarters trying to free those last collapsibles. But when the wave washed me overboard . . ."

Flora pressed a finger to his lips, drawing them to a halt. "Don't." Her eyes glinted with tears. "I know you didn't abandon them. The fact that you survived . . ." Her voice broke. "Well, it's a miracle. And I know Father and Charlie would never begrudge you that you lived, and they didn't." She shook her head. "I certainly don't."

"But your mother . . . How is she?"

"She's overcome with grief right now. My sisters and I are in agreement that one of us needs to stay with her at all times. At least . . . at least until she's more in her right mind."

Chess felt a pang hearing how distraught Mrs. Fortune was, the poor woman. He turned to look out at the sun-speckled ice.

"Do you blame yourself?"

He'd been unprepared for the question or the way it made him feel, but as always, Flora's brilliant gaze gave him no quarter. Though *blame* was perhaps too strong a word for what he felt, he acknowledged the guilt festering inside him.

The corners of Flora's lips curled into a sad smile. "I suppose this will be a weight we will carry with us all our lives. That we should have survived when so many others did not."

He was startled by her words. "But you're a woman."

"And that makes me somehow more worthy?" she countered angrily. "Worthier than Father, or Charlie, or Mr. Andrews, or Mr. Futrelle, or any of the others who perished?"

He grasped her hands between his, but she wasn't finished.

"It's not about worthiness or right, though the question will be asked and debated over and over again, perhaps for some time to come. Because in most instances there is no answer. No reason why this person was saved, and that person was not." She pulled her hand free to gesture broadly. "There *is* no *why!*" She closed her eyes tightly. "No satisfactory one, in any case." Then she turned her hands to grip his, her voice low and aching. "I'm sad Father and Charlie died. I will *be* sad for a very long time, and I will miss them always, but . . ." She hiccuped. "But I'm also glad you didn't."

Chess pulled her hands to his lips, pressing kisses to them, and wondering what he'd ever done to deserve this woman. He knew it was another question he would never have the answer to.

# CHAPTER 44

❧

*Tuesday, April 16, 1912*

Time moved slowly aboard the *Carpathia*. So great was the grieving and suffering of most of *Titanic's* survivors that one might have likened it to a funeral barge. When not suffocated by the cloud of her own sorrow, Alice spared some pity for the *Carpathia's* own passengers and crew who had been caught in the midst of it. Though they were all unbelievably kind and treated the *Titanic's* survivors with great consideration.

Much of the time, Alice remained sequestered with Mother, comforting her as best she could and urging her to do those things that grief stole the desire for, but were needed nonetheless for the body to carry on. Such as eating and drinking and sleeping. Alice had elected to take on the bulk of those duties, although Flora and Mabel helped whenever they could. But Flora had Chess to see to, making sure he also ate and rested in between getting up every two hours to exercise his frostbitten legs to try to save them from amputation.

Meanwhile, Mabel was determined to be useful, assisting with the widowed women and children, several of whom had become separated during the loading of the lifeboats.

"The sight of those mothers frantically searching for their missing children is one I will never forget," she confided to them one night as they lay in their berths after Mother had fallen asleep, with the aid of a healthy dose of bromide. "One mentally distraught woman even claimed another widow's baby as her own."

"How did they uncover the truth?" Flora gasped.

"The real mother recognized him by his cry, of all things. And then proved it by knowing about a small strawberry birthmark on his chest."

Mabel exhaled a long sigh. "Just two children are unclaimed. Two curly-haired boys."

"I believe I know them," Flora remarked. "They were put in my lifeboat by their father. They didn't speak English, only French."

"Yes, that's them," Mabel said. "Then you didn't see their mother?"

"No, only the father."

Mabel contemplated this. "Miss Margaret Hays has taken charge of them for the time being because she speaks French, but perhaps the boys' mother wasn't on board the *Titanic*. Though if that's true, then that might be because she was already deceased. Poor little mites."

"But what of the Allisons?" Alice asked. "Remember, the last we saw of them, they were desperately searching for baby Trevor and his nanny? Did any of them survive?"

Mabel's expression turned pensive. "The baby did. And the nanny, too. But neither Mr. nor Mrs. Allison, nor little Lorraine were among the survivors."

At this news, Alice closed her eyes, saying a silent prayer for all their souls.

"We did everything we could," Mabel said, her voice tight with emotion. But Alice could tell that, despite her sound reasoning, the loss of Lorraine Allison had affected her sister greatly. Perhaps it was because she'd tried so hard to save her. Or maybe it was because she was experiencing the plight of the orphans and the other surviving children firsthand by working with them.

Whatever the case, Alice was proud and pleased to see Mabel utilizing her skills and energy to such worthy ends. And this wasn't the only endeavor she'd undertaken.

Mabel had also been collaborating with several other women, including the Countess of Rothes, to help organize clothing for those who had been forced to leave the *Titanic* with very little. A number of orders had been placed by wireless to several New York stores for clothing to be supplied upon their arrival. In the meantime, many of the children in third class wore little but thin nightgowns, so a committee of women were working together to stitch clothes for them from whatever fabric they and the *Carpathia*'s bosun could find. This, at least, was something Alice could contribute to while she sat with Mother. Turning blankets into shirts and dresses also helped keep her thoughts occupied during those times when Mother slept but Alice couldn't.

Sleep didn't come easily to any of the Fortune women, but the sisters refused to take the bromide offered to them by the ship's surgeon. Though perhaps they should have. Flora suffered from nightmares and refused to share them. Mabel, on the other hand, seemed to feel the drive to keep moving. That by *doing*, perhaps she might find absolution for the anguish that haunted them all.

Absolution was something Alice also sought. For frittering away so much of her time on the *Titanic* instead of spending it with Father and Charlie. For stealing and gambling away Flora's pin money, even though all of it was now resting at the bottom of the Atlantic. For laughing at the fortune teller in Cairo. All of it weighed heavily on her mind.

On Monday afternoon, she'd seen Chess on deck exercising his legs. They had paused to watch as the bodies of four men who had died in the lifeboats, each sewn into a canvas bag, were consigned to the deep. Three of the bodies dropped into the water and slid down to their watery graves with the barest of splashes, but the fourth landed flat, with a strange *splosh*.

It was a sight apparently Sir Cosmo and Lady Duff-Gordon

had not been present for. Otherwise, they would not have had the poor taste Tuesday morning to insist on posing for a picture right there with their fellow occupants from Lifeboat 1.

"It seems they wished to make a presentation of giving the crewmen in their boats the five pounds they'd promised them each to replace their kits," Flora had explained after watching the tawdry event. "So they had everyone who escaped with them gather with their life belts. Which caused no small amount of distress to those watching the proceedings, making them fear that the *Carpathia* might now *also* be sinking." There was an angry glint in her eyes as she shook her head. "There were twelve of them. Just twelve, in their boat! And they decided to immortalize that. Lady Duff-Gordon, in her moleskin coat and purple silk kimono, even went so far as to have them all sign her life belt as a sort of macabre souvenir."

"I heard the five pounds wasn't just to replace their kit but a bribe to convince the crew not to row back for survivors," Mabel murmured so that Mother wouldn't hear.

"I don't know about that," Flora said, "But at the very least, they were being terribly callous and naive."

"A fact they'll no doubt live to regret if these rumors gain traction," Mabel proclaimed. She had already been hearing rumblings about the inquiries that were bound to be made into the sinking, and questions regarding a number of the claims beginning to circulate the ship were certain to be raised.

Allegations that either Captain Smith, Chief Officer Wilde, or First Officer Murdoch, or some combination thereof, had taken a pistol to their heads and killed themselves. That the captain had been attempting to take the Blue Riband for fastest Atlantic crossing, when everyone knew the *Titanic* had not been built to do so. That the crew had all been drunk and making merry the evening of the crash. That there had been more lifeboats, but they had capsized. And, most upsetting, that ice warnings had been received and unheeded.

This last rumor was one the Fortune sisters could give credence to, having overheard conversations regarding these warn-ings. Mrs. Ryerson told Mahala Douglas about her interaction with Mr. Ismay just several hours before the collision—an inter-action Flora had witnessed—in which he'd shown Mrs. Ryerson and Mrs. Thayer a telegram warning of ice, and soon the news of Mr. Ismay's potential duplicity spread throughout the ship. But Ismay had secluded himself in Dr. McGee's cabin and refused al-most all visitors, offering no defense for himself.

In the face of their grief, all of it was a bitter pill to swallow.

Chess could provide insight to some of the speculative claims, as he had been on the ship during its last moments. He'd seen Captain Smith, Mr. Andrews, and many of the ship's officers working until the very end to help as many passengers as possi-ble survive. If anyone had taken their lives, it would have been in the last seconds before they would have been swept into the water.

Alice encountered Mrs. Brown on deck Tuesday evening dur-ing her respite from caring for Mother and listened as she ex-plained about the committees that had been established that afternoon to create a fund for the relief of the destitute, as well as to express gratitude to Captain Rostron and the crew of the *Carpathia*. Several resolutions had also been passed in praise of the *Titanic*'s officers and crew in addition to everyone on the *Carpathia*. Alice promised her family would contribute some-thing to the funds.

Mrs. Brown wrapped her arm around Alice's shoulders as they walked. "I am so very sorry for you, my dear. How is your mother holding up?"

"Not very well, I'm afraid."

"Of course . . . to lose her husband and youngest child in one fell swoop . . ." She shook her head sadly.

"Yes, well, we lost them, too." Immediately, she wished her words back, ashamed of the bitterness of her tone.

Mrs. Brown did not berate her but merely squeezed her shoulders. "You did. And she will emerge from it eventually.

But it will take time. And, fortunately, you have your sisters to help console you."

Yes, she was grateful for that. Many of the survivors had no one except sympathetic strangers to lean on for support. Strangers who might not have their best intentions at heart. They'd already heard there was one reporter on board the *Carpathia* who had been sailing for the Mediterranean when the ship had been diverted to help the passengers of the *Titanic*. A reporter who, along with his wife, was gathering stories.

"And how are you faring?" Alice asked Mrs. Brown. "Are you sharing a stateroom?"

Many of the first-class women had paired up in groups to share accommodations.

"No, I'm sleeping in the Writing Room with a number of other ladies, and it suits me just fine. We are packed in like sardines and toasty as cheese over a fire." She shivered—either in mockery or in earnest, for the air was still biting. "After that night we spent on the water, being warm is something I shall never take for granted again."

# CHAPTER 45

❦

*Wednesday, April 17, 1912*

Flora jolted awake, sitting upright in her berth. It took several moments for her to recall that she was on board the *Carpathia*. That the *Titanic* had sunk. That Father and Charlie were gone.

*Crash!*

She nearly bolted from bed at the booming sound. Her first thought was that they'd hit another iceberg. But then she saw a flash on the wall at the edge of the curtains, and a second later the rumble of thunder. Climbing out of bed, she peeked through the curtains to see the wind driving rain against the porthole.

She pressed a hand to her chest. It was just a thunderstorm.

When the next flash of lightning came, followed by a crack of thunder, she was ready for it. She stood for several more minutes watching the atmospheric confrontation play out. The chill air settled around her shoulders, but her feet stayed warm inside her half-boots. She'd not taken them off since her arrival except to change stockings the day before, when someone had lent her a clean pair.

Though she knew it was ridiculous, she couldn't sleep without them, without knowing she was ready to leave their cabin at a moment's notice. Her coat, hat, and gloves were draped over the end of her bed. Removing them had been her only concession to comfort.

She hadn't been sleeping well, anyway. When she closed her

eyes, she saw Charlie reaching out to her from the water, calling her name. She stretched her hands out toward him, but no matter how hard she tried, he was always just out of reach. Other times she had nightmares plagued by ghostly moans, roaring waves, plunging ships, and frozen, hollow-eyed corpses. It was enough to make her fight the need to shut her eyes, but eventually her body gave in.

She rubbed her tongue over her teeth, cringing at the taste in her mouth. They'd been unable to find toothbrushes. The barber, who stocked some in his shop, had sold out quickly, and few of the *Carpathia*'s passengers had possessed extras, so most of the *Titanic*'s survivors had to make do with their fingers.

Flora sensed it was about midnight. Two days, then, since the *Titanic* had struck an iceberg. Two days since Father and Charlie had breathed their last. She tried to take comfort in the fact that they were in heaven, beyond want or fear or cold or pain, but it was difficult not to also think of the fact that their last moments on earth had been horrifying.

A clap of thunder rattled the window, reminding her of the distress rockets. She was glad her sisters and Mother were able to slumber through the noise. They were all restless and exhausted. None of them would be truly able to settle or begin to heal until they reached land.

Flora felt a flutter of anxiety about reaching New York. Here they were cocooned from the rest of the world, but once they docked, once they left the ship, they would be wading into the realm of telephones, telegrams, newspapers, and broadsheets. Something this enormous, this tragic . . . There would be no escaping it. It would extend its tentacles into every corner of their lives if they let it.

Compared with survivors like Madeleine Astor and Dorothy Gibson, Flora guessed, they would draw little enough interest from most of the world outside Winnipeg, especially if they stayed quiet. On the other hand, if the press found out about her connection to the tennis star and elusive bachelor Chess Kinsey, that might quickly change.

She wondered if he was awake. If he was as rattled as she'd been by the thunder. A sudden gust of wind hurtled the rain harder against the glass of the porthole. Surely, he wouldn't be out walking the decks in this weather.

Before she could think better of it, she grabbed her coat, and silently slipped from their cabin. The corridors were dark and quiet, just like the public rooms crowded with survivors. Pausing at the door to peer into the saloon, she could hear soft snores and voices mumbling in their sleep. She made her way to the entrance to the Forward Deck, peering out through the windows at its rain-lashed expanse revealed by flashes of lightning.

"Looking for someone?" She jumped at the sound of Chess's voice and whirled around. Searching the shadows, she spied him standing against the far wall.

"You don't honestly think me so foolish as to go out on deck in this weather?"

"No," she said, before confessing. "At least, I hoped not."

"Come here," Chess answered softly.

When she drew near enough to make out the features of his face during the next flash of lightning, he pulled her to his side, cradling her head on his shoulder. She could feel the tension in his frame and realized why he wasn't standing closer to the windows. The storm had unnerved him even more than it had her. For good reason.

She crowded close to him, absorbing his heat and comfort. Deeply breathing in the scent of his skin at the junction of his neck, she felt the knot of worry in the center of her chest begin to loosen. A few moments later, she was consoled when his muscles also relaxed. Still, they said nothing, merely held each other, their breaths seeming to settle into a rhythm. When he lowered his head to press his lips to hers, it was less a moment of passion and more a seeking of succor and solace.

"We'll have to take care, you know, when we reach New York," he said, after he'd tucked her head back beneath his chin.

She didn't pretend to misunderstand. "Yes. I don't think either of us wants reporters hounding us. That is, any more than they already will." Chess was certain to be pressed for interviews. "And . . . I would like to speak to Crawford first. I feel I owe him at least that. He shouldn't learn I'm jilting him for another man from the newspaper."

"Don't say it like that," Chess protested.

"But it's true," she stated bluntly. "We can paint it in as pretty words as we like, but the fact is, I *am* jilting him. And that's precisely what the newspapers will say if they catch wind of it. You know it's true."

He sighed wearily. "Sadly, yes. But you don't deserve to be labeled with such a term."

"Neither does Crawford." She grimaced. "But I shall have to face him in New York. That is, assuming Robert receives our telegram in time."

Though the wireless messages sent out from the *Carpathia* were being strictly limited by the captain, each survivor had been allowed to send one telegram to relatives to inform them of their status. Flora had requested a single message be sent on all four Fortune women's behalf to their brother Robert stating simply, "Mother and three girls are well, Charlie and Father missing." She hadn't been able to stomach writing the word *deceased* or the thought that it would be transmitted as such.

"We'll figure it out," Chess murmured, running his fingers through her hair where it tumbled unbound down her back.

She nodded against his chest. "How are your legs? Are you even able to sleep?"

"Possibly a little better. They're certainly no worse." He heaved a weary sigh. "And, no, I haven't slept well. But then, no one from the *Titanic* seems to be sleeping well. At least, not without either medicinal assistance or a liberal dose of brandy. I take it you haven't resorted to either."

"No." She hesitated before admitting. "I wish I needn't close my eyes at all."

He tipped her chin upward with his finger so that he could see into her shadowed eyes. "Nightmares?"

"A few."

"Me, too," he admitted.

She tightened her arms around his torso. "What a pair we make."

He tucked her chin against his chest again and they absorbed the comfort of each other's presence, listening to the rain lash the ship and the rolling thunder.

"Is there a place belowdecks where you can exercise?" she asked. "I mean, other than roaming the corridors."

"I should have asked one of the crewmen earlier." A note of humor entered his voice. "I found myself thinking your brother would be disappointed in my lack of curiosity about the ship."

Flora's lips curled reflexively. "Yes, Charlie would have pestered the crew into sharing every aspect of the vessel with him by now, wouldn't he? From the rigging to the boilers."

Her grin broadened, then abruptly fell. Charlie was gone. He would never sail again. Never annoy them with his recitation of facts about a ship or some other contraption. Never bend his intelligent mind to any task.

And her father . . . He would never again embarrass them with his buffalo coat. Never walk her down the aisle at her wedding. Never meet his grandchildren.

She wept against Chess's coat, soaking it with her tears while he held her.

He pressed a handkerchief into her hand and waited as she mopped her face.

"You need time," he said. "To grieve. To take care of your family."

"Mother needs us terribly," she admitted in a strangled voice. "I've never seen her like this. If we weren't here, I'm afraid she would simply give up." Flora hadn't dared mention Chess to her for fear of how she would react. She wanted her mother to be happy for her that he'd survived, but she suspected that would not be the case. That she would view any reference to him as a betrayal of Father and Charlie.

"And I'm rather worried about Alice. She seems to be keeping a lot to herself, and I get the sense that she somehow blames herself for some part of all this. Though I don't understand why."

Truth be told, she wondered if it had something to do with that fortune she'd received in Egypt. After all, she was bound to think of it, given how eerily similar the prediction had been to their circumstances. But that didn't mean it was anything more than a coincidence.

"Did I tell you Karl said Miss Newsom had a nightmare that something like this would happen the first night at sea? It troubles her."

"No, but I believe I've heard similar claims from no less than half a dozen people. It seems a quarter of the passengers on the *Titanic* were prescient of her doom, and yet sailed on her anyway," she muttered sarcastically.

"Maybe more like half. Earlier today I spoke to a fellow who was bringing home a prized French bulldog who claimed he'd had a 'bad feeling.'"

"Did the bulldog survive?" She knew of at least three dogs that had been saved—a fact that had upset some of the survivors, given that so many people had not. Even Flora, who adored animals, admitted to a pang of resentment that Mr. Harper's Pekingese had been rescued when her brother had not been.

"No."

Flora thought of Jenny, the ship's cat, and her kittens. They had likely never even had a chance.

"I fear I should feel more sadness at the discovery of another creature's passing, but I have nothing left to give."

She tipped her head so that her nose and forehead rested under his jaw, which at some point in the past few hours had been shaved smooth again. She took comfort in feeling his skin against hers—his warmth and sweat—and the pulse pumping in his neck.

# CHAPTER 46

❦

*Thursday, April 18, 1912*

The days on the *Carpathia* were the saddest and most disconsolate of Mabel's life, but were also the most fruitful. Never had she felt so useful and productive as she did in those hours helping Margaret Brown listen to the steerage passengers' plights and needs and searching for ways to meet them however they could. Or in cutting and stitching clothes alongside Noëlle, the Countess of Rothes, for those who had so little. Both women had big hearts, a marvelous sense of humor, and a decided lack of pretension. Noëlle had even snickered when she'd told Mabel how a sailor had claimed he knew she was a lady because she talked so much.

They were also unwilling to have men dictate to them what they could do when they could clearly see there was a need to be met. These same men decried them as meddlesome and interfering despite the good they were doing. Or, rather, they denounced Margaret as such. No one would have dared criticize Her Ladyship, and, admittedly, Noëlle went about her business with more tact and deference—whether feigned or real. Mabel suspected the former. Mrs. Brown, on the other hand, declared she had little use for tact except in her stitching, especially when it came to male vanities. Mabel had learned a great deal from both of them.

Thick fog rolled in on Wednesday morning, blanketing the ship and forcing it to slow down. It drove most of the passengers inside, out of the icy haze and away from the foghorn, which rang out dolefully at regular intervals, lowering spirits and fraying nerves. The fact that the mist shrouded the ship nearly the remainder of the journey to New York only heightened the sense that the *Carpathia* was a funeral ship.

However, despite the turn in the weather, matters were relatively calm, carrying on as they had before. There were still the downcast to console, the hungry to be fed, the cold to be clothed, and the injured to be seen to in the hospital and along the decks. Mabel had spent some time with a woman who preferred to lie flat on her injured back on deck rather than against the cushions of a settee or a hospital bed. She claimed the pain in her back was helped by the hard wood.

Mabel was relieved when they discovered that William Sloper had survived, and slightly aggrieved by the fact he seemed so intent on avoiding all the Fortune women, in particular Alice, with whom he'd been so close. However, he appeared at their cabin door on Thursday afternoon, hat in hand, asking for Alice. His usual loquaciousness appeared to have deserted him, though his eyes spoke eloquently enough of his empathy.

"I'm ever so sorry," William told Alice softly as Mabel and Flora eavesdropped. Not a difficult thing to do in such a tiny room.

Alice nodded and sniffled, giving way to a fresh spate of grief.

"I don't want to intrude on your mourning, but I also wished to offer any assistance I can provide in helping you obtain transportation or find accommodations once we arrive in New York."

"Thank you," Alice replied. "We're expecting to be met by my brother. And Father prearranged our rooms at the Hotel Belmont by telegram on Sunday."

"Then you'll be in good hands." He bowed his head solemnly. "My condolences again to you and all your family."

As he turned away, she asked, "You remember Cairo?"

It took him a moment to respond, and when he did, his reply was woeful. "I do."

She nodded and then closed the door.

Mother was sleeping again, otherwise Flora would never have ventured to speak so openly. "Is that why you've been so withdrawn?" She replaced the pillow she'd been fluffing and straightened the corner of her cover in preparation for their anticipated departure from the ship in several hours' time. "That fortune?" She shook her head and planted her hands on her hips. "Please, don't tell me you believe that soothsayer predicted this."

"No," Alice conceded. "I realize it predicted as many things wrong as it got right." She smiled sadly, tears still glinting in her eyes as she reached out her hand to her sisters. "After all, I didn't 'lose everything.'"

Flora frowned. "Then why have you been so taciturn?"

Alice dipped her head. "Aren't Father's and Charlie's deaths reason enough?"

She had an excellent point, but Flora still didn't look entirely convinced, and Mabel couldn't help but wonder herself.

While Flora and Alice helped ready their mother to disembark, Mabel went up on deck to find out how much longer they had to wait. She emerged to find their fellow survivors in a state of restless agitation, for they'd passed Lightship *Ambrose* a short time earlier—the familiar approach to New York Harbor. The fog had finally lifted and a heavy rain was now falling, accompanied by great flashes of lightning and rumbles of thunder. It would make disembarkation uncomfortable, but what was one more unpleasantness after everything they'd all endured.

Despite the storm, many of the *Titanic* survivors and *Carpathia* passengers lined the railings, eagerly gazing across the Ambrose Channel toward land. Mabel joined them and discovered that a veritable armada of tugs and small boats had surrounded them. In her surprise, she at first thought they were filled with anxious family members, but it became clear they were newspapermen. They hoisted placards asking questions such as "Is Mrs. Astor there?" and utilized megaphones to call out callous and downright unforgiving queries. They fired rockets in the air in attempts to better light the decks for their photographers. They even waved money above their heads to tempt survivors to jump ship and be retrieved by them to share their harrowing tales. What they didn't realize was that after lowering or leaping from the *Titanic* in fear of their lives, almost nothing—not even fifty dollars—could entice them to repeat the experience.

Mabel hurried below to tell Flora not to let Mother come on deck until they docked, which would be some hours yet, before returning to her place along the rail. Undeterred by the rain, thousands of curious onlookers crowded the Battery at Manhattan's southern tip as they passed. An even larger mob had gathered at Cunard's pier. But they sailed past, navigating farther up the North River to the White Star pier where the *Titanic*'s lifeboats were the first items unloaded. The last remnants of the magnificent ship.

Mabel had warned them. She had told them to be prepared for the chaos at the Cunard pier. But Alice was still shocked by the massive crowd gathered there—perhaps tens of thousands of people. By the police cordons and lines of ambulances and motorcars. By the swarm of journalists. At some point, the rain had stopped, though it still dripped from the eaves and formed puddles all over the ground, reflecting the lights of the ship and the flashes of the photographers' magnesium flares.

Alice had expected to be glad to reach land, to escape the sea and all its terrors. Instead, she found herself facing an abyss. Their rescue was at an end, and the path before them dark and uncertain.

Mother's face was grim and washed out, as it had appeared every day since their rescue. If she was disturbed by the spectacle before her, blessedly, she gave no indication of it. Though she needed Alice and Flora's support to stand.

Conversely, Flora's features were strained and tense. Her eyes kept darting to the deck several feet to her right, where Alice caught sight of Chess, trying, and failing, not to return Flora's looks. She knew they'd chosen to distance themselves from each other. At least until the tumult of the arrival of the *Titanic*'s survivors had ended. But that didn't mean it would be easy.

Mabel stood quietly and calmly on Alice's other side. Alice expected some sort of snide or irreverent remark to pass her lips, but she held her peace. The gangways were put in place and the injured passengers needing treatment at a hospital were taken to the waiting ambulances, and then the first-class passengers were allowed to disembark. As they processed over the gangway, Mabel proved herself to be the most composed.

The Canadian survivors had clustered together, and Major Peuchen and Mr. Dick—the only surviving Canadian men—escorted them collectively from the ship. But when Peuchen paused to speak with one of the reporters shouting questions, Mabel swept the Fortune women past the phalanx of newspapermen and photographers and into the Pier 54 shed.

Inside, friends and family of the survivors had been grouped behind placards bearing the initial of the survivors' surnames. Mabel guided them down the line toward F, but even before they'd reached the sign, Alice's knees threatened to give way at the sight of one familiar beloved face. A sob broke from her lips, and she stumbled into Holden's enveloping embrace.

He smelled of wet wool and peppermint and home, and she found herself weeping almost inconsolably at the feel of his arms around her. It was some moments before she was sufficiently recovered to even notice who else had been waiting there for them. Her eldest sister, Clara, wrapped her in a hug and so did Clara's husband, Herbert. Seconds later, she was hustled from the shed with Holden's arm draped protectively around her.

They passed several Salvation Army officers in their uniforms and doctors and nurses in white, as well as rows of stretchers propped along the wall, ready for use. The street outside was lined with limousines and other motorcars, and the Fortune family were helped into two sent by the Hotel Belmont. Mother, Clara, and Herbert climbed into the first, along with a Dr. Gibbons, while Alice, Holden, Mabel, and Flora occupied the second. It wasn't until they'd pulled away from the curb that Alice realized that not only had their brother Robert not come, but neither had Crawford.

She opened her mouth to say something to Flora, who was staring out the window on the opposite side of the motorcar, but then snapped it shut.

Holden swiveled to speak to them from the front seat. "Your brother Robert feared he wouldn't make it from Vancouver to New York in time, so he asked us to travel on ahead of him," he explained. His eyes lit on Flora, who hadn't turned to look at him. "And Campbell said he had some pressing business he couldn't delay, but he asked me to convey his apologies, Flora. That he would have come if he could."

"Thank you, Holden," Flora answered calmly, her eyes still on the damp streets rushing by the window.

"What rubbish!" Mabel exclaimed, expressing the same sentiment Alice held but didn't dare say.

He would have come if he could? Please! His fiancée had just survived a shipwreck. One in which more than *fifteen hundred people* had died, including his future father-in-law and brother-in-law. Yet "pressing business" had kept him away. It certainly removed any lingering doubt that Flora was doing the right thing by ending their engagement.

If Flora was angry, she didn't show it. Instead, she reached over to press a quelling hand to Mabel's arm. Mabel scowled mutinously as if she intended to say more, but then her gaze shifted to the rearview mirror, through which they could see the driver darting glances at them. It wasn't news directly about the

*Titanic*, but the papers would probably pay well for any sensational gossip about the survivors and their familial squabbles.

They passed the remainder of the drive largely in silence. Only once they were ensconced in their hotel suite, after being shown every courtesy by the hotel staff, did they dare to speak again.

"Dr. Gibbons has sedated Mother," Clara told them after she'd seen Mother settled in one of the bedrooms adjoining the parlor suite.

"How could any of this have happened?" Herbert demanded to know. "The *Titanic* was supposed to be unsinkable!"

"Obviously she wasn't," Flora replied listlessly. "We struck an iceberg. It scraped along the side. We saw it from our cabin window. We took to the lifeboats, but there weren't enough. There weren't nearly enough." She faltered before regaining her equilibrium. "And not enough time to fill more if we'd had them."

Holden sat on the arm of the chair Alice had sunk into, resting his hand on her shoulder. When Herbert continued to press them with questions, he intervened. "They've been through a terrible ordeal. Perhaps we should let them rest."

"But what arrangements have been made? Have they recovered the bodies?"

Alice winced.

"I suspect that's a question for White Star, not your sisters-in-law," Holden said firmly.

Herbert paused long enough to look at all four Fortune sisters' wretched faces and nodded, holding his tongue.

One by one, they dispersed to their bedchambers, no one giving any thought to leaving Alice alone with Holden in the parlor, something they would never have done before.

Holden led Alice to the settee, draping his arm around her and pulling her close. He pressed a gentle kiss to her lips before lifting his finger to tentatively touch their cracked and chapped surface.

"The cold and the salt spray," she explained.

He cradled her hand, now devoid of its bandages but still rough and peeling.

"From the oars."

"There weren't crewmen or even male passengers to wield them?"

She shook her head, and he pulled her close again, burying his head in her hair—her hair that had not been washed or dressed for days.

"When I heard . . . ," he began before breaking off. His throat worked as he swallowed. "Thank God you're alive."

There were so many things she wanted to tell him, so many things she needed to say. But for now, just being here with him was enough.

# CHAPTER 47

❦

*Friday, April 19, 1912*

Flora woke to a world in a frenzy over all things to do with the *Titanic*. Flags were lowered to half-mast. Stores were closed—in particular, Macy's department store, out of respect for the loss of Mr. and Mrs. Straus. Theaters were dark—at least, the ones that had belonged to victim Henry Harris. The newspapers and broadsides were splashed with all the latest news about the doomed Atlantic steamer writ in large bold headlines, and its pages yawned with harrowing tales from its survivors. Flora recognized some of the names, but not all.

Holden and Herbert had gone out to discover what information they could from White Star about the recovery of bodies and how to make property claims. They returned with a massive stack of papers, which they dropped onto the table in the parlor of their suite, and tales of being hounded by newspapermen in the hotel lobby eager to speak with the Fortune women.

"I caught one fellow lurking in the corridor outside our suite," Herbert informed them. "Somehow he'd sneaked past the lobby. Likely bribed a hotel employee for information."

There were other survivors staying at the Hotel Belmont as well—and some of them were not averse to speaking with the press and having their stories published in newspapers across the country and the world. The reporter who had already been sailing aboard the *Carpathia* when the *Titanic*'s distress call came in was rewarded for his scoop with a stay at the Belmont, compliments of his paper, the *New York World*. Perhaps it was only fitting that they'd put him and his wife up in one of the city's finest hotels, but his presence certainly caused a complication for the Fortunes.

Flora tightened the belt of the slate-blue dressing gown that Clara had brought her from Winnipeg. "I suspected the press attention would be bad"—she pressed her fingers to her forehead—"but this is far worse than I imagined."

Flora saw the way Alice and Mabel looked at her every time Chess's name appeared in the papers. Although he'd shared very little directly with the newspapers, he'd been touted as a hero, along with Jack Thayer and several of the other men who had gone down with the ship but had nevertheless survived. Word from some of the other survivors that Chess had helped them to escape merely added to his celebrity.

While Flora was filled with pride at these accounts, she worried that the greater his fame, the more difficult it would be to keep their relationship a secret.

Flora wished desperately that she could contact him to at least find out how he was faring. Whether his legs were continuing to improve or they'd gotten worse. But they'd already discussed what a risk it would be for her even to send him a letter, particularly during the days immediately following their arrival. Flora had been shocked by the idea of the press interfering with the mail or the telegraph service, or even a private messenger, but Chess knew better than she did what they were capable of. So she refrained from sending any correspondence, even to Crawford.

She wasn't completely surprised that Crawford hadn't rushed to her side here in New York, but it hurt, nonetheless. Especially when she'd seen Holden with Alice.

"I'm afraid you'll have to stay secluded in this suite until your mother is well enough to travel and we can make arrangements to return to Winnipeg," Holden told them all.

"That goes for you as well, Clara," Herbert said. "They might badger you just as severely."

"But I need to go shopping," she protested. "We all need mourning clothes."

"Then you'll have to ask the stores to come to you." Herbert's gaze traveled over his sisters-in-law, in their hodgepodge of attire. Mabel's dressing gown was too small, barely cinching at the waist, and Alice's hem was torn. "I'm sure the idea of dressing some of the *Titanic*'s survivors will appeal enough to convince them."

Herbert clutched the lapels of his coat. "I've asked the hotel manager to report that the physician has diagnosed that you are all suffering from shock and nervous fatigue and must have absolute rest. That should deter the reporters for the time being."

"It's more likely to whet their appetite," Mabel retorted wryly.

"Nonsense. Their attention will be diverted by the Senate inquiry into the wreck beginning at the Waldorf Astoria today."

The United States certainly didn't waste time! The survivors had only just reached New York and they were already convening an inquiry. Apparently there was some urgency to question Mr. Ismay and the *Titanic*'s crew before they sailed back to Britain and escaped their purview, perhaps for good.

Flora had little interest in it. The inquiry would not bring Father or Charlie back, nor would it rescue any of the other fifteen hundred lives from the depths of the ocean.

There was, however, one report that concerned Flora.

"Did you see the article about Mr. Sloper?" she asked Alice and Mabel after Clara and Herbert had gone to look in on Mother.

"Yes! Of all the scurrilous nonsense," Alice retorted angrily. "William would never have behaved so dishonorably."

"What did it say?" Mabel asked.

"That he disguised himself in a woman's nightgown in order

to escape the ship. But you saw him board the lifeboat, didn't you?" Alice demanded of Flora.

"Chess did." Flora's eyes shifted to Holden, wondering if he knew about him, too. "He said William boarded with Dorothy Gibson and her mother. The officers let him in without any fuss."

Mabel's expression was pained. "Poor William. Now that it's printed, there will be people who refuse to believe otherwise."

"Which is exactly my fear." When they all turned to look at Flora, she explained, "If we refuse to speak, if we don't offer them something . . . will the reporters make something up about us as well?"

Flora could tell the thought troubled them as much as it did her.

"Let's wait and see if the physician's statement placates them, as Herbert believes," Holden suggested.

The sisters exchanged looks, and Flora could tell Alice and Mabel were no more convinced than she was that this strategy would work. But for the moment, they had little choice but to follow Holden's advice.

# CHAPTER 48

❦

*Sunday, April 21, 1912*

On Sunday morning—nearly one week after the disaster—the family gathered in the parlor. Even Mother made an appearance, her head bowed and her shoulders slumped. Dressed in black, as they all were for mourning, they fairly resembled a flock of crows. As they did during inclement weather, the men read from the Bible and led them in prayer, while Alice directed them in a few hymns.

As their voices faded away following the final stanza, they sat quietly. Noise from the streets below filtered in through the windows, a background to their heavy thoughts.

Herbert was the first to break the silence. "I've received word from Robert." Their older brother who lived in Vancouver, and who was now ostensibly the head of the family. "He's decided to travel on to Halifax rather than come here. That's where White Star proposes to take the bodies they recover for identification and retrieval by loved ones."

Herbert had already informed the sisters that the White Star Line had hired several cable ships from the Canadian port to complete this arduous task, but Mabel wasn't certain Mother had been told. Even so, she barely flinched at the blunt reality.

"Robert was always a good boy," was all she murmured in response.

Mabel didn't envy Robert the task. It would not be an easy one. Particularly not after so much time had passed. She had to shy away from thoughts of what state the bodies might be found in.

Herbert and Holden shared a look before Herbert continued. "We've also made arrangements for us to depart New York by special train on Tuesday."

Had Mabel not been seated next to Flora, she might not have felt the tension that rippled through her frame. Plainly, she'd not anticipated their leaving so soon.

"Major Peuchen from Toronto is scheduled to testify at the Senate inquiry that day, and we decided it may be best to leave town before he finishes. We'll be traveling first to Montreal and then on to Winnipeg."

However, Mabel and her sisters knew this would not stop reporters from badgering them no matter where they went. So they waited for Mother to retire with Clara, and Herbert to scurry off to smoke one of his noxious cigars before addressing the issue with Holden.

Herbert's instructions to the hotel manager and his direct appeal to the *New York Times* for their privacy while they recovered from shock and fatigue had done nothing to deter the dozens of reporters still gathered in their hotel lobby. It was true, the call Mrs. Brown had paid them the previous day to collect their contribution to the fund for the destitute had not helped matters, but their continued silence was more the problem. Particularly considering that the other survivors staying in their hotel had already spoken to the press and, as a consequence, were no longer being hounded.

Alice slid forward in her seat. "Holden, little as we like it, we need to give them something more, or they will never give us peace. Not here or in Montreal or in Winnipeg."

"In Winnipeg, they can even harass our friends," Mabel pointed out.

They'd already received a telegram from Crawford informing them he'd been approached by newspapermen asking for information. The fact that he'd also asked them to write to tell him what they knew had upset Flora. She'd forbidden any of them to respond. An edict they would all respect, with the exception of perhaps Herbert.

"I suppose that's only logical," Holden replied, his concerned gaze trained on Alice. "Herbert and I could—"

"No Herbert," Flora stated flatly. "Only you."

It was clear Holden didn't like the idea of circumventing Herbert, but he conceded that the sisters had a valid point. Ultimately, it was his concern for their safety that won him over to their side, especially when they pointed out that there were not only male, but female reporters, who could go places he could not and ambush the sisters. Though he initially balked at their suggestion of what he should tell the reporters on their behalf.

"Just tell them you've refrained from asking too many questions about the wreck because when you do, we become hysterical," Flora said.

"Yes," Mabel agreed, knowing the newspapers would latch onto this explanation like a dog to a bone. "Tell them we're grief-stricken and . . . and physically prostrated. That's why we need you to speak for us."

"And then simply share the bare facts," Flora continued. Her jaw was tight, being as unhappy as Mabel that they had to serve up any portion of their family tragedy on a platter for the public's consumption. "No details. Just enough to convince them we've capitulated, so they'll leave us alone."

Holden blinked at them in perplexity. "You *want* me to tell them you're hysterical?"

"Disgusting, isn't it?" Alice concurred. Her rueful expression echoed her sisters'. "But it should be sensational enough to do the trick."

Flora's nose wrinkled in disdain, her shoulders slumping in weariness. "In any case, the rest is true enough. We *are* grief-stricken and exhausted. So, if letting them think we're too debilitated to be interviewed serves our purposes, then so be it."

Holden proposed that he write up what he intended to say and show it to them before moving forward, then departed the suite to do just that.

"He thinks we'll change our minds," Flora stated once the door had shut behind him.

"I can't blame him. We don't normally espouse such nonsense," Mabel said, and scowled. "But why is it that society expects ladies to be fragile blossoms incapable of standing up to even a stiff breeze? Any suggestion otherwise and the men ruffle up like offended roosters, telling us to mind our place."

"Not everyone is like that," Flora protested.

"No," Mabel acceded. "But enough people are that those women who don't crumple under pressure and instead intend to be useful are then decried as meddlesome or even less complimentary terms."

"Women like Mrs. Brown," Alice guessed.

"Yes!" Mabel sat forward in her seat, intent on making her point. "She and Lady Rothes saw needs that were not being met and set out to do something about it, but rather than be grateful for it, some of the men decried them as intrusive. How many of the needs of the world are seen and met by women without men ever taking notice of them? How many more needs could be met if men would stop telling women to mind their place when they do?"

"It sounds to me like this argument goes beyond what occurred on the *Carpathia*. Beyond what's happening now," Flora stated with her usual perceptiveness. She tilted her head in consideration. "Does it have something to do with why you kept disappearing aboard the *Titanic*? Does it have something to do with why you and Father quarreled?"

Mabel crossed her arms and turned away, uncertain whether to be honest.

"I thought that was over Harrison Driscoll," Alice said.

"I don't think so," Flora replied.

But if Mabel had learned anything during her time aboard the *Titanic* and since, it was that she had to stop hiding who she was and what she wanted. And who better to inform first than her sisters?

"I wanted to convince Father to let me attend university." When her sisters didn't visibly react, she pressed on. "But he said no. Numerous times. The last and most vociferous was that final afternoon."

"But I always thought Father was proud of how clever his daughters were," Alice said.

"He told me my place was at home with a husband."

Flora shook her head as if she didn't believe her.

"I assure you he did," Mabel snapped in defense.

She reached out to touch her arm. "I'm not shaking my head at you but at Father." She exhaled, closing her eyes briefly. "You both know how proud Father was that he'd built such a fortune from nothing."

"He certainly told us about it often enough." Mabel's mouth quirked. "It's why he insisted that Robert earn his living instead of simply inherit it."

Flora nodded. "When he was growing up, every member of his family had to work to help the family scrape by. Including his mother, his sisters, and even his grandmother." Flora grimaced sadly. "They toiled from sunup to sundown, and apparently his mother worked herself into an early grave. So, in his eyes, the ultimate mark of distinction was to possess enough wealth that the women in his family needn't work. Because it was what he wished he could have done for his mother. To ease her burdens. To help her live longer."

Mrs. Swift had said something similar, but this went beyond that.

"So when I told him I wanted to attend university, to do something other than marry . . . ," Mabel ventured.

"He thought of his mother and everything she'd endured, and took offense," Flora finished for her. "It was like telling him everything he'd done for us wasn't enough."

Mabel pounded her leg with her fist. "But that's not what I meant! That's not what I meant at all. Why couldn't he have just explained all that?"

"Because that was never Father's way," Alice answered softly.

Mabel grunted in acknowledgment. If only she'd known, if only she'd realized. She might have saved them both a great deal of grief.

"So what do you intend to do now?" Alice asked. "Do you still wish to attend university?"

"If I can." Mabel's eyes darted between her sisters, curious if either of them knew the terms of Father's will. Whether Robert would exercise control over their inheritance until they married.

But then her time aboard the *Carpathia* had shown her she already possessed the ability, the determination, and the wiles to be useful, even without a university education. That she was responsible for her own happiness and for finding a way to embrace the life she felt called to.

"Well, we are here to support you." A small smile creased Flora's lips. "Even if this means you're a suffragist."

Mabel frowned. "It's not all the terrible things you read in the papers."

"Of course, it isn't." Flora shared a look with Alice. "A man wrote those."

"*And* drew the caricatures," Alice added.

"You really must stop believing that just because we know how to be *tactful*, we don't hold opinions of our own. You might be surprised what we actually think."

Mabel realized she'd done her sisters an injustice. All this time, she might have confided in them instead of trying to conceal her every intention. How much easier would that have been? How much more productive?

Her irritation sparked. "Well, in the future, you might make your feelings plainer. At least in private. What you call tact, I call pretense."

Flora held up her hand. "Fair enough. I suppose we all need to communicate better with one another." She fastened her glare on Alice, who flushed.

"I don't know what you mean."

But Flora wasn't fooled, though she softened her tone. "Someday I trust you'll share exactly how you were spending your time on the *Titanic*." She arched her eyebrows. "And why it made you feel so guilty."

Alice arched her chin. "Meanwhile, we know how *you* were spending your time."

But Flora didn't rise to the bait, instead appearing rather forlorn.

Mabel could guess why. "Have you had no communication from him?"

She shook her head. "We can't risk it." She gestured toward the outer door to the suite. "Not while those reporters are holding us hostage, waiting for any news of the Fortune women."

"And we're leaving Tuesday," Alice murmured.

"So it seems."

It was their turn to console Flora, embracing her from opposite sides.

Alice hated it when Flora was right.

Remaining silent was no longer tenable. *Begin as you mean to go on.* Mrs. Brown's sage advice echoed in her head. So that evening, when the others had retired, she decided it was time to do just that.

Taking hold of Holden's hand, she led him to the sofa farthest from the bedroom doors and closest to the windows where the noise of traffic passing along Park Avenue below could be heard. This was not a conversation she wanted to be overheard. She gripped his fingers tightly with her own and, gathering her courage, she told him.

She told him how alive she'd felt during their travels. How each new setting, each new experience, had made her eager for more. How she'd thought she'd grow tired of it—had *hoped* she would—but how each new adventure had only whetted her appetite. She told him how she'd missed him terribly, but the closer they drew to their journey's conclusion, the more keenly she'd dreaded its conclusion.

"Well, I suppose that's only natural after you've had such a marvelous time," he remarked, his brow furrowed as he struggled to understand. He reached up to brush a stray strand of hair behind her ear. "Up until the end, that is."

She sniffed, swiping the tears from her face before reclaiming his hand. "Yes, but . . . I started to dread returning to my life with you. To the life you'd planned for us and laid out so neatly in your letters."

He stiffened, appearing both stunned and wounded. "Oh."

"I didn't dread *you*," she hastened to explain, shifting one of her hands to clutch his elbow, lest he attempt to leave. "I could never . . ." She broke off as a sob caught in her throat. "I love you," she squeaked as more tears spilled down her cheeks. "I love you so much. But I . . . I don't want to live a life where I'm coddled and cosseted, and never step foot outside of Toronto." She gazed pleadingly into his eyes, trying to guess what he was thinking, anxious for him to comprehend.

Now he seemed bemused. "What you're saying is that you wish to travel, isn't it?"

She sniffed. "Yes."

"Even after everything that's happened?" He arched his eyebrows. "Your ship sinking. Losing your father and brother."

She hesitated. Such things should make her want to stop, shouldn't they? But oddly, they did not. Oddly, they made her even more determined to do it. To not waste a single moment.

"Does that make me heartless? Heartless and foolish?" she asked.

"Do you think your father and Charlie would want you to stop living your life because they lost theirs?"

"No."

He shrugged one shoulder as if to say, then there you have it.

"But what of your seasickness?" she disputed. "I know travel on ships is uncomfortable for you."

"Well, then, I'll simply have to make do, or you'll travel with a friend or one of your sisters."

"You would do that for me?"

"Alice, I would do anything for you. Don't you know that all I want is for you to be happy? That all those things I wrote in my letters were what I thought *you* wanted. What I thought you needed to hear."

"They were?"

"You were sick so often as a child, and your family has always been so protective of you. I thought you needed to know I would take care of you as well."

Embarrassment welled up inside her.

"Have you been chafing against their protectiveness all this time and simply never said anything?" he queried. "Because that would be just like you. But you must *tell* me what you want and need." He smiled sheepishly. "And in the future, I will try to remember to ask rather than assume."

She pressed her hands gently to his chest, anxious to reassure him. "I haven't been chafing. Not awfully, anyway. But you are right. I'm not good at confrontation." She fiddled with his lapel. "But if I can be brave enough to ride a camel or explore ancient ruins, then I should be brave enough to speak my mind."

Instead of laughing at her jest, Holden cupped her chin. "Never be afraid to speak to me, Alice. To tell me the truth. I cannot promise I will never get angry. But I can promise you that I will always listen."

"I know," she whispered in earnest. "You are a good man." Tears stung the back of her eyes yet again. "Perhaps too good for the likes of me."

"That is most certainly not true," he refuted, but then paused, searching her eyes. "But it sounds like you have something else to tell me."

She pulled back and he released her, albeit reluctantly, as she gathered the words for her next confession. "I was so worried that our time on the *Titanic* might be my last chance for adventure, and I was so determined to squeeze out every last drop of excitement while I could, that I fear I became rather foolish." She risked a glance at his face before lowering her eyes to where she twisted her fingers in her lap. "I played poker," she confessed, squeezing her eyes shut as she continued. "I gambled away Flora's pin money without her knowing." She shook her head. "I didn't keep the best of company at all times."

"Did you kiss this Sloper fellow?"

Her gaze flew to his in shock. "No! Of course not."

His expression was somber.

"How could you . . . ?"

"Did you encourage him?"

Her face heated. "I . . . I admit at times he said flirtatious things to me, and on occasion I responded in kind. But he spoke to *all* the ladies that way. And I was always perfectly clear that I was spoken for, that my devotion lay with you."

"Just your devotion?"

She heard then the vulnerability behind his words and reached for his hands. "My heart also. You've always had my heart. Everyone knew how much I loved you. I couldn't help talking about you."

He didn't contradict her, but neither did he soften. Instead, his eyes seemed to be searching hers for something she wasn't certain how to give.

"I know I've disappointed you," she said, tears threatening

again. "That's the last thing I ever wanted to do. All I can do is say I'm sorry. I truly am."

He gathered her close then, cradling her head against his shoulder. "Oh, Alice. I'm not disappointed. Surprised, yes. But not disappointed. So, you tried poker. And discovered you're terrible at it, apparently."

She choked on a sound between a sob and a laugh.

"I presume it's not something you're eager to try again."

She shook her head.

"As for Flora's money . . . well, that's between you and her." He inhaled, as if bracing himself. "The issue that remains between us is whether you still wish to marry me."

She peered up at him in alarm. "Of course I do." Cold panic shot through her. "Why? Don't you wish to marry me?"

"I do," he assured her. "But with all your confessions, I wasn't sure if you were trying to tell me you'd changed your mind."

Alice wrapped her arms around his neck, scrutinizing his beloved features. From the widow's peak at his forehead and the patrician slope of his nose to his strong jaw and the cleft in his chin. "I love you, Holden. That will never change. And I cannot wait to marry you. The sooner the better."

His pewter eyes gleamed. "Then why don't we make it sooner?"

"Truly?"

"This summer."

Her heart fluttered in anticipation. "Yes!"

"I'll have to speak to your brother once he returns from Halifax, but I don't think he'll object."

She didn't think so, either. It would mean one less worry for him.

Alice beamed in happiness, and Holden's lips pressed to hers, sealing their promise. Oh, how she'd longed for this during the lonely hours of the night on their grand tour, when there was nothing to distract her from missing him. She felt so silly now for having feared how he would react when all it had taken was one honest conversation.

Holden ended their kiss, clearly not wanting to abuse Clara's good graces in allowing them to be alone together. They settled back against the sofa cushions, pleased to be seated side by side with her head cushioned against his shoulder. But her contentment reminded her that not all her sisters were so fortunate.

"Darling, I need your help," she said.

"Of course," Holden replied without hesitation. "What is it?"

"It concerns Flora."

# CHAPTER 49

*Monday, April 22, 1912*

Chess paced back and forth in a tight circle before the hearth, welcoming the twinge he felt with each step. It meant his legs were still there, attached to his body, and not amputated, as he'd feared. His family physician and the specialist he'd consulted had been optimistic about his ability to save both limbs if he remained on a similar course of treatment. However, it would be weeks or even months before they would know for certain. Either way, Chess had vowed to follow their instructions to the letter. If the worst happened, if his legs were amputated, then it would not be because he hadn't done everything in his power to keep them.

But his pacing in front of the fireplace in this handsome room at the Hotel Belmont was due not so much to his need to exercise as it was from anxiety. Anxiety that he might have been spotted by a reporter as Holden Allen sneaked him into the hotel from a side entrance. Anxiety that Flora might have changed her mind about him.

He supposed the last made little sense. He was here, wasn't he? Summoned to see her. But he also knew Flora was an honorable person. She would never end their relationship by letter and then slink away. She would do it face-to-face, just as she was intent on doing with Crawford Campbell. Or had been intent on doing the last time he'd spoken to her, four days earlier.

His mouth dried and his palms began to sweat at the possibility. He hoped that she remembered he loved her. Hoped that she understood why he'd stayed away until Alice's fiancé had contacted him to tell him the Fortunes would be departing for Winnipeg on Tuesday.

Chess had never anticipated that the press would be so ravenous for stories surrounding the *Titanic*. He knew he would be hounded for a day or two, but even a week after its sinking, they persisted. Especially after learning of the frostbite to his legs and feet. Somehow, they'd even discovered that he was at great risk of losing two of his toes, something he'd shared with no one. He had no doubt that whatever nurse or orderly had sold that choice piece of information had been paid a pretty penny for it.

Running the brim of his rain-speckled hat through his fingers, he pivoted sharply on his heel, noting his reflection in a mirror on the far wall. His dark hair was rumpled and standing on end, and he tried to repair it as best he could. Shrugging his shoulders, he scrutinized the folds of the worn and oversized coat he'd put on to disguise his appearance. Deciding to remove it, he tossed it over a chair and dropped his hat on top of it before straightening his tie. He felt like a green lad of sixteen, such was his nervousness to see Flora.

The door opened, and he whipped around in time to see Holden Allen enter, followed by Flora. She looked wan and tired, but even so, she was still the most beautiful woman in the world. The black silk of her mourning gown highlighted her elegance and made the copper accents in her hair stand out.

They gazed at each other, both seemingly reluctant to speak while Holden was present, though Chess's fingertips tingled with the need to touch her.

"I'll give you a few minutes," Holden told them before turning to address Flora. "I'm afraid Herbert departed on his daily ramble earlier than I anticipated, and I fear he might return sooner than expected."

She nodded in understanding as he turned to go, but she halted him with a hand to his arm. "Thank you."

He smiled at her fondly. "Lock it behind me just in case." His eyes flicked to Chess in silent warning before he departed, closing the door with a firm click.

Flora turned the key before swiveling to face him, her hands clasped before her waist.

"I take it Campbell didn't come to New York," Chess remarked.

"No. Only Holden and my sister Clara and her husband, Herbert," she answered softly.

Irrationally, he found himself furious on her behalf. "The rotten bastard."

Her face was composed in serene lines, but a measure of pain flickered behind her eyes.

"He never deserved you, Flora."

Her regard dipped to his legs. "How are they? I . . ." She broke off with a strangled sound. "I read about . . . your prognosis."

He realized then just how tightly she was restraining herself. In fear? In anxiety? In grief? Whatever the case, he hated seeing her like this. Like she'd been when they'd first met. Buttoned up, rigid, self-contained. Determined not to make a mistake.

Well, Chess was equally determined not to let her retreat into that shell.

Closing the distance between them, he pulled her into his arms and kissed her. Kissed her as if his *and* her life depended on it. Kissed her as if he might never have another chance. After but a moment of hesitation, she joined in, meeting him eagerly as she buried her fingers in his hair and melded her mouth with his.

In the end, he was the one to draw back, recalling his unspoken promise to her future brother-in-law as he'd departed. Even so, Chess couldn't resist placing three final kisses along the line of her jaw and behind her right ear, just to hear the sound she would make at the back of her throat. He had to firmly restrain his urges after that, but he managed it by forcing his thoughts back to his legs and the twinges they caused him even now, standing still.

"My legs are continuing to improve," he said, finally answering her question. "And I may or may not lose those toes. Either way, it shouldn't affect me overly much."

She inhaled a ragged breath. "I'm glad to hear it. Without being able to contact you . . ."

"I know," he assured her. It had been hell not to know how the other was faring. "And tomorrow you're leaving."

"Yes. We decided it would be best for Mother. Best . . . for everyone." They needed to return home. To mourn. To begin to mend. And she needed to end her engagement with Crawford.

"There's no need to explain. Little as I wish it, your place is in Winnipeg right now. And mine is here recovering."

"But for how long?" she murmured, her voice stark with sorrow.

"I don't know," he admitted. "A respectable amount of time after the loss of your father and brother and following the end of your engagement. A respectable amount of time for me to recuperate."

Her eyes scrutinized his every feature, perhaps memorizing them as he was memorizing hers. "Can we write?"

"*I* certainly intend to."

This brought a wobbly smile to her lips. Lips he couldn't resist capturing one last time.

She pulled away when there was a soft knock at the door, her eyes glittering with tears.

"Go on," he urged her gently, though he wanted to hold her tight and never let her go. He forced a smile. "I will see you soon enough."

She backed away, taking his heart with her.

# CHAPTER 50

❧

There was no shortage of press lurking about the Hotel Belmont the following morning when the Fortunes departed for the train station. Newspapermen and photographers crowded close and hollered out questions as the family was hustled into motorcars. But by the time they were riding out of New York on their special train, the interview Holden had given to two newspapers had already been published and read by thousands, if not tens of thousands, of people, hopefully granting the Fortunes at least a temporary reprieve. Of course, everywhere they went, they were still met by reporters, each clamoring for some new tidbit, but at least they weren't like the phalanx they'd confronted in New York.

After a brief stop in Montreal, the Fortunes sped on to Winnipeg, arriving on the first of May. An occasion that did not go unmarked. Friends and city officials met them with condolences and plans to honor Mark and Charlie Fortune, and four other citizens who had perished when the *Titanic* foundered. By the time the women were able to return to their home on Wellington Crescent—the one Father had so recently built them—Flora was greatly concerned her mother would collapse. The physician was summoned, and she was given strict orders for bed rest.

The sisters were also ordered to rest, but there was only so much sitting and reclining a body could withstand. At least on their own property, they could stroll behind the high garden walls, far from prying eyes, and breathe in the fresh air and the smell of spring flowers. They could surround themselves with memories of Father and Charlie and finally begin to heal.

A few days later, Robert returned from Halifax. Neither Father's nor Charlie's bodies had been recovered, and after two weeks in Nova Scotia examining the bodies of those who could not be identified by their effects, their older brother decreed he could no longer face the task. Flora's self-composure had shattered briefly upon hearing this. For if Robert had been this affected, then it must have been horrendous, indeed.

It was difficult to accept there would be no graves for Father or Charlie. No final resting places to mourn them. The plaque they planned to install in their memory at the city hall wouldn't be the same. The memorial service held in their honor at their church would have to suffice instead of a funeral.

In any case, Robert had another surprise for them. It seemed their father had taken out an insurance policy just one week before they'd sailed home on the *Titanic*. The policy, through Winnipeg's Great-West Life Assurance, also happened to be the largest insurance policy ever offered. Had Father had some sort of premonition of what would happen? Or had he merely recognized that in life there are no guarantees?

Whatever the truth, it brought tears to her eyes. Even in death, he was looking after them all.

Including Mabel. Who, true to her vow, had tried to convince Robert to allow her to attend university. Even when he'd refused, Mabel still pressed on in doing whatever she could to be useful to those causes she believed in. She presented an interesting dichotomy for some, working tirelessly in many of the efforts at church to help the widowed and orphaned and poor but also marching with her fellow suffragettes and pressing for equal education for women. Flora simply knew it was part and parcel for a woman eager for a fairer and more just world, and she was proud of her.

Alice and Holden were married on June 8, having been able to convince both Robert and Mother that it would be neither unseemly nor counter to their best interests. Alice made the most beautiful bride, and Flora had never seen anyone so happy, despite the tears glistening in her sister's eyes as Robert walked her down the aisle instead of Father. The sun shone brilliant that day, and Flora liked to think it was because their father had persuaded God that his Alice needed a bit of bright good fortune. Flora also liked to think the fox that had come scampering out of the pulpit and dashed down the aisle just before the service began was Charlie creating a bit of mischief in his own way.

Though she'd fretted and agonized for weeks over the task, Flora discovered that ending her engagement to Crawford proved rather straightforward. When he'd called at the Fortune home the afternoon following their arrival in Winnipeg, she'd simply pulled him aside and told him, and he'd accepted it with little fuss. He didn't even ask for an explanation. He merely wished her well and took his leave.

For a time, Flora wondered if she should feel offended but reminded herself that she'd gotten what she wanted. Given that, there was no reason to analyze it further. She would simply be grateful that Crawford hadn't contested her decision, and glad that Father had at least had the chance to approve of Chess before he'd passed. Which made convincing Robert of the wisdom of her decision that much easier, even if Mother hadn't yet fully accepted it. Chess's survival still rankled Mother, but in time Flora hoped she would realize that Chess's living had in no way caused Father's and Charlie's deaths, and that eventually she would choose to be happy for her.

Healing was a slow process. But as spring stretched into the long days of summer, and summer shortened into autumn, Flora became impatient for her life to move forward. She was ready. And she'd told Chess so in her last letter, though she'd yet to receive a reply.

They'd exchanged dozens of letters, but it wasn't the same as having him near. As being able to hold his hand or look into his eyes.

She had been relieved to learn his legs had recovered their full function, and that in spite of losing one toe, he'd still competed in his first tennis tournament since the *Titanic*'s sinking, placing fourth overall. Chess had also made strides toward setting up his sporting goods business. A fact that he said had bemused his family at first, but a few of them were beginning to come around to the notion that he needn't be a complete wastrel.

Mother had been less and less reliant on her in recent weeks, so in late September, on Flora's twenty-ninth birthday, she decided to take a long solitary stroll, past the churchyard and along the avenues where some of the prettiest houses stood, dreaming about where she and Chess might be in a year's time. Not here, she knew, but perhaps in New York or at a tennis tournament somewhere. Maybe she would even be expecting their first child.

So vivid were her imaginings that for a moment she didn't react when she rounded the corner to spy a familiar figure seated on the front porch of her family's home. It was only when he came trotting down the steps toward her that she realized he wasn't a figment of her imagination, after all, but a real flesh-and-blood human being. She hastened her steps, walking as fast as she could and then, abandoning all pretense of propriety, broke into an unladylike run, dashing down the walk toward him. He swept her up into his arms and spun her around.

"What are you doing here?" she gasped through her laughter.

"I knew today was your birthday," he replied, setting her down. "And after receiving your last letter, I simply couldn't wait any longer." His eyes burned with a fervor that made her flush with joy. "You aren't cross, are you?"

"Cross? Heavens no! Not when I've just been wishing I could trade all my birthday gifts simply for a glimpse of your face."

His teeth flashed white in his sun-bronzed face, telling her he'd been spending a lot of time outdoors. Even his dark hair had been bleached to a paler hue by the sun.

"Well, don't wish away all your birthday gifts just yet," he replied before extracting something from his pocket.

She gasped.

"I hope you haven't changed your mind," he said, suddenly sounding less sure of himself, and she loved him all the more for it. "For I've already spoken to your brother Robert."

"You have?"

"I went to see him in Vancouver before I came here."

She blinked back tears. "You did?"

He smiled softly. "And he gave me permission on your father's behalf to ask you for your hand in marriage." He lowered himself to one knee on the front walk for all her neighbors to see. "So will you marry me, Flora Fortune, and make me the happiest of men?"

"Yes!" she exclaimed, nodding empathically. "Yes."

He slid the diamond ring onto her finger and swept her up into his arms again. Only this time when he lowered her to the ground, his lips found hers as well. It was brief. They were standing on the front walk, after all. But it was no less ardent.

Then, taking hold of Chess's hand, she turned to stroll with him into the future. Whatever it might hold.

# Author's Note

❦

*Sisters of Fortune* is inspired by the lives of the Fortune family from Winnipeg and their journey on board the doomed RMS *Titanic*. When my editor approached me about writing a novel set largely on the *Titanic*, I knew that the success of the story would hinge on the main characters. So I delved into the passenger list, searching for someone who inspired me and fired my imagination. In fact, I found three of them—Ethel, Alice, and Mabel Fortune. No one I spoke to in those early days of planning had ever heard of them or their family—not even those friends I counted as *Titanic* enthusiasts—but a brief search turned up enough intriguing information about the Fortune sisters that I felt comfortable in pitching the idea that I focus my story on them.

However, once I truly began to dig deeper into the research, I discovered there is actually very little known about the Fortune sisters, especially about their time on board the *Titanic*. Even among family, they were notoriously reticent to speak of it. So when I tried to suss out these details, I was left with large gaps to fill in terms of action, personality, and motivation. I chased rumors—some of which I discarded because they could not be corroborated and were contradictory to other evidence—and scrutinized every first- and secondhand source I could get my hands on. Still the gaps remained.

This left me with both a blessing and a curse, at least from a storyteller's perspective. While it was frustrating not to be able to uncover more details to make a fully accurate depiction of each of the sisters, it also freed me to use greater creative license to flesh them out.

As such, I want to make it clear that while the core of the Fortunes' story and the fascinating anecdotes I uncovered about them form the backbone of this book, much of the rest of their tale is pure fiction. This is why it is important to note the distinction that these characters are *inspired* by the Fortunes and are not meant to be a comprehensive historical representation. In several notable instances, I have deliberately strayed from known facts for a number of reasons.

The first and most obvious instance is that I altered the story of the eldest daughter quite significantly. Because of this, I changed her name from Ethel to Flora (Ethel's middle name) in order to highlight the difference.

The real Ethel Fortune genuinely did postpone her wedding to Crawford Gordon (whose name I also changed, for obvious reasons) in order to embark on a grand tour with her parents and younger siblings, for whom she acted as a chaperone. She is reported to have balked at entering the lifeboats but was eventually persuaded to join her mother and sisters in Lifeboat 10. (Some sources list the Fortune women as leaving the ship in a different numbered vessel, but most state it was probably Lifeboat 10.) Ethel did not have a shipboard romance and returned home to eventually wed Crawford Gordon in 1913. By all reports, they enjoyed a happy marriage together.

So why did I elect to alter Ethel's story so greatly? Admittedly, including a romance in the book appealed to me, but the main reason is simply that Ethel's tale is so similar to her younger sister Alice's. Alice was engaged to Charles Holden Allen when the Fortune family set out on their grand tour, and she wed him when she returned on June 8, 1912. Because of their earlier wedding date and the fact that Allen is reported to have traveled to New York along with the eldest Fortune sister, Clara, and her husband, H. C. Hutton, to meet the *Carpathia* and escort the Fortune women home, I chose to keep Alice and Holden's relationship intact and modify Ethel's story instead.

In a twist stranger than fiction, Alice Fortune truly did receive that ominous fortune from a soothsayer in Egypt, and the main source for our information about this comes from William Sloper, who was with her on the veranda at Shepheard's Hotel when it happened. Most of the details about the Fortunes' travels, the Winnipeg Musketeers, Mr. Ross's illness, Mark Fortune's buffalo coat, Mabel's undesirable attachment to the musician Harrison Driscoll, and a few other details and anecdotes are also true. It is also known that Mabel married Driscoll in 1913 and they had one son, though the marriage did not last long. Mabel moved to British Columbia, living the rest of her life with another woman.

My other main character, Chess Kinsey, is the only fully fictional passenger in the book. However, he is based on two real survivors, both tennis stars—Karl Behr and Richard Norris Williams II. I chose to utilize Behr as a friend to Chess, partly because Behr's actual shipboard romance with Helen Newsom mirrors Chess's romance with Flora, but Williams is absent from my tale. This is mainly because I chose to have Chess borrow some of the details from Williams's struggle with frostbite after he escaped the *Titanic* in the swamped Collapsible A. Readers will be happy to know Williams also kept his legs and went on to play tennis for many years, even being inducted into the Hall of Fame.

As anyone who has ever chosen to write about an event that is now as famous and well scrutinized as the *Titanic* will tell you, it is not for the faint of heart. Despite my extensive research and efforts to do my due diligence, the eagle-eyed expert may catch me out on a number of errors. If so, I apologize. But please don't message me. Once the book has gone to print, there's nothing I can do to fix it.

On that note, I have attempted to include as many documented events, anecdotes, and conversations as I feasibly could, and as such I've slightly adjusted the timing of a few of these incidents in order to have my characters witness them. Many of these incidents were pulled from the recorded testimony and memoirs of *Titanic* survivors. The transcripts of the British and American inquiries can be found online, and I also recommend the website www.encyclopedia-titanica.org, which has a wealth of information on the subject.

There are still many mysteries surrounding the *Titanic*, and many hotly debated topics that we may never have definitive answers to. Did an officer commit suicide before the bow began its initial plunge? Did the band truly play "Nearer My God to Thee" during their last moments? When exactly did Lifeboat 10 leave the ship? There are dozens, if not hundreds, of details that are not uniformly agreed upon, and I do not profess to know the answers. In most instances, I've chosen to depict what I feel to be the most likely scenario, based on my research. Other times, I've opted to be deliberately vague. In many cases, my thoughts were most influenced by the research in *On a Sea of Glass: The Life and Loss of the RMS Titanic* by Tad Fitch, J. Kent Layton, and Bill Wormstedt—a detailed, in-depth analysis of all things *Titanic*, which I highly recommend. Their ship diagrams also proved to be an invaluable resource.

Now, to address a few matters I raised within the pages of the book but was unable to either resolve or further elaborate on because of my characters' limited purviews.

Francis Browne did, indeed, board the *Titanic* at Southampton and disembark at Queenstown. The photographs he took during his brief voyage are some of the best known. One of his most famous photos is of six-year-old Douglas Spedden spinning a top on the Promenade Deck. A scene that James Cameron also re-created in his movie *Titanic*. Browne is an interesting character, and I couldn't resist including him in some fashion.

It is true, Ella White had hens and a rooster brought aboard *Titanic* at Cherbourg, and her traveling companion, Marie Young, was escorted to look in on them every day by crewman Hutchinson. However, I could not find a definitive explanation for where they were stored. One resource suggested they were kept near the dog kennels on the Boat Deck, while another said they would have been stored in a cargo hold. Given this discrepancy, I chose to place them in the cargo hold simply to give one of my characters an excuse to visit this part of the ship.

The *Titanic* orphans were named Michel and Edmond Navratil. They were staying with their father, Michel Navratil Sr., over Easter weekend, when he decided not to return them to their mother, from whom he was divorced, and instead sail with them to America aboard the *Titanic* under the assumed name Hoffman. On the night of the collision, Navratil managed to get his sons safely into Collapsible D, but he perished. Neither boy spoke English, and they had been sailing under false names, complicating matters. After arriving in New York, fellow survivor Margaret Hays took custody of the boys while a search was made for their family. Understandably, they were a media sensation. Happily, because of this, back in France their mother saw a photograph of them in the newspaper and hastened across the Atlantic to claim her children. Michel Navratil Sr.'s body was one of those recovered from the Atlantic. However, because his papers listed him under an assumed name, his body went unclaimed, and based on his chosen surname of Hoffman, he was believed to be Jewish and buried in the Jewish cemetery in Halifax.

If you would like to learn more about the *Titanic* and the lives of its passengers, these are a few more of the sources I utilized during my research that I recommend: *Titanic: The Canadian Story* by Alan Hustak; *The Ship of Dreams* by Gareth Russell; *Gilded*

*Lives, Fatal Voyage* by Hugh Brewster; *The Band That Played On* by Steve Turner; *Titanic: Women and Children First* by Judith B. Geller; *The Story of the Titanic* as told by its survivors by Lawrence Beesley, Archibald Gracie, Commander Lightoller, Harold Bride, edited by Jack Winocour; *On Board RMS Titanic* by George Behe; and *Voices from the Carpathia* by George Behe.

# ACKNOWLEDGMENTS

None of my books would ever be completed without assistance from a large number of people. This book, in particular, proved to be a tremendous challenge, and I would never have been able to write it without significant help and support from others.

First and foremost, thank you to my husband for not only encouraging me to embrace this challenge, but also bolstering me when my self-confidence flagged, and stepping up to take on extra household tasks to help me make it to the finish line. I couldn't do any of this without you.

Thank you to my daughters for your amazing hugs and smiles, and for reminding me every day why I do what I do.

Thank you to my cousin, Jackie Musser, an amazing editor in her own right, for being a constant source of encouragement, wisdom, and guidance. I'm so blessed to have you as a sounding board and a friend. And many thanks to another cousin, Kim Ladouceur, for providing me with two invaluable resources, and for her never-ending love and support.

I am so incredibly grateful to my mother and father for helping me and my family in innumerable ways, be it childcare or cleaning up a flooded basement. You are life savers!

Heaps of thanks also go to the rest of my family and friends for your never-ending love and support, with a special shout-out to the ladies of my Mom's Group, and my agency sisters—the Lyonesses.

Many thanks to Kevan Lyon, my agent extraordinaire, for your always stellar counsel and support, and for always having my back.

Grateful thanks to Wendy McCurdy, my editor, for entrusting me with this project and for helping me see it through to fruition. Additional thanks to the entire team at Kensington for all your excellent work, as always.

Much appreciation to Rachel McMillan, who read an early manuscript, checking for any overt Americanisms I put in the mouths of my Canadian protagonists. (Any errors still contained in the book are my own.) I'm also grateful, Rachel, for your enthusiasm and support of my books, as well as so many others in the book community.

I also must thank all of the tireless *Titanic* researchers. So many of you have conducted such sterling research and analysis on the subject. Thank you for your dedication.

My heartfelt thanks to all my readers. It's because of your support that I get to take on such exciting opportunities and projects.

And lastly, thank you to God, from Whom all blessings flow. Your strength saw me through this, and Your grace gave me the will.

# SISTERS OF FORTUNE

## Anna Lee Huber

The following suggested questions are included to enhance your group's reading of Anna Lee Huber's *Sisters of Fortune*.

# DISCUSSION QUESTIONS

1. Which sister did you identify with more—Flora, Alice, or Mabel? How do you feel that you are similar to that sister? How are you different?

2. Prior to reading *Sisters of Fortune*, how familiar were you with the *Titanic*? Did you learn anything new? What surprised you most?

3. Many of the *Titanic*'s survivors reported receiving ill fortunes like Alice or having premonitions of doom before the ship struck the iceberg. Why do you think so many reported this happening, and do you think they were truthful? Do you believe in omens or clairvoyance?

4. Flora is seen as the dutiful daughter. This is something she has always prided herself on, until she begins to struggle with the implications of that role and a future she doesn't want. How is Chess the catalyst for her change? What do you think her life would have been like if she hadn't met him?

5. Alice has always been coddled, but she begins to long for adventure. Do you think her concerns about her fiancé were justified? Have you ever let fear drive you to do something reckless? What would you have done in her position?

6. Mabel longs to attend university and do something with her life other than marry and bear children. She struggles with her parents and society's expectations for her as a woman. How have those expectations changed since 1912? How haven't they? Were you surprised by some of the arguments against her achieving her goals?

7. Why do you think Chess found Flora to be so fascinating? Have you ever met someone who saw something in you that others didn't, and who inspired you to make changes

in your life for the better? Who were they and how did they encourage you?

8. Before reading this book what was your understanding of the *Titanic* wreck? How have your feelings about it and the facts surrounding it changed now that you've read this book?

9. Have you ever found yourself in a position similar to one of the Fortune sisters, when duty, expectations, or obligation prevented you from doing what you wanted? How did you handle it? What do you think of the choices the sisters made?

10. A reoccurring theme in this book is fortune and all its different forms. What are those different forms and how do they affect the characters and various passengers aboard the *Titanic*?

11. When a tragedy occurs, we can sometimes place great significance in little things that our memory latches onto. Such as Mr. Fortune's buffalo coat, the playfulness of a bulldog, or the use of a nickname. What other seemingly minor things did the survivors feel were significant? If you have ever faced tragedy in the past, what did you place significance in?

12. When a book is set on a ship, even one as enormous and opulent as the *Titanic*, the story is restricted to a defined space. What do you think the challenges are in plotting and staging such a story, especially one so well known? What are the advantages?

13. *Sisters of Fortune* features anecdotes about some lesser-known figures who sailed on the *Titanic*, as well as some of the more famous ones. Who do you find you identified with most? Who do you struggle to empathize with?